PROLOGUE

When Lyra is six, she crouches down at a truck stop while her mama goes inside to barter for cigarettes and finds a dead field mouse in the brown grass outside.

Lyra pokes at it with chubby fingers, unsure why it isn't moving. Nearby, in the shade of a big rig, her little brother Jackson plays with his favorite bright blue bouncy ball.

The mouse doesn't move when she pokes it, which feels...wrong. All the mice she had seen on the road had sprinted away whenever she got close, and this one isn't even breathing, isn't even twitching.

And then, something happens. Little Lyra frowns at it and feels something tugging inside her stomach.

The field mouse twitches against her finger.

Its back is crooked, like someone had thrown it against the wall like a rag doll a few days ago. So she pokes that, too, prodding it back into shape. Feels the tiny little bones like toothpicks, feels the tiny pocket of blood, barely kept in place by the fur.

It twitches again twice, three times, then springs up, its little feet scratching at the dead dirt for purchase before it dashes away. And she wasn't even done yet.

Lyra sits on her butt in the dirt and watches, until it disappears underneath a scrub brush.

The door to the gas station Quik Mart slams open, and her mama scrambles out, flip flops slapping on the dusty ground, her eyes wide, running towards Lyra.

Without a word of explanation, her mama grabs her, scooping her up from the dirt, then grabs Jackson by the arm, sprinting to the truck.

Jackson's ball drops, and he cries out, but her mama doesn't stop.

"Don't do that," her mama breathes, so quiet Lyra almost misses it. "Never do that."

Her mama throws her into the cab of the truck, heaving Jackson into his seat, not even bothering to buckle him in before starting the truck and roaring out of the parking lot.

All because Lyra wanted to help a mouse.

HER MAMA DRIVES through the night.

"Lyra," she says, after hours of silence and white-knuckle speeding, "Lyra, you can't ever do that again."

"I was trying to help the mouse," Lyra grumps, her eyes burning from the late hour. Jackson sleeps soundly in his car seat between them, tears from losing his ball still dried on his face.

Her mama takes a deep breath, but it doesn't look like it helps. "I know, honey, but you can't."

"How'd you even know I did it?" Lyra swings her feet against the truck seat. "You were in the store."

"I just know," her mama says, and the spare streetlight illuminates her for a brief second. "I'll always know."

Lyra doesn't want to answer, so she looks out to the starlit fields of Ohio instead.

"Honey, Lyra, if you do that, demons will come," her mama says, desperation in her voice, "they can tell you brought something back, and they'll come, and they'll hurt you."

THE GIRL WHO BRINGS THE DEAD

A NECROMANCY ROMANCE

ALESSA WINTERS

Sign up for her newsletter at: http://eepurl.com/dLfcFw

🏵 Created with Vellum

To 'A Brand New Chapter Writing Group', for making me change who died at the end of the book because they liked the character too much.

CONTENT WARNING

This book contains a fair amount of gore for a romance novel, and it's not sexy vampire gore.

There is sex in this book. Mom, please skip those chapters.

Demons are something found just in religious books and those gory horror movies her mama watches in motels when she thinks Lyra and Jackson are asleep, so Lyra gives her mama the most skeptical look she can muster.

"I mean it, honey, you can't. They'll come, and they'll hurt you until you're all taken up, and you die." Her mama takes her hand off the steering wheel to grip Lyra's, reaching across the car seat between them. "Promise me, Lyra, promise me you'll never touch the dead again."

HER MOTHER DIES when she is fourteen, and Lyra keeps that promise.

1

When Lyra is seventeen, she crashes her mother's truck.

Well, it's her truck by then, legally, and she finally has her license and the ability to roam once more, and many seventeen-year-olds crash vehicles when they really should have been paying attention.

But Jackson's in the truck with her this time, instead of their aunt, and it's the freest she's felt in years. Just the two of them, just them and the sky and the interstate across Arizona. No trees, just cacti and sand and rocks and an open road.

It's been six months since she's seen her little brother, and he's fourteen now and all knees and elbows. Their hair still matches, still the unruly dark brown that isn't quite a curl but isn't quite straight, but now he's far taller than her, and the chubby cheeks he's kept all through adolescence have melted away from his face, making him sharper, like a knife, while Lyra still looks vaguely soft and squishy.

If her mom were here, she'd say that Jackson looked like his father, if the old pictures Lyra found in the truck were any indication. Lyra probably looks like her father, too, but her mother didn't have any photos of him for Lyra to compare.

He's blasting some music he found on YouTube, some sort of

mood-enhancing noise that Lyra doesn't like but doesn't hate. He's belting along with his crackling voice, and with the sun overhead, they're easily going ninety on the blacktop. There's a tent in the back of the truck and some coolers with soda and ice and way more firewood and fire starter than they need.

It's good. It's more than good, it's great. It's phenomenal. It's everything Lyra missed about being sent away to school and him being in another state.

But as they're thumping along to the music, flying down the freeway with the windows cranked down, there's that single crystalline moment in time, that singular beautiful memory, where all Lyra can think about is how she hopes it never ends. That the rest of their lives is like this, this one moment, in a hot truck in the middle of the Arizona desert with nobody around for miles upon miles, just her and her brother and their mother's truck.

These things never last. If anything, she should have learned by now; any lesson from her life, any grand overarching thread of the story of her world, that everything around her is going to end. Is going to pass through her fingers, like she could never grasp anything fast enough or with enough strength.

The back-left wheel of her truck hits a nail in the road, and at the speed they're going it explodes, popping up the back end into the air, then sending it careening to the edge of the road. It hits the ditch, the blown tire spinning wildly as Lyra clutches at the steering wheel and tries to correct, before the back end of the truck tosses them around.

Jackson and Lyra lock eyes for that split second when the truck tilts, and the air is rushing at them at the wrong angle before glass shatters around them.

It's almost like music, the sound it makes, bright tinkling noises echoing as her hair gets flung in front of her face. Before the cab of the truck hits the pavement, and something crunches inside of her.

She can't tell what.

It might be just a few seconds, it might be hours, but when she opens her eyes once more, something drips onto her face and dribbles down her chin.

The entire world is pain, sharp, glittering pain, arching over her entire body.

She's upside down, somehow, and the only thing she can twitch is her arm. Her legs are pinned, halfway contorted between the seat and the steering wheel, and she can't feel them; it's like they're gone, and—

And Jackson's not breathing.

He's there, blood drooling down his face, his head tilted between the shattered windshield and the blacktop, and she can feel that he's dead like a kick in her gut.

She reaches for him, but her arm twitches. Something's broken inside of it, her bones scrape together in ragged edges, but Jackson's so close, so close, and he's not breathing.

"Jackson," she chokes out, and it barely comes out as anything more than a whisper.

The engine's whining drowns it out, still spinning, and the music, still thumping.

He doesn't move, of course, and she tries to whisper again, but nothing comes out.

Glass still tinkles from the car around them, and she hadn't seen anyone for miles; nobody would come to save her. He's not breathing. He's nothing.

Still, she can feel the pull in her stomach towards his body, and she shifts, just enough, so the tips of her fingers can graze against his cheek.

In an instant, with the pads of her fingertips against his bloody skin, she knows four things.

One, the small bones in his neck are not where they should be, in cleanly snapped pieces.

Two, blood is slowly pooling between his ears.

Three, his leg is broken in four places, but they're not critical places. They can be broken for a long time and nothing would happen.

Four, there's blood leaking from all over his body.

She had made a promise to her Mama all those years ago.

But Jackson's only fourteen.

She breathes out, and the air makes bubbles in some blood, but she keeps her stinging eyes open. She can't reach Jackson's neck, but she imagines the tips of her fingers thrusting down his face and to the bones, crunching them back into place, prodding the spine and the cartilage between them, connecting the electric current between his brain and his heart.

Her head pounds, and she doesn't have enough time to do this, doesn't have enough energy, like it's going to take everything and every little bit of whatever it is inside of her.

He gasps, but his eyes are still closed.

She reaches, again, prodding at his cheek, at the blood out of place inside his skull. She doesn't know where it goes, but there are leaking vessels, and she shoves it back into there, sealing up the cracks as she can until her eyes blur together and she can't hold her arm out to him anymore.

Her fingertips slide away from his cheek, and she can't tell what else she needs to do the moment she lets go. If there's anything else, if his leg bones need to be in place, if his blood is leaking too much, she can't tell.

But his chest rises and falls, like he's asleep.

So she watches that, for a few moments, or an eternity.

Until, outside the car, boots crunch against the broken glass, and she stirs again, somehow able to turn her head.

A man squats down next to the truck, hair sandy blond and cut short to his skull, and he smiles at her like she's a small animal at a zoo.

"Hello, little one," he says, shielding his face from the brutal sun.

In the shade, his eyes flash, and they reflect the light right back at her like a cat reflects a flashlight in the dark.

Still pinned in place, Lyra can't move. All she can do is blink.

"You're a young one, aren't you," he says, shifting, and glass tinkles beneath his shoes. He's dressed like a tourist, with a Hawaiian shirt and cargo shorts, but terror sticks in Lyra's throat. "Not often I get to see one of you."

His eyes flicker, just barely, behind her, to where Jackson breathes softly, then back to her. Again, there's the flash, and he's unreal. He can't be here, he can't, but—

Her mother had called them demons.

"You don't really want to die today, do you?" he asks, voice still laconic and calm. "You did such good work with him, and now you're all banged up."

"Please," she whispers, somehow, and she doesn't know what she's asking.

He reaches into the cab of the truck, like it's no big deal, like there aren't shattered edges of glass and plastic and metal all around her, and grabs the hand she touched Jackson with.

"Oooooh," he whispers, a smile breaking over his face, and it's the smile of someone who's just discovered something breathtakingly beautiful. "Ooh, you're in so much pain—"

He grips down hard, and her vision sparks white, and—

SOMETHING BEEPS AROUND HER, and her mind is a fog of cotton and muted lights, and it takes a few moments of struggle before she can pry her eyes open.

The ceiling above her is a cream color with dotted tiles, and she's hooked into some sort of IV line.

Lyra lets her eyes fall to her right arm, follow the line up to the bag, and it's almost empty. She fists her hand, and there's a delay, but her fingers bend to her will. Scraped, swollen, and puffy, but they work.

She's in a bed, a felted blanket covering her feet, but she can feel them. Feel them enough to twitch her toes and see the movement from under the felt.

Her head doesn't hurt, but she feels the far away sort of numbness that suggests that pain is somewhere nearby, lurking.

And she can't see Jackson.

She jerks but can't sit up, not fully.

"I would stay put if I were you," a voice says, bored, off to the side, and she has to tilt her head to see who it is.

It's the same man—demon—but his body is all different. The short blond hair now replaced by long and silky black hair, his skin is tanner, and he's quite a few inches shorter.

But, deep inside of her, where she felt the pull to Jackson when he was dead, she knows it's the same demon. Just a different body.

He smiles at her, and it's the same baring of teeth as before. His smile didn't change, at least.

"Hello, little Lyra," he says, and someone must've spoken her name, someone must've checked her ID. "The nurses say you're going to live."

If he's a demon if he's going to hurt her, drain her dry...

"You've been unconscious for about two days, sorry about that." He waves his hand as if it's his doing. "It's been ages since I've tasted necromancer. I got carried away."

"Who are you?" she whispers, and her voice is barely audible over the whir of the air conditioning.

He leans forward, steepling his hands.

"You can call me Melekai," he says, finally, as if evaluating her and what to say. "I saved your life."

"Where's Jackson?" With each word, she feels a bit more put together, a bit steadier, and she shuffles until she's sitting up.

Again, there's pain somewhere in there, somewhere in the background.

"Home already," Melekai says, eyes never leaving hers, still reflective, still eerie. "He only needed a cast and some band-aids after you were through with him."

She exhales, and he watches her struggle to breathe as she pushes through the tears prickling at her eyes and the lump in her throat.

"You're only here because of me," he says, finally, as if waiting for her to finish with whatever panic attack she's breathing through and for her to pay more attention to him. "I could have ended you. Could have taken away all of what makes you *you*, and no one would have ever known."

"My mom said demons steal your soul," she says, the words falling from her lips, as if that's a wise thing to say.

"She's not wrong," he replies and picks at a thread on the blanket, his fingers shifting through it like he doesn't exist. "A bit archaic, but not wrong."

She has to swallow past her throat again, and her head is magnificently heavy, now that she's sitting upright.

When her mom had warned her, Lyra had envisioned some sort of grand battle. A struggle, where a creature of darkness steals her soul and kills her forever.

Not...not a grim meeting in a quiet hospital room, with him sitting politely on a chair.

"I have a deal for you," he says, and the beeping increases on the machine hooked up to her finger. "I want to try something, something I don't think anyone has ever tried before. I want to keep you alive."

She looks back over at him, and his eyes had never left her.

"It'd be so easy to kill you, to take all of you," he murmurs, and she can barely hear him, "but then I have to wait decades for the next necromancer. Or..." He drapes his hand out, immediately touching her palm, and she flinches but doesn't jerk her arm away. "Or I can keep you alive and take small sips of your soul." He smiles again, and it's awful.

"What, kill me slowly instead of all at once?" she asks, and her eyes still sting.

Thoughtlessly, she lifts her left arm to her face, and it's in a cast, clumsy and large. She can't rub her eyes like this.

"You're still quite broken," he says, soft. "Demon's don't heal, not like you think we do. All I did was refuse your soul to die until the paramedics found you."

Lyra lowers the cast back down to the bed. It doesn't hurt, not yet, but the threat of it still lurks.

"If I did my calculations correctly," he starts again, "then you should recover in the interim. If I don't take too much." He sits back, and he's smug.

A tendril of terror winds its way down Lyra's spine, coiling around her gut. "If I say no?"

He raises a single eyebrow at her.

"I don't...I don't want that?" She manages out, past the fear and the numbness and the confusion. "I'm just...normal?"

"You knew that you might summon a demon from raising the dead, I think you know you're very much not," he says, and he has the gall to look amused. Like this is a joke to him. "I could just kill you now."

"That's not a bargain, that's just..." she trails off, the words escaping her grasp like dandelion seeds in the wind. "That's not fair."

He leans forward again, picking up her right hand in his, and draws circles in her palm—lazy circles.

Her skin prickles at his touch, swollen and numb from whatever drugs they gave her, but the pad of his fingertip never leaves her palm.

"Do you know how demons feed, little Lyra?" he asks, staring at her palm instead of her, then, before her eyes, lifts the finger, and a single golden thread of light connects her palm to him.

It should be terrifying, it should make her feel like she's about to cry, but instead, she's filled with a sort of detached wonder. Like, that came from her, and nothing so delicate or fragile should ever come from her.

"We can feed off of your pain, stealing it away in a heartbeat. We can feed off of pleasure, magnify it until your brain shuts off from the sensation." He rubs his thumb on the single golden thread of light like he's caressing it. "People have died to have that at their disposal. People have waged wars in times of old, just to glimpse it."

"Then why necromancers?" she asks, and the word feels odd in her mouth. "Why would we die?"

He twists his fingers, and the single thread detaches from her palm. In a snap, he winds it in his hand before it disappears.

And, suddenly, Lyra's eyes weigh a little more, and her head is a little heavier.

"Necromancers shine so bright, it's hard to stop," he murmurs.

She swallows again, then again because it doesn't help, and the door bustles open, and a pretty red-haired nurse shoulders her way inside, carrying a tray.

The nurse stops in her tracks, seeing Lyra sitting up.

"Oh, hello," she says, cheery, attempting to mask her surprise. "Here, let me get the bed upright for you." Setting down the tray, she pushes a few buttons on the side of the bed, and, thankfully, it adjusts up, so all Lyra has to do is lean back against it. "You can ring me with this button, whenever you need, 'kay?"

Lyra nods, her head heavy.

The nurse bustles about the small room, checking off paperwork, and never even once does she look over at Melekai. Not even acknowledging another person is in the room.

Lyra glances back to him, and there's a small smile on his face. Amusement.

"Can I have my phone?" Lyra asks, and her voice feels raw, speaking to someone who's not a demon. "My brother…"

"I think he has it, but I'll give him a call," the nurse says, and the kind smile never leaves her face as she crosses in front of Melekai, never noting his presence. "He was here just a few hours ago. He'll probably come back in the morning."

Lyra doesn't even know what time of day it is.

The nurse gives her a small barrage of questions about how she's feeling (weird), about her pain levels (far away), and about the car accident itself, and Lyra really does her best to answer but the weariness weighs against her eyelids, and Melekai doesn't speak, and the nurse doesn't react, and she doesn't know what's real, and—

IT'S ALMOST a year later before Lyra sees the demon again.

She's just getting home from a class at community college to the ramshackle apartment she shares with three other roommates when she climbs the rickety stairs to her attic room to find him standing there.

His body is changed again. He's taller this time, his face square, and has curly black hair styled almost fashionably.

His eyes flash, reflective, the moment she opens her door to see him standing inside.

She freezes, hand still on the doorknob, and for a few seconds, she strongly considers just stepping right back out again and pretending this never happened.

But instead he tilts his head at her, like she's a bug under glass.

She had half thought she made him up—a figment of the hospital bed and the trauma of the accident.

"Your pain got worse when you climbed the stairs," he says, neutral, like it's not something that Lyra knows already, like it isn't her body that's been so uncontroversially changed by the crash.

It's always hurting. It's always in pain.

The doctors never have a good enough explanation. They tell her the crash did something to her nerves, changed how her body processes signals, and switched everything around until her nerve endings didn't connect correctly.

Tentatively, she shuts the door behind her. Let her talk to this person without her roommates overhearing. Let her die— maybe— without them having to see.

"You look different," she says, instead of anything intelligent.

"I take the bodies available to me," he says, gesturing to himself. "Needs to be recently dead. Sometimes it's slim pickings."

She sets down her backpack on her tiny desk, happy to have it off her shoulders, and his eyes follow her movements. Hungry.

"Why are you here?" she asks, and her voice only warbles a little bit.

He doesn't move, still standing in the middle of her room, and it's surreal. This creature spun from her nightmares is next to her ratty twin bed and the power plug for her ancient laptop she pawned from a classmate.

"You...should be better by now," he says, and it takes her a few moments before she realizes that he's tentative. Asking after her.

"Well, I'm alive," she says, which is her standard prickly answer to when people pry into her health. "I think that's better than the alternative."

He absorbs her answer before abruptly striding over to her, crossing the attic room in two large steps, and is suddenly close. Close-close, closer than Lyra lets people be, and she cringes away, pressing her back to the door.

He freezes at that, hand halfway to her shoulder.

"I told you, I don't plan on killing you," he says, like her fear is puzzling.

"I didn't raise anything from the dead," she blurts out, hugging herself away from him the best she can. "I didn't do anything. How'd you find me, I..."

She's two states away from the car accident in Arizona, from the hospital that landed her in medical debt for probably the rest of her life.

He drops the hand away. "I know you now. I don't need any of your magic to find you anymore," he replies, shifting, so he stands next to her, leaning against the door.

It's far less threatening. But he's still a demon who could steal Lyra's soul without a second thought.

"This is part of the deal," he continues, and this close, she can see a tiny scar on the tip of the body's nose, "I find you when I need some power, and you get to live."

"I have a final tomorrow," she breathes out, because that's what's applicable. "I can't pass out for two days."

The corner of his mouth tilts up into a smile like she gave him far more than she had wanted to. "I'll only take enough for one night of sleep."

He settles his hand at the base of her neck, heavy, and she shudders.

"You can raise the dead if you want," he says, casual, as she shakes. "No other demon would dare take you."

"That's not reassuring," she says, looking down at the threadbare carpet on the floor, trying to focus on anything that's not the hand on her neck.

"If you ever do raise the dead, I will come along to check on you," he says, and the hand is unmoving. "You get threatened by another demon, kill a bug and bring it back. I'll be there."

Lyra doesn't know what she should say, if she should thank him for that, so she says nothing.

He exhales, and it's immediately strange, the idea of a dead body breathing like that. "You're in so much more pain than I thought," he says, and his voice is almost rapturous. "Let me..."

He trails off, and it's a little like the air is pressed out of her chest, but...

...But the pain in her legs, from walking home and carrying the backpack, abruptly ceases.

"Oh," she says, then blinks, her eyes heavy. "Oh."

SHE DOESN'T TRY to raise the dead again until ten years later.

2

She only gets to see her brother about twice a month now, and instead of any custody or court orders, it's because he's going to law school in Seattle, and she's living a two-hour drive away. She can't afford Seattle rent, and he doesn't have the time for a daily commute that long.

It had been a bitter fight when it first came down to it, but now, almost a year into his law school, Lyra is more or less settled into the routine of walking to the bus station, waiting for the bus to the light rail to the Amtrak to the other light rail, and then waiting for him at the little sandwich shop right off-campus.

She feels too much like an imposter if she steps onto the law campus after crashing so hard out of community college, so they reached an agreement on the cute little sandwich shop. It has everything they want; coffee for Lyra, tea for Jackson, and sandwiches that Lyra can only manage to eat half of, which means that she can take the rest of it home to eat when she's on her night shift at the store.

And it's overpriced, so it's almost always empty, except for the two of them and the grumpy clerk. So they can talk, actually talk, and not worry about who might overhear.

This time, however, there's one other person crammed into the far corner, his back to Lyra when she steps inside, so she tucks herself as far away from him as possible, ending up in a booth pressed against the glass window instead of further into the coffee shop.

The grumpy clerk brings her a cup of plain coffee without a word. They're almost a year into this every other week thing, and the clerk knows what's up.

And it never takes Jackson long to show up, and he always has a smile and a joke for the clerk. He even knows her name, though it escapes Lyra.

After his traditional greeting of the clerk, where she gives him some very fancy matcha tea she had already prepared, he squeezes himself in the booth across from Lyra, a smile lighting up his sharp face.

"Lyra!" he says, and his voice is bigger than the cafe. The man in the other booth even turns around and stares a bit.

His brush with death did nothing to dim the light around him, and Lyra hunches a bit deeper into the booth.

"Hey, you look healthy," she says, which is lame, but she could never match her little brother's energy in anything.

He's in his lawyer suit he bought with a scholarship, and his shoes are still just as scuffed as hers, which makes her feel less like trailer trash next to him, but it's only a small comfort.

And then...then they awkwardly stare at each other, sipping their hot drink of choice, as the clerk preps their sandwiches.

It's always a test, somehow, of who would ask a question first. Of who would break the awkwardness. Of who would ask something real, instead of just pleasantries.

They always got to it. It just took a little bit.

"So, done anything spooky lately?" He breaks first, stretching out his legs out the booth.

And this is why they chose this shop. The clerk could not give a shit about their conversation. Which meant they could talk about it.

It, the giant, capitalized word between them. Her powers, her nebulous deal with a demon, and the fact that her own brother had been dead for what was probably close to fifteen minutes before she brought him back.

Stuff like that gets real awkward quick.

"Nope," she says, popping the 'p' sound, which is her normal answer. "Saw someone get hit by a car, but they were…" she mimes a body getting torn apart. "Too far gone."

She never has anything else, not really, and Jackson knows it, but still always asks.

"Felt it like getting kicked in my chest from across the parking lot, though," she grumbles, which is more the information Jackson wants.

It turns out, when you get raised from the dead when you're fourteen, you get kinda obsessed with death for a bit. And even now, a decade later, with him in law school and far outpacing her in anything she's ever done, he still leans forward to hear her slightly spooky stories.

"And the…" he gestures, vague, but she knows his meaning.

"Still no word, not since last November," she says, nodding her thanks as the clerk drops off their giant sandwiches. "Almost a year now—it'll be any day."

Jackson scoffs. He doesn't have that high of an opinion of Melekai. They've only interacted about twice, and Jackson can only halfway see him, but either being related to Lyra and her weirdness or being brought back from the dead made him able to at least…sense him.

Apparently, once, they communicated with each other, but Jackson won't tell her what they said, and Melekai rarely speaks to her before doing whatever the hell he does.

"Ask him what he does when he's not…" Jackson gestures again, and really if he's going to become a lawyer, he'll have to learn how to stop thinking everyone knows what he's talking about.

Lyra usually knows, but still.

"We don't talk," she reminds him, prodding at the sandwich, which, again, he knows.

"Eh, he's a demon, you should trap him and chat," he says, light, before digging into his sandwich.

Lyra flinches at his directness, then lifts her eyes and instinctively checks the cafe.

The grumpy clerk doesn't care as she neatens up the depleted baked goods display case. She never cares, but Lyra always checks, and...

The man in the corner stares at her, eyes wide.

She flinches back, then flicks at Jackson's wrist. "Be quiet, there are other people here," she murmurs, to the rolling of his eyes.

"It's only bad if you act like it's bad," he says, but still, he lowers his voice. "Real people just think we're talking about books or something."

She glances up, and the man in the corner is still staring hard.

He's a strange sort of handsome, the sort of uncanny that comes from looking a hair too perfect. His skin is a bit too creamy and smooth like glass and immaculately highlighted. His hair is straight, black, and styled within an inch of its life, and he's dressed like he fell out of a street fashion Instagram account.

The hair on the back of Lyra's neck raises, and she ducks away again.

Jackson's watching her, a bit too close in a way that brothers always can.

"What?" she asks, still mumbling, still whispering.

"Need me to rough anyone up?" he asks automatically, like he isn't wearing a suit.

"Nah, just spooky guy overheard you talking about magic and is now intense," she says, eating a bit more of her sandwich and using the opportunity to turn her face more towards the window. "How are classes?"

"Long," he says easily, which is a better answer than he usually gives, "my reading hasn't let up, and I haven't had a date in months, and practicals are around the corner, and there's nothing I can do to prepare enough." He stares out the window with her, at the Seattle gloom and the rain trickling down the awnings. "Still got full marks on the last one."

Lyra smiles, just a bit, at the rain as well. Even with all the weirdness in his life, she still likes to hear about him doing well, still likes to hear him bragging.

As he should—he went from living out of a big rig with to a decent law school. He should get to brag as much as he wants when his entire class is full of rich kids whose parents were also lawyers or politicians, and he was only three steps away from homelessness for most of his life. It's a goddamn achievement, and Lyra is proud.

She still failed out of community college, but if one of them digs themselves out of whatever mess their mother put them in, then her failings are worth it.

He's still chatting at her, but her mind's wandered, so she grabs her attention with both hands and tries to focus.

"Patent law continues to be bullshit, and we keep on learning about it, but the Supreme Court just always says it's bullshit," he continues and doesn't even realize her mind had wandered off.

"Uh huh," she says, in a lull, and he grins at her. "Sure."

And he keeps on talking, and she keeps on trying to pay attention, and the man in the corner doesn't stop with his wide-eyed staring.

LYRA CATCHES a glimpse of the man as she walks to the light rail, and another as she gets off the Amtrak closer to her work, and she hugs her rain jacket a little bit closer.

But as much as she'd rather just walk the mile home from the bus stop, up the steeping roads and harsh seaside cliffs of Northern Washington, there's a reason why she and Jackson always met over lunch.

Namely, Lyra works swing shifts at Buggees, the last corner store, before the edge of her small town turns rural, and one slightly creepy person's never been enough to stop her from actually doing work.

And besides, Mr. Peters, the owner, keeps a shotgun underneath the counter. He says it's good for a soft girl like Lyra to know how to shoot.

She has to pass by a church on her way from the bus stop to the store, and she tucks her rain jacket in a bit tighter around her over-sized sweater.

The church itself is one of the hundreds of tiny bright buildings that dot this part of the Washington coast: all cozy structures and warm lights, but the pastor of this one always glares when he catches sight of Lyra.

Her mother had a rule, while they were out on their trucking adventures and staying in motels in small towns and camping when they weren't: never go into a place of worship. Her mother would tell ghost stories of the horrors that happen inside, of how the priest would manipulate and torture people like them. Like they could take one look at Lyra and know that she's something they would call evil.

Jackson, without a trace of the weird that Lyra inherited, went inside one megachurch in Utah on a dare and said it was tacky but otherwise fine. Lyra never wanted to risk it.

The bell over the door tinkles as she opens it. She nods to Mr. Peters as he counts off change for elderly Mrs. Rogers, who stops by the store once a week for a bag of rice and three cans of ravioli.

"And here, enough quarters so you can do your laundry," he says, with just enough of a smile that Mrs. Rogers gives him one in return. Mr. Peters has the look of a man who's fought in a few wars and found them bullshit but thinks that owning a convenience store is the epitome of living in luxury. He's missing a few teeth, has more hairs that are gray than aren't, and Lyra's never seen him wear anything but a pair of Carhartts overalls with his store polo.

Mrs. Rogers gives Lyra a wary glance as she passes, but she usually does whenever she sees Lyra.

Because despite Lyra's attempts at being normal, some people can just see the creepy.

Once safely away from disapproving old grandmas, Lyra changes from her nice sweater to the same bright red long-sleeved polo, tucking her dark brown waves into a matching baseball cap. It's still raining outside, and every time the door opens it'll bring wind and a chill, but she still has to wear the polo.

Contrary to the flickering fluorescent and the more expired than not products, it's not a bad place to work. In the history of Lyra's jobs, it's firmly above the time she worked in a warehouse, the time she had to be a waitress, and below the temp office secretary position.

"Lyra, can you stay until two today?" Mr. Peters calls back into the back room, which means that someone from the graveyard shift called out sick again.

"Yeah, sure," she calls back, tucking the polo into her corduroys, and dragging the stool from the storage room.

That's another reason why this job isn't bad. Mr. Peters allows her to sit for the long hours she's in the store alone, and standing all day makes the nerves in her legs shake. Waitressing didn't care about that.

Mrs. Rogers is gone by the time Lyra emerges, and Mr. Peters is counting out his till.

"Had three kids try to shoplift gum at about 3, they're Kyle's kids, keep an eye out for them if they return," he says, without looking up at her. "They're the ones with the red hair and freckles, about ten or eleven, and one's tall."

Lyra nods instead of responding because the kids are in about twice a week to buy candy and such.

"Nathan will come in early at two, so you don't have to worry about that," Mr. Peters says, then gives her a critical eye. "You went and saw your brother?"

"Yeah." She's never sure how he knows, other than the take-out container with the sandwich, but he can always tell. "Jackson says hi, he's still wearing a fancy suit"—Mr. Peters rolls his eyes at that—"and Seattle was, as always, soulless."

The one bit of obligatory niceties out of the way, it doesn't take too long for Mr. Peters to exit with the leftover daily newspaper, leaving Lyra alone.

There's a familiar rhythm to her day when she's at the store. There's the customers you see every day, the people stopping by to grab wine or snacks on their way out the road, the after-work rush at 6 PM of people buying gas and chips before their trek away, before it calms down by around 8:30, leaving Lyra with just the drunks and the loners and an empty store.

She likes the empty store more than anything else.

So when the doorbell tinkles again at around eleven, she raises her gaze from her phone to see the man from Seattle striding into Buggees like he owns the place.

There haven't been any customers for around forty-five minutes, so Lyra watches him as he idly strides down their three aisles, as if he's actually interested in buying a bag of chips, and rests a hand on the shotgun underneath the register.

Thankfully, he gives up the pretense after a few moments, making a beeline to the register.

"So, what are you?" he asks, and even his voice is cool and smooth, affectedly disinterested.

"That's rude," Lyra says, raising an eyebrow at him. He doesn't look like the sort of person who'd want to get his clothes dirty, but that doesn't mean anything. "Are you going to buy anything?

"I can if you need me to," he drawls, and he's examining his fingernails like they aren't immaculately perfect. "I thought I knew all the magicians in the Seattle area, even all the way out here. Are you new?"

She looks at him, hard, until he looks up from his examination.

"What?" he says, mild. "You are a magician of some sort, that much is obvious, and you were chatting about demons with your brother, so you're not"—he waves his hand, airy—"Not some ignorant hick with no clue of the world."

She's partially a hick and quickly decides to take offense to that statement, as her heart starts to pound.

Once, years ago, Jackson tried to encourage her to find more people like herself, but nothing came from her Google searches or library trips besides feeling more like a freak. And when she tried to snoop around witchy stores and pagan groups, they all either rejected her for some nebulous reason (she's creepy) or laughed her out for actually believing in this shit. The only person who ever seemed to have any knowledge of it in any real way... died when she was sixteen. And made Lyra swear never to do it again.

At her extended pause, he drops a little of the mask, just looking startled. "Wait, really?"

"I don't know what you're talking about," Lyra says, pushing as much boredom as possible into her voice. "If you want to loiter, you have to make a purchase."

He didn't, but the threat of it stops most people.

He immediately pulls out a slim wallet, yanking out a crisp hundred-dollar bill that she absolutely cannot split, then grabs a single pack of breath mints. "You don't have the look of most spell weavers," he continues, like it's a normal conversation, and he didn't just pull out the flashiest bill she's ever seen at the job. "Most of them look like they spend all their time in a craft store, not..." He gestures at the ballcap and the polo.

"Do you have any smaller bills? I don't think I can make change," Lyra says, and her brow is furrowing at his words. "What are you, then?"

All she can tell is he isn't a demon.

He stands up straighter. "You're looking at the Pacific Northwest's strongest alchemist," he says like she knows what that means. "Seriously, I thought I knew everyone."

He makes no move to grab the hundred from the counter nor to pocket the breath mints.

The moment stretches on, as Lyra doesn't know what to say. Doesn't know what she can think, whether revealing herself is at all smart or foolish or—

"Here, I'll give you proof." He taps his finger against the breath mints, and the hard plastic dissolves into a pile of glitter. Actual glitter, like he just poured out his pocket from a gaudy birthday card.

Unable to help herself, Lyra pokes at it, and there's a little bit of residual warmth. Like whatever it is, he transferred a little bit of heat over.

"So you're obviously not an alchemist, or that'd be very unimpressive," he says matter-of-factly, picking up a remaining Tic Tac and tapping it against the chipped counter. In between one blink and the next, it turns into a quarter, which he rolls between his fingertips.

"I can't trust this bill at all, can I?" Lyra says, crossing her arms, so she doesn't try to poke the glitter any more.

"I mean, it's not going to turn back into anything," he says, glib. "So, what are you?"

Somewhere in that, though, she stopped feeling threatened and started to feel annoyed. "Clearly not anything you know how to deal with," she says, then winces at her words. "Nothing. I'm nothing."

"Liar." He plays with the quarter like he's some sort of street performer doing sleight of hand.

She watches the quarter move with a sense of detachment that her mother would be proud of.

"How many are there?" she asks, and the quarter doesn't falter, though he glances back at her. "You said you were the top; how many are there that you have a...top?"

"Three in Washington." The quarter disappears into his pocket, which if he can just print money like that, it's a nifty trick. "I hear there's one in Idaho, but I've never met him."

"Top out of three isn't that impressive," she points out, and again, the mask slips for just a second, and he blinks owlishly. "Can you magic up paychecks that a bank could read?"

He hesitates, like the idea never occurred to him, and really, what sort of rich boy bullshit is that. Everything about him reeks of rich boy, and, quite frankly, Lyra doesn't want anything to do with that.

"I can tell when things die around me," she says, as blunt as she can. Because people usually wince away when they hear that. "It sucks."

He tilts his head, and the mask flashes to something resembling cunning. "Really," he states, and it's not a question. "Ever do anything with that?"

"No," she says, and, thankfully, the doorbell tinkles again, and Greg, one of the town stoners, stumbles in and heads straight for the chips and the salmon dip, just like he does at least once a week. "Is this all, or—"

He taps one of the Tic Tacs, and it transforms into a business card. "Call me if you run into any trouble," he says, then leaves, giving a nod to the stoner, who blinks blearily at him.

With only a few seconds before Greg comes to the counter, she sweeps the glitter and Tic Tacs into her pocket, then stuffs the hundred-dollar bill into the other one along with the business card.

The glitter streaks everywhere across the counter.

It takes her almost twenty minutes at the end of her shift to clean up all the glitter, though far less time to delete the entire interaction off of the security camera loop.

The business card is made of a thick paper, much better than most that Lyra holds, with a thin gold border around the words that read, in simple text:

AXEL MCLORRY

ALCHEMIST

MUCH MORE POWERFUL THAN YOU THINK

And his phone number.

And, after seeing him transform it in front of her eyes, she has no real idea if that's a normal business card for him or just...something he wished up out of thin air.

The moment she steps into the parking lot of the gas station, the flock of crows immediately takes off, but that's nothing new. Birds have been doing that since Lyra was a little kid, and it wasn't until Jackson pointed it out that she ever thought anything of it.

Animals generally try to stay away from her, but dogs and horses staying away bums her out more than birds. It just feels like she's less likely to get pooped on with birds, which is a plus in her mind.

It's just another thing in the vaguely uneasy feeling that the entire world seems to have around Lyra.

She deposits the hundred dollars into the ATM the next day but leaves the business card untouched on the little table she has pushed up against the window in her kitchen.

3

LYRA (12:02 PM): Hey, so a guy did some magic (like actual magic like transformed a box of Tic Tacs into glitter) at my store and asked me about my magic, any insight?

JACKSON (12:05 PM): Is this...is this a joke?

LYRA (12:05 PM): No?

JACKSON (12:07 PM): Did you talk to him?

Lyra sits in her favorite chair in the house, an overstuffed velvet green monstrosity that hasn't been moved since at least the early eighties, curling up her legs beneath her.

Her mother could have never afforded a place like this, but it turns out she had a father, too, and despite never getting a cent of child support, she was somehow his next of kin when he passed away.

It's a rather small mobile home, just a kitchen with an armchair in a corner and a bedroom stuffed with too many bookcases, but it's larger than most places Lyra's stayed since her mom died. The roof leaks in the heaviest of rain, the wind blows straight through the cracks in the walls, and there are splinters in the floorboards where the linoleum wore through, but Lyra loves it.

Mostly because it's hers, it's not a truck, it's not a set of toys or books she has to give up when Jackson gets to be the age, and she doesn't have to do anything but live in it.

She could sell it, of course, but it's in such rundown shape that they'd probably just tear it up and rebuild on the land, and she'd still be needing to find someplace stable to rent. The estimate the realtor gave her would pay for only a few years of Seattle rent.

And her mother raised her never to turn down free rent.

She rests the business card against the green velvet, snaps a picture of it, angling it, so the crack in the camera lens doesn't mess up the image.

LYRA (12:18 PM): See attached pic. I mentioned I could tell when things die, but not like actual creepy stuff. Can you sleuth?

Her brother doesn't reply immediately, which isn't entirely unusual, so she pokes at her phone while drinking her coffee.

JACKSON (12:34 PM): Sleuthing didn't find an Axel, but it found a Brent McLorry, who listed his job as an alchemist in 2014 on Facebook. See attached pic.

Lyra grins at her phone. Indeed, it is the same person, to a creepy extent: no aging, no change in hair, nothing.

JACKSON (12:38 PM): He disappears off the internet after that. Seems edgy for the point of edgy. He did actual magic?

LYRA (12:39 PM): Near as I can tell.

JACKSON (12:40 PM): Do you want to talk to him? Or do you need me to draft a restraining order that looks very official?

LYRA (12:41 PM): Maybe if he shows up again. I'll let you know.

After a night of sleep, her curiosity is piqued, and she mulls over telling someone. Actually letting another person know about the creepy, someone who seems at least base level familiar with what she's dealing with.

The only thing she'd have to fear is another rejection, just another person fearing her, another person skating around the edges of her life.

But really, if this new person does it, it might not be any big loss. She's seen him all of twice, and mostly because he followed her all the way from Seattle after a chance encounter in a coffee shop.

THREE NIGHTS LATER, close to midnight again, this 'Axel' strides back in, this time with another woman in tow.

She is tall and slender in all the ways Lyra is not, with rich, shining black-brown hair and gorgeous cinnamon brown eyes half-covered by gold-rimmed glasses. Her dress is neatly tailored and looks handmade, like she crafted the pattern herself, and she carries a messenger bag stuffed to the brim.

Lyra eyes them both as she checks out an out-of-towner driving through on his way to the Bellingham ferry, but they both hang in the back of the store, leafing through the aged magazines.

The moment the out-of-towner leaves with his bag of beef jerky and energy drinks, Lyra waves them over. "What do you want now?"

Axel gives up on the browsing and immediately makes a beeline to her front desk, the woman following more cautiously behind him.

"How are you still alive?" Axel says, picking up a stick of gum and twirling it in his fingers. Lyra watches it warily, in case it turns into something else. "We did our research, and you"—he points with the gum—"should be dead."

Lyra glances at the security camera as the out-of-towner gets into his sedan and pulls out of their parking lot. "The car accident wasn't that bad."

It's false, of course, the car accident was absolutely that bad, but it's her pat answer whenever anyone asks about it.

Both of them blink at her. "What car accident?" Axel asks.

Oh.

Lyra folds her hands on her lap, over her brown corduroys and her ugly long-sleeved red polo. "The car accident I almost died in?"

"I think you're misunderstanding us," the woman interrupts, and her voice is lulling. "Most people with the gift of necromancy die as children."

And Lyra remembers her mother's panic when she raised the mouse, at her terror, at how Jackson lost the bouncy blue ball. At how they never returned to Ohio. At her mother's fear of anyone around them. At how her mother forbade her from religion, forbade her from online forums. At how her mother obsessively tracked things for years, shuttling them from motel to motel, to campground to campground.

"My mama was overprotective," she says, simply, as if that answers all their questions.

They exchange a look, and in that look is years of baked-in experiences, of knowing each other for longer than Lyra's known anyone that isn't her brother.

"I understand if you're secretive, but I assure you, we're not going to harm you," the woman says, then she extends her hand to Lyra. "I'm Alette Jyotshi. I'm a spellweaver in Seattle and Vancouver."

Delicate tattoos, more than Lyra can track, blend into the dark skin on Alette's hand, and Lyra tentatively shakes it.

"Lyra," she replies.

"And I'm Axel, but I want to know how some demon didn't come by and"—he snaps his fingers—"just kill ya. You must be a walking target."

"Thanks," Lyra shoots back.

"Aaaaand you and your brother were talking about demons." He crosses his arms across his chest like he's got her on that one, like she hasn't obsessively replayed the conversation she had with Jackson over and over in her brain. "So, how'd you do it?"

Alette gives her a sympathetic look, the look of someone who's had to deal with this shit before.

The bell at the door tinkles and a gaggle of teenagers enter, despite it being well after curfew, heading straight towards the alcohol that they almost certainly can't legally buy.

"We find ourselves in need," Alette says, quieter, leaning forward on the counter so Lyra can hear her. "Especially from someone who could do the things necromancers can do."

"I haven't done much," Lyra whispers back, though she's tracking the one teenager who's reading the beer labels a little bit too closely. "Really."

Axel taps the gum against the counter, and she half expects it to turn into glitter or something, but instead he just taps it like it's a nervous habit. "If you have some way of talking to a demon without it killing you, mostly." His voice isn't nearly as quiet as Alette's, but the kids don't seem to notice. "We could use some power. Think about it."

"But what have you figured out?" Alette asks, then steps aside for the teenagers attempting to buy beer.

They have an ID that seems to be real. It's probably not theirs, but all Lyra cares about is that the ID is an actual ID. Her boss once got after her for not selling beer to just anyone with an ID, so Lyra just throws a fuss when it's anything stronger than beer.

The moment the teenagers leave, Alette and Axel immediately face her again, and it's worse than any of the doctors' prodding.

And, abruptly, she's tired of it, tired of dancing around these people, like if she plays dumb enough, they'll go away. Tired of half-truths and not knowing things and them just standing in her store.

"I raised my brother when he died, and a demon came, and we worked out a thing," she snaps and doesn't miss both of their eyebrows flying up. "Now, like once a year, he finds me and zaps some energy and then goes away, and I don't think about it until the next time."

It's quiet in her little Quik Mart, just the fluorescent lights buzzing and the far off sound of the mostly empty highway, as Alette and Axel stare at her like she's sprouted an extra head.

"You just...let him?" Axel asks, and joy of joys, his voice is disgusted.

Lyra looks down at her hands, at the little stool and the slight trace of glitter that's still on the floor, no matter how much they've mopped.

"The other option was dying," she says.

Out of the corner of her eye, she sees them exchange a glance.

"So you can talk to him, though," Alette says. "If you talk to him, can you bargain some more?"

Lyra lifts her gaze to them, and they're completely serious.

"You have access to a demon, a demon that isn't going to kill you immediately—" Axel starts.

"—Probably," Lyra injects because that seems to be a key thing they're missing. "Who knows, he might change his mind."

"And you work in a gas station quikmart named Buggees?" Axel gestures at the store, at the one broken fridge section, at that one questionable stain in the back, at the aging shelves and the dusty magazines. "You could ask him for unlimited money, unlimited power, and you work here?"

"I like this job," she replies, keeping an eye on the security cameras as a car drives by, but no one pulls into the tiny little parking lot.

Alette presses her thumb to the bridge of her nose, like Axel's giving her a headache. "May I contact you?" she interrupts, and for a split second, Lyra gets a glimpse of a much stronger, harder person than the impression Alette's given her. "Some time when you aren't at work, so we can sit and talk?"

"Why?" Lyra asks, immediately suspicious.

She's not as suspicious as her mother—she's not—but some things take longer to get un-ingrained from her psyche and trusting people who show up and claim to know random trivia about her is top of the list.

"In case we need your help, duh," Axel says, and Alette pinches her nose harder. "Do you know how rare necromancers are? Like, at all?"

Lyra just stares at him.

"We're facing a threat, and we're actively trying to find more people to help, is what he's trying to say," Alette says, then yawns because the nightshift isn't for everyone, and she clearly didn't sleep in until noon. "Can I have your number? I can contact you with more sources on necromancy if you'd like."

Lyra scribbles it on her scratch notepad for the job, rips off the corner of the paper, and hands it to her. "Don't give it to him," she says, jerking her head at Axel, who has the gall to look offended.

The scrap of paper disappears into Alette's immaculately tailored jacket, and Lyra gets a strong feeling she just made a huge mistake.

ALETTE (10:02 AM): This is for research purposes. How long has something remained dead before you raised it?

Lyra grabs at her phone from the stuffy old nightstand she still keeps by her bed and blearily peers at it.

All down her legs ache, like she had run miles the night before, like the small standoff in the Buggees entailed a race, and the muscle between her shoulder blades radiates the special sort of nerve pain that comes from sleeping wrong.

LYRA (10:04 AM): Mouse, I think a few days. Brother, about 15 minutes.

She thumps her head back down onto the pillow, squeezing her eyes shut.

Days like this are the worst, and it's always after her week of working. Always on her 'weekend'—which is Monday to Tuesday—and always makes her feel like shit.

One of her doctors a while back had told her that she should probably limit the number of days she works or even stay unemployed, but doctors like that have little idea about how money actually works.

ALETTE (10:07 AM): Is this an actual mouse, or is that a nickname for someone/thing?

LYRA (10:08 AM): Actual mouse. I was like six. I don't know.

ALETTE (10:09 AM): Fascinating.

Not getting any more sleep now, Lyra pushes herself up to slouch into the kitchen, press start on the ancient coffee machine, and curl up in the armchair to wait for it to brew.

Outside her kitchen window, mist drifts through the trees and rock cliffs, obscuring all signs of her neighbors just down the block.

That's another reason why she didn't sell the place. It's about as remote as she can comprehend being while still having no car, just a short half-mile trek from the Buggees, and yet...

And yet, she can sit at her window and not see her neighbors.

Granted, she's fairly certain the neighbors are cooking meth, and they have about five rusted out trucks and cars on their front lawn, but the mist makes it so she mostly doesn't have to look at them.

Her other neighbor is a tottering ancient man who makes the sign of the cross when he sees her, but otherwise only leaves his house once a week to sit on his porch and wait for his son to bring him groceries. Lyra leaves him alone, half expecting to wake up one day and feel the gut-punch of death towards his house and know that if she brings him back, she'd be unable to keep him alive for very long.

ALETTE (10:24 AM): Correct my assumption, but you have not been trained in any lore, correct?

And unless she's going to count her mother's ranting as lore, Lyra can't say she has.

LYRA (10:24 AM): Right.

ALETTE (10:25 AM): Do you want to meet for brunch? I can explain things without Axel.

Lyra doesn't usually eat breakfast until after noon.

LYRA (10:32 AM): Where?

THANKFULLY, Alette picks a restaurant in her little town, and since it's not a weekend, there are actually tables in the tiny diner. Lyra, knowing the place, dresses in a casual wide skirt cut at her mid-calf, with textured tights and an overlarge cable sweater.

It's what Jackson calls her 'cozy librarian' look, and he's not wrong. It protects her from any cold that'd cause her legs to cramp yet doesn't make her look like she's wearing a sleeping bag.

Alette is again wearing an immaculately tailored long jacket, one that's cut close to her body, and neat slacks that definitely aren't from any place Lyra can afford.

There's no one else in the tiny diner except for the waitress, and the moment they get seated, Alette pulls out a needle from a case, and it gleams gold in the overhead light.

With just a quick, raised eyebrow to Lyra, she uses the needle to sketch out a series of invisible lines on the little table, not even pressing hard enough to make a mark in the wood. Like she's writing a cheat sheet on a desk at school.

It scritches like a pencil, a soft sound that teases at the edge of Lyra's hearing, until…

All other sound drops away, leaving just the sudden sound of their breathing. Not the sizzle from the kitchen, not the scrape of the waitress's shoe as she waits at the grill line, nothing.

"Quick sound barrier, now we can talk in private," Alette says, stowing the needle back in the case and disappearing it into her jacket. "It's handy in public."

"Huh," Lyra says because it's way more practical of a magical thing than turning breath mints into glitter.

"And when we leave, the place will be…a little bit louder than it should." Alette fixes her with an almost severe look over her gold-rimmed glasses. "That's the rule of magic: what is done will also be undone."

"Creepy," Lyra says, and for once, she can say that about someone else.

Alette only nods in agreement. "It manifests in a lot of ways. If you can give something through magic, you can take it away. If something can use you, you can use it. It's never just a one-way street."

All this before Lyra's had any food for the day.

"Well, okay," she says, as neutrally as she can. "I just found out a few days ago that magic besides my…thing…exists."

"And you had to find out from Axel," Alette points out, and the corner of her mouth twitches up because he really is that annoying. "What did he transform in front of you? Was it his phone again?"

"Box of Tic Tacs," she replies. "Turned it into glitter."

"And somewhere in the world, a bag of glitter probably became breath mints," Alette says, and it's almost the most nonsensical conversation she's ever had. "Second rule: all magic takes energy. The bigger the effect, the more energy it takes. Did you pass out when you raised your brother?"

Lyra takes a moment to blink it out, to look at anything except for the over-serious Alette.

"It's hard to tell," she says, and her mind is racing back to that day, to the sensations, to all the things that she tries not to examine, to—"I did once the demon showed up, that's for sure."

"Right," Alette says, and to her credit, she looks visibly unsettled, her mouth turning downwards. She makes a motion, as if to reach back towards the needle case, but stops herself. "That would be...an additional drain."

The waitress drops off their food, and Lyra pokes at her poached eggs, feeling like the back of her neck is crawling with exposure.

"And you really have no additional side effects from him?" Alette asks, her fork hovering over a fruit salad and some toast. "That seems..."

She's had to talk too much about Melekai this week, and it's awkward. "I sleep for a night," she says because that's easier than anything else. "And usually don't have any pain for about a week."

Alette stares at her for far too long before setting down her fork to take a measured sip of coffee.

"Do you realize that demons are terrifying?" Alette says delicately, and Lyra must be better at bluffing than she usually is. "They are not...something to be trifled with. In any way or reasonable situation."

"I got that, yeah," Lyra says and takes a large bite of her eggs to stop herself from anything more awkward. "The option was to work with him or to die."

Alette stares at her, but she's back to the calculating stare instead of the incredulous stare, which is only marginally less weird.

"Do you...visualize your magic?" Alette asks, clinically. "Most do."

"No?"

Alette folds her hands like she's slightly overwhelmed at Lyra's lack of knowledge. "Picture magic as...a series of threads."

"Really, string theory?" Lyra says because she can't figure out anything more intelligent to say. "Pretty sure I heard that was debunked."

"From a physics level, yes," Alette says.

A man and woman breeze into the diner, but their footsteps make no noise, and despite their mouths moving, she can hear no sound.

In terms of magical powers, it's pretty damn odd.

"I would like," Alette starts, before frowning at the fruit salad, "given any sort of time or freedom, of course, which we do not have, to figure out a way to train you. There's next to no literature on necromancers—I looked it up—and what we have is... mostly through the lens of theory."

"What's the deadline?" Lyra asks, her curiosity piqued. "You said..."

And again, there's the little motion; she's about to reach for the needle case but realizes it before she does—a nervous twitch.

It makes Lyra feel a little bit better Alette is as unnerved by this conversation as she is.

Still, Alette measures herself. Visibly takes a moment to figure out what to say, to weigh out her words.

"A magical...thing...is trying to end the world," Alette says, blunt like they're not just sitting in a tiny diner in a northern Washington town that only has four stoplights. "We—myself, Axel, and my aunt —are trying to stop it."

The waitress swoops by, filling up Lyra's coffee and saying something inaudible before swinging away.

End of the world is a pretty strict time restriction, even Lyra must admit, and three people isn't enough. "Are magicians really that rare?"

"Very," Alette answers like it's an easy question. "And finding one as...old as you, with no additional training, is almost unheard of."

A big part of her, the part that keeps the job at Buggees and the house next to the meth heads and the part that refuses to drive her own car again, wants to just get up. Leave the rich girl with her golden tools to pay for the brunch and walk out.

End of the World is crazy stuff.

Worse than her mother's rambling, worse than the drunks who opine at her in the store, worse than the meth heads.

But...

But the world includes her brother, and she didn't give herself over to a demon just for him to die in some sort of pseudo apocalypse.

"So what can I even do?"

IT TURNS OUT, Alette has a lot of ideas on what Lyra can do, and they eventually leave the brunch restaurant and stroll around the twee little park that Lyra always avoids.

It's a nice enough day for late autumn. It hasn't snowed yet, so the ground isn't slushy, and the mist stays where it is, not falling into drizzle among the turning leaves.

"Really, the most important thing, the thing that could actually sway the battle, would be to see if you could convince your demon to fight with us," Alette says, after a lot of technical terms that Lyra doesn't understand and a lot of extrapolating with even bigger terms. "Sheer firepower, something that could match the...being...and possibly stop it."

"I doubt I could," Lyra says, scuffing her boots in the leaves on the dead grass. "We don't exactly talk."

"If what you've described is true," Alette starts, then scrunches her nose at the mist around them, "then you raising something from the dead should summon him almost immediately."

"He said that, yeah," Lyra says, unnerved that Alette could tell that without her giving that detail. "Said he'd show up to protect me."

"He'd show up because he'd have to," Alette corrects. "If he took some of your energy, then he's tied to you until you die. It's just... usually for necromancers that happens almost immediately."

"Not comforting," Lyra mutters and kicks at the leaves a little bit harder, ignoring the twinge of muscle pain in her upper back. If she doesn't take the rest of the day easier, she'll be in even more pain tomorrow, and it's not a cycle she wants to head down anytime soon. "So what, call him up, ask if he could help save the world and not kill me anytime soon?"

Alette's eyes are embarrassingly earnest over her glasses. "Yes."

4

～

ALETTE (10:46 PM): What time do you get out of work tonight?

Lyra raises an eyebrow at her phone as the fluorescent lights above her buzz. Technically, she's not supposed to have her phone at work, but Mr. Peters always keeps his plugged into the outlet under the till, so everyone else does as well.

LYRA (10:47 PM): Midnight thirty. That is an ominous question.

ALETTE (10:47 PM): Can we pick you up?

LYRA (10:48 PM): Why?

A small bit of her feels guilty, in some remote way, at being even that amount of rude, but she rubs her hands to warm them in the chilly convenience store. The heater always breaks in the first week of winter, and it's just cold enough outside that it's a big deal.

The three dots of typing appear and then disappear several times.

ALETTE (10:59 PM): With your permission, we want to test something. Test your sensitivity to things.

Someone drives by the Buggees, headlamps illuminating the glass door, but they don't stop.

LYRA (11:01 PM): Define 'we' and define 'tests,' and I'm game.

DESPITE THE ENTIRE exchange's vagueness, at 12:30, exactly, a pristine black Mustang pulls up to the Buggees as Lyra's counting off her till to the graveyard shift.

Her coworker Nathan gives the nice car a leer, then glances back to Lyra.

"You know someone with that nice of a car?"

"Only halfway," Lyra replies, counting out the dollars and placing them in the correct order, and facing up.

"One of your brother's friends?" Everyone here is skeptical of Jackson's friends, with his law school and their large amounts of money.

"Sure." She focuses hard on facing her bills, not looking out at the impressive display of wealth. For all she knows, it could be an absolute junker that Axel transformed into something else.

If that's even possible.

Once she locks up her till she gives Nathan a tight-lipped smile, then grabs her bag and trundles out into the wind and the mist.

Axel's even standing outside the car, leaning against it, like he believes himself to be out of a movie set, though Alette's clearly waiting in the passenger's seat where it's, you know, warm.

Lyra eyes him before opening the back seat and climbing inside. "Is he always like that?"

Inside it's the perfect temperature, not so warm she gets sweaty but pleasant, and the seats are a buttery leather, perfectly devoid of any crumbs or scuffs.

"Generally, yes," Alette replies, as Axel climbs into the driver's seat. Exhaustion rims the edges of Alette's eyes, even in the dim light of the headlamps. "Sorry for the late-night pickup."

"I'm not," Axel says, breezily starting the car. It doesn't rumble like a Mustang should, instead, feeling more like an electric car, and Lyra doesn't know enough to know about fancy vehicles to know if that's more or less expensive than a vintage Mustang. "It's prime magic time."

He pulls out of the parking lot, and the tires make no sound.

"Axel lives for midnight drives and energy drinks," Alette says, and even her voice echoes tired and...something worse. Something beneath the exhaustion, something Lyra knows very well. Pain.

She can't see much from the backseat, but Alette's gripping one of her wrists, like one would a sprain, and she's leaning to one side of the seat, all her weight shifted to one side.

A glance at Axel shows him favoring his shoulder, driving with one hand.

"I'm usually not in bed until two, anyways," Lyra says, though warning bells go off in her brain. "What sort of tests?"

She slips her phone out of her pocket.

LYRA (12:36 PM): Going somewhere after work. I will text you when I get home. Call if you don't get the text by the time you wake up.

And she turns her phone's meager location tracking on for Jackson to see.

Her phone doesn't always cooperate, so she generally keeps it off, but it's at full charge.

"I wanna see how much creepy you can sense," Axel says, and they pass under a street lamp, and the fabric on his shoulder glistens, wet. Like he's much more injured than he should be for someone driving a car.

"Remember how I told you about the person trying to end the world?" Alette starts, and her voice wavers, just a bit.

Axel snorts. "Fuck Terese."

"Yes, her name is Terese," Alette sighs, "she...set off a magical... thing. We want to see what you sense before we attempt to sanitize it."

Axel flips the turn signal on, and the click fills the quiet car.

"Is it safe?" Lyra asks, which seems like the most basic of questions she should be asking.

"It is now," Axel says, and his bravado almost, almost cracks, before he swallows it back down and shakes whatever it was off. "She's somewhere in the wind, but the location is...fine."

He turns down a gravel road out past Nugent's Corner, crossing over a rickety bridge over Nooksack River, and the entire car jostles as it hits an uneven board.

"If you kidnap me, my brother knows where to look," Lyra says, to the silence of the car.

Axel's eyes flicker to hers in the rearview mirror. "Yes, because what we want to do is piss off a necromancer who has access to a demon," he says, and just enough sarcasm covers up the quaver. "That's just the sort of smart thing to do."

Well, when he puts it that way, the little bit of fear feels foolish, but Lyra just shifts in her seat.

"Axel, don't," Alette says, quiet. "Lyra, if you want us to return, just let me know. We wouldn't bring you if there were any remaining danger."

They wind further upwards, as the mist turns to light rain, then to a steady, thrumming downpour on the roof of the Mustang. The road can barely be called one, more of a gravel and dirt pathway scarcely big enough for the Mustang, and berry vines brush against the windows and doors, scratching at the pristine paint.

Finally, Axel lets the car glide to a stop, and the rain lashes down harder. The only light is the headlights, so he leaves the car running as he steps out.

Lyra exchanges a glance with Alette before Alette nods at her.

"We mostly want to see if you can sense things," Alette says, not moving from her seat in the car, and Lyra's now not sure she can.

"I don't even know what to look for," Lyra says, but she unclips herself from the seatbelt, scooting out into the rain.

It turns her waves into an immediate bedraggled mess, soaking through her work polo in a matter of seconds.

"Eh, fuck that," Axel mutters, then digs in the trunk of the car and pulls out a plain t-shirt. With a flick of his wrist, illuminated by the headlamp, it's transformed into a cozy looking—and very fancy—

raincoat, which he hands to her with enough fanfare that she would think it's a ring.

Alette rolls her eyes through the windshield.

Still, Lyra shrugs it on, and somehow, it's exactly her size, which would be creepy if it weren't so warm, immediately cutting out the wind and the chill.

"So where are we?" she asks, flicking the hood over her hair and shoving her hands into her new pockets. "And will this turn back into a shirt at the stroke of midnight tomorrow?"

"I am not that much of an amateur," Axel says, then gestures for her to follow him into a tiny clearing ahead. "Clothing is easy."

It's like all of Washington's greenery, with the pine and the berry plants and the ivy suddenly...stops.

The hair on the back of Lyra's neck rises.

The edges of all the leaves are singed, evident even in the dim light of the headlamps.

Lyra hangs back, something inside of her shying away. "Do you have a flashlight?"

He digs his hand into his pocket, pulling out a granola bar, which he taps against his thigh, turning it into a mag light.

The light flickers, faint, and he thumps it again, but that doesn't help. He sighs, weary, like the exhaustion took his ability away.

The branches are all bent back, like something had forcefully inhabited their space, crunching down on everything in its path. It's more akin to a small, contained explosion than anything Lyra's ever seen.

"What happened?" The words fall from Lyra's lips as Axel swings the mag light to and fro, catching the rainfall in its flickering beam.

Something in her stops at the edge, stops her from crossing the invisible barrier into the detonation zone. Like there's a physical bubble, pushing back at her, preventing her from crossing its threshold.

"I was hoping you could shed some light," Axel says, pushing his soggy hair out of his eyes. "We think she tried to open a portal."

A portal. Because apparently that's something that exists.

"You're way overestimating what I know," Lyra says, and her legs lock in place, all but screaming at her, the aches and the pain ricocheting up her spine. Like every little motion and breeze from this place draws her pain in.

Axel watches her, and through the windshield, so does Alette.

Lyra forces her knees to unlock, to bend, to take a step into the little unnatural clearing.

Immediately, the unique pull of death punches into her gut, and the rain lessens before stopping.

Lyra blinks the water from her eyes and steps further into the bubble. The rain is almost gliding off of a little puff of air, sliding to the side. Outside, where Axel is standing with his flashlight, the downpour is the same.

"Well, that's neat," Lyra says and holds her hand out as if to catch the nonexistent rain. Even the air is warmer, the late fall chill headed off like she's wrapped herself in a fluffy, light blanket.

The pain in her legs is gone, too.

She exhales, watching the air puff up around her, then turns to Axel. "Is Terese a...what is she?"

He's staying well outside of the explosion radius, a hand pressing to the injured shoulder. "We don't know what Terese is, not really."

Because everything, the lack of pain, the gut-punch of recent death, is only something she's experienced with one person before.

Lyra scuffs her boot against the ground, against the dead moss and the dead branches, and tries to think. She tries to feel something, tries not to look like an idiot staring at the ground.

"Hand me the flashlight?" She holds out her hand. Axel gives it without a word.

She crouches down, looking at the ground, at the dead leaves and underbrush, at everything bent away in its path.

The twigs are broken and still fresh and green on the edges.

Slowly, she reaches out her hand and touches the bare earth.

It's full of dead things.

A dead ground squirrel, a couple of inches down. A dead snake, near the edge. A burrowing mouse.

It piles on, more and more.

Deeper, dead worms, dead insects, dead spiders, all suddenly gone, as if their life suddenly cut off just a few hours ago. An entire colony of ants, all dead now, in their tunnels where they were carrying food. The eggs of a lizard, off to one side, the yolks gone cold.

She could bring them back.

The thought strikes her, a sudden, chilly dagger into her back, and she jolts upright, jerking her hand away from the dirt, and blinks owlishly in the light of the headlamps.

Axel and Alette just watch her, grim.

"Was anyone...inside this bubble?" she asks, and her voice even sounds far away. "When it was...set off?"

Axel shakes his head. "Only Terese."

"And she walked out?" Lyra shakes herself as if she could shake off the creepy and the heebie-jeebies, to no avail, so she scoots out of the little detonation, back into the stinging rain and the wind and the vicious chill.

It's immediately unpleasant.

Axel jerks his head back to the Mustang, and she has no problem following him out, rushing out of the lashing rain and into the warmth of the car.

The water sizzles off of her as she does, and she flinches.

"Sorry," Alette murmurs, and the golden needle glints in her hand as Axel climbs back in. "I thought you would want to be dry."

"No yeah, thanks, that's good, that's good," Lyra says, and she's talking too fast, she's running her mouth, but the creepiness of all those dead things just crawls up her throat, as if it could choke her out. "Just surprised and all and what the fuck was that?"

Axel pushes his rapidly drying hair around, careful as if that is what matters right then when his shirt is still damp from blood as well as rain. Idly, he opens the car glove box and hands her a granola bar before taking one for himself.

"We tried to apprehend her. It didn't go well," Axel says, still raking his hair back. "What did you sense?" Finally, he starts the car, reversing down the dirt pathway.

"Everything in the ground, for as deep as I could tell, was dead," Lyra says, and her legs spasm with each bump of the wheels. "All the moss, all the bugs, a little snake, everything."

"Well, we didn't know that," Alette says, quiet.

"And my legs stopped hurting, and the rain didn't hit me anymore, and it was warmer, so I thought maybe a demon?" Lyra continues, wincing with the rough terrain until Axel pulls into a small turnaround and straightens the car. "The pain only goes away around Melekai."

"You named your demon Melekai?" Axel blurts out.

"No, that's...that's his name...he told me?" Lyra says because that's not the point. "But usually, the pain only stops when he uh..." she trails off because this sounds awkward no matter how she puts it. "When he feeds from me?"

It's silent in the Mustang for a long moment after that, as Axel navigates the car back to the gravel road, and Alette clenches the golden needle in her hand.

"So you're telling me that you're always in pain unless your demon comes along," Axel grinds out.

"Yeah," Lyra says, small.

"That's pretty astounding," Alette says, and thankfully her face is neutral. "I would have never known you were in pain."

"Yeah, well, I live with it," she replies, then winces at the rudeness. "It's not like I get to curl up in bed and stop whenever I hurt. Either I go to work or take a bunch of pills and be high off my ass all the time." This isn't the point. This is so far from the point. "But that thing, it...it killed everything in the bubble. Everything."

Alette takes a deep breath. "Terese put off a great deal of power when she did that. I'm not surprised everything died."

"And you guys were hurt." At their silences, Lyra scoffs. "Like I don't see the favoring of your shoulder, Axel, or you holding your wrist."

"We were a bit away from her," Alette says, her glasses reflecting the headlights as they pull back onto the rickety bridge and onto the freeway going back towards Lyra's town. "But...yes."

"Terese got away," Axel says, a scowl in his voice. "Any idea where she could have gone?"

"No?" Lyra says before staring out at the passing freeway. "All I could sense was the dead things."

The two of them exchange a grim glance in the front seat, leaving her alone with her thoughts.

THEY DROP her off at her father's little house, and all Lyra can do is send the all-clear text before collapsing into bed.

LYRA (2:04 AM): Home safe. Just some magical weirdness. Talk later.

5

Lyra doesn't hear from them for another two weeks, besides the occasional text from Alette with links to terminology-heavy research that she struggles through reading.

It's a quiet two weeks. The store is the same as always, with its ever-rotating array of customers and shoplifters, drunks and tourists, bored teens, and kind elderly. Lyra has lunch with Jackson and doesn't mention the End of the World, and he, in turn, doesn't mention his looming finals.

The weather slowly turns to slush, and Lyra's nerves feel like they're on fire each time she walks outside.

She tries not to worry about the End of the World, she really does, but honestly, it's a bit difficult. Even though she met Alette all of three times and Axel the same, the idea of the two of them being the last bastions of defense the world has is...troubling.

As is the idea that she could do something to affect it as well.

She's walking home one Sunday night, and the wind cuts through her jacket like it's made of butter. It's the first truly cold night of the late fall, the night where taking a breath makes her nostrils hurt and her lungs burn.

It's just about a half-mile walk up the sloping road from Buggees, but on cold nights after midnight, it feels like forever. She passes the animal shelter with its resulting kick of death in the gut, passes the graveyard with its old graves that still call to her, passes the last street lamp of their little town before it winds up into the hills. To where the sidewalk turns to gravel, then the road itself.

The first time Jackson visited her, she pointed out the amount of death at the animal shelter, and it just about broke his heart. Like death isn't incredibly common, if you know where to look for it, and an underfunded shelter with very little room in a community that's not wealthy wouldn't have to make the heartbreaking decision to put down animals.

Her phone buzzes in the pocket she's tucked her hands in, and no one calls after midnight unless it's an emergency, and her stomach flips when she sees Alette's number.

"Hello?" she answers, and the mist around her steals her voice, stopping it inches from her face.

"Yeah, Lyra?" It's Axel's voice, distinctive even over her tinny phone with its half-busted speaker. "We need you and your demon, and we need you quick."

Lyra looks around, but she's still a bit away from her house, and no one's driving this far up the hill this time of night.

"What happened?"

"Our big bad just tried to take over the world, and we need fire-power. We will have something dead for you to raise to call your demon. You have twelve hours."

"What could be so urgent but also give you twelve hours?" Lyra asks, shivering.

"We have to...we have to drive from Banff, I..."

And the phone clicks off, leaving her even colder than before.

LYRA (12:57 AM): Where's Alette? Is she okay?

ALETTE (12:57 AM): Busy. We will pick you up at 1 PM. Be prepared.

That's more ominous than she likes, and she stands still in place, the mist swirling around her, climbing around her and crawling into her lungs with each breath.

She'll have to raise something from the dead—ambush Melekai in front of who knows how many people.

Maybe die in front of strangers, if he doesn't take kindly to it.

She wouldn't take kindly to it, to being summoned someplace without warning. Heck, twelve hours of notice, and she's still feeling wrong-footed.

"What?" she whispers like the mist would give her answers.

It's too late to call Jackson for advice. It's too late to call anyone.

Her toes cold in her rain boots, she shifts, looking back down the road, towards the animal shelter to where she can still feel the pull of death deep in her gut.

Maybe, if nothing else, perhaps a little bit of warning.

IT TAKES her very little time to shimmy open the fence and find the small burial plot in the back. The pull in her grows stronger the closer she steps to it.

She grabs an empty cardboard box from the dumpster, then kneels at the burial plot. The ground is cold and wet, but thankfully there's just a thin layer of dirt thrown over a tarp, and...

The feeling of death scrabbles at her gut, clawing at her throat.

The bodies are too fresh for her to smell, thankfully, but the all-pervasive feeling of death makes her eyes water.

All she would have to do is reach a hand in and touch all the animals, and they could come back. They could all rise again; all be alive once more, and—

And something in the back of her mind knows that doing something so big, so massive, would end her. It would take all of her nebulous powers and energy and collapse her right then and there.

Gingerly, she uses the tarp to pick up the cat on top and set it in the cardboard box. The body is rigid, and even through the tarp, she can tell that the heart stopped beating but not caused by injuries or old age, just...got stopped.

Her skin crawls, and as quietly as she can, she shoves the tarp back into place and kicks dirt back over the animals.

Even for someone like her, this is up there on the sketchiest things she's ever done.

Still, even with the dead body radiating awareness in the box next to her, the grave pulls to her. She has to force her legs to stumble away, back through the gate and onto the main road.

When Lyra was back in community college, she had contemplated taking some pre-med courses, but even the brief glimpse of a cadaver she saw left her full of the awful sensation that she could reach to it and bring it back.

She never took anything above basic level biology after that.

With more speed than is good for her, she rushes back to her house, and the cardboard box grows heavier and heavier. She's more and more aware, until she can tell that the cat had pulled a muscle in his leg as well, before he got put down, and probably a limp. Until she can feel the whiskers bent out of place by being buried for about four hours. Until she can sense the very pinprick where a needle entered his fur, and where something cold stopped his heart.

She couldn't get home soon enough, and she scrabbles with her keys at her doorknob before shouldering open her door and setting the cardboard box on the table before backing away.

The sense of death stays there, on the table, and if she backs down to the hallway, she can think clearly enough.

The research Alette sent her mentions, time and time again, that if a magician is to do magic, they should do it after a meal when they have enough food and energy in their system that they can spend it and not suffer the consequences.

The very idea of food is repellent, but Lyra unclenches her muscles long enough to edge back into the tiny kitchen, to grab the box of cereal she keeps on the counter, and shove a handful into her mouth.

The cereal is powdery, supposedly chocolate flavored, and tastes like sawdust, but she makes herself crunch a few handfuls down before edging closer to her dining table.

Not since bringing Jackson back has she done this so deliberately.

"Okay," she whispers, then gingerly sets the box onto the wood floor. She just needs to raise this cat, tell Melekai, and then...

Then, knowing their interactions, she'll probably get knocked out for nine hours and then have to wake up and do it all over again, this time with an audience and the looming threat of the End of the World.

She fumbles with her phone and sets an alarm for 10:00 AM. Alarms won't always wake her after Melekai's done, but it's better than nothing.

Hands shaking, she drags the cushion from the overstuffed chair and sits on it, on the floor next to the cardboard box, and makes herself look inside.

The cat is still, of course, like she should expect, and three of the whiskers are bent, just like she sensed.

"Okay," she says, then takes a deep breath and dangles her hand against the cat's white fur.

Immediately, the overwhelming sense of just restarting the heart hits her, and she breathes out, blinking past the crawling and the confusion and the horror, and straightens her back.

Then, her legs aching from sitting cross-legged, she pokes at the cat's chest, against the breastbone, and imagines pouring herself into it, pouring whatever power and feeling behind her gut, and—

The cat's paws twitch, and a rumble kicks up, as the heart jumps a few times, then evens out, in time with the breathing.

And immediately, Melekai is behind her.

Lyra doesn't even have to turn to look. She just knows. It's like his very presence fills the trailer to the brim, stealing away air and light and everything good.

"Hello, Little Lyra," he says, and his voice is deeper than it usually is, words enunciated differently. "You've never called me before."

Not looking behind her, she withdraws her hand from the cat, folding it in her lap.

"It's been a bit," he says, and his hand rests, gentle, on the back of her neck, like he always does, but there's none of the familiar draw from her, none of the immediate numbing of pain. Like he's waiting for her. "What do you need?"

She exhales as a sudden fragment of nerves winds its way through her.

Keeping the hand on her neck, he crosses in front of her so that she can see him.

This time, the body he's in is young, closer to Lyra's age than before. His hair is a light brown and full of curls, pulled back into an artful bun, and his eyes match, a clear and light golden color.

Melekai looks halfway between an indie musician and a coffee barista at a way too hip Seattle Starbucks. He's dressed like one, as well, with a Henley and designer jeans and a jumble of hemp bracelets.

"Lyra," he prompts after she doesn't say anything.

"The World is Ending, and they wanted me to call you," she blurts out, and he raises a well-shaped eyebrow in response. "I found some magicians, they could tell I was...me...and they're trying to stop the world from ending."

He settles next to her on the hardwood floor, his long limbs folding up in an almost comical way. The hand lifts from her neck, but he's listening to her and not killing her. She takes it as a win.

So Lyra takes a big breath and tries to make herself slow down.

"They've...they've said they're fighting something, and something went wrong today," she says, and the vagaries and frustration just make it worse. "They wanted me to summon you tomorrow at 1 PM so they could make you help them."

"Make me," he says, neutral, but his eyes flash before he holds out his hand for hers.

She extends her hand to him, and he cradles it, a finger drawing a circle in her palm.

"I wanted..." she trails off because in front of him now, all of her actions seem rushed and hasty. "I dunno. To warn you, so you weren't...taken by surprise."

He tilts his head at that, continuing the soft touches on the palm of her hand. It almost tickles in that strange in-between feeling of sensation and feather-light touch.

"I don't...I don't know much."

"End of the World, that's new," he says, and there's a ghost of a grin in his voice. "Your friends must be...eager to get their hand on a demon, to say that."

He raises his finger, and a thin golden thread rises with it before disappearing into his hand.

It's not much compared to their usual contact, but some of the nerve pain in her legs lessens, and she stretches them out in front of her, nudging the cardboard box.

A tiny 'mew' sound erupts from it, and they both freeze.

The cat she stole from the grave pokes his head above the lip of the box, blinking at them both with green-yellow eyes.

"You raised a...cat?" Melekai says, a bit incredulous, but he leans over the little cardboard box.

The cat stares at him right back.

"I panicked. I had just walked by the pound, I could tell there was a lot of dead..." she trails off as he dips his hand into the box, scratching the cat behind the ears.

The cat leans into the touch, purring.

In the years she has known Melekai, she's never seen him interact with anything physical that wasn't...her. She had seen him walk through walls and doors and furniture without a second thought.

Tentatively, the cat steps out of the cardboard box before limping on his back leg like it's an old injury, and the cat has adapted to the point where he doesn't even notice it.

The cat sticks his cold nose on Lyra's hand, then purrs even louder, and Lyra's never had a cat not dissolve into a hissing mess close to her.

Careful, like she'd break it, even though it's a full-grown cat, she touches the cat right between the ears, and the cat just arches up against her hand. The fur is soft, like the cat had been brushed before being put down. Like the cat had been loved.

And Melekai's back to watching her, his eyes a bit too intense, a bit too hungry. Like he could devour her that second and not think another thought of it.

"I just went to the closest death I could find that wasn't in a century-old graveyard," Lyra replies again like she needs to justify herself more. "I didn't want to try a person."

"You could," he says, languid. "You have before."

Lyra takes a brief moment to think of the energy it would take to bring back someone who had been dead for a century and why Melekai believes she'd be able to do that, then moves the fuck on.

"So this is your warning," she says, with more confidence than she has in her entire body, and his eyes don't leave hers. "If you feel me raise a dead thing in twelve hours, they're going to ask you for help. Please don't kill me out of surprise."

The corners of his eyes crinkle up at her words, which is probably the best-case scenario. Better he finds her amusing than anything else.

"Do you really think the world will end, just like that?" he asks, almost absentmindedly reaching and cradling her hand again.

The cat protests the lack of petting, loud, so she scratches under his chin with her other hand. It's almost comedic, how much the cat leans down against the scratches, purring loudly.

"I don't even know," she says, shifting where she sits, and for the first time it's like Melekai becomes aware of their surroundings. He cranes his neck to look up at the creaky building, at the mist barely visible outside the window, at the oversized chair and the tiny table. "I saw the aftermath of one of their fights with this person. It was...dire." Something inside her stops herself from saying that it might've been another demon, with the dead creatures and the lack of pain. "I don't know if I could survive whatever they're fighting throws at me."

"Do you need me to take you somewhere else?" he asks, almost idle, focusing on the precariously screwed in light fixture above her kitchen sink. "If this world will end, I can always take you to a new one."

"Um." His words skip off her mind, twisting with the exhaustion of finishing a painful workweek and the oddity of the sentence. "No?"

He shrugs a casual, one-shoulder movement.

"Whenever humans start to say the world is going to end, they usually just mean their tiny little corner of it," he says, and it's a relatively clear dismissal. "I won't kill you tomorrow if that's what you're worried about."

"Thanks," she says, aiming for sarcasm but ending up embarrassingly sincere.

His eyes turn back to hers, reflecting in the dim light, and a chill goes down to her very soul.

There's never a time where she doesn't remember he's a predator.

He leans over her, the hand going to the back of her neck, settling like a collar, and she shivers.

"It has been so very long since I've seen you, Lyra," he says, voice rich. "It seems that much of your life has changed."

Even with his hand there, he's not drawing from her, he's not sapping her, he's just waiting.

"Jackson's in law school, now," she blurts out, awkward. "In Seattle. He got in."

"That's an achievement?" he replies, though she can hear the question in his voice.

It makes sense that a demon wouldn't care about that sort of thing.

The cat limps over to her lap, awkwardly climbing over her legs and curling up in the crook of her knee. The green-yellow eyes close, as though the cat has had enough for the evening and now wants to sleep, despite the four hours it spent dead and buried if the cat was even aware of that time.

Jackson wasn't.

So Lyra exhales, leaning back against his hand. "I just need to be able to wake up for tomorrow."

"I am very curious what they will have you bring back," he says, drawing a circle with his thumb on the nape of her neck, and her eyelids droop.

It's slower than he usually takes, and a tingling sensation drips down the muscle between her shoulder blades, unwinding it. "Me too," she says, the words falling from her lips. "They seem scared by me."

"They should be," he says, and despite his always changing voice, she knows him well enough to know that he's amused. "Any magician who knows anything should be terrified by you."

Through sheer force of will, she blinks her eyes open, turning her chin just enough to meet his gaze. "I didn't even know about them. This entire time, I could have been learning."

He raises an eyebrow at her, and the last glimpse of him she gets before she blacks out is a wide grin.

6

Something, somewhere, is beeping. Something is beeping, and something is vibrating against her stomach.

And Lyra's in a chair.

She pops her eyes open.

She's on her ugly green velvet chair, legs curled up beneath her, and weak sunshine hits her face from the window.

Nothing hurts.

She straightens her legs, and the small mound of fur on her lap lifts his head and gives her a plaintive 'mew.'

She stares down at the cat, who just stares back, purring.

"Right," she whispers, and lowers a hand to the cat's fur and strokes it. "You're here now."

As if understanding that she's talking to him, the cat just purrs louder.

She has a few moments of comfortable confusion before the beeping noise gets more and more insistent, and her phone is on the table, barely within arm's reach.

The alarm goes off, but it's at 9 instead of the 10 AM she set.

The lack of pain and the comfort that comes after every Melekai visit coats everything, like every light and sound is muted, wrapped in a blanket.

And Alette and Axel are going to pick her up at 1 to raise...something.

She thunks her head against the back of the chair, and the cat mews again, then jumps off her lap, sniffing around.

"I'm gonna need to get you food, aren't I?" Lyra says, and the cat blinks at her before continuing to sniff. "And litter, that's a thing cats need, right?"

Something inside of her bumps up against the idea of just turning the cat out, of abandoning something she brought back, even though she's...not an ideal person to have a pet.

Hell, most animals can't stand her.

"Do you have a name?" Lyra asks, finally standing and stretching and feeling the glory of no pain in the morning, even after sleeping in a chair all night.

Sleeping in a chair she did not get into.

She freezes mid-stretch.

The only possibilities are that she sleep-climbed into the chair, which she's never done before, or Melekai physically carried her to the chair and curled her up to be comfortable.

Usually, he leaves her crumpled up on the floor.

And he changed her alarm to an hour earlier.

Lyra eyes the cat, who's enthusiastically sniffing every little corner of her kitchen, then quickly changes out of her still-covered-in-grave-dirt Buggees polo shirt and into a chunky black sweater and matching jeans. She may as well look the part of a necromancer if she's going to do it, despite the fact that she has no clue what that would mean.

She sets down a bowl of water for the cat, and he enthusiastically dunks his head in it, in a way that she's pretty sure isn't normal for a cat to do, but...it was dead for four hours, so who is she to judge.

She needs food and litter for the cat, then food for herself.

Quick as she can (which is a lot quicker than usual because of the lack of pain), she strides the half-mile to Buggees, picks up a bag of generic cat food and a bag of litter and one of their stick-in-the-oven pizzas, and is back at her apartment long before she usually would be.

It's hard not to feel grateful towards Melekai in the few days after a visit, but this time a thin fizz of anticipation covers the usual relaxation.

She pops the pizza into her ancient oven and pours the kibble into a bowl, then empties the plastic bin she carried between foster homes and fills it with litter. The cat follows her every footstep in the house, limping from room to tiny room, letting out the occasional small 'mew'.

It'd be adorable if she didn't know it had died the day before.

LYRA (10:16 AM): I will be ready in about 30 minutes.

ALETTE (10:17 AM): Still not back in America. Will be there around noon.

LYRA (10:19 AM): Do I need a passport? I don't have a passport.

ALETTE (10:19 AM): I'll make one.

LYRA (10:20 AM): This is still Axel, isn't it.

There's no response, which settles it more than he probably thinks, and another layer of dread fits over the weird patchwork quilt that is becoming Lyra's day.

She attempts to busy herself with grazing on the pizza, puttering around the house, but very quickly ends up back in the chair, poking on her phone with the cat back in her lap.

Melekai hadn't said if he'd show up, just that he wouldn't kill her.

Which should make her feel better about the entire thing.

But all she can remember, now in the weak sunshine of a Washington winter, is the death in that clearing. The death that reached down into the dirt and killed everything around it. The death that hurt Alette, hurt Axel, and the mysterious woman named Terese who caused it.

And now they want to bring her in.

And Melekai.

The hours stretch on far beyond her patience, with the cat fast asleep on her lap, and everything is taking too long, and nothing she can do will pass the time.

LYRA (11:45 AM): Going to be doing some magic thing today. I'll have my phone tracking on. I might be in Canada.

JACKSON (11:46 AM): What?

LYRA (11:46 AM): I'll check in later today. I have been assured I won't die.

JACKSON (11:48 AM): That doesn't make me feel better.

LYRA (11:51 AM): Don't you have class? Focus on class.

JACKSON (11:51 AM): Fuck off.

The nameless cat jumps off her lap at that text message and starts batting at one of her hair ties left on the floor, and Lyra stretches her legs out of habit, despite the glorious lack of pain.

Impulsively, she snaps a picture of the cat to Jackson, taking care to focus it around the crack in her camera lens, then sends it over.

LYRA (11:54 AM): Any tips?

JACKSON (11:54 AM): How'd you trap a cat in the house?

She scowls at her phone.

LYRA (11:55 AM): I raised it from the dead, and now it likes me.

The three dots appear, then disappear, then appear, before finally, her phone rings.

"Lyra, is something up?" Her brother's worried voice comes through the tinny speakers. "Just ducked out of class. I have two minutes."

He's not wrong, but Lyra just taps the phone onto speakerphone and sets it on the table. "Well, remember the magic people I told you about?"

"Are they encouraging you to raise random animals for pets?" Jackson asks, "'Cause that is some ethical weirdness that I'm not prepared to condone."

The cat in question bats the hair tie underneath Lyra's chair and sticks his entire arm under the chair to try to reach it.

"It's okay, the cat was put down at the animal shelter," she says, knowing that it'll impact Jackson, "he was otherwise healthy."

At being unable to reach the hair tie, the cat gives out a sad noise, and Jackson coos through the phone, which she knew would fucking happen.

"But really, do you have any tips? Any names?"

"You just adopted a cat"—he *would* use that phrase to make himself feel better—"and you're going to head to Canada for a bit?"

"I'll let you know I'm safe," she says, reaching down to scratch the cat's head, but he doesn't give up on his quest for the hair tie. "Melekai told me he wouldn't kill me."

At the mention of the demon, Jackson puffs out a breath. "He'll be with you?"

"Probably."

"Jesus Christ," Jackson mutters, and she knows, she just knows this is probably not helping his law-school-crazy stress levels. "Check in like every hour."

It's fair, and she had made him text her every few hours when he first went off to college, so she nods to the room. "Yeah, of course."

"Take a picture of the car you drive in, take a picture of the address, all those things." It's a familiar refrain, one he's given her many times since his first criminal psychology course in undergraduate. "Tell Melekai to remember our conversation, I got...I got to get back...Jesus, Lyra, be safe?"

"Yeah, sure," she says and gets another huff in return before the line goes dead.

The cat gives another sad mew, so Lyra just gets a scrunchie from the bathroom and flings it across the floor, and the cat scrabbles after it, limp and all.

"If I get out of this," she says, to the cat that's viciously attacking the scrunchie, "I'm gonna go to the pound and see if you have a name, or like...a history."

He pays her no mind, just pounces on the scrunchie like an absolute bandit.

IT'S ABOUT thirty minutes after noon when the Mustang comes screeching up her gravel road, crunching to a stop right outside. Lyra's now had an extra few pieces of pizza and feels downright peppy as she locks the now sleeping cat into the house with an extra serving of kibble.

Axel looks...much worse for wear. His hair is undone, scraggly and unwashed, hanging over his face, and large circles ring his eyes, along with a bruise right over his right eye.

He doesn't stop clenching his hands on the steering wheel as she climbs in the passenger's seat, barely waiting for her to buckle in before tearing back down the street.

"My neighbors are going to think I'm getting involved in organized crime or something," Lyra says while thinking she should be much more nervous.

He flips a passport over to her, and it has her name, birthdate, address, and everything.

"We really going to Canada?" she asks, peering at it, looking at the watermarks and foil stamps and everything. "This is like...the most illegal."

"They won't catch it," Axel says, and it's close to boasting, so close to all her interactions so far with him that it's almost soothing. "I just took someone else's passport and changed all the details."

"Yeah still illegal," Lyra says, stuffing it into her purse regardless. "How'd you find my birthdate?"

"Easy." His knuckles are white on the steering wheel. "You were in foster care, apparently, so I just had Alette look you up there a bit ago in case we needed background." His voice breaks.

"That's..." she trails off, looking out the window. They're speeding, the trees of northern Washington streaking past them. "Can you, can you tell me what's going on?"

"Terese tried to wipe a logging village off the map," Axel says, and she can hear the exhaustion in his voice. "I don't know why, I don't know how, but she's escalated, and we can't keep up."

"How many...how many people died?" Lyra asks, and his words

are like a bucket of cold water on her good mood. "I can't... I don't think I can raise many."

He eyes her instead of the road. "I'm not taking you to the logging village," he says, and his voice cracks. "We're going to headquarters."

HEADQUARTERS IS A SMALL, neat-looking complex deftly hidden in the forest between British Columbia and Northern Washington, off any roads that may have markers on the border.

Axel's been silent for the last hour of driving like the very act has been meditative to him, like the rumble of the road beneath the quietness of the car brings him some peace, something to stop the incessant tapping that always seems to happen around him.

Lyra's lived in a car too long to find that sort of peace.

"Did you sleep at all last night?" she asks as they crawl along another dirt road, up past an impressive gate that sends chills down her back the moment they cross the threshold.

"Some," he says, which is a relief because she really should have asked this question before they were almost to their location. "Driving back from the village, we drove in shifts."

Lyra watches outside the window as the dirt road turns to gravel, then abruptly to pavement, and the trees clear enough that they no longer scrape the side of the car. It's as if someone decided they didn't need to hide anymore, so they made it more to their liking as soon as the building comes into view.

The building itself is squat and made of bricks, though a black-berry bramble is consuming one side. It gives the dual perspective that it's neatly socketed into nature without overwhelming the actual nature.

It's a pretty thought, especially considering what she's going to do in there.

"The dead thing's already there?" Lyra asks, and Axel's hands tighten on the wheel once more, like she's shattered his fragile inner peace.

He jerks his head in a nod, instead of answering, pulling into an open garage space.

The Mustang is the only car there, though it's big enough to hold probably around fifty, and the sound of them closing the car doors echoes around them.

She checks her phone. No signal, no way to let Jackson know she's safe.

The concrete pillars holding up the roof have words, letters, and symbols scrawled all up and down them, and they almost seem to dance in the garage's overhead sodium lights. Lyra reaches a hand up to touch them, and Axel jerks her arm down, gripping at her elbow.

"Don't," he warns, and she blinks at him in surprise. "We don't know what necromancer magic would do to those."

"So don't touch anything?" she asks, as he begins to walk across the large parking garage, and she has to hurry to keep up with him. "Just the dead?"

"Don't touch anything that looks magicky," he clarifies, which doesn't help too much. "When the world isn't ending, we'll let Alette run her experiments, but until then, assume that everything will explode around you."

Exploding. Great.

He strides through an ordinary-looking door and into a hallway that would be entirely in the norm in a nice mid-city office building if not for shimmering symbols hidden neatly in the wallpaper. Lyra tucks her hands into the pockets of her jeans to avoid accidentally brushing against anything, and she tries to keep up.

Even without any of her chronic pain, it's a struggle.

Axel blows through a series of doors, leading her down twists and turns, leaving her entirely unsure how she could get out without guidance. A purposeful labyrinth stuffed with more floors and hall-ways than the outside of the building accounted for.

Dread from the night before grows with each step—twisting inside of her, feeding into her unease and confusion.

It's a world she doesn't belong in, and it's undeniable. Lyra's never had a 9 to 5, middle-class life, and even seeing her in a place with a carpet this nice would send her mother laughing.

Granted, her mother would have scoffed at Jackson going to law school, would have belittled him until he quit or cut off contact, but the instinct is hard to curtail.

Axel walks like he doesn't even recognize it, like this is just a place to him, with no regard for how much money the very floor they walk on would be worth.

Finally, he draws to a large set of ornate wooden doors and pauses.

Even through the inscriptions carved into the dark wood, the familiar pull-punch of death calls to her.

"Are you ready?" he asks, and his voice cracks, before he digs out a granola bar from a pocket. "Have you eaten, you should eat, I forgot—"

"I had an entire pizza at home," she says, a little touched that he would remember something so outside of himself, but her eyes keep on straying to the set of doors. "They're behind there, aren't they?"

"Yeah, she is," he says, and she takes a moment to look at him, really look at him.

"This isn't a normal raising of the dead, is it, Axel?" she asks, and competing senses of sympathy and frustration war within her stomach. He's clearly been through something recently, something big, but still...something is off, and the fact that she hasn't been told settles wrong against her skin.

He ducks his head, and he lays a hand on the wooden door but doesn't push it open. "We needed a plan, and we didn't have enough power, and Terese hit her hard."

Lyra doesn't miss the pronoun.

"We do need the demon's help, and we need it bad, but..."

"Who's in there?" Lyra whispers as if speaking quietly would make this entire thing easier. "Who am I going to see?"

Instead of answering, he just pushes the door open, and something—magic—sparks off the wood of the door, glittering as the door swings.

Inside is a grand ballroom, with a mahogany conference table in the middle. At the head of the table stands a severe-looking woman, her graying hair scraped tightly into a bun at the nape of her neck. Her eyes fly over to Lyra, drilling down to her as if finding her wanting.

There are chairs around the large table, chairs that look like they're worth more than Lyra's entire house, but she ignores them.

On the table, with a blanket beneath her, lays Alette. Her dark skin is grey and dull, and her glasses are folded up and hanging on the breast pocket of her tailored jacket.

Lyra swallows down whatever fear she has and walks into the ballroom.

7

"How long?" Lyra asks, and her voice echoes in the tall ceiling room.

The woman just watches her, sharp.

Lyra draws closer, of course, with the pull of death so strong in her spine, until the tips of her fingers touch the large table.

This close, Alette's injuries are more obvious.

Something's wrong with her lungs. They're stopped, of course, but something blocked them for a bit, weighed them down, took away her ability to breathe.

There's a bone broken in her hand, one of the internal parts of her palm. Shattered, like something put all its weight on just that singular point.

"I think I'll need more than a granola bar after," Lyra warns Axel, who's still by the grand door.

He nods, a quick ducking of his head.

Still, the woman says nothing.

"A warning would have been nice, too," Lyra says, and her voice breaks. "There's a difference between raising something dead, so that you can talk to a demon and..."

"Will you do it?" the woman asks, and her voice is clear. "She's my niece."

"Jesus, yes, of course, I will, just..." Lyra pinches her nose, her thoughts racing.

She's raised a human before, survived it, despite the accident and the blood loss, and even after raising the cat last night and getting drained by Melekai, she feels...relatively fine, but there's a lump in her throat.

Alette looks so grey.

"How long has she been dead?" Lyra repeats, and everything inside of her quivers with a strange fear. If she can't do this, if Alette is gone, now for forever, what the hell can she do about it? Would the world just lose a kind and quiet person, just because she doesn't have enough power, and—

"Fourteen hours," the woman says. "We were told you raised something a few days dead."

"This is not...this isn't some test to run!" Lyra scrunches her eyes shut as if she could block out the sense of death in the room, the overwhelming punch in her gut, the crawling sensation of her skin. It does nothing. "Axel, Terese did this?"

Even with her eyes shut, she can sense him flinching at being addressed as if all his bravado and knowledge does nothing in the face of this anger. "Yes."

"Okay," Lyra says, then exhales, opens her eyes, and reaches out and grabs Alette's unbroken hand.

A million small broken blood vessels crowd Alette's lungs, and a rib is fractured. Blood pools on top of her lungs, around the rib, and Lyra tries to push the blood back into place, move it back into the vessels, seal up the cracks.

Alette's lungs flex, but there's nothing going between her lungs and her heart, so Lyra squeezes her eyes shut and imagines a spark of electricity hitting the heart, enough that it jumps in its place.

Her blood has pooled, cooled just enough, that Lyra's legs wobble as she tries to force the heart to pump it, to move the sticky liquid back around the body, through the lungs and up to the brain and—

Alette gasps, her eyes flashing open, and she screams. Screams then coughs, and blood pours out of her mouth, splattering over the mahogany table.

Even with a broken hand and still more vessels cracked, Alette jerks upright, flinching away from Lyra as she hacks out more blood.

Lyra wavers in place, her knees buckling, and immediately, Melekai is behind her, catching her under the arms as her legs give out.

Dumping her in a big expensive chair, he braces himself in front of her, his eyes reflecting the light around them. "Who touched you?" he all but growls, fingers going to her elbow. "Who grabbed you?"

He's still in the same body as before, bracelets and bun and curly hair, but the sharpness in his face is new. She's never seen that expression on him before.

Behind him, Alette hacks away, and the woman's wrapped the blanket around Alette's shoulders, helping her off the table. Alette's hands shake, and she clutches the shattered one to her chest.

Her mind races. The only contact she's had, the only thing, is maybe...maybe when Axel grabbed her elbow? Or the cat?

Black spots edge along the borders of Lyra's vision.

Melekai straightens. "Okay," he says, and he turns to survey the room, and Lyra takes big, gulping breaths.

His hand remains on her elbow, a steadying touch, and Lyra tries hard not to shut her eyes but to blink past the black, focus on something, anything.

Melekai scans each person in the room, methodical in a way she's never seen before, and she just wants to lean back against him. Draw some strength or some sort of comfort in the familiarity.

Axel rushes over, helping Alette settle into a chair across the table, and he's pale, too. He strips off his jacket, dumping it on Alette's lap.

Alette lifts her gaze to Lyra, and her cinnamon-brown eyes are wide, and except for her coughing, it's quiet in the room.

"Hi," Lyra says, even though her head swims. "Sorry I didn't fix your hand."

Alette's eyes just widen, and she clutches her broken hand closer, then her eyes lift directly to Melekai.

"You really did find a few magicians," Melekai says, his fingers gentle on her elbow, as he traces something only he can see against her skin. "Which one of them touched you?"

"Well," the woman says, and it takes Lyra a moment to realize, but it's not in response to Melekai. "Did your demon show up?"

Alette flinches with her whole body.

"Dr. Frisse, she just saved Alette's life, give her a mo'," Axel blurts out, and his eyes are wild.

Despite all his bravado and everything else, this isn't a magic he's seen before, and he's just as human as the rest of them, and Lyra's creepy.

"Yeah he's here," Lyra says, waving her hand at Melekai, who's evaluating the woman with a narrow focus.

"What happened?" Alette asks, her voice small, and all other noise in the room stops. "We were in that town, Terese was there, and then..." She locks eyes with Lyra, and Lyra can tell she already knows but can't bring herself to believe it.

Alette lifts her hand to her mouth, to all the blood still against her lips, before she scrabbles to fit her glasses back on. She shakes like a leaf, her fingers trembling and her shoulders quivering.

Lyra can't answer, not really, so she just sinks deeper into the expensive chair.

Melekai pauses in his scrutiny to curve an eyebrow at her.

It's a long moment before Axel speaks.

"We were near the bubble, you went in to try to help someone, and she hit you with that wave thing she does," he says, muted. "You just dropped, and we brought in Lyra."

"Wave thing," Melekai murmurs, so quiet and deep it's just for her.

"Two birds with one stone," the woman—Dr. Frisse—says. "We needed more firepower and needed you back." Abruptly, she claps her hands together, and everyone jumps. "Axel, order some food for the necromancer. This is clearly more than she's done in ages. Demon, can we talk?"

Melekai visibly bristles at her tone, and, impulsive, Lyra rests her hand on his, which snaps his attention back at her.

"Please?" Lyra whispers because she's exhausted, because Alette's been nothing but kind to her, because the spot in the forest still haunts her when she closes her eyes.

"So normal people can't see the demon, right?" Axel asks, a bit too loud, like he's trying to break the ice. "'Cause I can't see anyone else, and it's weird." He taps on his phone while doing so, desperately trying to appear nonchalant.

"I can," Alette murmurs, clutching the blanket to her shoulders and watching them through her golden glasses. "He's right there."

"That's good to know," Dr. Frisse says, with a pat on Alette's arm.

"Tell them," Melekai starts, "I don't appreciate any trickery. To you."

"Uh, thanks?" Lyra replies, then blinks. "He doesn't want you to trick me anymore."

Her head thuds with the same dull ache, and now she has to play translator, and Alette's still looking at her like she's a horror show.

"Understood," Dr. Frisse says with a nod. "We need your help. We have an adversary who is trying to rip a hole into the nature of our world, and we"—she gestures at the three of them—"are woefully underprepared to deal with her."

Melekai's attention flickers to Lyra, then back to Dr. Frisse. "What about the College in Europe?"

Lyra parrots his words even though they make no sense.

"They declined to help," Dr. Frisse says, and finally, she leaves Alette alone, striding around the mahogany table and towards Lyra.

Immediately, Melekai shoves Lyra's chair away, standing between the two of them, and Alette gasps.

"It's okay," Lyra calls over to her, and Alette's covering her mouth with her hand. Lyra can't tell what she sees, but Jackson once told her he found Melekai vaguely unsettling, and Jackson is prone to under-exaggeration. "Seriously, I'm okay,"

Dr. Frisse stops in her path, and her face doesn't waver, doesn't lose a bit of her composure. "I won't harm your pet," she says, and there's almost a patronizing tone, and Lyra's a bit agog. "I merely want to communicate better."

"Am I the pet here, or is he?" Lyra asks, and Melekai's not looking at her, all of his attention directed at Dr. Frisse, a hand still on her elbow, despite the protective stance. "Cause I'm not sure either one is gonna get you the result you want."

Dr. Frisse sighs, then steps back in a conciliatory way, settling into one of the fancy chairs far enough away that Melekai relaxes, just a hair.

"I apologize if I'm presumptuous," Dr. Frisse starts, and her tone sticks in Lyra's throat. It's the tone of countless rich people who think they know more than her about everything, just because of the size of their checkbooks.

Lyra's never liked those people.

Finally, Melekai looks back at her, and she's not used to this body, not yet, and he gives her an appraising look as if he could see right through her.

For all she knows, he might. She's never actually asked.

He curls his hand around her neck after a moment, and if he takes anything from her, she's going to pass out, but nothing happens.

"You wouldn't have raised that cat if you knew it was a person, would you?" he asks, voice low just for her.

She wordlessly shakes her head.

He's looking for something, she can tell, but what it could be, she has no clue. His thumb makes a circle on the nape of her neck as if trying to calm her down.

As if she is the one that needs calming right now.

Tears spring up in her eyes from the soft touch, tears from the stress, the lack of energy, the blood on the table, and the lingering death in the room.

She can't read his face yet.

He hesitates, and the motion of his thumb skips a beat.

"What do you need to know?" Dr. Frisse asks, and her eyes are unfocused enough in Melekai's direction that it's genuinely creepy.

"We don't talk until she's had food," Melekai says, still watching

8

F ood arrives after a tense twenty minutes, with Melekai remaining silent, perched on the table, while Alette continuously stares at him. After any question, Melekai just shakes his head, as if Lyra shouldn't answer, so she doesn't.

It doesn't take much encouragement, with her head swimming and exhaustion leaching into her bones, for her to sit back and close her eyes. Axel shatters the peace as he brings back a truly astounding amount of Chinese food and lays it out on the table, carefully avoiding any blood splatter.

Alette just stares at the fried rice that Axel puts in front of her. "Is it safe for me to eat?" she asks, and it takes Lyra a second to realize that the question is directed to her.

"What? Sure?" Lyra says, and Melekai nods along. "I mean, Jackson eats all the time?"

"Did he eat immediately afterward?" Alette follows up, and her voice is so small. "I know some magic can be disrupted by food—"

"You should be fine," Melekai interrupts her, and she pales even further. Lyra itches to ask her what she sees, what she experiences, but the takeout container of broccoli beef is more important.

Reluctantly, Alette takes the fried rice as if it'll bite her.

"I think Jackson was unconscious for a while. I passed out for two days," Lyra says in between bites of the broccoli beef, not sure if it's helping or not. "I don't know when he ate, it was...he broke his neck, it's a bit worse than suffocation, all I had to do was put your blood back in place and make your heart beat again."

The fork's frozen halfway to Alette's mouth, and the moment the words leave Lyra, she realizes how fucked up they are.

For the first time since she summoned him, Melekai cracks a smile. It's sharp, it's vicious, and it's very, very pleased.

The hair rises on the back of Lyra's neck. And they want to work with him.

"Sorry," Lyra mumbles into her food. "It's creepy."

Alette carefully sets her fork down.

"But you can tell those things?" Axel says, casually digging into his food, and Lyra's not well versed enough in fancy Chinese food to tell what he's eating. "That has some startling implications, right Alette?"

He's trying to engage Alette's studious brain, Lyra can just tell, but it's not helping.

"Yeah," Alette says, weakly.

A phone rings, and they all flinch, and Dr. Frisse steps out of the conference room, and it's like the air comes back in the moment she does.

Axel nudges another container of food towards Lyra when she finishes hers. "I should have given you a ton of energy bars for the drive," he says, and she hears the apology in it.

Melekai tracks his motion as he gets close to do so, but doesn't interfere, not as he did with Dr. Frisse, and Lyra just wants to know why.

"Was he the one who touched you?" Melekai asks, languid, leaning towards her.

She doesn't know if this is strange for him, being around so many people, but he's way more intense feeling than he usually is when she sees him.

But then again, he did feed from her the night before, and maybe this is just... part of it.

"Yeah, but -"

Melekai stands up in a smooth movement and stalks towards Axel, who can't see him, and -

"Wait, he was just helping me -"

"What do you mean, what -" Alette sputters, and -

Melekai pauses in his motions towards Axel, glancing at Lyra. Like he's considering her words, and Lyra grabs at that opportunity with both hands.

"He was just helping me. I almost touched something I shouldn't have. It's not a big deal," Lyra says, and Axel turns towards her, eyes wide like he's finally caught up that something is happening outside of his control, outside of his ability to sense. "Don't do anything to him, he was helping."

"What do you mean, what's going on?" Axel protests, eyes frantically scanning, as if he looks hard enough he could see where Melekai stands. He backs up, knees bumping into yet another one of the chairs.

Melekai considers her, and she hasn't seen this much evaluation since she was seventeen and in the hospital. At least it gives Axel a chance to scramble away before whatever the heck Melekai was going to do to him.

"Tell him not to touch you," Melekai says, finally. His eyes linger on her elbow. "Not without your permission."

"It was to help me," Lyra repeats, her heart pounding, acrid fear in the back of her throat. "Don't do anything."

The moment stretches out, and he's still, inhumanly still.

"Axel," Lyra starts, and her voice cracks from the exhaustion and the confusion over everything, "He doesn't want you to touch me without my permission."

Melekai nods, satisfied, before striding back to near Lyra, perching himself back on the conference table next to her food.

Axel looks like he's been caught in some headlights. "When did I..."

"You grabbed my elbow to stop me touching those weird letter things. That's what he's talking about." Lyra rubs her eyes, then grabs at the other container of food. "How could you even tell?"

"Easy," Melekai answers, fingers dipping down to trace her elbow. "It startled you, and your magic flared just enough to show me where."

"That's creepy," Lyra says because it is.

"And since he probably fancies himself some sort of alchemist"— despite herself, Alette snorts at that—"his magic instinctively responded. It's as clear as day." He lifts his hand from her, settling back, still too intense. "Nobody should touch you without your permission."

And that sounds great, but she's been a woman living in America for her entire life, and not a wealthy one. "Sure," she says.

"Am I...am I safe?" Axel asks, and there's panic laced through his voice. "Do I need to go?"

Melekai shrugs, like that wouldn't be a bad idea.

"You're safe," Lyra says, staring hard at the demon. "Just, I guess...don't do it again."

"No prob!" Axel says, a bit too enthusiastically, before grabbing his food and scooting his chair further away. "I don't want to anger Mr. Demon here."

Melekai pays him no attention, just returning his all-seeing gaze to Lyra, and she's not used to dealing with him at the same time as other people. It's overwhelming.

Across the table, slowly, Alette starts to eat, like the disruption in the room took away her fear of the food, and something inside of Lyra's chest unwinds. Like the small part of her that brought her back had worried. Had kept track, and Lyra didn't realize it until Alette moved.

"You still need to get your hand looked at," Lyra says softly. "I didn't get to it before you sat up."

"Can you heal it now?" Alette asks, in an equally soft voice, as she examines the wounded hand with some detached worry. "Or just when people are...dead?"

"Just when people are dead, I think?" Once again, Lyra feels like she should have much better answers than she actually does. "I haven't tried it, not in any great amount."

"You should try more," Melekai murmurs, and it's not helping.

Alette's eyes skitter away from him.

"How much of him can you see?" Lyra asks, impulsive, ignoring the raised eyebrow from Melekai. "My brother won't answer me."

Alette opens her mouth, closes it, then opens it again. "Enough."

"Great. He looks like a hipster with a bun to me," Lyra says, again too tired to be polite.

"He looks...human to you?" Alette asks, and she sounds just as awkward as Lyra feels right then, awkward and tired and stretched thin. "That's...not what he looks like to me."

"Gotcha."

Again, they fall silent, all eating what is probably excellent Chinese food with the same tasteless grunge of someone too tired to enjoy something. Axel keeps on shooting worried glances her way like she's going to compel Melekai to do something to him, and Alette seems to be trying very hard to not think of anything and fundamentally failing.

The door clicks open, and Dr. Frisse strides back in, all calm and collected, despite the blood still on the table and the exhaustion in everyone's shoulders.

"You're looking better," she says, and it takes Lyra a second to realize it's directed towards her and not, you know, her niece, who had been recently dead. "If you're to build up any sort of stamina, you will need to practice more."

"She's right," Melekai says.

"Will he talk now?" Dr. Frisse asks, taking her seat back, far enough away from Lyra that it feels intentional.

He gives the same, one-shouldered shrug.

"I think so," Lyra says, and continues to eat, still feeling a gnawing hunger in her stomach. "Go ahead and try."

Melekai leans over to her, hand cradling hers, and begins to draw circles in her palm again like he did the night before.

She lets him, as long as she has one hand available to eat some fried rice.

As Dr. Frisse visibly weighs her words, Lyra tries not to look at anyone, not focus on anything besides herself, on the gnawing in her stomach, at the lack of pain in her legs and back, and the whisper touch of Melekai's fingers.

"Axel, Alette, would you mind giving us the room?" Dr. Frisse says, finally.

"No," Lyra blurts out before anyone moves. "I don't...I don't know you. I'd rather they stay."

Both Alette and Axel watch her, eyebrows raised, and Lyra gets the feeling that people don't generally talk back to Dr. Frisse or deny her what she wants.

Melekai doesn't stop his touch, but he gives her a one-sided smirk, and this body even has a dimple when he does that.

"Very well," Dr. Frisse says, despite sounding like it is not, in fact, very well at all. "We are fighting someone we call Terese, but that is a misnomer."

Alette's brows furrow, and her scholastic nature seems to click into place like a setting on the stove. It's another small relief that Lyra didn't know she was looking for.

"We know the human body is named Terese, but not the current inhabitant." Dr. Frisse tilts her head to Lyra as if testing to see if she's having any reaction besides continuing to eat. "The current inhabitant is a demon we don't know the name of."

"That's why they wanted me," Melekai murmurs to her. "She wants to fight fire with fire."

"At least that makes sense," Lyra whispers back.

"That can't be right," Axel says, leaning back in his chair, and he too seems to have shrugged his casual all-knowing attitude back on, like it's a jacket to wear. He props his booted feet up on the fancy table like he owns it. "We can see Terese and touch Terese. She's not a demon."

Melekai raises an eyebrow at that.

Dr. Frisse inclines her head as if giving Axel the point. "She's a demon who has found a way to be in a live body," she says, and Melekai's grip on her hand turns briefly painful. "She has shoved herself into a body with an intact soul and is wreaking havoc on the world through that."

"Not possible," Melekai says, loud enough that Alette flinches.

"He doesn't think that can happen," Lyra says, in translation, and Melekai gentles his grip on her hand, but his fingers still hold tight.

"It's more than not possible, it's an abomination," he clarifies as if that word has special meaning to her. "The only way I can have this body, any body, is once the current owner is truly gone."

"She twisted herself in, that is all I know," Dr. Frisse says, and from the looks of it, neither Axel nor Alette were privy to that information. "Since doing so, she has been… unpredictable. She can warp the fabric of reality around her, causing mass death to every organism in her reach, and I believe she wants to take the rest of the world down with her."

There's a moment of silence as Melekai grips her hand like she's the one holding him down and not the other way around. Alette holds the blanket closer to her shoulders, and while she has more color to her now, she's still worrisomely gray. Still propped up on the table, Axel scowls at Dr. Frisse.

"Well, that's against every rule of magic I know," Axel says loudly. "And would have been good information to have before we, you know, faced her."

"My legs didn't hurt when you took me to that spot in the forest," Lyra says, and all attention turns back to her. "Where she had killed everything, even the bugs in the ground."

"What does that have to do with anything?" Axel asks, and Dr. Frisse waves at him to be quiet.

"The only time I'm not in pain is around him"—Lyra jerks her thumb at Melekai, not like they can see him—"and I thought it was a demon in that clearing."

"Was she there?" Melekai asks, direct, at her, and underneath his words is an undercurrent of panic. "Did this person see you?"

Lyra just shakes her head, and he relaxes abruptly. "It was just the aftermath."

Dr. Frisse gives her an appraising look, one that Lyra likes approximately not at all. "So you can tell," she says. "That could be useful."

"No," Melekai says, sudden. "No, she does not get to be useful to you."

"What?" Lyra asks, and he turns back to her, vicious. "Don't I get to make that call?"

"What'd he say?" Dr. Frisse asks, and Lyra barely hears her.

Melekai stands, leaning over, looming over her like he needs his height to intimidate her, a hand on each arm of the chair, bracketing her in. "You do not get to put yourself in danger for this person, not like this." Despite his words, there's something else in his voice, and his eyes are wide. "I can take you somewhere else, somewhere no one here can find you, and you can continue living."

For a second, Lyra's paralyzed.

But she exhales, and her body moves, so she curls her hand up Melekai's arm, in the way she does sometimes when first seeing him after a long time away. He twitches when she does.

"Can we hear her out?" Lyra asks, quiet, and her heart pounds, so loud he can surely hear. "Before you take me anyplace else?"

"Why?" His face is unmoving, so inhuman.

She doesn't have an immediate answer for him, so she lets herself think, her mind going back to that clearing in the forest, to the sense of death all around her to how nothing, nothing but her, was alive.

"The clearing," she says, and his eyes narrow in response, "was unlike anything I've ever seen."

"We don't know much," Dr. Frisse says, and from the scowl on Axel's face, he's resenting that she kept so much from them in the first place, "but we know she's in pain."

This catches Melekai's attention like a fishhook in the cheek, dragging his attention away from Lyra.

"What do you mean?" Lyra asks, guessing what he wants her to say. If this were going to work, her translating for him, they would need a system that relies less on her guesswork.

"Before everything went wrong," Dr. Frisse says, like that's not a loaded statement, "we spoke to her, and she kept on repeating she's in pain. That she just wanted the pain to stop, and that she'd do anything to stop it."

Melekai's hand settles over hers again, without even looking at her, like she's the one that needs calming.

"We tried to work with her, to figure something out," Alette says, small. "I tried so many spells, so many things, but nothing worked. She said she'd tear apart reality, just to stop the pain."

From the look Dr. Frisse gives her, Lyra gets the feeling that it's a step too far to mention that, like Dr. Frisse had wanted to keep that bit of knowledge to herself.

Melekai nods his thanks at Alette, but his lips tug down into a scowl, even more so than before. "We don't...we don't experience pain, not like humans do," he says, to Alette, but his eyes flicker to Lyra, and it doesn't take a genius to figure out why. "We have hunger, we have needs, but...but unless something tied her so tightly to the body she feels everything, there's no reason she can't just jump into a different one."

His face twists, like he's bumping against the language he has available.

"She said..." Alette glances to Dr. Frisse as if for permission, but without finding it, she forges on anyway, "she says she won't. And when we asked, that's...that's when she started doing things like the clearing."

"I want to see it before I agree to anything," he warns, and it was surprisingly easier than she thought it would be, but everything about him is coiled tight like he will spring a trap at any moment. "And I want their word that they will not put you in any more danger."

"We didn't know she was in danger then," Alette blurts out, then blanches when Melekai turns the entirety of his attention to her. "We just thought it was uneasy." Still, despite her very apparent fear, Alette keeps his gaze, her eyes wide behind her glasses. "Axel even made her a jacket to keep her dry. We didn't know."

"You didn't know," Melekai clarifies, eyes flickering to Dr. Frisse. "She did."

Alette falls silent at that.

Lyra uses the opportunity of Melekai not physically looming over her to grab another container of food. "He doesn't want you to put me in any danger," she tells Dr. Frisse. "And to see the clearing, to see what he can tell from it."

"The clearing can be arranged," Dr. Frisse says, and Melekai glares at her, pulling himself to his full height. It goes unnoticed, of course. "I cannot promise the lack of danger, only that we won't put her in unnecessary harm."

Melekai's eyes narrow further.

"If we drive fast, we can get to the clearing in less than two hours," Axel says, then puts up his hands when everyone turns and stares at him. "What, just saying, we can solve that one problem now."

IN THE END, Dr. Frisse stays with Alette back at the compound, and Axel carefully walks with Lyra back to his Mustang through the complex, and Melekai shadows her every step, a hair too close.

The moment they're out of the large conference room, Axel shoots her a genuinely overwhelmed look.

"I'm sorry, I didn't mean to grab you. I didn't know that was a demon thing," Axel blurts out, and Lyra still has to scramble to keep up with his stride. "I'm sorry I didn't warn you. Dr. Frisse said you might not come if you knew that you'd have to raise a person."

Her head swims with his words, but she follows him through the maze of the building, trying not to watch as Melekai's eyes jump from marking to marking, from strange lettering to strange lettering.

"I didn't know it was a demon thing, either," she replies, and Melekai shoots her a sharp look before getting distracted by the lettering again. "And why the fuck wouldn't I come?"

Axel stops in the middle of the hallway, and she almost bumps into him. "Because you had only raised someone once, and you seemed scared to do it again, and we didn't..." he swallows, visibly. "Look, my best friend was suddenly dead, and I would have lied to a hundred people if someone could bring her back."

Lyra could understand that.

"Still shouldn't have lied," Melekai says, though there's no snarl in his voice, not like before. "Still should have given you time and knowledge to prepare."

She doesn't know what to do with this random overprotectiveness from Melekai. All their interactions had been limited. All their interactions were him taking bits and pieces of her soul from her, not anything this sustained since she was in the hospital.

Keeping her hands far away from all the magical symbols, she follows Axel down to the garage, trying and failing to keep an accurate idea of the building's layout.

The moment they get to the car, Axel looks at her, then his eyes skitter away like he's trying to see something that's not there.

"He's right here," Lyra says, jerking her thumb at Melekai.

"Ah," Axel says, awkward, "uh, I have a lot of protections on this car, I don't know if they'll hurt you or if you'll hurt them," he says, apologetically.

Melekai smirks again, resting a hand against the roof of the car to no ill effect. "Tell him he's adorable."

"He says he should be fine," Lyra translates and opens the backseat of the car. "I wanna lie down."

Of course, Melekai squeezes in next to her. He tends towards having the maximum amount of contact with her.

She had always thought that was part of the stealing soul thing, but he's not even doing that right now.

"So I'm just like a chauffeur right now?" Axel asks, but it's without any sort of heat. "Can demons even ride in cars?"

"Clearly," Melekai says, so Lyra just nods at Axel through the rearview mirror.

They drive silently for a few minutes, and Lyra's entire body feels like it's buzzing from exhaustion.

"When this is a bit calmer," Axel starts, as they pull off of the gravel road and to the main highway, "talk to Alette about endurance exercises."

"I don't know what that is," Lyra says, and with Melekai in the backseat silently watching her, she has no place to lean back and rest, making her mulish.

"Little things, little bits of magic, that you can do to make sure you get stronger. Like doing lots of reps of little weights, instead of one big weight at the gym."

"Do I look like someone who goes to the gym?" Lyra asks, shutting her eyes against the afternoon sun.

How can it only be afternoon? It feels like the day has gone on forever.

"Well, maybe not with that chronic pain thing you were talking about with Alette"—Melekai snorts at Axel's words, and Lyra eyes him at that—"but still. Same principle."

"Sure," Lyra says, not wanting to argue.

Abruptly, once they reach the highway, her phone starts beeping, and she sighs before digging it out of her pocket.

Of course. The promise to Jackson.

JACKSON (1:54 PM): Hey. Check in.

JACKSON (2:44 PM): Lyra. Are you okay?

JACKSON (3:56 PM): This isn't funny.

JACKSON (4:59 PM): I will call the police.

LYRA (5:21 PM): Sorry, there was no signal. I'm alive and well.

"Good," Melekai murmurs to her, self-satisfied, clearly reading over her shoulder. "Why isn't he here with you?"

"Like I said, law school," Lyra says, watching as her brother types a reply, then stops, then starts again.

JACKSON (5:22 PM): Don't do that!

LYRA (5:23 PM): Sorry, a bit of an emergency. I raised a friend from the dead, and now my head hurts.

"The brother?" Axel asks, and he looks infinitely more comfortable behind the wheel of the car than he was in the compound. "What does he know?"

"That I'm creepy, and I was helping people," she says, stuffing her phone back into her pocket and ignoring the resulting dings. She rests her head against the cool glass of the window, feeling the buzz of adrenaline through her system, as much as she tries to ignore it.

The car is silent again, blessedly silent, for a few small moments, before Melekai lays his hand on her arm, touching the sweater.

"Here," he says, tugging her over, so her head rests against his shoulder. "You should sleep."

"Working on it," she says, grumpy, keeping her eyes open out of spite. "I wanted to lay down—"

Axel gives her a glance through the rearview mirror, blanches, then looks away to the road.

Melekai sighs, and his entire body moves with him, which implies that he still needs to breathe when inside a dead body and—

"Just sleep," he mumbles, touching a finger to her bare skin, and—

9

Lyra pops awake as the car rumbles over the rickety wooden bridge, her heart in her throat and a fizz in her veins.

She jerks upright, away from Melekai, who's watching her with his creepy eyes, and jolts her elbow against the car door.

"What the hell?" She breathes, eyes wide, and the blackberry plants are scraping against the car windows again.

It's night, the true night that comes from winter in the Pacific Northwest, though it's at least not raining this time.

"Oh, hey, you slept pretty hard; it was *real* weird," Axel says, cheery, and Lyra has to squeeze her eyes shut from the sheer volume of him.

Lyra instead stares at Melekai, who just stares right back.

"We're almost there. You timed your nap well," Axel continues, and she just wants him to shut the heck up immediately.

Lyra narrows her eyes at Melekai, who just raises a carefully manicured brow right back.

"Don't do that," she says, once she finds her voice again.

"Do what?" Axel asks, then, "Oh."

"You needed sleep," Melekai says with another shrug.

And she does feel better, but...

"Don't do that again," she says, and he just grins in return. "It's weird."

Axel coasts the car to a stop, keeping the headlights on, illuminating the clearing.

A few weeks have passed, but the clearing remains dead. No new moss, no new leaves, and Lyra climbs out of the car to avoid looking at Melekai one moment longer.

Melekai's immediately next to her, and she didn't even see him climb out of the car, so she shuts her eyes against the annoyance.

"Don't...make me fall asleep again," she says, a fission of worry going through her that she's even making this demand, that she's even asking something of him.

"You, yourself, said you needed sleep," he answers, and she can taste the irritation and confusion from him. "You were exhausted, and you overextended yourself. A nap was good."

And she does feel better, more alert in a way she seldom is from naps, but still.

"Just...ask first?" she says, scrunching her eyes shut again. "It's weird."

He shrugs, one-shouldered, and turns away, obviously inspecting the blast radius for something she can't see, and she takes that as a win.

"Can't demons teleport?" Axel asks, shutting his car door with a thunk, and pulling a flashlight out of his pocket and handing it to Lyra.

Melekai watches that with narrowed eyes; she can just tell, even without looking at him.

"That's something I never thought to ask," Lyra says, fussing with the flashlight. It's not a real flashlight, obviously something that Axel just transformed—there's no actual compartment for the batteries or anything. Still, when she clicks the button, a beam comes out anyway.

"Only if we've been there before or have someone tying us to a place," Melekai says, his eyes focused out onto the clearing. "Like you. I can always teleport to you."

"Sorta," Lyra says, because how else could she sum that up. "If he's been there before or...or if I'm there."

"So he literally could have stayed at the compound and joined us here, and instead, I had awkward driving while you're asleep leaning against nothing in the backseat of my car," Axel points out, and Melekai just nods.

"You came here?" Melekai asks, pointing to the broken branches like she could see something else.

"Yeah," Lyra answers, pointing the flashlight. "A few hours after it was...exploded."

His footsteps make no sound as he strides towards the dead zone, and even though it's been weeks, the scent of death still lingers in the back of Lyra's throat.

There are still the dead mice, the dead bugs, the dead snake, everything, and they buzz at the edges of her awareness, like an itch she needs to scratch.

"You know, you were creepy before, but this is even worse," Axel jokes, still hanging back from the broken limbs and branches. "The whole talking to yourself except not—"

Lyra flashes the light at his eyes, and he squints at her.

Melekai smirks, then strides directly into the little blast area, like he owns it, with none of the trepidation Lyra still feels from it.

His nose wrinkles, like the smell of the dead is even fouler to him than it is to her. He trails his fingers along the edges of the bubble, along the broken branches and the dead moss.

Hanging back next to Axel, Lyra lets him, trying not to shiver from the pervasive sense of death that it still has.

She's fairly certain no predators have tried to eat the bodies, and no scavenger attempted to eat the meat left behind—no ants crawling through the soil, no bugs over the dead moss. Not even the hint of worms crawling towards it to decompose anything.

"Terese did this in a village?" Lyra asks, after a silent moment.

"Just about," Axel says, voice somber. "It'll be in the news, I'm sure of it."

"And everyone...fell?"

"Everyone. They all died." He nods, and they watch as Melekai inspects the forest floor, pads of his fingers crumbling the moss.

Or, rather, Lyra watches, and Axel stands there awkwardly, clearly looking for something, anything, to focus on.

"Is he...is he doing anything?" Axel whispers, finally.

"He's looking around," she says, and Melekai shoots her a glance before continuing to inspect.

"You should come here," he says, quiet, but the hair on Lyra's neck rises at his tone.

With a glance to Axel—who, of course, didn't hear it, so he has no input—she steps inside the radius.

Again, it's a buffer of warmth, a puff of air, and the sense of death just gets worse. Usually, after a certain amount of time, bacteria move in and start to eat away at the dead creatures, taking the edge off of the buzz to her senses, but this is just as bad as it was the first night.

He reaches to her the moment she crosses the barrier, his hand caressing her wrist. "Tell me what you feel," he murmurs, and it's the voice he usually uses on her, right before he takes from her, but no glimmer of gold rises between the two of them.

"It's warmer," she says, and his eyebrows raise again. "It's like... walking through a grocery store door where there's that puff of air to keep out all the bugs."

His hand is still on her wrist, the same hand that handled the moss, and some crumples against her skin.

He can't interact with most things, but he can touch the moss, just like he could touch her and the cat.

"Nothing is alive here," she says. "Everything that died the first night is still dead, untouched."

"Well, that's creepy," Axel says, shifting, still outside the bubble.

Melekai's face pinches together like he ate something sour, and the grip against her wrist tightens, briefly, before he relaxes into just holding her hand.

He leans in close to her as if Axel could even overhear. "I don't like this," he whispers, and Lyra doesn't like it that much either, so it's fair. "I don't like this one bit."

"I mean, I don't either," Lyra says, but—

Between one blink and the next, they're no longer in the forest. No longer in the dead zone where nothing has grown in three weeks, no longer amongst all the death, but...

But in her little mobile house, next to the overstuffed chair and the velvet cushion still on the floor, the cat she raised curled up tight in a circle in the middle of it.

Lyra staggers, her feet taking a moment to catch up to the idea that she's not on the forest floor, and Melekai catches her by the shoulders.

It's brighter, far brighter, than in the forest, and she squints against the light she apparently left on all day.

She gasps, taking big shaking gulps of air, and the air inside her lungs came from the forest, and now she's here and—

"You asked about teleportation," he says idly, releasing her to bend and scratch the cat behind the ears. "Now you don't have to suffer through a car ride back with that little alchemist."

Lyra sits heavily back onto the armchair, and her hands tremble, her heart pounding.

The cat—the cat she still hasn't named—stands, arching into Melekai's scratches. It's been less than 24 hours since she raised it back from the dead.

All that happened in less than 24 hours.

"Shit," she says, scrambling for her phone in her pocket, "I've got to warn them, let them know I'm okay."

"Why wouldn't you be?" Melekai says, giving up all pretenses and folding himself on the floor to pet the cat. Like that's been the most important thing with all of this. "Clearly, you're with me."

Between raising the cat, raising Alette, and the tense whatever-that-was conversation with Dr. Frisse, Lyra's heart pounds and her eyes sting, and she presses the heel of her palm to her face.

She takes a moment, in her warm little house, with the familiar noises it makes in the rain, to try to gather herself, gather something, anything, resembling a composure. A thought, properly stated, to accurately convey what she's feeling, and...and she can't even tell what that is right now.

LYRA (8:49 PM): Tell Axel I'm safe. Melekai took me back home.

ALETTE (8:49 PM): Yeah, I still have her phone. I should've given it back.

ALETTE (8:51 PM): So will he help?

Lyra lifts her eyes to the demon, who watches her with reflective eyes while petting the purring cat.

LYRA (8:51 PM): I have no clue.

"I won't," he speaks up, without her prompting, which also isn't great. "If a demon can inhabit a living body and do that sort of magic, I want no part of it."

"Even if it ends the world?" Lyra asks, rubbing her eyes.

"I doubt it would," he says, stretching his legs out on the cheap wood of her floor. "But anyone who can do that"—he waves his hand as if gesturing towards the clearing in the woods— "on any bigger scale could obliterate me, and I'm not interested."

"Great," Lyra says, hollow. "Great."

He raises an eyebrow at her, and she gets the uncanny feeling he can see right through her. See right through all her worry and exhaustion and confusion.

Instead of saying something, however, he unfolds himself from the floor, crossing to the window and tracing his fingertips around the sill.

"Is this some sort of demon magic?" she asks, too weary to feign disinterest.

"Some sort, yes," he says, neutral. "I had your last place well protected. I don't know why you moved."

It's new information that he would bother to protect her, bother to put anything in place. "Free rent will tempt me," she says, gesturing at the mobile house.

It's strange to discuss something so mundane as housing with him.

He looks askance at her, then continues onto the little window over the sink, tracing something along the edge, and she watches, tucking her legs underneath herself on the velvet green monstrosity.

"When did you get a house, anyway?" he asks, leaning up to trace around the vent above her little two-burner stove. "I thought you were renting a room from that couple."

"Inherited it," she says and closes her eyes against the awkwardness. "Does this even help?"

"It'll make it substantially more difficult for someone to enter without you wanting them to," he says, which is just confusing enough to be true. "It won't stop everyone, won't stop me, but it could help."

"Did you do this everywhere I've stayed?"

"Yeah," he says, still focusing on his work, before he crosses to her doorframe. "Unless you moved more than once in between me seeing you, then I didn't."

It's too early for her to go to sleep, especially with the nap she had, but everything in her just wants to rest, wants to close her eyes to the world, and ignore the demon busybody in her house.

The cat jumps on her lap, butting her chin with his head. Because, of course, she has an additional responsibility in all of this, to this creature that decided it likes her, despite everything else.

"What do I do if she comes here?" Lyra asks, giving in and petting the cat's soft fur and getting rewarded with a deep purr.

"Do you have any guns?" he asks, not looking over.

"No?" she says, incredulous.

"Well, if the body she's currently in is alive, kill the body," he says with a shrug. "I don't know what it'll do, but it'll be distracting, that's for sure."

"Not comforting," Lyra says, and he flashes her a smile. "What if she goes after Jackson?"

"You've brought him back before. You could bring him back again," Melekai says, and it's almost dismissive, almost. "And she'd have to know where he is, how he relates to you, and how you're involved at all. And she shouldn't."

Suddenly, he turns back to her, leaning in close, looming over her.

She swallows down, hard, at the natural instinctive fear of a predator in front of her but refuses to sink lower into the chair.

"Don't get involved," he says, dipping his voice down low as if anyone else could overhear them. "Don't go helping people who don't matter, don't go gallivanting around with strange magicians."

It galls something inside of her to be ordered around like such, but she knows that giving voice to that instinct at that moment would be unwise, so she just holds eye contact with him.

"I don't like anything that can cause demons pain," he says, his voice light, like they're talking about the weather. "And I can't imagine that someone would stop at anything to make it end."

He scowls at her like he can tell what she thinks before he looks to the side and disappears.

Leaves her there with a lapful of cat and nothing else to do.

10

ALETTE (8:14 AM): I have substantial bruising across my front. Is this normal?

Lyra peers at the phone, bleary-eyed, immediately happy that she's not working that day.

LYRA (10:41 AM): How would I know?

ALETTE (10:42 AM): Did your brother have any?

Lyra thunks her head back against the pillow.

LYRA (10:45 AM): I probably didn't put all your blood back correctly

ALETTE (10:46 AM): That is objectively terrifying.

LYRA (10:48 AM): Look, I could tell it was wrong, but I didn't know exactly where it belonged. I was caught off guard and had to improvise.

ALETTE (10:49 AM): When things aren't dire, I want to figure out just how much of the human body you can sense.

LYRA (10:50 AM): Only works when they're dead.

ALETTE (10:50 AM): Terrifying.

The cat butts his head into Lyra's chin, and it takes her a moment to remember that, oh right, she has a cat now.

"Do you need food or something?" Lyra whispers, and the cat just rubs his face against Lyra's. "I don't speak cat. What do you need?"

The cat just snuggles up underneath her chin, and Lyra finds herself completely unwilling to get out of bed all of a sudden.

LYRA (11:01 AM): In related news, do you know anything about taking care of cats?

ALETTE (11:02 AM): ...no.

LYRA (11:02 AM): Usually, they hate me, but I raised one to let Melekai know that I'd be calling him, so he wasn't surprised, and now this one is cuddling a lot.

ALETTE (11:03 AM): There are so many parts of that text I don't know what to respond to.

That's fair, so Lyra just lets her phone fall to the side and snuggles the cat back, doing a mental sweep of herself, the calculation she faces on most days to see what level of activity she feels up to.

Her legs don't hurt, but that's easily chalked up to seeing Melekai so recently, though her back feels a bit tense from all the weird positions she's slept in recently. Like, if her legs feel this good, a nice walk could unwind the muscles in her back enough.

The only thing she had planned for her day off was to do laundry and maybe see about going to the dive bar for a drink with a book if she felt so inclined, but in the face of a lack of pain, she wants more.

She should just stay inside, rest up after the craziness of the last day. That'd be smart, at least.

The cat nudges her again, and she can't believe that everyone else gets to interact with animals like this all the time. Just unfair.

"Do I need to take you to the vet?" Lyra asks, scratching under the cat's chin. "Make sure there wasn't something else that made them put you to sleep?"

The cat just purrs in response.

She rolls over, twitching the curtain open next to her bed, and snow falls from the sky, blanketing the blackberry brambles and the spruce trees in a pale white.

It's quiet, in the way that only comes from new snow, and she just lays there, breathing in the silence, with the cat purring and nothing hurting, and tries not to think about the End of the World.

THE WORLD DOESN'T END during the next two weeks. The pain slowly eases its way back, creeping up her legs like the most insidious exhaustion, before winding its way into the muscles in her back until she needs the stool again at work and has little energy to do anything but lay on the bed at home with the cat.

ON A FRIDAY NIGHT, objectively the worst night to work the late shift at a gas station convenience store, she's dealing with an unruly crowd of college students on their Thanksgiving break when a woman strides in, and all the air immediately goes out of the store.

Not literally, of course, but the students all shift uneasily, leave without purchasing anything, just leaving their pickings on the shelf nearest to them. The drunk over by the cold wine section closes the door, leaving without picking up his favorite three-dollar bottle, which Lyra's never seen him do.

The moth that had been buzzing around her fluorescent light even lands, stilling its motion.

The woman herself even looks out of place, with white-blond hair shorn severely short and her face sharp and pointed. She wears a leather jacket, but the sort that would be more in place in a motorcycle club than in snowy northern Washington. She could be anywhere from nineteen to thirty-five, completely indistinguishable in age.

She watches Lyra with pale, almost translucent, gray eyes as everyone else leaves without even glancing at her, like everyone else's eyes skitter away, sliding off this person without realizing it.

Lyra swallows.

"Hello?" she says after the last college student files out, their cars squealing out of the parking lot.

The woman just gazes at her, unmoving from her stance at the front of the store.

Deliberately, Lyra puts one hand on the shotgun underneath the till. She pulls her phone out of her pocket with the other.

"Do you need any help?" Lyra asks, again, because she's seen creepy before that wasn't meaning to be creepy, and checking is better than not.

The woman's colorless eyes flicker to Lyra's legs hidden behind the counter, where she's perched on the stool. "You're in pain," she says, and her voice is melodic. Like she's trained to be a singer.

Lyra reflexively crosses her legs. "I'm okay," she says, sliding her phone next to the gun under the till and thumbs her text messages.

LYRA (11:58 PM): Someone not normal at the store.

Without appearing to move, the woman is suddenly next to the front counter, and Lyra flinches, but the woman only stares down at her. She's several inches taller than Lyra is, even if Lyra had been standing.

But instead of saying anything, the woman just watches her.

"Are you okay?" Lyra asks, instead, though her heart pounds at the strangeness.

A glance at the security cameras shows no other car in the lot. The woman must've walked, or...something else.

ALETTE (12:01 AM): What does she look like?

Lyra lets her eyes fall to the phone, then back up, but the woman can't see her phone, not from that angle, not unless the colorless eyes can see through plastic and wood.

LYRA (12:02 AM): Short blond hair, leather jacket.

There's a small, minute movement in the woman's eyes like she's tracking something that Lyra can't see.

"You're a necromancer," she says, finally, in the same melodic tone. "That's why you're so easy to see."

"Well, that's odd of you to say," Lyra says, staring hard at her phone, willing for another message to come through, but it remains blank. "Do you need any help finding anything in the shop?"

For the first time, she wishes she had an actual phone number to text Melekai. There's nothing in the store that could be raised, not even a dead mouse in the storage. The closest thing she's aware of is the collection of dead bugs near the far light by the gas pump.

Because this might be nothing, but...everything in her body, all her instincts and adrenaline tell her it's not.

The woman's eyes narrow, just a hint, like she's sizing Lyra up.

"Did Frisse already talk to you?" she asks, and there's a thread of frustration weaving its way through that soft voice.

Lyra exhales, keeping the hand on the gun. "I spoke to her. It was weird," she says, not sure what answer the woman is seeking. "I swear, I'm just some person."

Feigned innocence didn't work too well last time, but hey, she wants to try it again. The best way to get through conflict is to pretend it doesn't exist.

"Don't trust her," the woman says, which no problem there, "she'll say things, and then go back on her word."

"I believe that," Lyra says, "I swear, I don't have anything to do with anything."

Lyra could swear the woman relaxes, just a hair, her shoulders coming down just enough to make her seem more natural, less still. Less like an immovable statue, less like a creature from the deep, more like a person.

"You went to my clearing," the woman says, and the floor drops out on Lyra's stomach. "I felt a necromancer there, some stirrings, with that spell weaver and alchemist."

Lyra resists the urge to grip the gun tighter, just keeps her hand on it, and only years of customer service training stops her from yanking it off its shelf and taking aim. "I'm sorry, I didn't mean to intrude."

So. This woman, with her soft voice and colorless eyes, is Terese. Supposedly a demon in a live body, supposedly in pain, supposedly wants to end the world.

The woman, Terese, doesn't look away, just continues to size her up.

"Did they try to deal with your demon?" she asks, and, deliberate like it's much more significant than the action would suggest, sets her hand, palm up, on the counter like she's bidding Lyra to hold her hand.

Lyra's seen it enough times from Melekai to recognize the motion.

She nods, instead of anything else, not trusting her voice in this time of fear.

"Don't do it," she says, keeping her hand there. "Whatever she offers you to help, don't do it."

"Noted," Lyra says, swallowing past the moment of terror. "I don't control what my demon does."

There's something, a little spark, and Terese's eyes flash, just like Melekai's, before it disappears. "You could," she says, and her voice is just a hair sly, in a way that sets Lyra's teeth on edge. The palm of her hand twitches like she's begging Lyra to recognize what she's doing. "You could command him to go in, to kill the Doctor, to rid the world of her."

"I'm not down for murder," Lyra says because that seems like an important distinction to make. "I just work at a gas station."

"I could take away your pain," Terese says, and the words are so similar to Melekai's that her skin crawls like Lyra's been dumped into a vat of ants. "I understand it, I understand what it means, to never be comfortable. To have the hurt burrowing inside, unceasing. I could make it go away."

Lyra exhales again because that seems like the proper thing to do when someone offers you an existence without pain. "I'm okay," she repeats.

"No, you're not," Terese says immediately, and her eyes flash again. She extends her hand a little closer, and Lyra scoots the stool away. "I could tell, it's clouding the room, it's clouding the very fabric of your being. Imagine what you could do without it."

"Thanks, but..." Lyra shrugs, despite her pounding heart.

"Please," Terese says, and her voice starts to plead. Like she watched a movie where someone begged and decided to emulate it.

It's the freakiest thing Lyra's ever seen, and she's seen some shit.

"Please, you need to help me, she hurt me," Terese begs, her voice hitching up.

Her phone lights up, and Lyra glances down. And that is all the space Terese needs.

Terese jolts forward, grabbing at Lyra's chin, vaulting over the store counter, hitting the cash register, and knocking it off its till. It bursts open when it hits the floor, coins clattering everywhere in an explosion of glittering cacophony.

The gun skitters away, outside of her reach.

The stool tips over, sending Lyra and Terese crashing to the tile, and Terese claws at her face, gripping her chin and jerking Lyra's head to the side.

There's a bright flash of gold, the same gold as the thread that Melekai pulls, and her legs go lax, outside of her control.

Pinning her down, Terese gasps, the sound ripped out of her.

"You're so..." she says, then turns Lyra's chin, so Lyra looks at her instead of the money spilled.

Terese's eyes reflect back at her, just like Melekai's, and they're wide, euphoric.

Lyra struggles, but everything is heavy, her limbs weighted to the ground, panic coating her throat.

"Stop," Lyra croaks out, reaching out to grab something, anything, that could be a weapon, but her hands just close over loose change.

She usually passes out by this point.

Still holding her chin, Terese sits up, eyes aglow. "Is this why necromancers are so rare?" she marvels, and her nails dig into Lyra's cheeks.

Not letting go of Lyra, still pinning her down, Terese raises her free hand, and the golden glow shines from her palm. She inspects it like a surveyor would inspect a fine gem.

Lyra tries to push her away, she really does, but her eyes struggle to keep open, which isn't how she wants to die. This isn't how she wants to be discovered, dead at work with a wake of destruction around her.

She might not be found until the graveyard shift comes in, unless a customer stops by and calls the police.

"Interesting," Terese murmurs, above her, "I could do so much with this—"

There's a bang, and Lyra's ears pop, and there's a rush of warm air, and everything on the ground around them gets thrown back.

The stool shatters, splintering into a million toothpicks and suspending in the air, and the very tile beneath Lyra's back dents down. Coins hang in the air around them, glittering in the light of the fluorescents.

And the sense of death fills the air, fills Lyra's lungs, and she gasps.

Everything, every little bug and ant and bacteria on the floor, the mouse in the basement, everything is dead.

The moth that had been buzzing hits the dented tile, just out of reach of Lyra's hand, not even twitching.

Terese pays the chaos no attention, just smiling down at Lyra. "That usually kills humans," she says like she's some sort of freaking supervillain. "Something must be really different with you."

Lyra rips her eyes away from her, stretching her fingertips to the moth. Just a little bit more, just a few bare fractions of an inch away, and—

The pad of her finger brushes against the moth's wing.

The wing is broken from the fall, and the thorax doesn't move, not like it should. She doesn't know bug physiology, she doesn't know, but—

Her eyes flutter shut, and she pours whatever she can into that little moth, into the thorax and the wings, and all of its little broken parts.

It sparks against her eyelids, and the moth moves.

Terese makes a sound in the back of her throat, something between a sigh and a scoff.

"You shine so bright when you do that," she says, voice musical. "I can't believe you're not dead yet." She gentles her hand on Lyra's chin, patting her cheek where her nails had dug in so severely.

And Melekai's not there.

Terror winds anew around Lyra's spine as the now uneven tile beneath her pushes into her back.

"I don't know what you want," Lyra whispers, and the weariness weighs against her, wrapping her up in a fog of unrealism. Like she's watching herself in a movie, watching from outside a misty glass, seeing the scene play out from afar. Like the swinging fluorescents, the shattered chair, and the hanging coins are just dressings on a set.

Terese raises her hand from Lyra's cheek, and a thin gold thread rises with her.

All discomfort from the tile evaporates, like Lyra's laying on the softest bed.

This is what her mother had warned her about.

And now, all she can do is lay on the floor at work, staring at the moth with the broken wing flutter and twitch against the floor. She brought it back, and she didn't even heal the wing enough for it to fly away.

"I wanted you to help kill Dr. Frisse, but I think...I think otherwise," Terese says, and there's a smile on her lips that chills Lyra's blood.

She hopes Jackson doesn't quit school if she dies. She hopes he doesn't find out until after his finals, until after he succeeds.

Terese lowers her hand again, and—

Like a gale-force wind, something slams against Terese, knocking her back, her knees coming off of Lyra's middle.

Lyra gasps, a high-pitched keening noise from her throat, one she can hardly believe comes from her.

She rolls over, somehow, and everything's shaking. Her legs shake, her hands shake... the floor shakes.

The floor is shaking.

The coins clatter to the ground, pelting Lyra, and she curls up in a ball as the splinters of the chair fling in every direction, embedding themselves in the wall, in the counter. A bottle of wine shatters along the far cooler, then another.

A splinter slashes her cheek, blood spraying across the dented tile.

A crash and Lyra lifts her head just enough to see Terese struggle to her feet, and in front of her, arms outspread, stands Melekai.

He's still in the same body as she saw him last, and his face stretches into a grimace. He's coiled like he's ready to spring if Terese makes another move.

Terese glances at Lyra with those colorless eyes, then back to Melekai. "I was hoping to speak to you," she says, oddly formal despite the dust covering her motorcycle jacket and the new rip in her jeans. The left side of her face looks like she scraped it along the broken tile, like she could be hurt. Red blood mixes with something black, something oily, on the side of her face.

Melekai actually snarls at her.

"Dr. Frisse hurt me, you need to help me," Terese says. Her pleading voice hitches up, and Lyra's blood goes cold.

If she hadn't just seen her flip away from it, she'd buy it this time.

Her limbs heavy, everything heavy, Lyra drags her way to the shotgun, now clattered just outside of the dented tile.

Melekai's eyes flicker to her, brief, and she might be imagining it, but his head dips down in a brief inclination. A nod.

"Please—" Terese says, and Melekai moves.

Lyra can't think of any other words for it as the entire store explodes in some crazy, chaotic whirl of motion.

It's bright, her eyes can't make sense of it, but she squeezes them shut and crawls until her hand closes around the familiar butt of the shotgun.

She cradles it to her, pushing herself up, and black spots swim around her eyes. Melekai and Terese stand close, and a strange wind whirls around them, light streaking around the small Buggees convenience store.

Magazines rip from their stand, clattering around, their pages flinging around the store, and one of the windows shatters, sucking in cold air and sending snow spiraling in.

Sirens sound, close, and red and blue lights reflect off of the shards of glass. Too far out.

Lyra squints, her hands shaking, and aims.

She's her mother's daughter, and her mother taught her to shoot when she turned twelve, but soda cans on a fence are a hell of a lot easier than this, with every bone in her body trembling with exhaustion, on uneven tile, with light and wind and swirling snow, but Mr. Peters keeps the gun loaded with birdshot, and when she squeezes the trigger the shot goes wide, but the birdshot strafes Terese, drawing bloody lines across her shoulder, and the wind and light abruptly stop as she gasps, colorless eyes wide.

There's a brief moment of sudden silence, like the fog in Lyra's head turns out to the rest of the world.

Before the police burst in with their guns drawn, Terese turns.

With a flash of her hand and a bright bang of light, the tile rips up before her, and she disappears, right before the police's eyes.

Leaving Lyra huddled on the ground.

11

Thankfully, the police take the time to pull the security tapes and call Mr. Peters, and someone drapes a blanket over Lyra's shoulders as the police scuttle around the store, taking pictures of everything and generally exclaiming about how surprised they are.

Melekai stands close, snarling at anyone who comes near her, but nobody can see him, so they pay no attention. His golden-brown curls have mostly fallen out of the bun, framing his face, leaving it wild.

An EMT squats next to where she's sitting, still in the dented tile, and starts disinfecting Lyra's cheek, on the cut she still can't feel.

Well, she can feel the blood crusted and pulling along her skin, she can feel the grime and the sawdust and splinters, but not any actual pain-like sensation.

Melekai looks like he wants to vibrate into another dimension. An injury, something, a line of thick black blood oozes from a nick in his hand, and he notices her looking at it.

"It's not like we bleed red, we're not like you," he says, gentle.

Terese had. At least partially.

"I don't know what happened here," the EMT says to her, "but you're lucky you weren't hit by anything bigger."

Lyra blinks at her, but she's just a normal EMT, wearing a uniform, her dark hair pulled neatly out of her face.

The EMT takes her lack of talking as an invitation. "I saw that video, any of those bigger chunks of wood, that'd be bad."

Someone had placed a bottle of sugary drink in Lyra's hand, and she takes a sip instead of saying anything.

"Yeah, 'cause that's good bedside manner," Melekai mutters under his breath, and she feels more than sees him shift behind her. "Let me just take you home."

And while her bed and cat sound excellent, she just shakes her head minutely, watching the EMT deftly search through her bag for something.

She can hear Mr. Peters' distress, at the store, at the tapes. Though his words seem to blend around her, she can hear his concern for her, worry for her injuries.

The EMT fits her phone in her hand, and, dumbly, Lyra looks at it, to avoid looking at anything else, to avoid figuring out emotions, anything.

ALETTE (12:12 AM): Get out of there right now.

Of course, the message had come too late, and if Lyra had any energy she'd chuckle.

Then, later:

ALETTE (12:46): Are you okay please text!

Finally, after Mr. Peters and the detective have enough time watching the tapes, the EMT packs up her little kit, and she can hear generalized amazement coming from the store office, she closes her eyes, just a bit.

"Oh no," she hears Melekai mutter with a bite of acid. "You don't get to do that."

His hands, strong, grip her shoulder, and something between a zap of static electricity and a sudden cramp of her muscles sparks inside of her, and she gasps, her eyes flying open.

The fog in her head disappears like it was never there, and the cut on her cheek blazes into her awareness.

"Fucking ow!" she says, slapping a hand over the bandage, and the EMT looks back at her.

Her hand had moved easily, too easily, and her legs ache.

"That's why I didn't do that sooner," Melekai says, scowling down at her accusing look. "What? You'd be in pain."

There are police and Mr. Peters and EMTs in the tiny store so she can't do anything but stare at him before she pushes herself up to standing.

Fuck, even her back hurts.

Before she knows it, the EMT is back at her elbow, as if worried she'll wobble. Melekai stands back, the hint of a smirk on his lips.

"You should sit down again," she says, voice professional. "You're in shock."

"Uh, this"—Lyra looks at the label—"sugary drink helped. Do they need my...statement or anything?"

One of the police officers glances at her, and at the EMT who's frantically shaking her head. "We're going to contact you in the next few days," he says, firmly.

Mr. Peters rushes over, however, and for a horrible second Lyra thinks he's about to hug her. "Do you need the hospital? You should go—"

"—No," interrupts Lyra, because health insurance is for rich people.

"You need a ride home, something, anything—"

There's a small sound at where the front door used to be and the small bell still tinkles, and Lyra and Mr. Peters both instinctively turn towards it.

Alette and Axel are standing there and something inside Lyra unwinds at seeing Alette still doing well. Her hand is now in a brace instead of a cast, and it looks like she actually has movement in her fingers again.

Axel's looking around, his eyes falling from the dented tile to the piles of glass and sticky pools of wine, to the pages of magazines ripped from the stands.

"We can take her home, we're her friends, she was texting me earlier," Alette says, and her voice wobbles as she glances between Lyra and where Melekai broods near the wall. "We can..."

The police officer nods, and within a few moments, she has given her information and Alette and Axel help her to the black Mustang.

Melekai follows, which she expects, a glowering specter just inches away.

Of course, he climbs in the back with her, too close, and she has a million questions for him, a million things she wants to blurt out, and her skin buzzes with whatever he did to her.

The door's barely closed when Axel turns to her, all chill gone. "Oh my god, are you okay? How are you alive?"

"Melekai attacked her back," Lyra says, and she should be exhausted, she should be nigh unable to move, but it's like she's just taken five shots of espresso. "I raised a moth."

"Uh, thanks," Alette says, painfully polite, with just a thin covering of horror over her words. "What—"

"How'd you survive the death bubble?" Axel interrupts, as he pulls the Mustang out of the ruined Buggees parking lot.

She's not going to be able to go back to work.

"Uh..." She looks to Melekai, who's watching her with the intensity of a thousand suns but doesn't say anything. "I don't know?"

Axel breathes out, long, as he drives up the winding road to her little house. "Do you need to stay someplace else?"

"No," interrupts Melekai, and Alette flinches.

"Uh, he says no?" Lyra says, and she feels like she could easily walk this, despite the ache in her legs and the muscles in her back. "How'd she find me?"

"That's what I want to know," Melekai all but growls, and for a brief, fleeting second Lyra is scared, before it's immediately banished from her mind.

He saved her life, in possibly a few different ways, he's not going to kill her after that.

She doesn't miss the glance between Alette and Axel, and from the tensing of his muscles, neither does Melekai.

Lyra lays her hand on his knee, and he twitches in surprise.

"We know she's hunting down magicians of all types," Axel says, finally. "She killed a spell weaver in Oregon yesterday, and a scholar in NorCal the day before."

Melekai relaxes, just a hair. Which is...interesting.

The road turns to gravel once more, and Axel has to grip the wheel of the car.

"She wanted our help to kill Dr. Frisse," Lyra says, because while she doesn't want to be in the car that seems like the minimum amount of information she should give them. "And she was trying to convince me before she did the whole...death bubble. Then she was trying to uh..." she trails off, looking to Melekai, as if he'd have a better way of describing things. "Steal my soul? Eat my life essence? Do demon things?"

The car is silent, just the churn of the gravel beneath the wheels.

"I'm going to come by tomorrow," Alette says like she's steeling herself up to say it, "and teach you some basic self-defense against magic."

Melekai opens his mouth to respond but looks to Lyra instead and closes it.

Which again is unusual.

"Thanks for the ride, sorry you had to drive all this way to do it," Lyra says, as they pull past the meth house and to her meager driveway.

"Oh, we're going to sneak back into the crime scene and investigate," Axel says, and his voice is forced light. "I'll make up some badges—those are easy—and Alette will have a charm or something that'll make them forget we were already there, it's simple."

"Simple," Lyra says, then shakes her head. She has more energy than she's had in months, and...

She kicks open the door, with all the strength of someone who's really damn frustrated with all this shit, and Melekai follows her out, close, like he's guiding her into the house, like it's safer, and—

And the moment the door closes behind him she whirls, staring back at him, almost backing him against the door.

"What did you do?" she asks, almost accusing, and her blood fizzes inside her veins. "How did you reverse that...whatever that was?"

"She took some of you, I just gave it back," he says, and he pulls himself up to his full height, which is odd because this isn't the tallest body he's inhabited before, so the effect is somewhat lessened. "You were about to stop breathing."

"How could you—" She pinches her nose, and a scrape across her hand makes itself known. "So this whole stealing my soul thing can go both ways."

"That's really inaccurate," he says, because accuracy is totally something she's concerned with right now. "I am protecting my investment in you—"

"Investment," Lyra repeats back at him, and his eye twitches.

"And I made sure you didn't die," he says, raising his voice a bit to talk over her. "I don't know why that's something you're upset with." They're standing so close, so close she can see every breath he's taking, see his chest rise and fall, feel the anger radiating off of him.

So she takes a step back, gives herself a little bit of breathing room, takes the time to shuck off her snow boots, and stack them in the entryway, and everything hurts. Everything hurts and she's hyper-aware of the pain, of every sensation, of every scrape of fabric across her skin, everything.

"I didn't even know it was possible," she says, once she's taken off her winter gear and hung it up on its hook. And he watches her with rapt eyes. "Does that mean you're...hungry now?"

He shrugs. "I'll definitely survive. I'll take from you in a few weeks when you've recovered."

"How kind," she says, and the sarcasm in her own voice makes her wince.

He raises an eyebrow, just a small movement that seems to reveal so much about Lyra, lay bare all of her inner thoughts, and she hates it.

So she turns away, to get greeted by her cat with a small meow, to busy herself in her small kitchen.

She's starving herself, utterly starving, like she could eat an entire feast just by herself. Her back aches where the tile detonated beneath her and a million small scrapes brush against her clothing.

Her cat winds his way between her legs, already purring, so she dumps some food in his bowl as she putters, trying to figure out something to eat.

"So you kept the cat," Melekai says, neutral like he's reading something in that action as well.

"I was not going to give the cat right back to the shelter that put it down," she shoots back at him, irritation crowding under her skin.

"I suppose," Melekai says, still watching her too closely.

She should be grateful, she supposes, that he took the time to come and save her, to do...whatever it is he did to Terese, whatever destruction he caused.

But instead, she just feels gross. Gross and hungry and irritable, like everything is too much and everything is rubbing her the wrong way.

She's filthy, covered in tile dust and Cheeto crumbs and dirt and blood, so she sets her ancient oven to preheat and, completely ignoring Melekai, strides to her tiny shower to clean off some of the grime.

Her shower may be tiny, as most showers in mobile homes are, but at least it always has obscene water pressure and heated water that can steam up her entire place if she's not careful to shut the door behind her.

Her cat, of course, finds the whole process intolerable and will likely yowl at the top of his lungs at her while she showers, but there are worse noises in the world than a cat that desperately wants to save you from drowning.

So she shuts the door with a click, leaving her cat and the demon staring at her from the living room, and examines herself in the mirror.

The cut along her cheek is by far the grossest, but the edges are clean and the EMT didn't put any stitches. She's pale, of course, because it's winter, but she also has the bone-deep pallid skin tone of someone who's been through way too much that day.

Her polo shirt is almost an entirely different color from the tile dust, and blood obviously splattered down it at one point in the evening, so she strips it off directly almost immediately, and turns to examine her back.

It's already a mess of bruising, bright red scrapes warring against the deep purple that will absolutely hurt more the next morning. She's not sure she's been this bruised since...

Since the car accident.

"Oh fuck this," Lyra mutters, then steps into the shower and yanks the curtain closed, and for one long moment everything is a tangle of stinging skin against hot water, and she hisses under her breath until it calms down just enough that she can start actually rinsing off the muck of the day.

"If you're in this much pain I could just take some back," Melekai says, somehow in the room without opening the door.

Lyra stares at the pale yellow/white of her little shower tiles, breathing out of her nose.

"I didn't exactly use exact measurements, I was estimating," he says like this isn't a huge violation of privacy.

"What are you doing in here?" Lyra asks, still staring at her shower wall.

"You came in here, I could tell you had pain, I...followed you?" he says, and he sounds so genuinely confused that she pokes her head out from behind the curtain to stare at him.

He's just leaning casually against the closed door, looking unconcerned.

"I'm naked," she says, in case he didn't put that together.

"Most humans are, when they shower," he says, completely unruffled. When she stares at him, he sighs. "I've seen your entrails spread across an interstate in Arizona, this is no more revealing than that."

She yanks the curtain closed again, so she can breathe hard out of her nose, before scrubbing herself down with perhaps a bit more force than necessary.

It stings her skin, which she knows he can sense, but does it anyway.

"Why'd you take so long with the moth?" she asks when the questions just build up more and more pressure inside of her until it comes tumbling out.

"Had trouble sensing it," he says, after almost too long of a pause. "It got masked by her...explosion."

That almost makes sense, so she scowls at her shampoo bottle, before trying to scrub out the caked-on dust in her hair.

It's beyond weird, talking to someone through a shower curtain.

"Instead of being a bright pinprick of light on the horizon," he continues, and she stills, "it was like the entire area got lit up. Here until Mount Rainier, all one big splash of necromancy, like there were thousands of you."

"Well that's terrifying," she says, trying to squeeze out some of the dust still in the curls of her hair. "It was just a moth."

"Good call on that," he says, and again, there's something odd in his voice. "I could tell before something was wrong, but not...not anything concrete. The same feeling I got when you broke your hand five years ago, or when that train almost hit your bus."

"I didn't tell you about that," Lyra says, washing off her hair, feeling a bit more human. A bruised, over-sensitized human, but a human.

"Or when you lived in the house with the faulty staircase for six months," he continues, "or when a drunk stalked you between your work and your bus back in Iowa."

She stands under the hot water, blinking at the wall once more before she pokes her head around the curtain again. "When was that?"

He shrugs. "Two years ago? Maybe? Human time is odd."

She stares at him, and he stares right back.

"What? I made him go away," he says as if defending himself. "I didn't think you'd want to be jumped in an Iowa parking lot."

"Thanks," she says, unsteady, and from the other room, she can hear her oven chime to being done, so she twists off the shower, blindly grabs her towel, and as securely as she can, wraps it around her. It scrapes against the skin on her back, but it's better than walking outright in the nude in front of him.

His eyes still follow her, too closely, as she breezes by him and into her room, but she closes that door with a click and a warning glance, and he thankfully stays on the other side. She can hear him settling against the door, leaning against it.

"I didn't know you did those things," she calls through the door, quickly getting into her coziest of plaid pajama pants and a tank top so she can stick a lasagna into the oven. "I didn't know you could, I dunno, tell that sort of thing."

"Of course I can," he says, muffled. "What, did you think demons couldn't?"

She shoves her feet into slippers, then opens the door just enough to squeeze out, and his eyes go directly to the abraded skin on her back.

"You didn't know," he declares as if reading her answer from her back, following her back into the kitchen. "You couldn't tell I was there."

"Not at all," she says, taking a frozen lasagna out of her freezer and shoving it into the oven. "Didn't know you could tell anything about me being in danger at all."

She settles into her giant green velvet chair, and he folds himself into the one other kitchen chair she has, to watch her as if she's a beetle underneath a glass.

"Didn't know you could give back life essence, didn't know you could teleport until three weeks ago, and didn't even know that other magicians existed at all. Didn't know that demons could do a death bubble"—he rolls his eyes at that—"or anything else that's been going on."

He obviously mulls that over in his mind, as if weighing his options.

"I didn't know you were going to be so...overprotective, either," she says, watching his reactions. "I appreciate the protection, but...but I'm confused by it."

He leans forward in the rickety kitchen chair, so he's leaning towards her, close.

"Necromancers are rare," he says, after a long pause, and she's never seen him so slow to talk. "Taking all of a necromancer's life essence at once could sustain a demon for decades, but I've only met four in my entire life."

Lyra doesn't want to ask what he did to the other three.

Or how long he's lived.

"Demons...don't really have contact with each other, we're solitary, but," he pauses, and the cat winds his way around them, rubbing against the legs of the chair, "to the best of my knowledge, no one has ever tried keeping a necromancer alive."

This isn't quite new information, so Lyra nods along.

"From what I understand, my awareness of the world is different than yours," he says, and that might be the understatement of the year, "but I thought...I thought you could tell when I helped out. When I sensed things from you."

"Well," Lyra drawls because there is no proper reaction to that sort of statement that her brain can scramble together, "no."

He stares at her for a few moments again, like she's actually surprised him.

"Only times I've been aware has been when you've shown up to zap me," she says, trying and probably failing to not sound frustrated. "I know nothing, and I want..." she trails off, the ire suddenly gone from her, as if the frank conversation steals it all away.

"You want...?" he prods, steepling his hands, and the oft familiar look of hunger appears back in his eyes. "Tell me what you want."

Her mouth is dry, so she looks away, blinking for a few seconds, at the kitschy decor in her inherited little house, as her cat brushes against her plaid pajamas and purrs.

"I want to not be surprised," she says, finally, and it feels wholly inadequate. "I want to know all there is to know about me, about demons, about all this, so I don't worry about being caught off guard.

I don't want to find out about my weirdness from creepy research papers from Alette, I don't want to read about things in ancient terms, I want to just know."

He smiles at that, and Lyra can't figure out what to make of it.

"And you said your brother is the scholar," he says, finally leaning back, and her cat takes the opportunity to jump on his lap, startling a laugh out of him.

The tension broken, Lyra lets herself sink more into the green velvet chair, the fabric downright luxurious against her sore muscles.

"Well, he is," she says, and everything feels less dire, now that she's gotten that out. "He can read something, anything, and just automatically know it well enough to teach it to someone. It's crazy. I have to read the same book three times to get what he knows after a quick glance."

"Weren't you in college, though?" Melekai asks, resting his hand on the cat, who just purrs louder. "I could have sworn you were."

"Yeah, well, when your nerves don't really cooperate and you miss too many classes, they don't really let you stay for very long," she says, pulling over the plush blanket she keeps thrown over the chair to cover her arms. "Only so forgiving for so long on that."

He scoffs. "Ability to show up to classes has nothing to do with someone's intellect," he says like he could condescend her college professors from this far away, "and the amount of things you've picked up by just existing suggest that you're far from dim."

"Thanks," she says, snuggling into her blanket, and every little brush of fabric sets her senses buzzing. "Why do I feel high out of my mind right now?"

"What?" He blinks at her like he didn't notice.

"Ever since you zapped me back," she says, "I can feel all the pain —thanks for that—but also it's like I had three shots of espresso and my skin feels everything."

Automatically, he leans over, dislodging her cat from his lap, reaching out his hand to hers, palm up.

Just like Terese did only a short time ago.

She hesitates a second, then rests her hand on his.

Immediately, his eyes reflect back at her, but the numbing loss of pain doesn't come like she's grown to expect.

"Well," he says like that's a full sentence. "You are full of sensation."

"Yeah," she says, unsteady, unsure of what exactly he's feeling, "that's what I meant." Then, remembering the conversation they had literally moments before—"tell me what you can sense."

He raises his eyebrow back and rubs a circle into the palm of her hand with his thumb. "Your back hurts more than I thought," he starts, focusing on her hand, his voice low. "The skin is competing with the bruise on what is the most distracting."

She nods because he's not wrong.

"You're far too aware of your skin against the blanket, of your wet hair, than you should be." His thumb against her palm raises goose-bumps on her arms. "You could just as easily succumb to pain as be overwhelmed by sensation right now."

That sounds more ominous than she feels, but not entirely wrong. "I guess I succumb to pain a lot."

"Hmm," he murmurs, then lifts her hand to his mouth and presses a soft kiss against the center of her palm.

She shudders at the touch, her stomach going tight, and snatches her hand back.

"I must've miscalculated how much Terese took from you," he says, and his voice is back to normal, back to what she thinks it should be. "The effect will wear off in a few hours, you can sleep through it if you wish."

Lyra doubts she'll be able to get any sleep, and a glance at the clock on the microwave shows it to be hovering near two AM, and she still has the lasagna in the oven.

"So I have more soul than I should have right now?" she forces out, her heart thumping in her chest. "I didn't even know that was possible."

"Soul is archaic and boring," he says, leaning back. "You need to find a better word."

"Sure," she says, because what else can she say?

12

He sticks around as she eats way more than she needs to of the lasagna, and despite the pounding heart and the fizzing in her blood, she conks out on the green chair sometime around three-thirty.

HE'S THERE, in the morning, standing at her window next to her sink, and Lyra makes herself take a few deep breaths before reacting to someone standing in her house as she wakes up.

"Your phone has been going off," he says, without even looking at her, just staring out at the snow falling in her overgrown yard. "The little magicians are contacting you."

"I would pay you money to call Axel that to his face," she says, instead of reacting to any fear or anything.

She stretches her legs out, and they ache, right before her back sends a pang out to her, and she lets herself drape over her legs in the chair. The cat jumps off her lap, immediately batting at a dust bunny in his weird limp run of his.

"Ow," she mutters, because of course her back would hurt, she got blasted into some tile.

"I don't need it," he says, off-handedly, and it takes her a moment to figure out what he's talking about. "Money, that is."

"Right, I don't know what the demon economy runs on," she says, blinking through her exhaustion enough to hobble over to the coffee machine. "Are there even enough of you to have an economy?"

"Yes," he says, bland.

She doesn't have a reply to that, so she just stares at the coffee machine, willing it to work faster.

He turns towards her, finally, and his attention is like a laser, cutting through the fog of sleep, so her mouth goes dry and the small part of her brain that's focused on survival snaps awake.

"Terese is one of us," he says, and she doesn't particularly like the use of 'us' in that sentence, "but I don't know how she did it."

"Did what?" The coffee is taking forever to percolate.

He leans against the counter, still looking at her, still too still to be real. Idly, she realizes this is the first time she's ever seen him in the same body for so long, and a bit of her morning focus goes down the rabbit hole of wondering just how often he has to switch.

"She's in a live body," he says, and another part of her kicks awake. Just like Dr. Frisse had suggested. "There are two souls inside her, the...original inhabitant, and the demon."

"Sounds unpleasant," Lyra murmurs, as finally the coffee finishes percolating, and she pours herself a large mug. "Can the body..."

"Completely aware," Melekai says, which doesn't sound good, in this quiet moment with the two of them standing in her kitchen and the snow falling outside. "Feels everything. Torture for the demon, too."

"Huh," she says, staring out at the snow, warming her hands on the mug, before wincing as her leg gives a twitch. "I can call out work, this should count as a sick day or something, I mean, I got attacked."

"Don't go back," he says, quick, and it's enough that she shakes herself loose from staring at the snow and raises an eyebrow at him.

"If she's seen you there before she could see you again. Don't go back."

"I don't want to look for a new job," she murmurs, instead of any of the hundreds of things flying through her brain.

Her job is good. Her boss treats her decently, it's close and pays enough, and the idea of Melekai ordering her around because of this...

Though she doesn't want to die for it. Doesn't want to deal with seeing Terese with her colorless eyes stride back through that door.

"It'll probably be closed for a few days, anyway," she says, instead. "I doubt he could repair all the windows overnight, insurance is a bitch and his isn't that good."

He clearly looks like he wants to demand more, but he nods instead, his hand going to her arm, in the small motions he always seems to make.

Lyra exhales at his touch, clutching the mug closer, then strides out of his reach, back to her phone on the table.

ALETTE (3:52 AM): We just finished at the store, are you still awake?

AXEL (4:01 AM): Yoooo Lyra you up we have questions?

ALETTE (4:09 AM): We are packing up but will be by tomorrow afternoon. I hope you're okay.

And a missed call from Mr. Peters.

JACKSON (7:02 AM): Your boss just called me. Are you okay?

LYRA (11:03 AM): Sorry, just woke up. My back is very sore.

LYRA (11:04 AM): I didn't even know Mr. Peters had your number.

"I could help with that if I'm careful," Melekai says, suddenly, and of course he's peering over her shoulder. "Take just enough to edge some of the pain out, not enough to knock you out or harm your heart."

She grabs the cereal box and sits down with it, instead of immediately reacting. "I want a list," she says, finally, "of weird side effects and limits of this, so I can understand it."

He looks nonplussed. "That should be possible."

So she shoves a handful of dry cereal in her mouth and holds a hand out to him.

He drifts around, directing all his attention to her hand, studying it, like it's a complex puzzle and not an entirely standard hand that everyone has. He cradles it, examining it like it'd break if he isn't incredibly careful.

It's just another reminder of how weird he is.

Her phone dings, but he doesn't look up, so she checks it with her free hand, brushing off the cereal dust.

JACKSON (11:09 AM): Are you safe?

LYRA (11:10 AM): Who knows.

JACKSON (11:10 AM): Not a cool answer, Lyra.

"Yes, you're very fucking safe right now," Melekai grumbles, though she didn't read it aloud and he's not looked up from her hand.

LYRA (11:11 AM): Mel says I'm safe, he's here. It was a demony thing last night, don't tell Mr. Peters.

JACKSON (11:12 AM): Tell Melekai to leave you out of it.

Melekai lifts his eyes to hers, very briefly, at that, before he continues examining her hand, turning it over in his.

LYRA (11:13 AM): I think he agrees with you bro.

JACKSON (11:14 AM): Don't call me bro.

"Here," Melekai says, placing a finger at the base of her wrist, and, deliberate, drawing a single golden thread from her skin.

It glimmers in the light from the snow outside.

Her breath caught in her throat, Lyra swallows.

In comparison, the gold flash from the night before seems insurmountable.

With a twist of his finger, the thread snaps from her, and the pain in her back lessens a level. Not gone, not even remotely, but...but a little less.

Like she took an Advil or something light. Like a normal good day, not a day after Melekai visits.

"I don't want to take more, not for a few weeks," Melekai murmurs.

"Can you tell my...levels or something?" she asks, past the lump in her chest. She didn't even feel fatigued at that, didn't even feel like she lost any sleep.

"Or something," he says, standing back, and it's suddenly, without warning, very awkward.

"Uh, do you want to be here when Alette and Axel get here?" she asks, because what else can she do.

"I can tell how bright you shine, and I know how much to take to knock you out," he says, instead. "I now know how much it takes to get you to stop breathing because Terese was irresponsible. All else is guesswork."

She blinks at him because she didn't expect such a specific answer. "It's a visual thing?"

"More or less," he says, then paces the length of her little house, the cat skittering in his footsteps, batting at his feet. "Do you want to fight Terese, or do you want to run?"

It's too much to contemplate before the coffee has kicked in, so she takes another gulp, then another handful of cereal.

"I can't just stay here?"

"Not easily," he replies, "I've jury-rigged some protections, but any demon would know their way around them if they thought hard enough, I just don't think Terese has encountered them yet," he pauses, "she seemed...unnaturally young."

"Huh," Lyra says around a mouthful of cereal. "How so?"

"She fell for a very basic attack, one she shouldn't have."

"She also sorta suggested she hadn't seen a necromancer before," Lyra points out, and he quirks an eyebrow at her. "When she pinned me down. She was monologuing..."

He hesitates, visibly so, like his very being stutters, before he resumes his pacing. "That's good," he says, begrudging, "then we can trick her if we need to."

They sit in silence for a few moments, as she drinks her coffee and eats her cereal.

ALETTE (12:01 PM): Is the demon still with you? We have questions.

LYRA (12:01 PM): Yes.

ALETTE AND AXEL SHOW UP, idling in the black Mustang outside of her house in the snow for too long, visibly arguing about something.

Melekai hovers around Lyra like he's worried she will break, as if her pain drives him almost to distraction, and it bothers the edge of her awareness.

Through the window, she sees Alette crane her neck to look at the house, then blanch when she sees Melekai.

"What does she see when she sees you?" Lyra asks, resisting the urge to wave back at them.

A small intrusion of irritation inside her grows, at them, which feels rather unfair, but...

They were the ones fighting the monster, not her. Until Axel happened upon her in a cafe, nothing like this happened.

"Hopefully something ridiculous," he says, "hopefully something terrifying."

Her cat jumps to the window as well, pressing his nose against the cold glass, as if he could also sense the two outside. Or is just curious as to why all the attention is on something else besides him.

She scratches between the cat's ears, and he settles a bit, purring.

"Did you ever name the cat?" Melekai asks, glowering out the window.

"Couldn't think of anything," she says, then blinks up at him. "Wait, can you read my mind?"

He shrugs, which is very not helpful. "A little."

"Don't," she blurts out, then rubs between her eyebrows. "I mean unless I'm in trouble or something."

"It's not an active effort," he says, still glowering at the car, "you just project a lot."

She stares at him, then promptly decides to deal with it later.

"Besides," he continues, "it's not so much reading your actual mind as it is observing what you observe. An additional set of eyes."

"Weird," she says, because it is, "but I guess a little better."

This time he does look at her, a puzzled tilt to his eyebrows, but before he could say anything Alette slams the door shut to the Mustang and stalks to her front door, with Axel trailing behind, a wounded look on his face.

"This'll be fun," Melekai murmurs, right as Alette knocks.

The cat races to the door, faster than Lyra's seen him run with his limp, and Lyra scoops him up, so he doesn't escape before opening the door.

There are two red splotches on the top of Alette's cheekbones, but otherwise, she is as collected as she usually is, her wool jacket crisply tailored to her slim form, her gold glasses pristine. Even her wrist is in a sleek brace that coordinates with her outfit.

"Good, you're upright," she says, then steps in, her eyes immediately going to the door jam, then over to Melekai glowering next to the window. "You put up protections," she says, quick.

"Of course I did," he snaps, and she doesn't quite visibly shrink down, but it's a near deal.

"Ooh, you have a cat!" Axel says, clomping through the door after Alette and immediately petting the cat in Lyra's arms, not even bothering to take off his snow boots.

The cat tolerates it for a second, before jumping out of Lyra's arms to wind around Melekai instead.

Alette crowds around the doorway, peering up at it like she can read something Lyra can't. "Does that one actually work?" she asks, tapping a thin finger against the door jam.

"Of course it works, why wouldn't it?" Melekai snips and Lyra sighs, making her way back to her green overstuffed chair, as the two continue to talk in a language that sounds half made up.

Axel is, of course, already puttering around her tiny kitchen, way out of place in her ratty house.

"Do you need anything?" Lyra asks, already feeling tired from the sheer amount of people in her house. It's tiny, it's not really designed for more than two people, and four is downright claustrophobic.

"Nah I'm just curious," he says, before glancing over to Alette, "so am I the only one who can't see the demon?"

Oh, right. "I think so, yeah, even the cat can see him somehow," she replies, as Axel pokes at her broken microwave. "That doesn't work."

"I can tell," he says, opening the door and peering at it, before tapping the roof of the microwave with his fist.

It makes an odd thunk, and Alette cranks her head over, the conversation with Melekai immediately forgotten.

"Axel, don't fix things without permission!" she says, and gets a scowl in return. "So sorry, he just...does things."

"You fixed my microwave?" Lyra says, not finding the energy to get up and inspect it herself. "How?"

"Magic," he says, with a wide smile, and Lyra rolls her eyes. "What, you have to admit you're curious."

"What are you two doing here to begin with?" Lyra asks, and that finally pulls Alette's attention from her very normal looking doorjamb. "What did you find?"

"You really should be dead," Axel says to her, and Melekai snarls. "There's no real way for someone to survive the death bubble."

"It's not a death bubble!" Melekai says, frustration coating his every word, and he stalks back over to Lyra, perching himself on the table right next to the chair, maximally close.

An idea percolates through Lyra's mind, and she lays her hand out next to him, and he immediately rests his hand against hers, without looking.

"And I would really like to do some measurements to see why," Axel continues.

"Why don't you call it a death bubble?" Alette asks, a little bit intensely, and Lyra's not entirely sure she's gotten over her fear of Melekai or if the quest for knowledge is just too much for her to resist.

"Okay, this isn't cool if the rest of you can talk to him and I can't, uh, Lyra do you have an old cell phone laying around?" Axel asks.

Alette sighs, and takes a seat on the one other chair in the room, pulling out the golden needle from its case. "Don't transform any of her belongings," she warns like this is an old, old argument. "One of us will play translator."

"Next time I'm bringing some tech I can mess with," he says, and Alette rolls her eyes but doesn't say anything in return. "Lyra, how'd you live through the bubble?"

All three sets of eyes turn towards her, and her cat skitters across the floor, chasing something she can't see.

"Uh," Lyra says, "I don't know?"

"You were pretty messed up last night," Alette says, gentler. "When we got there, you looked about to pass out." Awkward with the brace, she pulls out a single strip of fabric from a different pocket, a rustic fabric, something linen-like. It's an off-white color, with single gold threads running through it at random intervals.

Melekai narrows his eyes but doesn't butt in, so Lyra has to assume it's safe. His hand doesn't even twitch on top of hers.

"No that was because she tried to steal my soul," Lyra says, and both the magicians blink at her, "uh, consume my life essence? Demons do that."

Alette is very obviously not looking at Melekai. "But you survived the blast?" She threads her needle with a shining gold thread, having to hold the needle with her broken hand and painstakingly guiding the thread with her other. "Can I touch your hand?"

"Does it matter which one?" Lyra asks, unnerved.

"Not particularly," Alette says, so Lyra offers her the hand not currently touching Melekai.

The touch seems to at least keep him still, keep him a little bit calmer than before. She doesn't know exactly what to do with that information, but...but it's something.

"I'm going to test to see if she left any magical traces on you," Alette says, wrapping the linen around Lyra's wrist like a soft bandage. "Now, I know you have Melekai, but we've found a unique residue on several people and things she's come in contact with, that I believe is separate from a demon residue."

"You leave a residue?" Lyra asks Melekai, who just shrugs, watching Alette's motions intensely.

"Most magic does," Alette says, and deftly pulls her needle through the fabric, stitching it like a bracelet against Lyra's wrist.

Even with the broken hand, this motion seems like second nature to her.

Axel seems to bounce on the edge of his toes, a sharp contrast to Alette's focused care. Like staying up so late did nothing to hurt him, like it did nothing to harm his energy.

Alette still has deep circles underneath her eyes, like she hasn't slept well in ages. Since Lyra raised her.

Lyra frowns, thoughtful, at that. "Alette, have you had trouble sleeping?"

"Some." She doesn't look up from her stitching, and the golden thread seems to shimmer under her gaze. "I always have."

"Yeah, she's always staying up reading," Axel says, from where he's fiddling with what looks like a walkie talkie that definitely didn't come from Lyra's house. "Her Fitbit just might have a fit if she loses anymore sleep."

"No, I meant since...since three weeks ago?" Lyra asks, skating around the obvious events.

Melekai looks at her, sharp.

Alette pauses, a moment's hesitation in her stitches. "Some," she says, and her voice is neutral. "It's not...exactly good night sleep material to know you were dead for fourteen hours."

"Jackson had some insomnia, too," Lyra says, wracking her brain for back when this had all started. "I think it went away after a few months, he said his leg hurt and he couldn't sleep, but..." She shrugs. "It might be a thing."

"A thing," Alette repeats, hollow, and puts her needle down for a second to rub her eyes. "Thanks."

"Once a human brain has known death, it doesn't want to return, even in something so benign as a nap," Melekai says, like he's trying to not scare Alette, "but the human brain adapts, relearns bad habits."

"Okay, see, you'll sleep okay again," Lyra says, and squeezes Melekai's hand in thanks, "you just seem tired."

Alette takes a moment, her fingers still on the golden needle, before she picks it up again, her hand softer against Lyra's wrist. "Can you sense things about your brother's health, after all this time?" she asks, and the thread woven through the linen starts to glow, more than just a shimmer.

"Yeah," Lyra says, staring at the golden glow because even that is a more tangible example of magic than she's seen in a while, "but he's my baby brother, of course I can."

"What about the cat?" Alette asks, deft fingers twisting the thread.

"Wait, the cat was dead?" Axel asks, looking up from his walkie talkie. "Why? And when?"

"He's fine," Lyra says, looking down at the cat, who had grown bored of the new people in his house and is now pacing the length of the hallway, patrolling for bugs. "He limps but he's happy."

"So that's a yes," Alette says, then, before Lyra can tell that anything's done, snips the end of the golden thread with a pair of tiny sewing scissors.

The linen grows warm against Lyra's wrist, spreading up her arm, racing down her back and across her shoulders.

Melekai tenses and she squeezes his hand again, and miracle of miracles, he relaxes.

The golden thread spreads across her skin, trailing down her blood vessels, leaving just a warmth, skittering away from the scratches on her back and the slash across her cheeks.

Both Alette and Axel watch her like this isn't anything special to them.

"She definitely grabbed your face," Axel says, pointing, and if Lyra had a mirror easily available without getting up, she'd look. "Jesus."

"So yes on the residue?" Lyra asks, and despite the warmth of the magic or whatever, she shivers. "What does this actually tell us?"

"Sample size," Alette says, confident. "More data means more ways to combat her means, more ways of getting ahead."

Melekai scoffs, and Alette flinches.

Axel finishes fiddling with the walkie talkies, and a loud, high-pitched whine fills the room, and Lyra's cat dashes away, down the hallways and into the bedroom. With a thump, Lyra can hear the exact moment he dives under the bed, into the spot he hid the one time Lyra vacuumed.

Melekai stands, stalks over to the walkie-talkies, and pokes one.

Nothing happens.

"Good lord, Axel, that's annoying," Alette murmurs, taking out a little notebook and jotting down notes.

"Sorry, sorry," he says, taking one of them directly away from Melekai and twisting the knob, "didn't know it'd be actually audible. Lyra can you make your demon say something?"

Even with his back to her, Lyra just knows that Melekai's eyes are narrowed. "Make is a strong word," she replies.

Axel waves his hand at her. "You know what I mean." He fits an earbud into his ear, and even the earbud is glowing.

She can't even know if it's from whatever magic from Alette that's crawling over her skin, or if it's his own magic, or what.

And it burrows inside her, a little bit frustrating and a little bit annoying, how little she knows about all this.

"Not until you tell me what that does," Lyra says, and there's a spike of heat at her words, on the linen at her arm, and the gold glows anew. "I don't like this random experimentation"—Melekai turns to her, a wide grin at her tone—"and some clear answers would be good once in a while."

Axel blinks. "It's just something I made up so I'm not left out from the demon talk," he says, bewildered, like he hasn't figured out that Lyra doesn't exactly like her things changed around her. "It's not...it's not going to harm him or you or anything."

"Is there...is there anything you want to know?" Alette asks, and she pulls out a golden seam ripper from her little packet of tools. "I'm not meaning to keep secrets."

Lyra offers her wrist back, and Alette starts to pick at each little stitch she put in place, and the warmth decreases with each little motion.

"Why does Terese hate Dr. Frisse?" Lyra asks, and Melekai nods, still grinning at her, like she did something correct. "Why did Dr.

Frisse keep it a secret from you that she's a demon? Why is Terese going around and doing this?"

"Yeah, Dr. Frisse hasn't told us that yet, so we don't know," Axel says, as Alette continues to pick a stitch, then write down whatever it is she's observing, then pick another stitch. "Frisse isn't exactly the type to let on what she's thinking on the best of days, and definitely not when she's under any pressure; it's not her style."

"And you just...follow that just 'cause?" Lyra says, and Melekai's smile is wide, wide and vicious. "That's...foolish."

"She's a vastly powerful experimental magician who's willing to teach others," Alette says. "Those aren't common, especially in America."

"She called you her niece," Lyra says, and Alette nods.

"She was briefly married to an uncle of mine," Alette says, neutral. "It's technically correct."

"And they trust this person," Melekai mutters, before Axel lets out an excited squawk.

"Got it!" he says, and Melekai eyes him, and Lyra can tell he's reevaluating his promise to not kill any of them. "I could hear you that time!"

Lyra watches Melekai glower, watches Axel bounce on the balls of his feet, as Alette continues to pick at the seams she just put in.

"Can you defend yourself against her?" Lyra asks as the linen comes unraveled on her wrist. "Can I?"

"Absolutely," Melekai all but purrs, and it's such a different tone of voice that Lyra looks up at him, wide-eyed. "Do you know how devastating necromancers can be?"

"Woah," Axel mutters, as Alette blanches, then quickly tries to hide it.

"That makes sense," Alette says, once she recovers, though there are lines next to her lips, some sort of tension. "The first rule of magic is what you can give, you can take away."

Lyra looks between the two magicians, at their grim faces, and at Melekai's grinning in delight. "You mean I can kill people, right?" she says, a sinking feeling in her stomach. "That's what that means."

"Easily," Melekai says, like he thinks that's a good thing and not yet another thing on the long list of evidence proving how awful Lyra is.

Leave it to a demon to be happy about that.

"Hopefully there are some shades of nuance between just killing and bringing people back," Alette says, though her eyes dart to Melekai. "I wouldn't even begin to know how to safely experiment."

"We'd need space," Melekai says, and Lyra can tell, she can just tell, he's all but bouncing from the excitement of the idea. "Space and some way to stop you from running out of energy."

"Protein bars," Axel interrupts, and he looks ridiculous, with a single earbud in, completely at odds with the rest of his ultra-fashionable outfit. "Protein bars, 5-hour energy shots, and a block of cheese."

13

So Lyra finds herself bundled up in her snow stuff and tucked into Axel's car once more. Melekai takes one look at the car, nods to Lyra, then disappears.

"Uh, I guess he'll meet us there?" Lyra says, already tired of all of this.

"I sure hope so," Alette says, the strip of linen in her hand. She sits in the car, running her fingers along it and alternatively jotting down notes, like she can read something from it that's just completely unapparent to Lyra.

AXEL TAKES them down a rugged dirt and snow path in the middle of nowhere Pacific Northwest, before killing the engine somewhere completely surrounded by trees.

"Near as I can tell, there's nobody for miles," he says, before digging into his glove box and tossing Lyra a hand warmer. "Let me know when that gets cold, I'll charm the chemicals to being warm again."

"Nifty," Lyra says, unease coating her throat, and she tucks it into her gloves. "Wish I could do that, all I have is the creeping death power."

"I mean, I'm grateful for that," Alette says, and it's enough of a joke that Lyra feels a panicked giggle in the back of her throat. "If nothing else, an emergency medic is a good thing."

"Medic, yeah, I like that a lot more," Lyra says, stepping out of the car and into the untouched snow.

It crunches underneath her old boots, like no one's ever stepped on this particular path before. Like the snow wipes away everything that happened, every foot that's crossed it, every animal that found its way.

Following behind her, Axel hands her a 5-Hour Energy shot.

Buggees sells them, and the morning crew is downright addicted to them, but Lyra's never developed the taste. "Gross," Lyra says, but takes it anyway.

"I agree," Alette says, fervent, "but if you're going to expend too much energy, they're a good stopgap."

"You just don't have taste," Axel says, taking one of his own, and Lyra's seen him do tons of casual small amounts of magic on the way here, so it makes sense. "They're delicious."

She tucks her fingers around the handwarmer, her legs aching, her back chafing against her snow jacket. The cut on her cheek peeks up over her scarf, the edge of the bandages turning icy.

"Am I...supposed to just wait for Melekai?" she asks.

"You can sense dead things, right?" Alette asks, instead of answering her questions. "Try to focus on that. What dead can you feel around us?"

Lyra sighs, then scuffs her boot against the snow.

About three inches down, there's a slew of dead bugs, some spiders, and a few feet away there's a dead mouse, curled up around some acorns, that didn't dig deep enough. It's frozen solid, has been for at least a month. Its tail had fractured in two places, from something stepping on it without realizing.

Axel and Alette watch her.

"Uh, there's some bugs and a mouse," she says, because they're actively waiting for an answer. "And maybe something that used to be a bird, hard to tell."

She really doesn't want to raise something to summon Melekai. It'd only die immediately anyways, and that feels vaguely unethical.

"What's it like in a hospital?" Alette asks, voice wondering.

"Horrible," Lyra says, because it is. "Haven't gone since I was seventeen."

"You probably should have again," Melekai says from behind her, and all three of them jump, "you've broken so many bones."

"Hospitals are for rich people," Lyra replies automatically, hugging herself close, as if that could stop the sudden jump in her heartbeat at his appearance.

He rolls his eyes, then sweeps forward, a hand going to the back of her neck and another to her left wrist, guiding her a few steps away from Alette and Axel.

"In case you have less good aim than I think you do," he whispers in her ear, barely audible over the snow crunching under her boots.

She lets him, the hand on the back of her neck, at least, familiar. And, somehow, warm.

Even though he's still wearing just a Henley, jeans, and the bracelets.

"You don't feel the weather?" she asks, stating the obvious.

"The body is dead, Lyra," he says because of course, he has to remind her of that. "The only reason you don't feel like you could bring it back is there's another occupant."

"Still very creepy!" Axel calls to them, tapping the earbud.

The corners of Melekai's lips twitch, like he doesn't know if he should laugh or scowl.

"Yeah, he's pretty much always like that," Lyra says, and gets a smile out of Melekai. "What am I supposed to do?"

He evaluates her for a second, the hand still on the back of her neck, halfway between an embrace and a guide. "Can you feel anything alive, under the snow?"

She thinks, tries to calm her heartbeat enough to listen, but there's no sound besides just them, and the restless noise of Axel shifting in his shoes and Alette's quiet breathing.

"Nothing," she says, and the pad of his thumb rubs soothingly at the base of her neck, teasing out the tense muscle there.

"I gotta make glasses to see him now," Axel mutters.

"You really don't want to," Alette says in return, and she shouldn't really be able to hear them so clearly, with how quiet they're speaking and how far away Melekai's guided her.

Underneath that, there's a scratch of something, something creaking in the branches, and Lyra lets her eyes flutter shut.

"A bird," she says, unsteadily. "A bird in a nest, it's...slow. Almost asleep."

It rustles in its nest, packed down with feathers and down, a protection against the winter wind and snow. It doesn't want to move, even though they're standing underneath its branch, could be predators. Doesn't think it's worth the energy to move, not with how high up in the tree it is and leaving the tree without reason when there's no food would be foolish.

Lyra blinks, and Melekai's hand is a bright point of warmth against the cold of the wind, and she shivers, as if she is the one up in the nest in the wind.

"Was that you?" she asks, wrong-footed. "Did you make it so I could do that?"

He shakes his head, minute.

"Okay, that's...spooky," Lyra says, then turns and waves to Alette and Axel. "He had me sense something alive this time."

They both stare at her because of course, she's the weird one.

"So what do I do now?" Lyra asks, shifting in her boots. "I don't wanna sense everything alive all the time, that'd be annoying."

He shrugs at that.

"I'll teach you some compartmentalization techniques later," Alette calls over to them. "They're simple."

Lyra gives her the thumbs up, barely able to do so in her gloves because that'd be nice. It'd be nice and no one's bothered to tell her that so far, which feels patently unfair.

If she could move around without having the sense of death so close to her at all times, that'd be a miracle.

"We could probably let them leave," Melekai says, voice low, so only she can hear. "Practice in private, where you don't have to be judged."

"Why would they judge?" Lyra asks, looking up at him.

"Because I want you to reach out and kill that bird," he says, like he's reciting poetry at her. "From all the way down here, I want you to reach out and stop its heart."

Lyra's blood freezes. "What?"

"Don't worry, you can bring it back if you want," he says, languid. "But if you can give something, you can take it away."

Axel and Alette are still, so still behind them, like they're frozen in place as well.

"Or," he continues, and Lyra feels like she's about to collapse from relief that there is an or, "just kill its wing."

That seems almost worse, to the tiny bird that's worrying about flying away because they're being loud but doesn't want to waste energy for food. Its foot twitches in the nest, and there's an old hurt there, where something grabbed it, but it got away, and healed wrong.

"Can I do its foot instead?"

Melekai's face wrinkles, as if he finds her charming but utterly confusing. "Sure?"

So Lyra exhales, finding the bird in its little nest again, and she shifts over, resting the palm of her hand against the tree, since there's no way she'll be able to climb the tree up to the nest without spooking it.

"If I just do the foot, I can heal the foot, right?" she asks, squeezing her eyes shut against the exhausting brightness of the snow around them. "Is that how it works?"

"Most likely," he says, crowding close to her, as if to shield her from the wind. The wind she's feeling half on her own face and half in the feathers of the bird above her. "I've never trained a necromancer before, just seen them in action."

That's almost helpful.

"I once saw a man kill the left ankle of a charging enemy," Melekai says to her as if trying to pep her up. "The enemy crumbled to the ground, his leg in sepsis."

"Super weird," Lyra replies, not opening her eyes to face that. "Okay, let's try this."

In the snow, with the bird restlessly shifting above them in the tree, Melekai leans close.

"Pay attention to how this feels," he murmurs to her, and another shiver winds its way down her spine.

"Why?" she asks, tilting her head towards him, as if their secrets are for them and them alone.

"Well, always observe how you feel after magic," Alette calls from the other side of the clearing like they aren't being as quiet as she thinks. "That way you can know if you replicate results!"

And that sounds about science-right, but Lyra raises an eyebrow at Melekai.

"Because if you"—he rests his hand on her waist, gentle, but like he's bracing for something—"if you can manage this, manage the energy, then that's how we bring down Terese."

Lyra exhales, a little puff of air collecting in front of her face. "That's how to kill a demon?"

"With a lot of power," Melekai says, and for once, the smile is gone from his voice. "Even a demon isn't impervious to that. Even a demon would be forced apart, given enough power flooding through them."

It's a grim thought, what that would look like, so Lyra refocuses on the wood of the tree beneath her palm.

She can hear Alette and Axel hold their breath, all this distance away.

"Will this call to her?" she asks Melekai, instead, and his eyes narrow down at her. "I know when I do anything, it calls to you, but will it call to her because she took some of me?"

"She's not in any state to track you, not after last night," he says, and it's a little bit vicious, a little bit satisfying.

"Okay," she says, then settles her eyes closed again, focusing on the tree.

The bird is about twenty feet up, in its little nest, far above where she would ever be able to climb. There are needles all the way around the branches even though it's winter now, and frost clings to them.

She breathes out, feeling the little twitch in the bird's leg, in the restless stretch that comes from something feeling fundamentally wrong but being unable to fix it. Of the cold on the feathers and the warmth of the little nest, and—

Without touching the leg, without a hand to the little body of the bird, it's like she's trying to read something from far away, far away enough that the letters blur into an indistinct shape, but close enough that if she just concentrates hard enough, squints long enough, she'd be able to figure out the words. Piece them together from context clues and the words around them but would leave her with a headache.

She's been using the sense a lot, lately, and the instinct to reach out with it comes more readily than before. Like a muscle she's actually working, instead of a warped and twisted little division of her soul that she works to ignore.

Next to her, Melekai gives a little sigh, barely on the edge of her hearing.

She takes another breath, against the cold and the frost and the self-doubt, and reaches out with that muscle.

The bark underneath her palm shifts once, then—

With a bang, the entire tree flies apart, disintegrating into splinters.

Lyra stumbles back, and Melekai catches her before she falls, and the bird on the branch squawks as it flies away, panic in every flutter of the wings.

"Woah," mutters Axel, behind them, and Alette makes a wordless noise of wonder.

Lyra fights to get her feet back underneath her, eyes popping open.

The tree is...gone.

Twigs and branches spike the snow around the stump, fractured into a cone moving out from where her hand had rested. Like something inside of her blasted it to pieces.

Pine needles stab into the snow everywhere, and the little nest lays empty, a good thirty feet away.

Melekai all but lifts her by her armpits, setting her back upright. "So you have some control problems."

THE NEXT DAY, after Lyra spends a glorious night in her bed, sleeping sounder than she has in ages, she gets woken up by the news that she has absolutely lost her job and a text from Alette.

ALETTE (10:43 AM): Dr. Frisse has some ideas if you would be okay coming back to the headquarters.

Lyra listens, but all she can hear in her little house is her cat purring beside her, no sound of Melekai or anything.

LYRA (10:44 AM): Can I get a ride? Aren't the headquarters in Canada?

ALETTE (10:45 AM): You really don't drive?

Lyra rolls her eyes, and pets her cat instead, entirely unwilling to leave the warm cocoon of her blankets.

After the destruction of the day before, Melekai had disappeared without an additional word, leaving her in the snow with Alette and Axel, and she can't quite figure out if it's from something she did or if it's just his general...demon-ness. Like it gives weight to the weirdness of all his actions in the last three weeks.

There's now an exploded tree in the middle of the Washington forest, a bird that got entirely too spooked and flew way far away, and the lingering sense that she did something...wrong.

Well, she obviously did, by exploding the tree, instead of the little harm she was supposed to, but it worries its way into her mind.

The very real possibility she could be asked to do that to a person sits underneath her skin, and she has to breathe through it, breathe through the little bit of panic squeezing at her heart.

Even with Terese's hand on her chin, even with the impact into the tile, she's not sure she could have done it right then.

If it could be done to a demon at all. Or if they're immune like she was immune to Terese's crazy little death-bubble.

The skin on her back still itches, the scrape healing, so she just burrows deeper underneath her quilt. Her back is magnificently bruised, still, and probably will be for quite some time, if she knows her healing rates at all.

LYRA (10:51 AM): Not a chance.

ALETTE (10:52 AM): I'll send Axel and we'll try to set up a faster transportation situation for you.

LYRA (10:53 AM): Is that a magic thing?

ALETTE (10:54 AM): Yes.

Lyra lets herself stretch underneath her covers, her legs cramped as if they had been twisted underneath her all night, and her cat lifts his head and mrrrs at her.

"I know," she murmurs, before pointing her toes, trying to work through the pins and needles.

Whatever little bit of pain relief Melekai had given her the day before is long gone, and the muscle between her shoulders is tight, tighter than it's been in ages.

So she stretches in bed, in the half-yoga half-physical therapy prescribed to her so long ago, working through the aches and the twinges and the shakiness.

If she hadn't just been laid off via email, if her workplace wasn't still completely destroyed and under shoddy insurance, then she'd call out sick. Or bring out the wooden cane Jackson had given to her years ago, the one she keeps tucked into the hall closet out of some sort of pride.

Maybe it's the walking over untouched snow that did it.

It's nice to think of that, that it could be something as simple as a stroll over snow that she chose to take, rather than an unpredictable and violent attack.

She pauses in the stretches, staring up at the vinyl ceiling.
LYRA (11:12 AM): Could Terese track me to my house?
ALETTE (11:13 AM): Axel'll pick you up in thirty minutes.
ALETTE (11:13 AM): It's something to worry about.

14

The moment Lyra steps out of the Mustang and into the parking garage, she wishes she had taken the cane.

"Any way we can...I dunno, take the elevators this time?" Lyra asks, resting a hand against the Mustang, as her legs feel like they're going to give out on her.

Axel raises an eyebrow at her, one that quickly morphs into something strangely eager. "Do you need me to transform a wheelchair?" He looks around the parking garage as if searching for something easy.

"Hell no," Lyra says, as sharp as she can, and he blinks at her. "I mean, no. No thank you."

"I've never transformed a wheelchair before," he says, bouncing on his toes. "That could be fun!"

"No." Lyra sighs, and pushes herself away from the car and concentrates on not limping. "I got blasted into the tile, like, two days ago, I'm sore."

"Sure," he says, glib, but keeps pace with her. "Think I could make it out of something without wheels?"

"I don't have the faintest idea how your bullshit works, Axel," Lyra reminds him, and thankfully he steers her to a bank of elevators instead of the stairs. "Near as I can tell you think of something and it happens."

The door beeps open, and Lyra leans against the mirrored wall.

"Easy, I can switch the components of things around to give them new functions," he says as if it's really that simple. "Most things are made up of similar atoms, it's all about switching around. Like I can make most electronic readers out of cell phones, or receivers out of the walkie talkies, or—"

"Or glitter out of Tic Tacs?" Lyra supplies, as the elevator moves at a glacial pace.

"I made the glitter out of the plastic box, and just disintegrated the actual mints," he says with a wave of his hand. "It was just for show."

"There was still a glitter streak when Terese blew up the store," Lyra points out, and he blanches. "So your glitter stuck around."

"But making things with wheels is easier when the thing"—he gestures with his hands as if Lyra could picture that in her mind— "Already starts with wheels. Full and complete circles are tricky, they never seem to line up how I want them to."

"Huh," Lyra says, as the elevator comes to a stop.

"So I'd probably take some roller skates, or a bicycle or something," he continues, pacing out of the elevator way faster than Lyra can keep up

"Please don't," Lyra says, again. "I really don't want one."

"Now it's just a thought exercise," he says, though he slows down to keep pace. "Did your demon show back up again yesterday?"

"No," Lyra says, nettled for some odd reason, "this is the most I've seen of him ever."

He raises an eyebrow as they approach the same foreboding wooden doors as before. "You keep saying that," he says, hesitating before opening the doors, "but he shows up to save your life."

She doesn't want to repeat Melekai's words about investment back, so she smiles thinly.

He opens the door, and she hobbles in, concentrating on not limping.

The grand mahogany table is pushed all the way to the side, the chairs rolled next to it, leaving the wide-open room hollow, empty. Like an old school gym, emptied of all its bleachers, strangely devoid of purpose.

Alette sits on a yoga mat off to one side, and she lifts her braced hand and waves. There are a few other yoga mats scattered around the floor, sending Lyra's stomach plummeting.

Everyone always tells her to do yoga. Everyone always forgets that nerve issues aren't really solved by yoga.

It's a toss-up between yoga or weight loss 'well-meaning' doctors seem to like to prescribe to her when they're confused by her body. As if weight had anything to do with her nerve endings.

Still, she joins Alette in the middle of the room, sitting down on the yoga mat as carefully as she can, though her left leg shakes more than she would like, in front of these people who know her enough to teach her magic, but maybe not enough to call friends.

The edge of the mat is decorated with golden thread, carefully sewn into the edges in a scallop pattern.

"Do you meditate?" Alette asks, and she's casually cross-legged on the mat like this is something she does all the time. Like sitting in a conference room she once laid dead in is as natural as breathing.

"Not if I can help it," Lyra quips, and Axel takes a seat on another one of the mats, crossing his legs despite his severely skinny jeans. "Just seemed like fancy sitting and thinking."

"She's not wrong!" Axel says, and he's so hyper she just wants him to tone it down a touch.

"Well," Alette says, and Axel gives her a cheeky grin, "I would argue that you meditated last night before...the tree happened."

"That was just me concentrating," Lyra says, running her fingers along the gold thread edging.

"Concentrating is just focused meditation," Alette says, almost smugly. "And this room"—she gestures to the vaulted ceilings, to the table pushed to the side, to the strange markings along the walls—"is built to focus magic further."

"There's a reason why we brought you here, instead of her to you," Axel says. "We didn't exactly know how difficult it would be."

"And Terese can't teleport in," Alette points out. "The only way a demon can get in is if you"—she points to Lyra—"intentionally bring them in. Or if Frisse lowers the wards, which I think she also did for that time."

"So if you need alone time away from him, come here," Axel says, and even cross-legged he's bouncy. "Even if the world ends, they couldn't get to us in here."

"That is wholly inaccurate." From the door, Dr. Frisse's voice booms over the vaulted room, and she strides in, giving Lyra an almost appraising look. "I heard your power can be destructive. That's good."

"Not so good for the tree," Lyra says, tucking her hands underneath her to prevent herself from giving finger guns.

"If you can focus that, you could turn the tides on this entire thing," Dr. Frisse says, taking a seat in one of the grand comfortable chairs, well outside the little circle of yoga mats they've created. "Just need to put you near Terese."

"I don't..." Lyra trails off.

"I don't know what you gave her, but she's been...powerful since she visited you," Dr. Frisse says, leaning back in the chair like she's in control of all of this. "Injured, frantic, but powerful. I had to repair a rip in the world in Baie-Trinité yesterday, one I didn't think she'd be able to do for months yet."

Lyra notices Alette and Axel's silence.

"Well, sorry 'bout that, it wasn't so pleasant for me either," Lyra says, and is probably more sarcastic than she actually needs to be. "I almost died."

"And yet you're here," Dr. Frisse steeples her hands, like a goddamn super villain. "Can I see you concentrate?"

She considers refusing, but it is in fact why they drove over the border to Canada and it would be silly to pretend otherwise. Still, irritated, Lyra lets out a breath and closes her eyes.

Tries to reach out, feel that strange sense.

There are a few dead bugs, the floor below, and what may be a mouse skeleton near the basement. Her mind immediately goes to those dead bugs—ants, fallen from some sort of poison they ate with sugar—and dwells there. There's a cluster of them, about ten or twelve hard little bodies, tucked away under some tile, never to be found by any cleaning crew.

She exhales again and feels Melekai settle in next to her, leaning against her back, one long line of pressure and support.

She leans back, without opening her eyes, less stress on her back immediately, at not having to sit upright on her own.

Alette's breathing hitches, across the little yoga circle, but Lyra doesn't let herself look.

The mouse skeleton is old, possibly as old as the building, all flesh decayed away, leaving just the bones and a few sinews behind. It's in a crawlspace, near a vent, probably enclosed inside by accident. The bones give an echo of a hunger so strong it's painful, of a dizzying need for food.

Starvation. It died of starvation.

"Focus on something alive," Melekai murmurs into her ear, leaning his head against her shoulder. His arms wrap around her middle, a physical stabilization, something for her to rest against.

It's difficult, to redirect.

But slowly, Alette's and Axel's breathing becomes apparent, deep inside of her. Axel's foot twitches, like he can't keep still, like if he keeps still it'll hurt, and twitches again. It's not real pain, not like the nerves in her legs and her back, but it echoes a sort of discomfort. Not an injury, not a defect, but a restlessness.

Alette's entire front is still a mess of bruising, but older, like it's yellowing and fading away. She can't feel it when she breathes anymore—she never mentioned to Lyra that it hurt when she breathed, but it must've.

"Easy," Melekai whispers, and she shivers, but lets the idea go.

Alette's hand, however, is healing quite nicely, bones starting to grow along the shattered edges, knitting themselves back together. It aches, but it's the ache of growth, of building something anew.

Further away, there's a strong pillar of presence that's Dr. Frisse. Her shoes are uncomfortable, pinching at her toes and rubbing the back of her ankles, but there's layer after layer of skin there, like it's all happened before. Everything else about her is comfortable, in control, a single long line of a vaguely uneasy power, and—

"Please stop scanning me," Dr. Frisse says, and Lyra's eyes pop open.

She squints against the light, much brighter than it should have been, and shelters her brow.

Dr. Frisse is still sitting, bored, on the chair across the room, her face impassive.

"Uh, sorry?" Lyra says, uncrossing her legs and rubbing out the tense muscles. "Could you guys, uh, tell?"

Alette and Axel look at each other, and Axel shrugs.

He's bouncing his foot, ever so slightly.

"I could," Dr. Frisse says. "Is that what a necromancer looks like when meditating?"

"Um."

"Tell us what you felt," Alette says, which is a much more productive way to think of things.

"There's a dead mouse in a crawl space a few floors away, there are some dead ants that were poisoned, you still have bruising, Axel doesn't like to sit still, and uh..." Lyra lets her eyes slip over to Dr. Frisse. "Your shoes are hurting your toes and the back of your heel. I think."

"Surprisingly astute, if incomplete," Dr. Frisse says, and Lyra's not sure if it's a compliment. "And did the demon tell you any of that?"

Lyra glances at Melekai, who just tightens his grip on her, scowling. "I don't think so."

"I didn't hear anything from him," Alette says, thankfully, and Lyra can't believe she's been running around like crazy when it probably hurt just to breathe, "just some...encouragement."

Dr. Frisse's eyes narrow, even across the room, and it's not anger and it's not frustration, just...evaluation. "Demon," she says, and her voice is calculating, "demon, could you sense her doing that?"

She could feel Melekai's tension rolling off of him, so she leans back a little harder.

"Yes," he says, after a moment, and both Alette and Axel nod to Dr. Frisse. "It's...abundantly obvious."

"So at the very least we could draw her in," Dr. Frisse says, and Melekai tenses again. "Somewhere we can control." She sits back as if signifying that train of thought is done. "Alette, can you walk her through something a bit more guided?"

"Yes?" Alette says, though her eyes are a bit wide, then, "What? Yes, of course. Lyra, can you sit like this?" She uncrosses her legs, touching her feet together in a way that is possible for Lyra, but going to be more than uncomfortable.

Lyra sighs, but imitates the pose. It's a classic yoga pose, one she's seen several times in the classes and YouTube videos people try to get her to do, and it never works.

"You can refuse," Melekai grumbles, and Alette pales further. "Sit how you want to sit."

"Uh, yeah, sit how you think you'd be the most comfortable," Alette says, then shudders, "The point is to have no distractions, to have it just be your mind."

Lyra sighs, leaning against Melekai instead of anything else, and closes her eyes once more.

AFTER A FRUSTRATINGLY LONG session where Alette has to constantly talk to Lyra to 'imagine' powers instead of immediately going to the dead bodies, Dr. Frisse leaves and Melekai immediately springs up, starting to pace around the cavernous room, like all this energy had been pent up and he just needed a place to purge it all out.

Alette's eyes follow him, wide.

"We need a break?" Axel asks, loud, and they all jump. "I don't know about you, after like twenty minutes of trying to meditate I just want to scream, and you've been at it for...way longer."

"Yeah, that's about right," Lyra says, stretching her legs out in front of her, and Melekai's attention is immediately on her, sharp, like the twinge of pain draws him.

She waves because it's far weirder to not acknowledge it.

"What I want," Alette starts, then frowns, thoughtful, as Melekai resumes pacing, "what I want is some ethical way for you to practice."

"Well I could find those dead ants and bring them back, one by one," Lyra says, only a little bit sarcastic.

Now that she knows the ants are there, they're goddamn annoying.

"A bit less...focused than that," Alette says.

"Wait, so would the ants see Melekai, too?" Axel asks.

"Yes," he snarls back. "And I don't like you being forced to do unnecessary things just to satisfy their curiosity."

Alette sits back on her heels, but Axel just taps the earbud he has in, contemplative.

Probably helps that Axel doesn't see whatever it is that Alette does. All Lyra sees is an angry-looking hipster pacing around a conference room.

"Lyra," Axel starts, and she's already not feeling great about him starting a conversation like that, "do you want to learn how to mind control a demon?"

"Axel!" Alette hisses, but Melekai's face turns thoughtful.

"Go on," Lyra says, once it becomes clear that Melekai isn't going to chime in.

"There are ways—don't look at me like that—there are ways to actually have some bit of control over demons if you're close to them," Axel says, and he too bounces to his feet. "It's tricky, because usually it's hard to get them to stay still, and if you can't see them it's even worse, but there are ways."

Melekai just watches him, but he's not outwardly upset, so Lyra shrugs.

"Then why didn't you do it to Terese?" Lyra asks because that seems like the logical next step in whatever it is that they are trying to do with her.

"Because everyone who's gotten close enough has died," Alette says, quietly, though she too relaxes.

So whatever she can see is enough to see body language.

"And since you haven't yet, it might work," Axel says, then looks wildly around the room. "Uh, demon—"

"—I have a name," Melekai interrupts.

"Uh yeah, Melekai, would you let Lyra practice with you?" He still doesn't know where to look and has ended up looking off in entirely the wrong direction.

Melekai crosses his arms, but Lyra's seen this motion before and it's never been confrontational. "Which process?"

"There's more than one?" Alette asks. She rolls over onto her stomach, propping herself up, and she immediately looks younger.

And Lyra can still feel the vague pull of the bruising across her front.

"Uh, a little tie and bind, that sort of thing." Axel gestures, vague, but Melekai nods like he knows what he's saying. "Nothing permanent—obviously—but something just to teach her the ropes, so to speak. Give her a safe way to practice, so maybe she could stop Terese a little bit easier than just relying on blowing someone up."

Melekai's gaze slides over to Lyra, and then sticks there, like he cannot look away.

"Would it hurt him?" Lyra asks because that seems like an important bit of information no one else is bringing up. "Or me, rather?"

"No," Melekai says, and he's still staring at her. "It would be no more painful than tying your hands with a rope, and about as easy to undo." Without breaking eye contact with Lyra, he tilts his head. "She's not that well educated in manipulating power," he says, conversational, to Axel. "I don't think she would hurt me, I know her power too well for it to react to me, but I don't know if she could manage the finesse."

Lyra debates feeling insulted, but he's probably right.

"That gives us a place to start, at least," Alette says, still propped up like a schoolgirl, "instead of exploding things."

All three of them look to Lyra like she's a bug under a glass.

And Lyra...Lyra doesn't know what to think.

On one hand, not exploding things seems like a decent way to go about practicing something. Not focusing on just the dead ants—they're like an itch against the back of her mind now—seems smart.

On the other...

"I'll let you know I flunked out of college, I'm not gonna be a great student," she warns Alette and Axel, and Melekai rolls his eyes. "And I was homeschooled the rest of the time."

"Do you learn better by doing something, by reading something, or by seeing someone else do it?" Alette asks, then looks askance to Melekai. "Not that we'd necessarily have an easy time showing you unless Melekai lets us."

"No," he says, short.

"Okay, so, reading or practicing," Alette says, visibly steeling herself to not flinch at Melekai's words.

Lyra shrugs, because truth be told, who knows.

"You do well when someone walks you through something," Melekai says, still watching her, still intense. "Following along with instructions, more than being lectured and then practicing."

"Don't know how you know that, but sure," Lyra says. "All the creepy stuff I've done is through instinct." She waves a hand at Alette. "I couldn't tell you how I raised anything I've raised, it just seems...right."

"Like a pull in the back of your stomach?" Axel asks. "Like you'll crawl out of your skin if you don't?"

"Like if you don't do something you'll shake apart into many pieces?" Alette asks, resting her chin in her hands. "That's what it is for me. If I don't do some charm, some spell weaving, it's like the worst sort of espresso and upset stomach."

"If I walk next to a burial site, I can feel it in my gut," Lyra says, and somehow, they both nod, like it's something they know. It's something they experience. "Or if flies get in my house and die, I just...automatically know where they are, and I have to throw them out or else they'll drive me nuts."

"Exactly," Alette replies, nodding into her hands. "That's fairly standard."

"That's like...exactly normal," Axel says, bouncing on his feet again, and Melekai takes a moment away from staring at Lyra to eye him distastefully. "So you're just untrained."

"Only reason why it's odd is that usually magicians are found at a young age," Alette continues, "and because...well...necromancers usually aren't found."

"By humans," Melekai interjects.

"By humans," Alette agrees, then pales.

"Okay then," Lyra says, squashing down an inappropriate giggle at Alette abruptly remembering to be uncomfortable around Melekai. "So I can get trained. Then what, we trick Terese into getting close to me so I can tie her up, then what? We leave her tied up with some of my nebulous power for forever?"

"Then we kill her," Melekai says with a shrug.

"Or we figure out some other way to stop her from destroying people and things," Alette says.

"And then we kill her after that." Melekai narrows his eyes at Lyra, thoughtful, evaluating. "You should be able to handle your part, I'll work with you."

"Great," Lyra says.

Great.

15

After a few hours of fruitless practice imagining a rope, Melekai walks her outside the bespelled complex and whirls her away, and she's back in her little house before she even knows what he's going to do.

Lyra's knees buckle, at the movement, from standing on uneven ground to her straight linoleum, and he stabilizes her by her elbow, his eyes alight.

"It's been ages since I've trained a magician," he says, and she gets the sudden sinking feeling that he's speaking literally, that 'ages' isn't just a figure of speech, "and never a necromancer, this will be fun."

"Cool," Lyra says, and he pauses, abruptly, then softens the hand on her arm, just holding her there.

"You are...unwilling?" he asks, and his voice tilts up enough that she can tell he's checking, not that he's stating. "Most would jump at the chance to get better at something."

He's not wrong, but it still rankles at her, so she pulls her arm away and sits down in her chair, and her cat immediately jumps up on the side of the chair, butting its head against her.

Melekai hovers near her, brows drawing together.

"I don't want to kill anything or anyone and I don't like feeling stupid," she says, finally.

"You're not stupid," he snips back, quick.

"I know, but someone telling me to stand there and imagine things sure makes me feel that way," she says, then rubs her eyes with her hand. "And now I have no job and everyone in town will know that somehow I caused the weird explosion things at Buggees and no one will hire me."

"She would have found you eventually," Melekai says, leaning against the countertop. "If she was out there, looking, it would have only been a matter of time."

She stares at him, lets him be the subject of an uncomfortably long gaze for a few minutes, until he shifts.

"Since when are you all gung-ho about helping them, anyways?" she asks, after watching him squirm for a good little while. "Last time you were all...'no, absolutely not', and now you want me to explode things and kill people."

"I don't want you to kill people, I want you to kill one specific person, and it's because she came after you first," Melekai says, indignant. "She came after you, I am going to go after her, and anything to help tip the balance over to my side is going to be something I like."

"So this is more of 'protecting your investment'?" Lyra asks, and his lips twitch into a frown. "Some sort of demonic pissing contest that I'm in the middle of?"

"I thought you wanted to help them?" he says, again tentative. "You were the one last time who asked me to not kill any of them and to help."

"That's not answering my question," Lyra points out, and he scowls. "Of course I want to stop the End of the World."

"I am far less concerned with saving the world and more with making her pay for trying to kill you," he says, folding his arms. "The world will spin on, existence will continue, there are other realms, but there's only one of you."

The words hit like a ton of bricks, so she sits with it, blinking out her window, her jaw working.

"Well," she says, after probably taking too long to respond to such a statement. "Thanks?"

He shrugs, like that statement cost him no more than the air it took to speak. "So any way she ends up dead is good in my book. If I thought the little magicians were capable enough, I would just whisk you away someplace safe until they're done, then bring you back, but they aren't, and I don't trust that doctor to do anything."

"Yeah, she seems sketch," Lyra says, clutching onto that instead of the emotionally weighty conversation. "Makes my skin crawl."

"I'm fairly certain it's because she wants more power and Terese is flaunting power all over the place," Melekai says, seeming to accept the shift with something resembling grace. "Or, rather, thinks she can gain control of the power vacuum afterwards, and I don't like any human who likes to think that of us."

There's some history there, she can catch a bare glimpse of it, a bare glimpse of something in his past, but it's gone before she can put a finger on it.

"I mostly think she just doesn't...care," Lyra says, and again stretches out her legs, grimacing. "She used Alette."

"So we agree," he interrupts, "we don't trust her."

When put that blatantly, Lyra blinks.

"I don't know why you trust the little magicians, but they're probably harmless to you, but her, her I don't like." He pushes himself up off of the counter top, and paces in front of her, all long lines and frustrated energy. "I don't know what it is, I don't know why, but we don't trust her."

"Axel thinks she's trustworthy, but Axel also thinks that transforming something into a hundred-dollar bill is okay," Lyra says, relieved at the thread of the conversation turning, the sentimentality prickling at the back of her neck. "Alette is...kind."

"Kindness doesn't win battles against demons," he says, and he probably has a point. "Kindness didn't stop Terese from killing her."

"Thanks," Lyra says, swallowing that down, swallowing the memory of the blood pooling in Alette's chest cavity.

It's like being shoved into cold water at even the memory.

"And kindness didn't stop Terese from trying her explosion on you," he says, and he's worked up, she can tell, something deep inside of her...

She narrows her eyes at him, but he doesn't stop his pacing, the small room barely able to contain him and all of his energy. Like the ratty linoleum and the cheap countertop would shake apart from the force of whatever the hell is going on with him.

So the next time he paces near her, she reaches out and snags his hand, just like he always seems to do to her.

He stops in his tracks, abrupt.

"Is there anything we can do about this right now?" Lyra asks, as he stares down at her, eyes reflecting all the light in the room.

"Not until you learn more techniques," he says, but his hand cups hers back, gentler than his pacing would suggest.

"Yeah," she says, then squeezes his hand. "Maybe calm down a bit?"

"Why?" he asks, eyes narrowing.

"Because you're just spinning yourself up?" she says, and she doesn't know how that would affect a demon. If they even burned energy like that, if they exhausted themselves, any of it. "Because I'm tired and you're pacing everywhere like a madman."

"I'm not going anywhere," he declares, like she's kicking him out, and his hand twitches in hers. "I'm either going to be here with you or actively tracking her down."

"That's fine," she repeats, and a small part of her marvels that she's not encouraging him to just go away for a bit, leave her to rest. "Do you...do demons sleep?"

He hesitates, like she's asking a far more complicated question than she actually is, then perches on her table, close enough that he can still hold her hand.

"Only by a limited definition," he says, and she rubs her thumb over the back of his hand to encourage him. "It depends on if we are in a body or not, and how that body died, and what we are doing with our time."

"So would you need to sleep right now?" she asks, tilting her head up to him. She could certainly use some sleep.

"No, not now," he says, and she can tell he wants to jump up and pace again, but he remains still. "Maybe in a few days, if I'm not careful. This body is...in good condition, it doesn't take much to sustain it."

There's a whole slew of other questions that come with that, and she's not sure what to think, so she just moves right the heck on.

"And how often do you need to switch? Bodies, that is?"

"Are you trying to get information out of me?" he asks, but his voice is more bewildered than anything else. "Which of the little magicians asked?"

"I'm asking," she says, and he wrinkles his nose at her, as if not believing that the questions could come from her. "What, you always look different and now you haven't for like three weeks." At his continued silence, she sighs. "I've always wanted to know, I just...haven't had the courage to ask."

"You don't need to be afraid of me," he says, and he had all but professed dedication to her safety, so she knows that, but—"I've told you how many times—"

"Probably like four times," she interrupts, raising her voice to talk over him, "and it's rather recent that I had more evidence besides just your word."

He grins at her, at her speaking over him, like that little bit of fire amuses him, and the oft familiar thrill of danger winds its way down her spine.

"Depends on the condition of the body," he replies, examining his free hand with a sort of detached curiosity. "This one died from accidental carbon monoxide poisoning—I think it's accidental—so it's easy to inhabit. I'll probably stay in it for a year or so, maybe a small amount longer." He shrugs, and she's finally getting an answer to one of the weirder wonders she's had about him. "The worst are when they die from sickness, those barely last a few weeks."

"I don't feel them as dead, not really," Lyra says, looking at his hand in hers, and, for the first time, tries the trick on him. Tries to slow her breathing, see what she can sense, see what she can tell.

His fingers twitch, in hers.

But his blood flows through his veins, just as it would a normal person, with oxygen pulling in from the stuffy air in her little home without a hitch. There's a little scar, on the underside of his palm, and calluses on his fingers, like the body played guitar.

"That is," he breathes, "so incredibly strange."

She ignores him, trying to figure out more about the body. There's an old injury in the left shoulder, something that left the muscles a little bit warped, a little bit smaller than the other side. Probably ached when it rained.

He has less muscle mass than she anticipated, and his heart thumps a little bit out of rhythm, like his death caused it to beat a little bit strangely. Like whenever Melekai forced his way into the body and restarted the systems, it didn't quite go according to how he wanted.

She's going to have to check Jackson's heart, now that she knows how to, next time she sees him. Make sure she did it correctly, that it healed just fine. That she didn't fuck up his spine in a way that'll become too evident in a few years as he ages.

"Do you feel pain?" she asks, finally.

"Not how you do," he responds, and his eyes are alight. "I've told you that, that's why Terese is doing this."

"Well, do you feel it in your shoulder?"

His face goes blank, and he lets go of her hand just long enough to roll his shoulder back, contemplative. "Almost?" he says, and he's marveling. "It feels more like a tightness than anything like the pain you feel."

He would know.

"Well whoever it was who actually lived in the body definitely horked it up," Lyra says, sitting back in the chair. "Poor guy probably tore a ligament or something."

He says nothing in return, just regards her thoughtfully, and it moves from the casual conversation to more of his usual staring, his usual intensity, and Lyra decides that the emotionally correct thing to do is ignore him and go about her day.

16

T he next morning, she's acutely aware that Melekai's watching her with carefully narrowed eyes, but instead of dealing with whatever the heck it is, she just pushes past him to grab a protein bar and some coffee.

"You're going somewhere," he says, after a few minutes of taut silence, and there's a tentative nature in his statement. Like he wants to ask a question but can't bring himself to do so.

And Lyra's already brushed her hair and put on more than one layer of fleece-lined tights, so it seems a bit obvious.

"It's Jackson's day," she says, between sips of coffee, and they both eye each other. "Every two weeks, we get lunch."

"That's it?" he asks, and his manicured brow furrows, like this is a puzzle that doesn't quite make sense. "He would really do that?"

"It's not like lunch with his older sister's that big of a trial," Lyra says, a bit hurt.

"No, why doesn't he come out more?"

That's not really better, so Lyra just scowls into her coffee.

"He's busy," she says, because he is. He's actually gone above and beyond whatever anyone could have thought that he could. "He's busy and he's in classes all the time."

"You raised him from the dead," Melekai says. "You think he could visit more than twice a month."

She doesn't have a response, so she goes back to ignoring him and his narrowed, careful gaze.

He follows her out of her house as she locks her door and then locks the screen, still narrowed-eyed and thoughtful.

The snow on the ground is the soggy mess that comes in early winter, and she wraps her snow jacket tight against the chill, before starting down the gravel road.

"You're not seriously walking, are you?" Melekai says, finally, as she passes the neighbors with their snow-encrusted rusty cars on their dead lawn. "He couldn't come to pick you up?"

"He doesn't have a car, either," Lyra says, irritation grating under her skin. "And public transportation's pretty good now."

She can just feel him seething behind her, and it doesn't help her mood.

"How far away is it?" he asks, finally, like it's bursting out of him. "How far away, and have I been there before?"

She looks back at him, finally, and he scowls at her like she caught him unaware. "Seattle," she says, "near twelfth and Madison street."

He watches her, blank.

"I have no clue if you've been to Seattle or not," she follows up, still crunching down the road, past the pull of death of the animal shelter, past the church graveyard. "How the heck could I know?"

"If I knew, then I could just take you, and you wouldn't have to do whatever this public transportation is," he says, but he falls in next to her, sticking his hands in his pockets, as if he's affected by the weather and could get cold fingers. "Is it safe?"

"Well I've never been mugged on the light rail," Lyra says, and the sarcasm misses its mark as his eyebrows raise. "I mean, I've never had anything bad happen on this trip."

"I meant from Terese," he says, still trodding along with her, and thankfully the bus stop is in view. "Could she track you?"

"How would I know?"

He frowns, but not at her, still keeping close.

Walking by Buggees is like dousing her in cold water.

It's roped off behind police tape, and half the windows are boarded up. Still, outside, shredded magazine pages flutter on the ground, and shards of glass glitter in the slush, like they had been pushed out in a perfect circle.

A few coins shine on the ground, on the grody concrete, and the store stinks of death.

Even though the only death was the moth.

She idles by the sidewalk, as if she could wait for it to get better. As if just by standing there, it'll return to its old glory.

"This place reeks," Melekai says, where he stands back a few steps. "The entire place."

"I don't get it," Lyra says, the words falling from her lips, "the only thing that died in there was that moth."

He scuffs his shoe against one of the coins, and it nudges aside. Like it's contact with Terese had made it malleable to him. "I don't know," he says, and it's quiet. "I don't know what happened to her, and I don't know what else she can do."

Lyra shivers, though with her coat she's plenty warm.

"Let's go," Melekai says, and his jaw is tight. "I don't want her to come searching."

THEY'RE the only ones at the bus stop, at this non-commute hour, and the damp wind is harsh.

"I don't wanna look crazy on the bus," she says, and he shifts close to her as a car drives by, "so tell me to pick up my phone if you want me to talk to you."

His eyes track the car as it speeds away, and somehow, she knows he's going to be exhausted with all of this when it's done.

If demons can get exhausted.

The question sits odd with her, as he stands too close to her, closer than she'd tolerate from anyone else. But somehow, she knows, can tell, that he'll be on high alert through all of this and it will wear on him.

She doesn't have a reason for this knowledge, but it's there, in the back of her mind.

So, despite the irritation and the fact that she very much so does not need a babysitter, she shifts closer to him and fits her hand into his.

Immediately, his entire attention is back on her, blazing in its intensity.

"If you don't want to, you don't have to follow me all the way to Seattle," she says, squeezing his hand in a way she hopes is encouraging. "I do this every two weeks."

He scowls, but not at her, though he entwines their fingers together. "She might sense you, and you're outside of the protection I put up at your house," he says, and has a stubborn tilt to his head. "She found you at your store, she could find you on this 'public transportation'."

"Melekai, have you ever taken a bus or train before?" Lyra asks, a smidgen delighted.

He shakes his head.

"This is gonna be a disaster," she says, fervent, and he raises an eyebrow at her tone. "You're gonna hate this."

True to form, the bus pulls up right then.

THE BUS RIDE wasn't that bad, but the moment they step onto the light rail, she feels his entire body tense.

"Lyra," he whispers, and his voice is so tightly controlled it wavers, "Lyra what are you doing?"

She just grins at him, then limps to the single open seat, and has to squeeze herself between two business men.

Melekai stares at her, then stalks to her, bracing her in, like she's going to go flying off the train.

The doors close, and he flinches. "I don't like this," he says, and she has no real way of offering him comfort, so she presses her knees against his.

The train starts to move, and he scowls down at her, one hand gripping the overhead pole, the other tight on her shoulder, like she's the only thing keeping him in place. Like she's the only stable factor here.

Under the pretense of tucking her hair behind her ear, she grazes her hand against his.

He nods at her, still frowning, his brows drawn together, and she rests her hand back down on her knee, barely able to touch his leg without making it obvious.

Usually on this trip she reads a book on her phone, or browses Pinterest, but this time she remains like this, managing the soft touches to Melekai as he appears to have several breakdowns over the course of the hour-long ride.

THE MOMENT she stands for her exit, he shudders with something resembling relief, and Lyra steadies herself on the overhead pole right next to his hand.

"This is madness," he whispers to her, like he thinks other people could hear and needs to prevent it. "Please tell me you don't do this every two weeks."

She just nods, neutral, as if nodding along to music only she can hear, and she feels his scowl more than sees it.

The train slows to a stop, always a little bit of a jolt, and he keeps a hand on her arm to steady her, even though she's done this a hundred times by now.

But it's harmless and he's way more upset than she is by all of this, so she lets him, before gently tugging him off the train and onto the platform with the lunchtime crowd.

He stares, wide eyed, at everyone who brushes by Lyra, at everyone who gets a little too close, at everyone who's entirely focused on getting where they're supposed to, just like she always is.

Sighing, she digs her phone out of her pocket and holds it to her ear as she walks.

"Really, it's not that bad," she says, and his hand twitches in hers.

"Any one of those people could be a threat," he counters, and he's not exactly wrong, but her mother was the paranoid one, not her. "You would have no way of knowing."

"It's just as likely they would be a friend," Lyra says, and squeezes his hand to emphasize her point, slowing as they draw close to the sandwich shop, with its blue awnings and it's display case of confectionery. "I can't live like I'm afraid of everyone."

He looks at her sidelong. "I need to teach you more magic," he says, like they hadn't already come to that conclusion the night before, "so you're less of an open nerve walking around."

"I'm okay with that," she says, something small and very similar to relief welling inside her stomach. "But I'm not gonna just hide away, not like my mom."

She pushes open the door to the coffee shop, and the grumpy lady just nods at her.

The booth in the back is entirely empty, so she squeezes herself deep enough inside of it that Melekai can scoot on the bench next to her, and she puts the phone down in relief.

"We always meet here," she tells him, and he's so tense he's practically vibrating, so she rests her hand on his leg, and all his attention immediately goes to the point of contact. "Only sketchy thing that happened here is that Axel found me once."

"You got involved in all of this because you ran into a magician at lunch?" he asks, skeptical, and that's fair. "A magician found you, exactly when he had a crisis to be solved, on a random lunch?"

"Yup."

The grumpy waitress swoops by, and leaves Lyra her coffee, before disappearing back behind the counter, already preparing Jackson's fancy matcha.

Melekai lets his hand settle over hers, like he's willing himself to relax. "Can I teach you how to blow up people, instead of just trees?"

"Please don't," Lyra says, but at least he grins at her in return. "That sounds messy."

Through the windows, she spots Jackson walking up, in his suit with scuffed up shoes, and he stops short, staring into the store, directly at Melekai.

"I should have warned him," Lyra murmurs, and that is the thing that finally gets Melekai to cough out a laugh, to relax just a hair. "This'll be fun."

Jackson visibly shakes himself loose, then shoves the door open, striding in. "What the hell?" he asks, and it's not at Lyra. "What the absolute—hi, Cynthia, thank you I'm doing well—but what the hell?"

He slides into the booth, staring down hard at Melekai.

"Lyra," Jackson asks, voice tentative, "do you have a crick in your neck?"

Melekai immediately casts a worried look at her, as if checking for pain.

It's an old code, one they formed when their mom was drunk, to see if the other needs a rescue.

It means they need the other to drop everything and get to them. The only time he had used it was when their aunt got too drunk and left him outside after his high school football practice for three hours in winter, and the only time she used it was when a roommate had pulled a knife on her, so she had to leave immediately without having time to grab her wallet.

"No, I'm good," Lyra says, a bit touched that he would be so worried, "all's good, I'd text you if I did."

"Your neck always hurts," Melekai says, puzzled, and Jackson and Lyra get that amazing moment where they can lock eyes and keep a secret.

"What are you doing here?" Jackson asks, finally.

"You're less of a child," Melekai says, leaning back in the booth.

"You let my sister get attacked by a demon, don't try to deflect," he says, then looks, guilty, to Lyra. "Sorry, I'm glad you're okay."

"Just some bruises," she says, bemused. "He's paranoid, he insisted on coming along."

"She was at risk eight times during her little trip through public transportation and she had no idea," Melekai tosses over at Jackson. "And you don't come out and visit her."

"Oh my god, stop," Lyra says, as the grumpy waitress sets down the matcha and their two sandwiches. "Melekai, this works for his schedule"—he scoffs, but she pushes on—"Jackson, he's concerned and wanted to make sure I was safe."

For a few seconds, they sit there, with Melekai and Jackson making hard eye contact, until Lyra reaches for her sandwich.

"So, update, I got fired," she says, willfully ignoring the stare down. "Buggees won't reopen for at least a month and the police have no idea how to categorize this, and now I know how to blow up trees with magic."

That gets Jackson's attention, and he sits, frozen, like she hit him over the head.

"There is actively a demon thing who tried to kill me, I know other magicians now, and I've raised another person from the dead so you're not special." She kicks him under the table, and he jumps. "How are midterms?"

"Finals are in three weeks," he grumbles, but takes his sandwich anyways with a distrustful look to Melekai. "Is he hurting you?"

Melekai pulls himself to sit taller, as if he could loom from across the table, and Lyra puts her hand on his arm to derail whatever confrontation that is about to happen.

It works, but now both of them are staring at her hand on him.

"He's the only reason why I didn't die a few days ago," Lyra says, removing her hand as smoothly as she can.

"And you raised a moth," Melekai says, like that's an important detail. "I wouldn't have known if you hadn't raised the moth."

Jackson sits back in the booth, running his hands through his messy black-brown hair, and he immediately looks more like an awkward teenager than the kid who's going to law school in the big city.

"Are you safe?" he asks, finally, staring down at his sandwich like it's going to betray him too. "Do you...do you need me to come stay at your place?"

"Not during finals," Lyra reassures him, though Melekai shoots her a narrowed-eyed glare. "Or, uh, not sure if you could help a lot."

"Thanks," Jackson says sarcastically.

"If Terese finds a way to infiltrate her house, can she stay with you?" Melekai says, finally leaning forward. "Even during 'finals'?"

"Of course?" Jackson says, dazed. "She's, Lyra, you're always welcome."

"Good," Melekai says, dark.

The awkward pause stretches on, and Lyra focuses down on her sandwich, because she's never had a boyfriend to bring home to a dad, and this entire encounter feels too much like what the media says it is.

"How was she in danger?" Jackson asks, finally picking up his sandwich and actually taking a bite. "You said eight times."

"There were three people on the trip with hidden guns on them, one man under the influence of something that had a knife in his pocket, two tweakers who eyed her phone, and one man stared at her for twenty minutes and thought impure thoughts," Melekai lists off. "And the bus was only half a second away from getting hit by a truck that would have hit her behind the head."

"Jesus," Lyra says, and she doesn't want to give up her sandwich but she's a lot less hungry after that.

Jackson sits forward, tenting his hands, and it's his lawyer pose. "You can read people's intent?" he asks, suddenly scholarly. "Can you read everyone or just those in relation to Lyra?"

"Relation to Lyra," Melekai says, immediate. "I knew you wouldn't hurt her."

It's almost, almost an olive branch.

"Good," Jackson says, still in his lawyer pose. "Can you take care of this 'Terese' problem before it hurts her again?"

"Working on it," Melekai almost snarls.

"Can you guys not posture?" Lyra asks, pressing her knee against

Melekai's in some hope to calm him down. "Jackson, is there anything new with you?"

It takes a few minutes, but they both unwind, just enough that it turns into a relatively normal lunch punctuated with occasional too tense topics.

And, since she has her brother in front of her, and he's just…talking, speaking about his classes, Lyra settles deeper into her chair, and tries to slow her breathing.

In front of her, her brother is strong, his lungs steady with every motion. His blood pumps through his heart, as easy as anything, though there's a muscle in his neck that's a bit stiff, like he slept wrong on it.

Melekai's hand shifts against her arm, and she blinks her eyes back open.

Jackson hasn't even noticed, but still.

He's healthy.

IN THE END Jackson wraps her in a tight hug, so tight that her ribs ache.

"Please be careful," he whispers into her hair, as he clings to her in a way he hasn't done since he was fifteen and she was going off to community college. "Please don't put yourself in harm's way."

"Yeah, stay out of trouble too," she says, patting him on the back.

He releases her, but his brows remain pushed together as they walk out of the little shop, her little takeout container with her half sandwich in her hand.

Melekai strides after them, eyes immediately scanning around. "I don't want you back on the train, not today," he says, stopping both of them in the tracks. "Lyra, let me take you back?"

"How…" Jackson trails off, and he grabs at his hair again. "What is…"

"He can teleport, but only to someplace he's been before."

"Or where you are," Melekai interjects.

"Or where I am," Lyra follows up, which isn't quite better, and Jackson's eyes narrow. "But it's handy."

"Can I see?" he asks, the lawyer voice coming back out. "I want to see."

Melekai jerks his head down the street for them to follow, and leads them down the short street, to a barely disguised alleyway.

"Text when you get home?" Jackson asks, and his voice wavers, just a bit.

"Of course?" she says, and, formal, Melekai holds his hand out to her.

With one last comforting smile to her brother, she takes Melekai's hand, and has only a breath to prepare herself, before they're back in her little living room, her cat twining around her legs.

"I hated that and I never want to do that ever again," Melekai says, almost petulant, but still holds her hand as she texts.

LYRA (1:32 PM): I'm home safe. What did you see?

"What, a simple trip on the light rail is what got you?" Lyra says, then stretches her neck, her back twinging.

JACKSON (1:32 PM): You just vanished.

JACKSON (1:33 PM): When things aren't crazy I want to video tape it. Maybe over Christmas break?

Melekai squeezes her hand, and the pain lessens, just enough to be noticeable.

She eyes him, but his gaze is locked outside their window.

Outside her window, down the gravel driveway she never uses and into the road, stands Terese.

Before she can register what's happening, Melekai shoves her back, blocking Terese from seeing her.

Terese doesn't move, just stares through the window at them, her jaw jutted out.

She locks eyes with Lyra, from behind Melekai's back, but remains still. Remains frozen.

The line of muscle in Melekai's shoulders stiffens.

"She can't get in," he murmurs, and she mostly feels like it's for himself, not for her. "The protections are holding."

Lyra shies close to him. "She can't get any closer?"

He shakes his head, all of his attention out the window.

A frightened meow echoes from her bedroom, and she would bet actual money her cat is under the bed again.

She can see nothing actually stopping Terese from crossing onto the meager patches of dead grass and ice she calls a lawn, but Terese doesn't move forward, her pale eyes just watching Lyra.

"Do I need to call Jackson?" Lyra asks, and her voice wobbles. They had spoken of it just that morning, though it seems so very far away.

"No," Melekai says, lifting his jaw.

Terese's head tilts, like she's considering something, and around her feet the pebbles on the ground stir.

It's too much like the coins from the till in Buggees that Lyra makes herself look away, reach for her phone, anything.

There's nothing stopping her from moving like normal in her house, so she swallows down her fear, pulling her rickety kitchen chair across the room so she's sitting as away from the window as possible, but still able to see outside.

Tucking her knees underneath her, she carefully, ever so carefully, takes a picture of Terese out of the window.

Melekai twitches at the sound of the fake shutter on her phone, but otherwise doesn't react.

On the cracked phone screen, there's a dual image in place. There's the body that Lyra sees, with the white blond shorn hair and colorless eyes, but overlaid like a smudge is a vicious, blurry figurine. Like the skin exists only to cover up a far more sinister creature, with glowing eyes and a mouth drawn wide in agony.

She stares at the pic for a few seconds.

"Should I do anything?"

"No," Melekai murmurs to her, though he doesn't break his eye contact. "She can't get in."

"Am I...trapped?" Lyra asks, hugging her knees to her chest.

"Hardly," Melekai says, though there's a bead of sweat on his forehead. "I can get you in and out, and she...she cannot cross over your yard." A hint of a smirk forms on his lips, a hint of some control.

The pebbles at Terese's feet stir, and her face twists into a snarl, before she abruptly disappears, and Melekai sags backwards.

For a brief, crystalline moment, Lyra's heart jumps in her throat, with the thought that Terese would appear inside, appear next to her, but Melekai just glances at her and relief is obvious on his face, as he sits down hard on the velvet green armchair.

"Are you okay?" Lyra asks, still hugging her knees. She probably shouldn't sit in that position for too long, but damn it, it's comforting.

"I'll have to reset the protections soon," Melekai says, with a half-hearted wave of his hand. Like he wants to be flippant but doesn't quite have the energy. "But that cost her more than it cost me, and I have you."

Lyra doesn't understand, it just looked like they were staring at each other, but she nods anyways.

"Could she hide out there?" Lyra asks, small. "Wait for me to come out, then ambush?"

"Not easily," Melekai says, and he swallows, his throat sounding dry, before he pushes himself up from the chair, crossing to her in three large steps, pulling her gently up.

She allows him to pull her with him, but all he does is dump her on the armchair instead, before curling a hand on her neck.

"I won't take much," he says, voice low, and for the first time she gets that he's asking permission. "Just enough to reset the wards and make it very uncomfortable if she returns."

Lyra nods, and his thumb rubs a circle on the back of her neck, soothing. "Will it hurt with the...uh...death bubble thing she did?"

"I won't take that much," he says, almost a whisper. "You might feel a bit tired, that's it." His eyes track to her face, to her neck, like he's reading her pulse.

"Are you okay?" Lyra asks, again, because he never answered that question, and his thumb stills on the back of her neck. "I couldn't see anything, just you two standing there. What even happened?"

His lips part, but then he pauses, like he takes a moment to think of the answer.

"You couldn't see anything?" he asks, tentative.

"Just some rocks moving," Lyra answers, then pokes at his arm. "Answer my question."

"I don't like her knowing where you live," he says, which is another example of him not answering. "But I am glad my protections held up against such a rookie demon, and it will take her some time to regain strength." Finally, he looks at her, and his eyes reflect the light back at her. "I'm okay."

"Good," Lyra says, before giving him another nod.

He exhales, smooth, and the tell-tale pressure on her chest kicks in, a little bit of a gold flash behind her, reflected in the plastic of her cupboards.

But the pressure relaxes after a few moments, and her legs tingle, as if relaxing suddenly, but she doesn't pass out, black spots don't crowd her vision, and her head doesn't swim.

He releases the back of her neck, gentle, and watches her for a few tender seconds, before looking back towards the window.

Lyra pulls her leftover sandwich to her, as Melekai sets about tracing things she cannot see into every surface of her house, to the doorframe, to her windows, then outside, along her driveway, along her lawn, every bit of it.

And wonders what it is she cannot see.

17

The next day, when Terese is nowhere near her house, according to Melekai, he casually suggests she should dress warmly, then whirls her away the moment she comes out with a snow jacket, to the dead clearing in the woods.

There's still no life in the bubble, still no ants crawling or bacteria decomposing, and for all she knows, it might never.

No snow falls in the bubble, and it's barren, just as much a warm puff of air as it was the night she first came. There's a clear edge of snow, along the side, like snow piled up against a glass window.

She scuffs the toe of her snow boot against the barrier, at the snow propped up, and it gives her no difficulties. It crumbles against her foot, but when she pulls back from the border, none of it falls inside of it.

"Some scientist is going to stumble on this and be really confused," Lyra says, turning towards Melekai.

He's inspecting the bubble, so incredibly obvious with the snow sliding off, his chin tilted back, the golden curls still tied up.

She wonders if he has to do his hair every day. It hasn't been in the exact same bun, it had fallen out, but...

Without looking at her, he reaches out his hand, and she grasps it.

"Don't be scared," he murmurs, so quiet she can barely hear, and she gets a brief warning with a squeeze of the hand, before...

The entire world around explodes into light.

No, not quite.

The entire world reveals its light.

Golden strands weave through the border of the bubble, moving, always wavering, like it's knit together from a thousand moving, shimmering strings. They react, when flakes of snow hit them, pushing the flake off and sliding it down to the ground.

Lyra looks down. Her footsteps shine gold, like a trail, leading directly to her boots, and it extends far beyond the bubble, where she had gotten out of the Mustang those months ago, paced around the edges.

"Why..." She points towards them, and her snow gloves ride up, revealing a little sliver of her wrist.

It shines. Gold encircles her skin, glowing.

She strips off her glove, and her entire hand shimmers with the same gold light.

It's the same strands that she sees whenever Melekai takes from her.

"Do I...look like this to you?" she asks, unable to break her gaze from her own fingers.

"Yes," he says, his voice deep.

"Uh..." She waves her hand in front of her face, and the motion leaves a trace behind it, like a ghost image of her hand, blurring her actions. "Huh."

"Yes," he says, this time impatient. "Now tell me what you see with me."

She glances up at him, and it's almost two images. There's the hipster face, with the bun and the manicured eyebrows and the high cheekbones, but underneath it, like a bad movie hologram, is...

Is another face. Something more terrifying, the eyes sunken, the mouth larger and full of sharp teeth, the skin more uneven. Something restless, something always moving, like his very features morph beneath him.

She reaches her hand to his face, cups at his chin, and there's the hint of scruff from the human body, but his eyes slip shut and he rests against her palm. Both parts of him, the human and the shadow self beneath, all leaning into her touch.

There's an echo, something strange, like she's feeling her touch twice. Like she's getting it from him, not just from the nerve endings from her palm.

"I'm seeing your face, aren't I?" she asks, and he nods against her hand.

There's a moment, as the snow falls onto the bubble and slides down, as it's warm, with just the two of them standing together, silent.

But then he opens his eyes again, and takes a step back, moving all contact away.

Still, she sees the golden light everywhere. Not touch-activated.

"Tell me if I'm going to accidentally do something dangerous," she says, and he just nods, and she reaches out and rests the tips of her fingers on the edge of the bubble.

It's rough, like a burlap sack, and the threads move and morph where she pokes at them.

It doesn't feel like death, not how she feels it at least, but she twists her fingers in between the strands, and they wind their way around her hand, like a living and breathing creature.

"When we said to visualize a rope, we meant like that," Melekai says, nodding at the threads in her hand. "Imagine them twisting around my wrist, keeping me in place.

She tugs the threads free of the woven bubble, and snowflakes drip in. It's a small bit colder, the moment she does, and the warm air whistles, puffing up immediately outside the bubble.

The sense of death, the gut punch of the snake and the mouse and the ants, immediately lessens. Not much, not a lot, but lessens.

"Can I store this and use it later?" Lyra asks, rolling the strands between her fingers. It's still rough, coarse.

"You can, but it's not the best way," he says, tilting his head at her, eyes hungry.

When she sees the reflected light, it's not light, it's his actual eyes seeping through.

Unsure if she's unsettled or not, she tugs a little bit more of the threads free, opening up a gap in it. Snow piles up, already, on the ground beneath the gap.

"Hey so those creatures will decompose now, won't they?" she says, and she can even see where she had crouched down and touched the dead moss, two perfect little fingerprints of gold. "So they won't be stuck like this for forever?"

He smiles. "Probably."

"Good," she decides, then looks straight at him. "Then how do I do this rope thing?"

He grins, wide, wild, and it sits well on his true face.

"All magic, fundamentally, is made of threads," he says, and she nods along. Alette had told her as much, in her scholastic texts and lectures. "That's why spell weaving is the most common out of them all, it takes less inborn talent and more concentration and study."

Sounds about right.

"To use the metaphor, alchemy is taking the threads from somewhere else and slamming them into the threads they hold. A rapid substitution from somewhere else in the world, leading it to change. Necromancy," he pauses, reaches out, and touches her elbow, "finds the threads in people."

With his touch, she can see the thread between them, but he doesn't take from her, not this time, and he breaks the contact without any of the telltale symptoms.

"So, to tie this rope," she ventures a guess, "Alette would have to pull from the world around her, and Axel would basically summon from somewhere else."

"Relatively," he says, "though they most likely do not think of it that way. It isn't...visual for them, not like I'm showing you now." He holds out his hand again, demonstrating, and with a twist of his fingers a golden string appears. "To control someone quite thoroughly, using this to tie them is the key. Around the wrist or arm is easiest, around the torso is more effective, around the neck is the best, but I'm not sure you want to get close enough to Terese to do so."

He's not wrong. "So I just keep some magical rope with me in case I encounter her again?"

He shakes his hand, and the string disappears. "Not that easy," he says, and begins to pace around the little bubble of dissipating warmth. "In most cases, manifesting energy like that will just be absorbed back inside, unless you do something with it." It takes him only four strides to cross the bubble, then back. "Your body needs its energy, holding it outside of your body for an extended period would be instinctually difficult and logically unwise."

He's sounding more and more like a scholar himself.

"So I create the rope, use it, and then take it back when I'm done," she reiterates, and he nods. "Then how the heck do I create the rope?"

"Well," he starts, still pacing, "how do you raise the dead?"

The question stops her cold, and she looks away, at the snow starting to pile in the one spot of the bubble, and the wind swirling the flakes into the hole.

Outside the bubble, the wind has picked up, the tree branches bending and rustling against its force. If she had to walk there, walk out, it'd be difficult to see, difficult to pick a direction.

It's not a proper blizzard, not like how Washington can get them nearer to Christmas, but it'd be strong enough that she wouldn't want to walk to work or take a bus into Seattle.

"I guess I imagine it," Lyra says, and his eyebrows flash up. "I imagine the heart beating again, imagine the blood going in the right place, imagine all the electricity sparking correctly, and I touch them until it does."

He hesitates, and, somehow, she can just tell she surprised him. Even with the human face impassive and the demon face still.

He's almost never still.

"I think, this entire time," he says, "I assumed your mother trained you."

She scuffs her snow boot at the edge of the golden barrier, where the snow props up against it. "She was much more about scaring me to never do it than teaching."

"Well that's foolish," he scoffs, and his hand drifts towards her.

"We never said she was a good mother, just that she was there," Lyra says, and watches as the warm air continues to puff out of the hole she made, as the temperature gets colder and colder inside. "Better than finding out your dad lived in a trailer this entire time and never sent any child support."

His nose wrinkles, before he shrugs it off. "Human things," he says, airily, and she cracks a small smile at him. "Can you still sense the dead snake?" At her nod, he continues. "Use whatever sense from that to summon the rope, and tie around my wrist."

She nods again, taking the moment to shove some of her wavy hair behind her ear. "And you're okay with that?"

"Little Lyra," he starts, his voice dipping down low, "do you think I would be here if I wasn't?"

"Right, right," she says, shaking out her hands and trying to ignore how much her heart jumps when he says her name like that. "I just...wanna check."

"It matters to you," he says, and it's almost tentative, like he's working out a puzzle piece of her. "It matters to you what is done to others."

"Yeah, generally," she says, then shakes her hands out again. "Alright, okay."

She doesn't need to close her eyes, not when everything is outlined in gold, to feel the snake. To feel the stillness in its scales, the autumn's warmth still in its body.

"Instead of raising it," he interrupts, as she can already feel herself listing that way, "take what you sense and create a rope."

She exhales, and her vision blurs for a second, before clearing, abruptly, and the gold is gone, leaving the world a bit darker, a bit more barren, but...

But in her hand, somehow, she can feel some coarse thread. Like a bundle of twine, cupped in her palm.

He's watching her, and it's just his human face, with the sharp jawline and the high brows.

Tentative, with the ball of twine she can feel but no longer see, she unravels it between her fingers.

She can no longer tell the snake is there. It's no longer an itch, no longer an intangible scent in the back of her throat.

"I can't raise anything I use for this, can I?" she asks, and he wordlessly shakes his head. A few curls tumble from his high bun, as if bringing her here and showing her this takes up his energy as well.

She fumbles to the end of the twine, and approaches his outstretched hand, feeling worse than at any of the high school dances she attended in foster care.

But still, she somehow manages to tie a knot with an invisible string, and a small spark thrills down her arms when she does.

Melekai inhales, sharp, as if he felt it too.

"There," he says, and his voice is gentle, "that's the basic idea."

"Wait, just like that?" Lyra says, blinking up to him, and his amber eyes watch back in return. "What...I can just order you around?"

"Some," he says, making a fist with the hand and then releasing it, like he's testing things. "It won't make me do anything I can't innately do, and if I had severe enough impulses, I might be able to fight and delay it. It won't last for forever, you're not that practiced yet."

Her heart drops, and she stares out at the snow around them, at the sudden lack of golden threads, everything.

"Can you...try to help me tear down the bubble? Now that I can't see it?"

"Is that a question or an order?" he asks, voice silky low.

"Uh," she starts, then squints at him as he grins wide. "An order."

Almost immediately, he reaches his hand to the edge of the bubble, where she had started the hole, but his hands come away with nothing, and no new snow falls.

"It seems I cannot," he murmurs, though his brows raise at his hands. "It seems that whatever energy she has put into it, mine cannot undo." The side of his face twitches, like it irritates him, before he grabs her hand for a brief moment and the entire world glows golden again. "Does that count as helping you?"

Lyra blinks through the sudden light, at the bubble back in vivid color again, at the shimmering thread sloppily tied around his wrist, nestled between the other bracelets that came with the body.

"I guess?" she says, and almost imperceptibly, his shoulders relax, so she reaches out and takes another chunk of the bubble with her, the threads dissolving into a mess on the ground underneath her. "So the gold vision, any bad side effects for me?"

"Are you ordering me to tell you?" he asks, and there's a smile on his face. Like he's enjoying this weirdness.

"Fuck off, I'm just asking," she says, and he grins. "I just want to know."

"Don't stare too hard at it, your eyes will get tired," he says, stretching his arms over his head so he barely touches the top of the bubble. "Don't ask me to do it all the time, I'll get hungry too fast, and need to feed." He gives her a sidelong look, one much, much more terrifying with his real face. "This doesn't take from you, it takes from me."

"Gotcha," she says, deliberately turning away and tearing out another piece of the bubble, rolling the threads in her hands before dropping them to the ground. "Is it a necromancer thing to undo demon things?" He opens his mouth to say something obviously smartass. "I'm asking for conversation!"

He grins, still. "Yes."

She rolls her eyes and uses her boot to scuff away some of the bubble again, and the snow leaning against it plops onto the ground, sizzling a bit at the comparative warmth.

And bit by bit, the gut punch of death fades away, until the only part of the bubble still constructed is the bit immediately over their head, immediately keeping them dry. A chill wind blows through the clearing, scouring Lyra's cheeks and turning them red.

She turns towards him, and he's still watching her, eyes intent, like she's the most important thing in the world, now with the string around his wrist.

"Take me home?" she asks, and immediately they're in the warmth of her house before she can even blink.

Her cat twines between her legs, and her cat shines gold, too. Like whatever energy she put to bring him back stayed there, inside the tiny little cat body.

She strips off her snow jacket, and there's even a handprint on the wall next to the coat tree, where she braces herself on bad pain days.

Her footsteps cover the entire building in a thin layer of golden dust, her handprints on the wall, on the handle of the microwave, on the smudge next to the light switch that she fumbles with in the dark.

"And you see like this all the time?" she asks.

Melekai stretches, then sits on the kitchen seat, casual, the thread still shining around his wrist. "More or less."

She squints at him. "Do you want me to untie the string?"

He stills, at that, like he's unsure of what he heard. "It'll work its way loose in a short time," he says, instead of answering the question. "It makes no difference to me at this moment."

That feels like a trap.

"Stop me seeing the gold for now, it's disorienting in my house," she orders, and without a single word it's gone, leaving her with just her familiar linoleum floor and her still purring cat. "What do you want?"

He looks up, startled. "What do you mean?"

She gets an idea, and it might not be the smartest of ideas, but she tilts her head at him and narrows her eyes, and he sits up straighter out of confusion.

"Can I order you to tell me the truth?" she asks.

His lips split into a grin, wide, which is not a helpful answer. "Little Lyra, you can order me to do anything right now and I would happily do so."

She resists the urge to squirm, at that.

"How long, exactly, will this last?"

"About thirty more minutes, with this tie job," he answers, easily, grinning up at her, like this is fun. Like this is a joke to him and not incredibly uncomfortable.

"Okay, tell me the truth," she says.

He shivers, like the order compels him, which is just strange, and her mouth suddenly goes dry. Like she's lost on what she can actually ask him, actually get from him. "What do you do when you're not...feeding from me?"

"Destruction and mayhem," he says, cheekily. "The world of demons is vast and full of politics, and nobody understands how I am steadily so well fed."

"Terrifying," she says, then lets herself settle into the green monstrosity directly across from him. He leans forward, towards her, like the string on his wrist guides him to her, and they stare at each other for a few long, uncomfortable seconds, before he picks up her hand again.

Idly, he traces his long fingers along her palm, and she's almost used to it by now.

"Why do you do that?" she asks, and he doesn't stop. "Do you get something from that?"

"Not food, if that's what you're asking," he says, and his finger dips up her wrist, at the delicate place where her veins sit close to her pale skin. "It's a cruel thing that demons cannot interact easier with more humans, so when we do, it's a bit of a marvel." He traces up her veins, pushing up her loose sweater sleeve to the crook of her elbow, then back down. "Humans are a...glut of sensation, and touching one is akin to glory."

She shivers at his touch, and he looks up to her, quick, before he looks back down at her hand.

"Even when we are in a human body, it's not quite the same," he continues, the pad of his finger resting at her pulse point, like he's testing her. "Now you tell me the truth—does it bother you?"

"Not...really?" she says, voice lilting up. "It's...strange. Not bad, but strange."

"Order me to stop, if you need to," he says, and lifts her wrist to his lips, pressing a kiss against her skin.

She shivers again, and his eyes flicker to hers, before he presses another kiss deeper on her arm, then at the crook of her elbow, to where he pushed up the sleeve of her overlarge sweater.

"The thing about humans," he says, his lips still against her arm, so close she can feel the shape of his words as he speaks, "is that every little bit of them is a new sensation." Another small kiss on her wrist, as soft as air, before pulling back.

"What does that mean?" she asks, and he shifts, so his knees are pressed against hers.

"Demons, without the extra body, do not have the nerve endings that you do," he says, and his other hand flutters to her leg, to where the muscles ache and the nerves send sparks up her back. "The pain that you always feel, that is as foreign to us as another language would be to you. We would never experience it, unless..." he traces a small circle on her knee, and she suppresses a shiver. "Unless we can touch a human. Then we get a glimpse of it. Like viewing through a telescope at a vast array of colors you can only halfway see."

"So you hold my hand whenever you're here," she says, and he nods, reaching up and settling his hand on the back of her neck. "Or touch there."

"This is because it's easy to pull your pain away, so close to your spine," he says, and she wouldn't really mind that right about now, but every part of her is abuzz against his touch. "It's expedient."

"Expedient," she teases, "is that like protecting your investment?"

"Somewhat," he teases back, and it's playful, certainly less all-consuming than his usual intensity. "If you find a lifeline thrown out to you in the grim dark of existence, you'd protect it too."

"You...you're speaking literally, aren't you?" she asks, and his thumb caresses the side of her neck. With the shining gold and every-thing, she realizes he means actual light in actual darkness. "Is that why Terese could spot me immediately?"

The playful glimmer fades from his eyes, just a little bit. "Any demon who would happen to stumble on you would know," he says, but he doesn't stop the twin points of contact, a hand on her knee and a hand on the back of her neck. "It's a miracle you weren't dead before I found you. A miracle and sheer luck."

"You're still telling the truth, aren't you?" she whispers, and he nods. "Well, uh...thanks? For keeping me alive?"

He smiles, soft, at that, and her heart thumps.

"Another question, then," she says, mind reeling around, skirting around the awkwardness of the moment. "If you can jump from body to body, why are you always a guy?"

He sits back, startled, and she misses his hand against her neck.

"I can take a female body," he says, puzzled, "if that's what you'd prefer? Usually..." he shrugs. "I took them before and people didn't take me seriously, so I stopped. It was...bullshit."

"Yeah, it is bullshit," she says, then shrugs, trying to mirror him. "You don't need to change, I'm just curious."

"The gender of the body doesn't matter, ultimately," he says, relaxing back down, "Some take the female body specifically to mess with humans, but I don't have the patience for it."

"Wonder if that's why Terese is..."

He stills. "I don't think so," he says. "Whatever happened to Terese, I don't think she had a choice in it."

That falls over the two of them, and he looks away, like he's regretting the truth that time.

"Tell me when the bracelet's about to fall off," Lyra blurts out to him.

"You'll be able to tell," he says.

There's a lull, in their small conversation, with them sitting knee to knee in her tiny dining room with the snow swirling outside, and she could command him to do anything, command him to tell her anything, and her heart is pounding with the proximity. Pounding with how close he is, with the hand still on her knee, with how tender he's being, with how soft everything is about him.

He leans closer and presses his lips against hers.

18

At first, she doesn't know what to do.

She's been kissed before, of course she has, but never by someone she knows so well and for so long. All her meager sex life has been with near strangers, with people she only met for just one night, without any of the following complexities or awkwardness.

Not a lot of people can deal with the day in, day out of her with her pain. Too many people bounce the moment she has a day lying in bed from the agony and exhaustion.

But Melekai's seen that, many times.

Not to mention any of the baggage she has around her family. Around her mother. Around her lost job, the job she's going to have to replace before her next phone bill and—

But his lips are soft, in this body, and it's been a long time since someone had taken the effort, so she leans into it. Leans into him, into the space between her green velvet monstrosity and the rickety kitchen chair.

She could stop him, if she needed to. If she wanted to.

He makes a small surprised noise, deep in the back of his throat, and for a brief second, she wishes she could see the gold everywhere, to see what expression he's making on his true face. See if he's truly surprised.

If he's been around as long as she thinks he has, the idea that someone as small and insignificant as her could surprise him sends a thrill up her spine. That she could do that, just by leaning in.

His hand comes up and cradles her chin, drawing her closer to him, and she braces her hand on his thigh, leaning. The muscle in his leg twitches at her touch, as if he has never been touched there before.

He might not have, in this body at least. And if precious few humans can actually interact with him, he may not have ever been held by a human.

She could stop him at any time.

So she trails the hand up, until it's against his chest, and she can feel the thump of the heart, beating hard against the ribcage.

She doesn't understand how that would work, in a stolen body, but she splays her fingers over his breastbone, with the blood coursing through the veins and the nerves firing.

Just like they do in a real person.

He inhales against her lips, then presses down, tilting her chin up towards him, like he would consume her right then and there.

"Your heartbeat spiked," he mumbles, mouth still next to hers, "are you scared?"

And the answer to that is honestly...maybe. She might be, it is rather terrifying, to say the least, to be kissing a demon who steals sips of her soul.

But more than terrifying, it's exciting. It's a gorgeous thrill down her neck, like she's speeding in a car almost out of control, like there's loud music thumping in time with her pulse, like she's about to shake apart from the sensation and the expression of it all.

So instead of answering, she just opens her mouth to his, and lets him sweep her away.

He makes a sound, deep in his chest, and she feels it through her fingertips more than hears it, before he climbs into the green monstrosity chair with her, bracing himself over her.

She could get him to stop if she so wishes.

But her heart jumps, and she just grins at him.

"You're playing with fire, Little Lyra," he says, and his voice is low, low and teasing, "Many people have tried to tame a demon, not many are still alive."

"You won't hurt me," she whispers back, and their faces are close, so close, and she just wants more. More of the contact, more of the kissing, more of everything. "I could stop you anytime I want."

His eyes alight, his fingers trail from her chin down her neck, dancing across her collarbone, above the edge of her overlarge sweater. It's milder than the things she used to do at high school dances, but her skin buzzes.

Instead, he studies her, eyes intent, like he's looking over every inch of her skin. Every speck of her, all that he can see, while his thighs brace on either side of hers on the chair. It's a tight fit, the two of them, but moving would mean to the bed, which is daunting, and this contact would have to stop, and she'd rather gnaw off her own arm than lose the touch of his hands.

Slowly, making sure she doesn't dislodge him, she pulls the sweater over her head. She's wearing her normal lounge-about-the-house bra, a simple black band with soft cups, and he gazes at her with the same intensity as before.

A hand settles on the curve of her waist, where she's hardly ever touched, and she shivers.

"Kiss me again," she whispers, and she can feel the grin on his lips against hers, a second after the words leave her.

Too soon, he breaks the kiss, before pressing a series of kisses down her neck, into the hollow of her collarbone. "You didn't say where," he says, tilting her head to the side and kissing where her neck meets her shoulder. "You should be more specific."

She shudders again, and his hand toys with the edge of her bra strap as he nuzzles her neck, like she's the softest thing he's ever held.

"I don't see the problem," she says, and it's halfway between a sigh and a squeak. He laughs, an almost soundless breath of air between them, before he slides off the chair, kneeling in front of her. Both his hands settle on her upper legs, as if holding her in place by sheer desire.

Careful, as if he is the one that would break, she winds her fingers through his curly hair, undoing the hair tie. It's such a mundane thing, a hair tie, and it might even be one of hers that he picked up around the house.

He shakes out his curls, like a horse shaking off a fly, then smiles at her. It's almost unfair, how perfect the golden-brown ringlets are, that he could just jump into the body and find one so perfect, so catered to his uses, and not have to deal with all the complexities that come with actually maintaining one.

A small, selfish part of her, wonders if he picked it just for her.

"Do you feel this?" she asks, twisting her hand in his hair, almost a sliver too tight.

He nods, pushing his head against her hand, so she does it again. Again, it's not something she'd do to other hookups, or other lovers, but his eyes slip shut at her movement, like she's placing a spell on him.

"Melekai," she starts, and his eyes open to languid slits, "this is an order. If you don't want me to do this, you need to tell me."

He nods, then swallows, his Adam's apple bobbing. "Don't worry," he says, low, "I will." A smile curves his lips, and he's kneeling in front of her with her hand tight in his hair, and it's such a pretty picture.

"Then tell me," she says, and she's the one in just her bra and pants, but he's way, way more vulnerable, "what do you want to do?"

He doesn't answer, at first, instead leaning more into her touch, like he's mulling over his answer. Like he's figuring out what to tell her, like he's figuring out what exactly he actually wants. Like it's not something he knows.

"I've tasted so much of your pain," he says, and his voice is a bit raspy, like she's affected him this much. "I want some of your pleasure."

She shivers, at his voice, and he presses a kiss against her knee, over her corduroys.

"I want to see you fall apart," he continues, leaning against her, "I want to hear you scream until you can barely speak, I want to overwhelm you until you cannot think, and then I want to do it again."

"That's...more than I was expecting," she says, and he smiles at her, the moment broken. "What does that even mean?"

His hands on her legs gently tease them apart ever so slowly. "May I show you?"

And there is the question, the one that washes over her with a rush of chills. Would she let him do what he wants, do what every nerve in her body is vibrating for, is yearning for?

His hand trails up the inside of her thigh, so gentle it might be a tease, might be a feather.

"Will it hurt me?"

He hesitates. "Not if I'm careful."

There are a million things that could mean, a million possibilities in front of her. Does he mean her nerves and her injuries, still apparent after all this time, or something deeper, something more like her soul, like her abilities?

Something more like her ability to stay alive. To draw breath. To live to see this through.

His eyes flash, as he watches her, intent. A reminder of the shadow self beneath.

"Then be careful."

There's a stillness to him, when she says that, like his mind is computing her words, before he takes her hand in his, and presses a kiss to her palm.

It's a strange moment of peace with him, surrounded by all the chaos in the world, just the two of them in her trailer home.

He guides her up off the chair, like she's a princess. His hand settles on her bare back, and goosebumps raise along her spine.

Outside, the snow still falls. She can't see past her meager driveway, can't see the neighbors or the gravel road, just soft white snow and mist.

His thumb drawing small circles on her back, he pulls her towards her bedroom, and his footsteps fall silent on the old orange linoleum.

He's far too pretty to be in a place as rundown as this, with his hair hanging around his face, and his high cheekbones. Like he's as remote as the wilderness outside, as out of place as she was in the forest.

But then he looks down at her, and his lips turn upwards, before, right there in her hallway, he swoops down to give her a kiss. Like he couldn't make it to the bedroom.

She tangles her hand in his hair again, and he makes a sound deep in his chest, and she marvels at it. Marvels that she's the one causing it, causing him to react in such a way.

She spares a thought, quickly, for his changing motivations, for what this means for him, for how it's different, it must be different than what she's feeling, before his hands rake into her hair, pulling tight, pulling so close to pain that she arches into him against the wall.

"Oh, you like that," he says, and she can just tell he's amused. "You like it when I do that." His hand tightens in her hair, and she moans, a bare breathy exhale, and he grins.

It's heartbreakingly beautiful.

Before she knows it, he's maneuvered her so the back of her knees hit the bed, and he guides her down, every inch of him controlled, before he buries his face in the crook of her neck, climbing over her.

"This isn't fair," she breathes, and tugs at the hem of his shirt as he cups at her breasts, as if she's worthy of worship. His eyes reflect the light back at her, eager, and it stirs a strange mix of exhilaration and terror inside of her.

Sitting up, he pulls the shirt off of him in a long, smooth motion, and the body underneath it is all long lines and lean muscle, more akin to a runner than a weight lifter. Like whoever the body belonged to took care of it, took good care of it.

He watches her, his lips shining, before he grabs her chin and kisses her again, hard. Like he's pushing against all of her guards and walls that she's put up over the years.

A hand floats between her thighs, pressing up against the seam of her pants, and she gasps against his mouth.

"How far can I go?" he mumbles, not pulling away, but his long fingers trail up, to the button of her fly. "Tell me, how far can I go?"

"Yes," she replies, breathless, even though that's not really an answer. "Yes."

Pulling away from her as if it will kill him, he undoes her pants, tugging them off her in a motion that belies untold practice, until she's in front of him in just her underwear.

It's nothing fancy, it's nowhere near something she'd try to wear if she knew this would happen today, but he consumes her with his eyes, dark, as if the very sight of her leaves him famished.

It's a long, still moment, as his eyes rake over all of her, from the surgery scars on her legs, to the red marks still left from the shattered pieces of glass from the accident, to the scrapes and bruises left by Terese, and she tries hard to not be insecure. To match his stare.

"You," he starts, after too long, "are beautiful."

She lifts her chin into his gaze.

He hooks a finger on her panties, pulling them away, and his eyes go to the small dark patch of hair between her thighs.

He exhales, as if the sight left him breathless. As if he isn't a demon, isn't someone who has caused untold pleasure.

With just a quick glance up to her, he pushes her thighs apart, trailing his hand up in a way that's almost ticklish, almost, and she breathes out a laugh.

He gives her a lopsided grin, then kisses her there, a quick motion of his lips, before he licks her clit, startling a gasp out of her.

"Somehow I knew," he says, and she wishes he'd stop talking and keep doing that, "that you would like that." He kisses her over her clit, directly, and she thumps her head back against the pillow, shivers racing down her body. Like he worships her, like the very act is exalting her, until she moans, embarrassingly high.

He presses a kiss into the side of her thigh, then with another glance to her face, he sticks his finger in his mouth for a brief second, the very picture of sin, then presses his finger against her entrance. "May I?"

"Yes," Lyra repeats, almost a bit impatient.

With a grin, he kisses her again on her clit, pressing his finger inside of her and crooking it just so.

"You're so responsive," he whispers, before licking her again, and she moans. "I should have done this ages ago."

She squeezes her eyes shut against the onslaught of sensation, her breath caught in her chest as he traces love letters with his tongue against her. It's building, it's so much, like she's going to burst or cry or—

Too soon, he pulls his finger out of her then looms over her, grabbing her chin, and presses a deep kiss against her lips, such a thorough claim that Lyra finds her heart in her throat all over again.

She can taste herself on his lips.

In a deft move, he unclips her bra, immediately palming her breasts, like she's a treasure. Like her bare skin is a glory in and of itself.

She has a brief thought, a brief moment of wondering if he experiences any of this how she does, so she reaches out, finds the edge of his jeans, and dips her hand towards his crotch.

He makes a sound, deep in his throat, when she does, so she presses her palm against his erection until he breaks the kiss.

"Yes?" he says, but his voice is pleased.

He's pleased with himself.

"Wanted to see," she says, and her voice is embarrassingly flustered.

He stands back, a smile tilting his lips, satisfied, and undoes the button on his fly. "You can see anything you wish," he says, eyes shining back at her, reflective even in that moment.

So she sits up, half drawn closer to him, propping herself up. "Do you...feel sex like I do?" It's a wholly too clinical of a question for such a heated moment.

He hesitates, his head tilting to the side. "Probably not," he says, a hand dipping into his boxers and pulling out his cock.

His cock is long and lean, just like the rest of him, and her eyes immediately fall to it, her breath catching. He sheds his pants, standing in front of her, just as naked as she.

"But just because it's different"—he puts a hand back on her bare upper thigh, pressing her backwards, and she moves with him as he climbs on top of her—"doesn't mean it's not worth it."

She grabs his dick, and he hisses out a breath against her neck.

"Stop me if you want me to stop," he says, and there's nothing further from her mind, with him on top of her like this. "Tell me you'll stop me."

"If I want to, I will," she says, and it half comes out as a growl.

Almost before she can even guess what he's about to do, he grabs her by her wrists, pinning her down, looming over her. They lock eyes, and he moves, and—

His dick presses into her, and she arches up into the motion.

It's like the world stops, and all that exists is the three points of connection between them, his cock inside of her, and both hands on her wrists, holding her down.

As if it's just a brief thought, all other sensation escapes her, just narrowed down to the points where they meet. She gasps, she must have, like all the air in the world would never be enough to satisfy her lungs. Like the entire earth is insufficient.

He groans, moving against her, and she shatters again, pleasure coursing through her body, sharper than any pain, sharper than any panic. Like every part of her body, every part of her broken body, is made for this. Is made for these sensations, is made for his movements.

She's straining at his hands, but she doesn't want him to move them, like she'd float up without him holding her down, like she'd disappear into the ether of the world. Like he's holding her down to earth, against her too large bed in her small little trailer in the tiny town.

His hands are gentle, still clasped around her wrists, and as he thrusts, he presses kisses down her neck, kisses across her collarbone, kisses on her shoulder. Like he just can't help himself.

It's beyond sex. It's beyond anything she's ever felt, more intense then the car accident, more intense than raising anyone from the dead, more intense than—

With a snap she feels in her soul, the twine tied around Melekai's wrist breaks.

He freezes, still inside her, and all the sensations stop.

She blinks her eyes open at him, and he mouths something at her, as if intending to speak and finding himself unable. His hands fall away from her wrists, his long fingers trailing down her arm as if he's unwilling to do so. He's still propped up over her, and his gaze roves from her chest to her stomach to her cheeks, as if unable to look away. As if savoring a moment, to remember it for forever, to hide it away in his memory.

They lock eyes, in that long moment, her heart pounding, and she cranes her neck up, capturing his lips in hers.

It's bruising, it's vicious, but he pulls away.

"Do you need me to stop?" he asks, and his voice is wrecked, like he had been yelling.

"No," she says, simple, honest, and clenches herself around him.

His breath hitches.

"Not unless you need to," she amends, and his lips break into a surprised grin, more real than any she's seen, and now she knows that it would fit his real face so well. She thrusts at him, as best as she can with him over her, and he breathes out.

Without him holding her down, she trails a hand up his bicep, across his shoulders, then cradles his cheek.

Just like he did in the forest, he leans into the touch, eyes fluttering shut.

Then he presses her deeper into the bed, thrusting into her until she cries out, and he shakes apart.

AFTER, he pulls himself out of her and immediately snuggles next to her, arm thrown over her middle, face buried in the crook of her shoulder.

Lyra doesn't quite know where her skin ends and the bed begins, but his arm is hot against her stomach, almost like a brand.

It's...very similar to the feeling of being wrapped in clouds that she gets after he feeds from her, where there is no pain, nothing wrong, and the world feels kinder.

She turns her head, impulsive, and plants a kiss against the crown of his curls, and he responds by just pressing his face deeper against her skin.

"Are you okay?" she asks, after the moment stretches on, the only sound his ragged breathing.

He nods, still against her, and she's not used to being cuddled after sex, not like this, but he tightens the arm around her middle, as if she's threatening to get up.

She's not entirely certain her legs work, after that.

So she leans into him, curling her body towards him. She's not tired, not like she is when he feeds from her pain, but there's a thin layer of contentment, of being so incredibly cozy, that she just wants to lean against him and close her eyes. Forget the rest of the world out there, forget about the magic and the threats and everything.

So, for just a little while, she does.

19

Her phone beeps, too early for her, and Melekai makes a wordless noise of protest as she rolls over to grab it.

ALETTE (6:01 AM): We have some additional intel for you and Melekai, are you awake?

His arm tightens around her.

"Did you really sleep here?" Lyra asks, turning back towards him. "Like, the entire night?"

He sighs, a brief exhale, before he pulls away from her just enough to look at her. His curls are rumpled, half flat against his face, before he rests his head back against the pillow.

He's still naked.

"That was...a lot more than I anticipated," he mumbles, shutting his eyes again. "I didn't think about how different it would be...with you."

"Hmm," she says, and he peeks one eye open, before closing it again. "In a good way or a bad way?"

He just grips a bit tighter. "Some day you're going to have to develop some self-esteem," he says, but it's playful. "Of course it was good, it's you."

Her phone beeps again, saving her from having to figure out how to feel about that statement.

ALETTE (6:05 AM): Dr. Frisse has a theory about trapping Terese.

This time, Melekai pushes himself up, all long lines, running a hand through his hair.

"What sort of theories could she even have," he mutters, and it's hard for Lyra's eyes to not slip lower on his body.

LYRA (6:06 AM) What is it?

ALETTE (6:07 AM): We found a pattern in her attack, besides the one on you.

ALETTE (6:08 AM): Can we meet? Can Melekai bring you here, if we lower the wards?

"I can bring you there even with the wards, I've been there before," he grumps, but he's leaning over to his discarded clothing, pulling the Henley over his head.

She stretches out, and his eyes linger on her skin, before he raises an eyebrow at her.

Right.

"Let me clean up, then sure?" she says.

It's so early the sun hasn't even risen yet.

But it's not like she has a job she has to stay awake for. It's not like she's going to fall asleep at the till, not anymore.

She pulls herself out of bed, and his eyes follow her to the bathroom, as she cranks on the shower to blistering hot for maximum effect.

This time, she doesn't even jump when she hears him sit on her tiny little sink counter.

"If you break that, I'm going to need your help repairing it," she warns him.

"I won't," he says, through the shower curtain.

Her stomach twists at the sound of his voice, at everything that happened the day before, and it's been ages since she's been awake at six that it doesn't feel real. Doesn't feel like a time that actually exists.

"Terese is outside again," he says, in the same tone of voice, and her breath hitches. "She still can't get in."

"And you're okay?" she asks him, staring at the pale off-white of the shower walls, at the water dripping off her hair, instead of out at him.

"I may be a bit overpowered today," he says, still neutral. "I doubt even an old demon could get where I don't want him."

She blinks the water away, aggressively shampoos her hair, then cranks the water off, trying to wade through the connotations of all of that.

"I don't feel like you took too much of me," she says, grabbing a towel and trying to dry off as much as she can. There's a chill in the air of the trailer, like she needs to make sure the heater's working. "Or is it different?"

"It's different." He watches her as she steps out of the shower, eyes dark, like half his attention is elsewhere. "You'll return to pain much sooner, and I'll have to burn through this faster than I normally would."

She trails to the bedroom, and he follows her. Somewhere during her shower, he tied his curls back, looking neater than before.

"So will that hurt me? Or you?" she asks.

"Only if I'm not careful."

It's an echo of his words before, and she gets dressed with a speed she usually can't muster up, then flicks her curtain aside, looking towards her driveway.

Outside, shoulders hunched against the wind and the blowing snow, stands Terese.

Lyra stills, and Terese's pale eyes lock onto hers.

"How long has she been here?" Lyra asks. It's the sort of winter morning where the sun doesn't so much rise as it gets gradually less dark, fully committed to the gloominess of the season.

There are snowflakes on Terese's shoulders.

"Since you woke," Melekai says.

Lyra sits on the edge of the too large bed, staring out the window, and pulls the fuzzy blanket from the bed around her shoulders.

Small eddies of wind buffer the snow, around Terese's feet.

"Melekai," she starts, and his name falls off her tongue like it never has before, "can you make me see her power again?"

"You don't want to," he says, but his hand slips in hers, and he squeezes, once.

Her entire lawn blazes in gold, a rippling, undulating flame.

Save for Terese.

She's outlined in black, like the gold can't quite touch her, like it nears her then shies away, like a magnet to the wrong pole.

Underneath the human face, however, another face lurks. But instead of the contained power of Melekai, the face stretches out into a frozen agony, into a rictus of pain.

Lyra glances back to Melekai, to the shadow self beneath him. "Is my entire house in a death bubble?"

He has the audacity to roll his eyes. "No."

She looks back at Terese, then does a double take back at Melekai.

He's standing taller, his features less uneven, his shoulders broader underneath the human skin.

It takes a second, but he notices her staring.

"What?" he asks, puzzled.

She doesn't exactly know what to say, so she shrugs, puzzled back.

He did say he had more power.

And it's from fucking her.

She blinks back out at Terese, entirely unsure of how she should feel.

"Is she cold?"

This time, he rests his hand on the small of her back, and she shivers from the touch.

"It depends," he says, neutral, like his attention is elsewhere, and since there's currently magic fire outside on her lawn she believes it. "If I was out there, I wouldn't be, but she's...more tied to the nerves of the body than I."

"I don't know, you seemed pretty tied to the nerves last night," she says, and he turns his head to look down at her.

"That's different," he says, disgruntled, "human flesh feels entirely different than snow."

Her brain skips a beat, then another, and to avoid doing anything else she pushes herself up off the bed and putters into the kitchen. Her cat twines around her legs, mrrring at her for being awake so early.

LYRA (6:32 AM): How urgent is this? Terese is outside my house again.

ALETTE (6:33 AM): Again?

ALETTE (6:33 AM): Are you safe?

ALETTE (6:33 AM): Can you escape?

"Hey Melekai," she starts, because he's still standing in the other room.

"Yes, we can leave," he calls back. "I'm not a child."

"I don't know what that means," Lyra responds, and the gold dust is still everywhere around her kitchen, brighter where she just walked from the bedroom, and no wonder Terese found her so easily.

LYRA (6:35 AM): Melekai says we can leave, apparently it's no big deal to teleport out.

LYRA (6:35 AM): Can there be food?

Impulsively, Lyra takes a picture out the window, but none of the gold flame shows.

Just Terese, hunched in the snow, looking miserable.

Still, she sends it over to Alette.

ALETTE (6:36 AM): Oh no.

LYRA (6:37 AM): Melekai says I'm safe.

She ducks to her fridge, grabs a soda because her stomach twists with hunger, and even the items she put away the day before have the thin sheen of gold.

She blinks twice at her fridge, then at her shining cat. It's disorienting, still, now that she knows this exists. Now that she knows how Melekai sees her, now that she knows how she's found.

The cat purrs at her feet, so she stoops to pet him, and he arches into her hand. A small spark of gold shifts between them, as natural as breathing.

It doesn't leave her feeling any more drained, doesn't reduce any pain or discomfort, just...

"Anything you bring to life, you'll have that with," Melekai says, and he's leaning casually against the window, and she didn't see him move. "It's nothing you should be concerned with."

Her cat seems fine, leaning up against her as she stands with the fridge open, and gives a little meow.

Another glance out the window, and Terese is still in pain.

"Why is she still here," Lyra starts, "if she can't get in because of you?"

Melekai follows her gaze out, then reaches to her, cradling her hand. It would be awkward, if her kitchen wasn't so small.

She lets him, of course, and his touch feels the same as it always does. As if the day before hadn't happened. As if she hadn't tied that slip of magic string around his wrist, as if he hadn't kissed her.

She doesn't know how to think of that.

How if things are going to change, or, perhaps worse, if they are not.

"Desperation, maybe," Melekai says, finally, and Terese looks to where their hands are joined. "Looking for a way in, looking for some relief from the pain, might think a necromancer could bring it."

"Could I?" Lyra asks, and he looks at her, sharp. "I mean, is there something I could do—"

"No," he interrupts. "She thinks killing you could."

"How far out does it go?" Lyra asks, and he gives her a mildly puzzled look. "The protection?"

"Why?" he asks, almost immediately suspicious.

She shrugs, because she doesn't have a great answer.

"No," he says, brisk.

"I want to know if it's safe for me to, I dunno, get my mail or something," she says, gesturing at the mailbox halfway up her driveway. "Get picked up by someone driving, something like that."

"Have them pull up to the edge of your stairs, if you see her out there," he says, pointing to the narrow spot of her driveway right in front of the stairs. "I can guarantee I'll cover you on your stairs, even when I'm weaker." His lips curve up into something almost a smile, and she wants to shiver again, but for an entirely different reason. "Now, now you could walk within five feet of her and all she could do is snarl."

The snow flurries around Terese's feet, against the wind, and the only thing that tears Lyra's gaze away is her phone beeping.

ALETTE (6:42 AM): Axel told me to tell you that there will be food.

"Excellent," Melekai says, standing with a burst of energy, and before she knows it his hand tightens on hers.

This time, she braces herself, and the rush of power as they blow through whatever barrier doesn't double her over, and her feet hit the floor in the grand conference room in the headquarters with only a small amount of sliding.

"See, I told you it was weird looking," Axel pipes up, from where he lounges in one of the chairs.

Blinking the stars from her eyes, Lyra turns to look.

Alette shines the same gold as her cat, brilliant and obvious and somehow exactly matching her glasses, and a gold smudge is still visible on the table where she lay dead. Axel is less so, a much more shifting red haze around him, though...though he looks shorter. More rumpled, with his skin a bit ruddier and his shoulders a bit thinner.

Lyra blinks, and Melekai touches her lightly on the back of the neck, and the gold sight vanishes.

Immediately, Axel looks normal, all smooth and polished and perfect-skinned.

Lyra glances up at Melekai, and he nods.

Axel digs in his pocket, pulls out the earpiece, and sticks it in his ear.

"Dr. Frisse is getting some food," Alette says gingerly, "we didn't quite know when to expect you." As always, her eyes flit to Melekai then skitter away.

"That seems...strangely beneath her," Lyra says, trying and failing to get the sarcasm out of her voice.

"She's not that bad," Axel says, and after seeing him with the gold vision, it's strange. Like the perfect skin is too much, too unreal. "I think she likes shopping, when she gets a chance."

"She's usually too busy for it," Alette says, though her eyes are still narrowed at Melekai. "When she was married to Tau Dev, when I was little, she would make fanciful dinners for us once a week. Spend all day in the kitchen."

"Huh," Lyra says, trying to fit the idea of Dr. Frisse cooking in her mind and failing. "Wouldn't have pegged her for that."

"Her cookies at Christmas are top." Axel says. "She claims she doesn't use magic for them, but she must. They're too good."

"She doesn't use magic, just shortening," Alette says, light. "Shortening and chai in the dough. Melekai," she starts, switching the topic and visibly steeling herself to talk to the demon, "what do you think of the sigil bonding method?"

Lyra blinks, then folds herself into one of the overpriced office chairs, tucking her legs beneath her without pain. It's cozy, it's comfortable, and she wishes she could sit like this forever.

Without the looming edge of doom, the seats are almost decadent.

Melekai drifts closer to her, like he's unaware he's doing so. "It would take far more power than you three have," he says, and Lyra gets the distinct feeling she's not included in that number. Like she can read bits of his mind, after the night before. "I've seen it before, but rarely."

Alette worries her bottom lip for a few seconds, weighing her words. "How much would be needed?"

"I've seen it with a group of twenty," he replies, easy. "It locked a demon for fifteen minutes."

"So that's not great," Axel says, propping his feet up on the table. The table that still bore the magical remnants of Alette's death. That probably would, for the rest of Lyra's life. "Lyra, get anywhere with the rope and bondage method?"

She flushes. "I got the concept."

"Cool," Axel says, oblivious to Alette's single raising eyebrow. "How long did you last?"

Melekai and Lyra glance at each other, and her face warms even more.

"Thirty-eight minutes, twenty seconds," Melekai says casually. "Or twenty-three, if you take out how long it took to tie."

That's a lot more precise than Lyra would say, so she just nods.

"Did it work?" Alette asks, and her tone is odd, just ever so slightly, as she regards both of them. "Lyra, could you control him?"

"Yeah, I think so," she says, and her voice is small, like she could barely squeak out an answer. Which is bullshit, she's a grown woman with a private life, but this is the most embarrassed she has felt in years.

"Yes," Melekai interrupts. "I didn't resist too hard, and her orders were vaguely worded, but they held true."

She eyes him, at that, as if she could intuit what orders he tried to resist.

"Classic mistake," Axel says, from where he's leaning so far back, she briefly worries he'll tip the chair. "Always use language that a lawyer couldn't get out of."

"I'll ask Jackson, next time," Lyra says, still blushing. "I, uh, didn't expect it to work so I didn't think anything would happen, so I didn't plan ahead."

"Well, you're lucky you have Melekai to attempt with," Alette says, and Lyra blushes further. "Any other demon would probably eviscerate you for trying."

Melekai just nods, and the whole thing is just unfair. Just entirely unfair, that he's so unaffected when she's so brilliantly red in the face.

"I just asked him to take me to that clearing, and help me take down the death bubble," Lyra says, and this time he shoots her a deeply amused look. "So the area decomposes, that sort of thing."

"Creepy," Axel says, still staring up at the ceiling. "Wait, so Terese makes it so things stop decomposing?"

That, finally, sparks his attention enough that he moves his feet, stares at her.

"Uh, yeah, no bacteria or anything had moved in to start eating the dead, that sort of thing," Lyra says, and Melekai shifts even closer, resting a hand against her arm, like he's almost unaware he's doing so. "So it doesn't just...stay dead."

Alette finally blinks to her, to her red face, to Melekai standing too close. "I never thought of death that way."

"This could be...nifty for figuring out Terese's power," Axel says, still oblivious. "If we understand it, we can reverse it."

Melekai sets two fingers on her arm, like he's grounding himself.

"I doubt you can reverse anything with a demon," Alette says, and Melekai nods along, "but still, if she's stopping natural processes like decomposition, that's worthy to note."

The door opens, and Dr. Frisse strides in without even touching the grand doors, her arms laden with bags of food. With a flick of her head, they shut behind her with a nice and even click.

She doesn't even break stride at seeing Lyra sitting in the chair, and Lyra wonders what it would take to truly surprise her.

"This part of Canada has a truly appalling amount of actual bagels," she says, setting down the bags with surprisingly little pomp. "But that diner you liked Alette was open for takeout."

Alette smiles, actually smiles, and it's startling in comparison to how reserved she is the rest of the time.

She unpacks the bags, and an overwhelming amount of breakfast food comes out of them, all steaming warm, like they were prepared in the very building.

"Warming spell," Melekai murmurs to her.

Bacon, eggs, perfectly done toast, even fried rice, as well as a few dishes of spiced potatoes, a rolled flatbread, and a dizzying array of dips, all food that Lyra's never seen before.

"Ooh, did you get roti?" Axel asks, leaning over and grabbing one of the flatbreads. "Is there enough for all of us?"

"Of course," Dr. Frisse says, then her eyes land on Lyra, cutting through anything she may have thought she's hiding, and hands her a takeout container full of eggs benedict and an extra side of bacon. "Oh good, you slept with him. That will help things."

Axel's hand freezes, holding the flatbread halfway to his mouth, and Lyra's face blazes anew. She grabs the takeout container as if it will protect her.

Eyes wide behind the golden glasses, Alette turns to Lyra.

Melekai, however, narrows his eyes at Dr. Frisse, and fear punches through the embarrassment as he takes a step forward.

"Wait," Lyra says, and Melekai actually pauses. "What?"

Melekai turns to her, eyes regarding, before he actually stands back, leaning against the table near her instead.

"You clearly slept with him, it's all over you," Dr. Frisse says, then portions out some of the sauces with the flatbread and spiced potatoes, half for her and half for Alette, who takes the proffered food with a detached sense of shock. "That's good, that helps with loyalty."

"He's standing here," Lyra says.

"Clearly, you couldn't get here without him," she says, then hands Axel a container with mostly scrambled eggs, plus fried rice and extra flatbread. "What do you think of a modified sigil method?"

Nobody speaks, and Lyra just stares down at her food, eyes wide.

"He said that it won't work with less than twenty people," Alette says, quiet, "And then it'd only hold for a few minutes."

Dr. Frisse, who's clearly been up for hours and is completely unaffected, shrugs. "It's a starting point, we can work something out." She nods in Lyra's direction, like this is normal conversation and normal ways of speaking to people before they've eaten anything in the morning. "The coffee's still in my car, I'll be right back."

And she strides right out, like nothing ever happened, leaving the three of them holding plates of amazing smelling breakfast foods.

Before Lyra can figure out what to do or say, both Alette and Axel turn to look at her, and, thankfully, Melekai grins.

"What?" Lyra says, taken off guard, still not sure what to say. "I'm an adult."

Alette blinks at her, rapid, like she's trying to fit the picture she has of Lyra in her head with the person in front of her, and failing. "I don't want to know."

"I do," Axel says, finally taking a bite of the flatbread. "Like, what the fuck?"

"Axel," Alette hisses.

"What?" he says, casually dunking the flatbread in the sauces on Alette's plate. "That's at least something different. Never heard of that before."

"You clearly don't know demons, then," Melekai says, and instead of being mortified or horrified, he's amused. "You clearly don't have any idea of us."

Axel listens through the earpiece, and very clearly has a moment where his brain skips a beat, before he nods. "Fair point."

"Are you okay?" Alette asks, horridly earnest.

"Of course she's okay," Melekai bristles, and Alette quails.

"Yeah, I'm fine," Lyra says, though her face might never return to its normal color. "I'm an adult, it was sex, it's none of your business."

Melekai gives her a grin, and his dimple is deep.

To avoid looking at them, Lyra stares down at the eggs benedict and the bacon, and tries not to think about how Dr. Frisse knows her expensive breakfast order.

"Well, that's fair," Alette says, looking down at her own breakfast, full of foreign foods that Lyra's never seen before, and it's horrifically awkward. "I'd probably respond that way, too, if people were suddenly asking me about hooking up with...with anyone."

"No, you'd come gossip to me, like you've done since we were seventeen." Axel points at her with the flatbread, which just serves to make Alette blush. "Like that time you hooked up with that apprentice out of Brazil."

"Oh my god," Alette says, closing her eyes briefly, before opening them and determinedly starting to eat her breakfast. "You're the worst."

"Or that time you slept with that museum curator behind the ancient Egyptology display so you could see what was written there," Axel continues, and, thankfully, it's taking all the embarrassment from Lyra and placing it directly on Alette's shoulders. "You gossiped a lot about his—"

"Okay," Alette interrupts, but at least the attention is off of her.

"Point taken." Delicately, she rolls up one of the flatbreads, dunking it in one of the sauces.

And it descends to silence, as Lyra tries not to look at any of them even though she can tell that Melekai is smirking at her.

The breakfast is delicious, of course it is, and probably costs more than Lyra would ever pay for food, which dredges up another question.

"Do you two have any...actual jobs?" Lyra asks, after a few seconds of eating glorious eggs benedict and bacon done perfectly. "How do you pay rent?"

They both blink up at her.

"I mean, I definitely lost my job at Buggees," Lyra continues, which she'd prefer not to, but once she started speaking her mouth won't let her stop. "The entire place is trashed, and they don't know when they'll reopen."

Axel and Alette share a glance, and it's a glance that shows a lot of years of friendship, of knowing what to say to each other, and of knowing what not to say.

"When you get to a certain level of magical knowledge, people pay you to help them out with things," Alette says finally. "I haven't ever worked a normal job."

"If I need money, I just transform some paper and take it to the bank," Axel says with a shrug. "It beats having to talk to stuffy people about theory all day."

"Though you do that, too," Alette says, with only a hint of bite behind her voice. "You're just not as good at it as me."

"So no, you don't know anyone hiring," Lyra says, and Melekai all of a sudden directs all of his attention to her, and it's brilliant like a beam, cutting through her focus.

"Ready," he murmurs, and Alette and Axel look up, right as Dr. Frisse walks back in, effortlessly balancing a tray of coffees that definitely came from someplace way more expensive than Starbucks.

She hands Lyra a spiced hot coffee, and it's way better than anything Lyra's ever had and ages better than her cheap coffee at home, then a giant iced drink to Alette, and another hot drink to Axel.

"I'd offer you something, Demon, but for the life of me I couldn't find any knowledge about what your type would prefer for coffee," Dr. Frisse says, and it's almost, almost, a joke.

Melekai bares his teeth at her in response.

"So you've blown up a tree, you've managed to tame a demon, anything else?" Dr. Frisse says, casually drinking her own iced drink, like she didn't mortify Lyra the last time she walked in. "Have you ever brought back more than one person at a time?"

"No and I don't want to try," Lyra says, though Melekai tilts his head at her. "That feels like...too much."

"Four weeks ago you never even used your abilities to scan others," Dr. Frisse says. "I don't think it's much of a stretch to believe you could do more."

Melekai tilts his head, like he agrees with her but doesn't want to say it, which doesn't help things.

"Terese has been...showing up at my house," Lyra says, still looking down at her food to avoid anyone's eye contact. "Just outside, staring."

"Of course," Dr. Frisse says, nonplussed. "There's not exactly a plethora of necromancers known in the world—she probably thinks she can use you to rip whatever hole she's trying to rip and escape."

Dr. Frisse sits, prim, in one of the chairs, eyes intent on the space near to where Melekai stands, unfocused. "Demon," she starts, "I want to plan."

20

Dr. Frisse, Alette, and Melekai argue plans in such an obscure vocabulary that Lyra's head spins after too long, and she stops asking them to define words after the first thirty minutes.

They argue until the coffee goes cold, until the clock ticks over to roughly when Lyra would actually wake up after her night shift, and, somehow the tense muscle in the back of Melekai's shoulders unwinds during it, like this is actually productive. Like this is a conversation that settles something in him.

After a long bit where she could swear they were talking in more Latin than English, Axel catches her eye and scoots his fancy chair over to her.

Melekai briefly turns his head to glower at him, before being drawn back into the conversation.

"I had to give up my earpiece to Dr. Frisse," he says, leaning back in the chair. "I can barely keep up with Alette and Dr. Frisse when they're like this, not even taking into account missing a third of the conversation."

"I took German in my high school language class," Lyra says, waving her hand at the three, "not whatever this is."

Axel bounces his foot against the table, then narrows his eyes at Lyra. "Wanna go to the practice rooms and have you blow up some dummies?"

Melekai's attention immediately snaps over to them, like he was never paying any sort of mind to the conversation in front of him. Alette gasps at his movement.

"Uh," Lyra says, and all of a sudden everyone's attention is on her, "they're not alive or recently dead so probably not."

"Interesting facet of necromancy, if that's true," Dr. Frisse says, and her eyes are like a laser, cutting through whatever boredom-induced comfort that Lyra had developed. "We could bring in some animals, if you need to practice on something alive."

Her stomach turns, at that.

"Or more plants, we can grab some pots from the greenhouse," Alette says, which is monumentally better than imagining blowing up some animals, "but really, we should have an actual written plan with sigils before we just unleash Lyra to go blow up things, have an actual escape route—"

"Why would I be blowing up things?" Lyra asks, taken aback, because she had not caught that in the snippets of conversation. "I don't want to blow people up."

"You could," Melekai says, low. "You'd be able to."

"I don't..." she trails off, squeezing her eyes shut. "Okay. Fine, I'll blow up some potted plants."

Melekai drapes his hand on her shoulder, sending a thrill up her spine, but she doesn't exactly feel better, so she pushes herself up to follow Axel back down the hallway, and Melekai's eyes burn into the back of her skull the entire way.

She follows him down the stairs, deeper into the building (and closer to the mouse skeleton), until they come to a room with deeply padded walls and floors.

"Right, because this doesn't look creepy," Lyra says, staring at the easily three-inch-deep foam.

"You get blasted into the wall once because Alette miscalculated a rune, and you'd be happy for it," Axel says, light and breezy. "Stay here, I'm gonna go get some plants."

Thankfully, he leaves the door open as he disappears, leaving Lyra in the room alone.

It's...somehow worse than she thought it would be, and she carefully sits against the wall on the padded floor. The foam absorbs all sound, leaving her in a ghastly vacuum of noise.

Her mama used to say she'd get locked up someday, and Lyra always half believed her. Jackson used to whisper that he thought her mother had already been locked up once, though he wasn't sure if it was a psychiatric hospital or, you know, actual jail.

But still, she sits there, staring up at the ceiling.

There's a scorch scar near the top of the walls, like something caught fire but burned out before igniting the foam, and a deep groove along the opposite wall.

Like a war had been fought in these walls.

"Okay, here," Axel says, shoving the door a little more open with his hip, carrying two rather large potted plants as if they weigh nothing. "We have much more, but they're ingredients for things so I don't think they'd want you to blow them all up."

Lyra eyes them as he sets them down on the padded ground. They're healthy, with plenty of large green leaves and cheery colored pots. "They're okay with me hurting these ones?"

"More like they're cheap to rebuy at Lowes," Axel says, standing by and dusting off his hands. "Go ahead, give it a try, this room'll contain anything."

"Right, just go ahead and blow something up, that'll be great," Lyra says, before scooting so she sits next to the smaller of the two plants.

Without the bird to focus on, it's more difficult. Like her heart doesn't beat in time with whatever it is in the plant, with whatever systems and life it may have. It doesn't have blood, it doesn't have lungs, but...

But there's still something moving. Something so sluggish, she can barely feel it.

Axel is immediately more distracting, a bright brilliant body of blood and electricity and air moving back and forth, like all her attention just focuses on the nearest living creature before her...instead of this inert plant.

She definitely needs to take more biology classes.

"Are you scanning me?" Axel says, taking a step back towards the door. "Is that what that is?"

Lyra's eyes pop open. "Yeah," she says, scowling at the plant in front of her. "When I blew up the tree, I was concentrating on a bird."

"What about a bug?"

AFTER AXEL SPENDS an awkwardly long time hunting for a bug in the greenhouse, Lyra's left alone again, and the excitement and the happiness of the day before has waned substantially.

Without even a pop of displaced air, between one moment and the next, Melekai appears next to her, staring down at her seated against the wall.

Without any other reaction, just staring down at her, Lyra waves.

"Yes?" she says, feeling a little bit sour, when he still doesn't say anything.

His eyes narrow, but his head tilts up, and he folds himself to sit next to her again.

"You're unhappy about something," he says, with a downturn to his mouth. "I could feel it all the way from upstairs."

And that just feels loaded.

"I'm not exactly jiving with the plant," she says, gesturing at it still in its cheery pot. "And don't exactly know what I'm doing."

"And the little alchemist?" He leans against her, just enough that it's noticeable.

"He went to go look for a bug, to see if that'll help," she says, and the corner of his mouth twitches up into a smile at that. "What? Sorry I'm not some ultra-practiced magician who knows Latin and how to blow up Mr. Basil here."

"Do you want to leave?" he asks, and it's just enough of a question that it gives her pause. "We could leave. Go somewhere else, leave them behind, keep running."

"All the Latin talk that bad?" she asks, and he bares his teeth at her at that.

"I have no interest in forcing you to blow up plants," he says, loftily, and if she squints it might be a joke, "or any more danger."

"Right," she says, hanging her head, looking at her hands. "That."

It's quiet, for a few moments, in the room made out of foam. Not even the lights buzz or the air moves.

"She'd just find me again, wouldn't she?" Lyra says, thinking of the person in front of her house, of standing in the cold in misery.

"Most likely, but we could always run again," Melekai says, his attention settling on the plant in front of her with a scowl. "Just run for forever."

"Yeah, no," Lyra says, stretching out her legs, even though they still don't hurt. Idle motions and all that. "That sounds hellish."

"Just know, that's always available to you," he says, and his voice is low, but he's leaning so close to her that it doesn't matter. "We can always find someplace else."

A chill runs down her back, and his eyes reflect back at her.

"What...what do you want to do?" she asks. "You keep on offering that to me, what about you?"

He tilts his head back, his eyes tracking the scorch mark. "I want to kill her."

"Right," she says, hugging herself.

He glances back to her, face impassive, and it's so different than all the emotion from the night before that it is as if she dreamt it. As if it never happened.

Lyra swallows down something distinctly uncomfortable.

But then, something in his face softens, just a hint.

"You don't...quite understand the world of demons, not yet," he says, as if that helps anything, "but her trying to go after you"—he touches her arm, as light as a feather—"after I am already here with you, is unforgivable."

"Right," she says again.

This time, he looks at her. Really looks at her, his eyes narrowing. "You keep on saying that, and you're still distressed."

"And people keep on telling me I'm gonna have to blow someone up," she shoots back, then pinches her nose. "Sorry."

He's silent for a long moment, just sitting next to her. His arm is pressed against hers, his clothing against hers, skin warm where they touch.

"I can't tell, are you trying to make me feel better?" she asks, after the silence stretches on.

He nods, neutral, but the corners of his lips tug downwards.

Biting back her first instinct to snipe at him, to bristle, Lyra takes a deep breath in, then another. If he's trying, if he's actually trying and not just giving her words he hopes will work, then she owes him that, at the very least.

"Making me feel like a commodity will not make me feel better," she answers, and winces a bit at the honesty.

Giving words to stuff like that is...not something that just comes easily or naturally to someone like her. Not as a girl who watched her mother die, not as a woman who's avoided friendships and relationships and everything in between, and not as someone who had the need to fear built so deep within her from so, so young.

He's still, so still and inhuman. "Understood." She knows he breathes—he gasped for breath the night before—but right now she could swear the heart isn't even beating. "I was trying to show you that you're important. To me."

It's far more than he's said before, but still, she nods, less agreeing with him and more showing him that she heard him, so he wouldn't have to wait for her to say anything. So he wouldn't feel tension, or nervousness, or whatever the hell else it is that he feels.

In her silence, he picks up her hand, and starts to trace along her palm, and somehow, it helps.

"There's not much in this world that would make me go intentionally against another demon," he says, staring down at her hand, at whatever shining gold he sees. "I've seen too much of it to need land, or territory, or any regional power, and fights between demons are too...destructive...to engage in battle without reason." His finger skips along the skin on her palm, as if a stutter in his thoughts. "I want to for you."

"Is this you being sappy?" Lyra blurts out, and he cracks a smile at her awkwardness. "I mean—"

"Somewhat," he says, but his shoulders are lower, more relaxed. "This is me trying to get you to stop pouting because you're important and it's hard to concentrate when you're like this because all I want to do is make you stop being upset."

"Thanks," she says, and means it that time. "I guess...thanks."

She leans against him a bit more, and he sighs, a gentle release of breath. Her cheek meets his shoulder, and he leans his head against hers. Something between the constant contact he always has with her and the passion from the night before, something gentler.

"But I do want to kill her," he says, startling a laugh out of her, as the door opens and Axel strides in, carrying another few plants.

Axel freezes at her position, and she straightens.

Melekai nods at her, before he disappears. Like he really did just come find her just to cheer her up.

Axel blinks at her, owlish, before he sets down the potted plant. Some sort of miniature rosebush.

"This one had a marker saying that it had aphids," he says, unsteady. "I figured there'd be something on it."

"He went back to whatever meeting," Lyra says, somehow still knowing beyond a shadow of a doubt that he's still in the building.

"I'm not judging," he says, which is generally something that people say when they absolutely are judging. "I just know that Alette says he's very creepy-looking so I don't get it."

She's seen Melekai's true face now, and while creepy isn't the word she would use, unsettling kinda is, so instead, Lyra just closes her eyes, tilting her head back into the foam, and tries to feel the plant in front of her.

There're hundreds of little bugs, all little pinpricks of life, all over the inner stems of the plant, and even a few small dead ones, so tiny they hardly stir her stomach.

"Yeah, I think this'll work," Lyra says, because the rose plant is so thrumming with life that it stands out almost as much as Axel. "This one should have...definitely not been with any other plants."

"Cool," Axel says, and breaks off a branch and puts it with the basil. A few bright bugs climb onto its wide leaves. "So we can duplicate."

Lyra feels a lot less bad about possibly killing some aphids versus killing a bird.

"Am I supposed to kill the plant or the bugs?" she asks, opening her eyes to look up at Axel, who stands as far away as possible in the foam room.

"Try with the bugs," he says, examining his own hand. "If you can bring things to life, you can take it away."

"People keep on saying that," she replies.

The dead bugs at the base of the plant tug her closer, but she shuts them out, looking towards one of the crawling ones on an outer leaf. It's a white dot against the dark green.

Focusing on something so tiny is almost difficult, and her eyes cross with the effort. It's surprisingly spherical, with spindly legs so small they're invisible to her eye, but with concentration she can get a feather light sensation that it's crawling, jittering over the leaf. Its eyes don't see well, not like she does, and it's dizzying with the lack of focus.

She can't tell if it actually has blood, or just a fluid, but something beats from its mouth to its stomach, turning the plant sap into something it can use, and she should really take some more biology classes. Maybe a class on bugs, if the community college up here could do that.

Tentatively, she touches her finger to the leaf, and the bug skitters around, but she holds still, still enough that it pokes back into the leaf with its mouth-thing, and she can rest the very edge of her fingertip against it.

"A cockroach might've been easier," she says idly, but still staring at the tiny white dot on the leaf. "They at least have blood."

"Do...do aphids not have blood?" Axel asks, and even without looking she can tell he's aghast.

"I can't tell, it's too tiny."

"Wait, is all your stuff around blood? That's..."

She closes her eyes, as if that could block out Axel's voice, and imagines the bug...stopping. Whatever liquid is inside of it to freeze into place, for the little pumping heart to stop moving it, for the muscles inside its dorsal to wither up.

Even though it's so small she cannot physically feel it, it flares bright against her awareness, with a gut punch of immediate death. Leaves rustle in the foam room, like the plants sensed it as well.

She blinks her eyes open, and the tiny white dot is still.

Half the leaves to the miniature rosebush lay crinkled up and dead on the ground.

She ventures a glance up at Axel, whose eyebrows are so raised they're practically disappearing into his hairline. "I killed the bug."

"So creepy," he says, and she can't really blame him.

There's a shift of air, and Melekai's standing beside the plant.

He gives her a quick up and down, with a raised eyebrow, before vanishing again.

Some sort of little check in.

Somehow, whatever it is that crinkled up the rose leaves, left all of the other aphids alive, with just the new dead one bright against her awareness.

So she picks up one of the leaves, and a chunk of it crumples in her hand, as if it's been decaying for some time.

With the bright little spot of death, from the aphid, she imagines it like the rope she brought with Melekai, and...tries to push it into the leaf in her hand.

It's hard, it's not coursing with sap or liquid, and grows warm against her fingertips, but eventually, it flattens back out. The waxy sheen comes back, the serrations popping up, and the color smooths from brown back to green.

The chunk that crumpled away still remains dead, on the ground, and the remaining leaf has a cutout of that area, so clean and perfect it's like someone cut it out with an Exact-o knife.

Axel takes another step back, and he has literally seen her raise a person from the dead and explode a tree, and yet this is somehow worse for him.

"Probably useful, still weird," Axel says, sitting down on the opposite side of the room, but off to the side. Like he doesn't want to be caught in any blast radius, like it's some sort of strange calculus he's used to making around magic. "Are you still good on energy?"

She is, somehow, so she nods.

"Then let's try a few more things."

AFTER A FEW MORE GRATEFULLY UNEXPLODED plants and a few more dead aphids, Melekai appears in front of her again with a meticulously arched eyebrow.

"The Doctor is sending Alette here to come get you," he says, instead of any sort of greeting, then smiles, wicked and sharp. "Bring a plant, I want to scare her."

"Why?" Lyra asks, standing up and dusting herself off. There's a fair amount of plant dirt and matter on her hands, and she feels as if she just went on a long walk over mildly challenging terrain.

"Why what?" Axel asks, also scrambling to his feet, and Lyra just jerks her thumb at Melekai.

"She's being dismissive of you, and I want to wipe that smile right off her face," Melekai says, and there's a snarl underneath his words, buried beneath the sharp grin. "As if you didn't raise her own niece from the dead."

There's a polite knock on the door, and Melekai just raises the eyebrow at the remaining plant with aphids, before vanishing again.

"What did he want?" Axel asks, though his tone is forced, like he's trying to be casual instead of panicking, but she appreciates the effort. He twists the door open, letting Alette in.

"Just to say hi," Lyra lies.

L<small>YRA MAKES</small> Axel carry the basil plant with roughly twenty aphids on it up the stairs, back to the grand ballroom and the giant mahogany table that still feels slightly of death, despite Alette being almost bouncy and her hand now in a slim brace that she—or someone, but Lyra has her money on Alette herself—decorated in swirling gold runes.

Dr. Frisse watches Lyra like a hawk, and Lyra feels an irrational rush of gratefulness for Melekai's warning. Like, she could deal with her, as long as she had that little bit to mentally prep.

Melekai gives her a private smile, dark, before he drifts over to her, a hand trailing up her arm. It's deliberate, somehow, much less unconscious than it usually is.

Alette shudders, as if her skin is crawling from the touch on Lyra's arm.

"Blow it up," he whispers to her, so quiet it's almost a breath.

And after all the careful isolation of each tiny bug for the last hour or so, that sounds really good. Really fucking good. Like being able to yell after being forced to whisper.

And she wouldn't necessarily have to focus on killing the bugs. Just…taking the pitcher that is her power and dumping it in the area, instead of using an eyedropper to parcel it out, bit by bit.

"How'd practice go?" Dr. Frisse asks, almost flippant. But it's not directed to Lyra, not at all.

She's expecting a report. It chills Lyra's blood, just a bit.

"Good, she killed some bugs and brought back leaves," Axel says, and he slouches into a chair. "Really cool the first time, really odd the second few times, perfectly boring after that." He winks at Lyra, though, as if to show she shouldn't take his words to heart. "Just like all practice should be, hardly any explosions."

That little bit he tossed at Alette, who actually rolls her eyes. "I haven't exploded anything in ages," she says to Lyra, as if she has to convince Lyra of her abilities, "he just won't let it go."

"Ah, well," Lyra says, because explosions aren't something she really knows how to respond to there. "Do you want to see something impressive?"

Dr. Frisse stills, and she can't tell if it's from surprise or what. "Yes."

"Alright," she says, still feeling mulish over the casual reveal that she slept with Melekai, and the casual reporting, and she grabs a leaf of the basil plant, where a cluster of aphids have tentatively climbed up.

They squirm against her hand, barely large enough to feel, and Lyra...pours.

Imagines the gut punch inside of her, imagines whatever gold spark Melekai sees, imagines all of that.

The leaf shreds itself in her hand, the pliable stems of the plant detonating, sending shards out.

This time, with her eyes open, she gets to see it.

The porcelain pot it's in crumbles away from the plant, spraying the dirt everywhere across the table. The leaves fly apart, ripping from the stem as if from a gale force wind.

All at once, all the aphids on the leaves die, with bright pinpricks of light.

And there, right there, Lyra has a choice.

With the bright little punches of death, she could take them, she could use them. Add them to whatever little bit of power she has and magnify it by hundreds.

Coat the entire area in death. Like a wave.

She hesitates, just a moment, then cuts off the power, shaking the basil shards out of her hands.

The room is quiet around her and smelling vaguely of Italian seasoning.

Axel and Alette stand back, their eyebrows raised, and Melekai's grinning, sharp.

"So you do have some spite in you," Dr. Frisse says, and she doesn't look at all unsettled. Like she expected it. "Interesting."

Lyra almost wobbles on her feet, but squares up, resting a palm on the mahogany table instead.

21

W hen Melekai takes her home, Terese is still standing
outside the house, despite hours and hours and a fair
amount of snow falling around her.

"Do you think she felt me doing...whatever that was?" Lyra asks,
staring out at the rapidly setting sun and the demon in front of her.

"Probably," Melekai says, languid, and he doesn't even look out
the window towards the obvious threat in her yard.

The cat immediately jumps from the green monstrosity chair and
rubs against Lyra's legs, purring, and it's rather nice to have an actually enthusiastic animal to greet her after coming home.

She's really going to have to get a job to come home from. Or
something.

"You could've done much more," Melekai mentions, as Lyra
twitches her curtains closed, eliminating the view of Terese. "I felt it."

Figures that he would.

"All the bugs died at once," she says, sitting on the chair and
getting rewarded by a lapful of cat. "I could've maybe taken them
and...used it?"

"You could've," he says. He's watching her, his eyes reflecting
back, but he's obviously thinking of something else. "Frisse said

something today, let something slip. She thinks, but she won't outright say, that Terese the human and Terese the demon knew each other before whatever happened."

Lyra resists the temptation to look out the window again.

"And some of her powers seem to be less...demon, and more of a demon accentuating natural human powers," he continues, and he's leading towards something, Lyra can tell, but it's ever so slightly out of her grasp.

"So there's more she's not telling us," Lyra supplies, and Melekai nods, perching himself on her table so he can be close. "I don't like that."

"She let a lot more through her filter today," he says, draping a hand against her arm, and after the night before she flushes. "I don't know if speaking to her puts you in more danger, or if the information she presents is more useful."

She hears the tentative nature in that.

"I think Axel and Alette are good," she says, then hesitates again. "What I did to the plant, how different did that look to the death bubble?"

He stills, and stares. Like her sentence needs time to compute through his brain.

Lyra sits back at that, lets him, and pets the cat purring in her lap, checking her cracked phone.

He flickers away, between one breath and the other, and somehow, she knows he just went to check.

Because in her hands, it felt like the death bubble, and she doesn't want any part of that.

Her hands still smell of basil.

Her phone dings.

ALETTE (5:38 PM): Can we do brunch tomorrow? I have a question.

Lyra raises an eyebrow. They spent all day together, and now this.

LYRA (5:39 PM): Sure?

It's not like she has work tomorrow.

ALETTE (5:40 PM): I noticed something that I don't want to talk about with everyone else.

LYRA (5:40 PM): Ominous, but okay.

Melekai flickers back to sitting on the table. "No, but I see your point," he says, without preamble. "There's some fuckery happening."

It's such a modern usage of the word that she smiles at him, and, almost startled, he smiles back, before disappearing once more.

HE DOESN'T SHOW up for the rest of the night, but he's in her front room when she putters out of bed, her sleep schedule all messed up.

There's no sign of Terese outside her window, but still, Melekai has the curtains open and is staring.

He's unmoving, so she just sidesteps him to feed the cat, who ignores her for staring out the window as well.

"Is it something I can't see?" she asks, and he turns towards her, keeping his gaze out the window.

"She just left," he says, and his voice is deeply, deeply suspicious, "and I don't know why."

"Great," Lyra says, staring at the coffee machine, trying to figure out if it'd be better to make her own or let Alette buy her some at the brunch place. The brunch place would absolutely have better coffee, but it's still a 20-minute walk. "Is it safe for me to walk to brunch?" she asks, only half expecting an answer.

"I can take you," he says, distracted, which isn't an answer.

HE ENDS UP STANDING, half distracted, with her as she waits for Alette in the warm foyer of the brunch place. Their little diner is now completely bedecked out for Christmas, with tinsel and glass balls and twinkling lights everywhere. Melekai pokes at one of the many tiny plastic Christmas trees with a sort of idle curiosity, of course not impacting it at all.

He's far more flighty than usual, like his eyes are tracking things she cannot see, and he's not twitchy, per se, but it's a close deal.

Alette comes bursting in the two doors with a whirl of wind, snowmelt clinging to her boots, and though her eyes flicker to Melekai, she doesn't look as frightened, just...frustrated.

"Thank you," she says, ever polite, shedding her tailored jacket and wincing as it tugs against her brace, such a small movement that she probably doesn't even realize she's doing it. "I'm glad you're here, too." It's formal, and definitely directed towards Melekai.

With a quick nod, as if assuring herself that Lyra is, in fact, here and going to follow her, she strides to the same table they sat last time, tapping the same place she sketched out the runes before, and the same buffer of silence falls over the table.

"Nicely done," Melekai says, his long fingers tracing over the invisible marks. His eyes unfocus again, like he's only half paying attention.

"Thanks," Alette says, still on edge, and Lyra raises an eyebrow at her, but she says nothing else until after the waitress has taken their order. "Look, can you or your brother see...other things?"

That gets Melekai's attention, and Alette doesn't wilt under it.

"Uh, what?" Lyra asks, none too smartly.

"Other things. Other, non-demon things, that are like demons but obviously not." She lays her unbroken hand on her needle case, a restless drum of fingers. "I swear that some of them are following me."

"How can you tell they're not demon?" Melekai asks, lips curving up into a smile, like this is delightful.

Alette opens her mouth to answer, then hesitates, "They aren't as terrifying as you," she says, like she's going to actually offend Melekai and not just amuse him. "But they're still...off, and no one else can see them."

And Lyra's seen a lot of strange people in her life and has no idea how she would even remotely be able to tell them apart without the eye glow thing that Melekai does. "Off how?"

Alette shifts, then rests her hand on the needle case again, as if to comfort herself. "Like they have a stirring of power around them," she says, unwillingly, like it's being pulled out of her. "Like the world is a sea of currents and winds, and they are an unmoving post. It all parts around them."

It's poetic, but it also makes no goddamn sense.

"I made eye contact with one of them, and now he keeps on showing up outside the headquarters, and chatting at me," Alette says, and she's looking out the window, as if she's afraid of being followed. "And another showed up at the library, and was just...asking questions, and poking at my hand." She lifts her unbroken hand, as if to show them something different. "I feel like I'm going crazy."

Lyra doesn't have another word for it, so she shrugs.

"Well," Melekai drawls, "sounds like you discovered Wights."

"I've never seen those," Lyra says. "Probably."

"You have," Melekai says, with complete and utter confidence. "You just didn't notice the magic around them."

Alette looks like she's about to vibrate out of her seat with tension, and when the waitress drops off the food and coffee, she doesn't even look at it. "But what are they?"

Lyra immediately dumps sugar into her coffee.

Melekai touches Lyra's elbow, and it's so slight she doesn't even know if he knows he's doing it. "Halfway between a human and a demon," he says with a shrug, "obsessed with territory, obsessed with keeping magic flowing in the proper directions, mostly harmless. To me."

"And I've seen them?" Lyra asks, and even if Alette isn't eating, she's going to. "And just...not known?"

"At least two would stop by your work, their markings were everywhere," Melekai says with a shrug. "They get lonely, probably just spoke to you out of curiosity. They wouldn't have harmed you, I could blow them out of the water without a thought and they would know it."

All of the strange people who would sometimes pass through the store multiple times without actually buying anything flashed through Lyra's mind, but she wouldn't be able to pick out which one would be different from a normal human if you put a gun to her.

Alette takes a steadying breath, then another, then another when those didn't work. "How many other types of...beings are there?" Her voice is strained.

"Many," he says, and touches Lyra's arm again, where she had stopped eating, as if to remind her. "Most do not interact with your world, you don't need to worry about them."

"But I can see them now," Alette says, and her voice tilts upwards at the end of the sentence. "I think I need to worry."

Melekai just shrugs, which isn't helpful.

Alette takes another deep breath, then pulls a notepad and fancy fountain pen out of her bag. Gold swirls in the body of the pen, flakes and flecks and it's probably worth more than Lyra's entire house and anything that's ever been in her bank account.

"I want a list," she says, uncapping the pen. The nib gleams gold, with a few drops of blue ink on it. "With comprehensive knowledge on what each type can do and how I should be aware of them."

"Has Jackson seen any?" Lyra asks, curious. "He never told me."

"Probably," Melekai says, still unconcerned that he just told a scholar about an entirely new world and source of magic, "unless he's developed any magical sense to him—which I doubt—he probably just thought they were normal people."

Alette looks like she's about to die of curiosity, still holding her pen.

Lyra nudges Melekai, just a little.

"That'd be like asking yourself how many types of animals there are," Melekai says. "It's not useful to list them all out. Keep your own notes and I can tell you what they are."

That, at least, seems to be actionable data for Alette, who caps the pen back on.

"Will they hurt me?" she asks, finally.

"Probably not," Melekai says, and he's back to being flighty, back to looking like nothing can keep his attention. Like he keeps on expecting Terese to pop out at any moment. "Probably not more than any normal human could—I haven't exactly studied their effects on actual humans—carry a gun if you're concerned"

"That is...astoundingly not helpful," Alette says, and she's blinking so rapidly that Lyra gets a smidgen afraid that she's going to cry. "You're telling me there's no literature, there's no lore, there's nothing?"

Melekai throws a look at Lyra, like he's hoping she'll rescue him, so she takes an obnoxiously large bite of eggs.

"They might have some," he says, instead, with another bewildered shrug. "Ask one of the ones hanging out."

This time, Alette gives Lyra a look, like she wants her to still play translator, as if she could make sense of it.

And Lyra sighs, casting around to change the subject. "It's...necromancy's a lot easier than I thought it would be," Lyra says, poking at her egg dish, aware that Melekai is watching her with eagle eyes. "It's a lot less foreboding than I thought it would be."

"With the note that so little is known about necromancy, I'm not entirely surprised," Alette says, though her voice is still strained. "Often, when magicians are found late in life, there is a steep growth in their powers."

"That makes the opposite of sense," Lyra says, sitting back, "muscles decay. Things atrophy. I should...if it's like I've never walked before, wouldn't baby steps be more reasonable?"

Melekai scoffs, but says nothing, though both Lyra and Alette look at him.

"Think of it more like a battery, one with a capacity we have no idea about," Alette says, then her face twists. "Axel is far better at explaining it than I, but if you've been building up charge for a while, then you have more power to use, and some batteries, simply by using them, you can increase the capacity faster and longer really quickly, until you figure out the limits."

"I don't think batteries work like that," Lyra says.

"I don't know, Axel's the one that actually knows computers, not me," Alette grumbles. "I make him set up all my laptops. But," she pushes onwards, "magicians who start later in life sometimes find themselves growing at a rapid rate, before finding an equilibrium."

"So I'm normal?" Lyra asks.

"Normal enough to be within the statistical mean." Alette smiles, and it's just as prim and proper as most of her smiles. "It might seem like you're racing past, but it's only because we don't know the applicable milestones for necromancy. It would be great"—here she swings all her attention to Melekai, who's almost startled by it—"if we knew someone who had primary sources."

"Primary sources on necromancy don't exist," he says, smooth.

"Secondary, then?" Alette gives him a smile, and this one has nothing proper about it. "You're a demon, you've experienced other necromancers, you could always tell us."

"For research sake," Lyra chimes in.

"Exactly. For research sake," Alette finishes, and it's more blood-thirsty than Lyra's ever seen her.

Melekai shoots Lyra a wounded look, like she's the one that put him in this position, but she just bats her eyes at him instead.

"When we have time," he starts, and Alette grins, "when we have time, I'll see what I could...tell you?" He waves his hand, and it's only through their years together that Lyra can tell he's actually uncomfortable. "When I don't have to think about defeating another demon?"

With a sigh, Melekai stands, pushes himself up, then disappears.

Alette flinches back.

"He does that," Lyra says. "I think he didn't know how to answer your question and felt awkward."

"He's a demon," Alette breathes, "why the hell would he feel awkward about questions?"

And that is a question and a half, so Lyra just shrugs, and, tentatively, Alette picks up her fork.

"Seriously, though, am I in danger?" Alette whispers, despite the silence charm she has in place, like someone will overhear them. "One followed me all the way from Headquarters to the grocery store. I was driving, and it just...kept up with the car."

"Did they say anything?" Lyra asks.

"He was talking the entire time," Alette replies, tucking her long hair behind her ears and starting to pick at her bowl of fruit. "About nonsense, asking me about why I go in there, asking me why I can see him, all of that. I just...pretended he didn't exist."

The thought of prim and proper Alette studiously ignoring a magical being is...rather amusing, but Lyra knows better than to ever suggest that aloud.

"I thought it might be a subsect of demons, and that I might be in danger, or you would be, or they were pawns of Terese, or something. Some didn't even speak a language I've ever heard of, and I've heard...most of them."

"And probably fluent in a few?" Lyra asks, teasing.

"Only a few," Alette brushes off, then rubs her forehead. "I can't tell Dr. Frisse, not until I know more."

Lyra hears the request in that, so she nods, eating more of her eggs. "I'll see if I can get more information from him," she promises. "He might be better when he's not put on the spot."

"If the writings and lore are even in a language I can understand," Alette says, verging on despairing. "I don't have time to learn another language right now, I'm just trying to find established lore on binding demons—" she shuts up, abruptly, with a guilty look to Lyra.

"I already knew that," Lyra reminds her. "I did manage to control Mel for a bit."

Alette takes that in, absorbs it, like it's a bit of knowledge to be broken down and dissected. "Is that what led to you..." she trails off.

She's not wrong, but it feels misleading.

"Not really," Lyra fibs. "That was after."

Alette blinks at her, rapidly, then just goes back to her fruit bowl.

"I don't know how Dr. Frisse could tell," Lyra says, because once she started talking it seems like she can't stop, "I mean, I wasn't exactly going to...tell anyone."

"Sleeping with demons has a long history," Alette says, as if that makes it better. "Especially in antiquity. People would do it all the time before making deals for the battlefield. Some sort of...ancient magic sealing the bond or something."

Or, rather, Lyra suspects it's mostly that the demons wanted the touch. Wanted the sensation.

But that seems a bit too private to share.

"Well we didn't make any new ones," she says, "so unless it's the old 'he can stop by and take bits of me' one, I see no difference."

"You should...still probably be careful," Alette says. "Demons are not known for responding to things with subtlety or emotional depth."

"That sounds about right," Lyra says. "I thought he was gonna kill Axel that time."

"I forgot about that," Alette says, which is understandable because she had other things on her mind that day, like being dead for fourteen hours. "Is he just...hanging around now?"

"Mostly?" Lyra says, and there's something strange unwinding in herself, at just sitting and chatting with someone. "I'm not sure if it's because of Terese, or protecting me, or—"

"Or because he slept with you?" Alette asks, almost coy. "That might have more to do with his reasoning than anything else."

"That's recent," Lyra points out.

WHEN THEY BUNDLE up and leave the restaurant, Melekai's waiting a few steps away, close to a completely non-descript car.

Next to him is a tall man, with black curly hair shorn short and the most brilliant blue eyes Lyra's ever seen, leaning casually against the car, and Alette stops.

"Found your Wight," Melekai says, jerking his thumb.

The man—Wight?—nods at Lyra. It's not a friendly nod, but there's no immediate animosity.

He's almost familiar, like he buzzes along the edges of her memory, like he's stopped by the Buggees several times but not enough times that she knows his name.

"He won't hurt anyone," Melekai says, languid, and the man scoffs. "He controls the territory, wouldn't want anything to disrupt that."

Alette looks pale, but also like she very much wants a knife. "Please don't follow me," she blurts out, then turns to Melekai. "What do you mean, territories?"

Melekai and the man exchange a glance, before Melekai reaches a hand out to Lyra and—

And in the blink of her eyes, they're back in her home.

"Did you just..." Lyra trails off, getting her feet underneath herself and shedding her jacket.

"She'll be fine, the Wight is just curious," Melekai says, a hand on the small of her back as she undoes her snowshoes, a steadying force. "He keeps track of anyone going in and out, keeps track if anyone does any disruptive magic, tries to ruin anything."

"So did he know about Terese?" Lyra asks, tugging on the laces with more force than necessary.

He bares his teeth at her in a grin. "More than you think."

"Huh," Lyra supplies, intelligently, pulling out her phone.

LYRA (11:23 AM): Ask him about Terese.

"I doubt he'll say anything without proper...motive," Melekai says, and his hand stays on the small of her back as she straightens, and a thrill goes down her spine. "He doesn't want to cross a demon. That includes me, but also includes her."

ALETTE (11:23 AM): Why did you leave??????

Melekai smiles down at her, as if daring to see what she'll say.

LYRA (11:24 AM): I didn't mean to.

Then, almost tentative, Melekai pulls her close to him, half in a hug and half in a captive embrace. Like he's unsure of the motions, of how to hold her against him. Like he's never just hugged someone before, never let himself have that comfort.

Lyra stills, stills her instinct to squirm away, waits. Sees what he's doing.

Careful, he presses his lips against her wavy brown-black hair, and it's a quiet moment. Almost peaceful, but for the whir of her lights and the purr of her cat in the other room.

She lets her eyes flutter shut.

"You don't have to worry about any Wight hurting you," he says. "That one...assured me that everyone knows you are off limits."

The words seem heavy. Weighted. Like she's leaning through a wispy curtain to grasp the meaning.

One of these days, they are probably going to have to talk about all the weirdness between the two of them, but for now, Lyra just rests her head against his chest and lets herself be held.

22

Two days later, he takes her to practice controlling him again, takes her out into the woods, somewhere completely unfamiliar.

This time, before he even says anything, she closes her eyes, and thinks. Feels.

There's a dead animal, some sort of racoon, a little bit away, so she lets herself drift over towards it, letting the pull of death guide her way. Melekai follows, and the only sound is the crunch of their footsteps on the slushy snow.

There's not much left of it. Something ate most of its innards, leaving bones and stringy fur underneath the coating of snow and ice, and its blood has frozen in its veins, but there's still the stirring in the back of her stomach.

If she brought it back, it wouldn't live too long. Moments, maybe, before it dies all over again, from its lack of guts and from the ice and from the broken shards of bones and from the decay eating at its brain.

It gives her the same pull as the centuries-old graveyard.

Without even saying a word, Melekai holds out his wrist to her again, veins pale against his skin, rope bracelets still in place.

"Right," Lyra says.

It's substantially more difficult, without seeing the literal gold thread, but she stoops to touch the tips of her fingers to the bare edge of the racoon's fur and tries to visualize it anyways. Instead of pushing life back in, she...pulls it back out. Coils it in her hand.

It's colder than before. Less of it, like the snow and the ice leeched parts of it away.

Watching her, intent, Melekai nods.

She steps close to him, with whatever life essence of the racoon chill in her hand, and he doesn't look away.

"Tell me how to do it better this time," she says, still holding the coil. "You said it was sloppy."

"Next time, try to pull it from as close to the wound that caused the death as possible," he says, his eyes alight. "Newer death would be better, but this...this isn't bad."

He withdraws his wrist, mimes pouring the string between his two hands, and she copies the motion.

The icy coils pour from hand to hand, like a chain of a necklace, warming slightly.

"For most, they will have done study down to incredible details. For you, you're probably going to have to focus on intention. What do you want this to do, and how can you personally guide it?" he says, wrapping his hand underneath hers that holds the strange rope of power. "It takes years of study for some of this, I doubt you have that before you'll need that."

"Right, intent," she says, staring down at her hand. To her, it's empty, but she feels the weight of it in her palm.

"So focus on what your intent is for right now," he says, like that's not a loaded statement, because what the hell does she want? "Focus on that before tying any part of you to any demon."

"Would that work on Alette's Wights?" Lyra jokes, feeling for the edges of the rope.

This one is less like twine and more like cord, like the length of the death tightened it up.

He tilts his head, his curls falling to one side. "Probably, but I would advise against it," he says, light. "They get territorial and that would give them mixed signals."

"Is the territorial like your investment?" she asks and gets a bared-teeth grin in return. "Or would this work on any non-regular human creature?"

"In theory," he says with a shrug. "Only ever seen it applied to demons."

The conversation naturally drifts off, as she feels the cord in her hand, as she focuses on what her intent could be.

For this, for this it would just be making Melekai listen to her commands, like the practice. Bend him to her will, however strange it may be.

For Terese, it'd probably be something to stop her, stop her cold. Prevent her from moving, from using any powers, from doing a single thing without Lyra allowing it.

Long enough for whomever to pour enough power in her to...permanently stop her.

She swallows, and Melekai rubs his thumb along the back of her hand.

"Whatever you're thinking, this is just a practice," he says, and his voice is almost embarrassingly gentle with her. "Go easy, even if it's ridiculous."

Ridiculous.

"Can I impose the time limit this time?" she asks, as a slight breeze stirs through their wooded spot.

"You can always just untie it," he replies.

She exhales, and her breath puffs up in the air around her.

Intent.

Quick as she can tie something without actually seeing it, she ties the cord around his wrist, imagining him being without any sort of powers until it comes off. Just like she would with Terese, if the time comes.

See if she could stop that.

Immediately, he jerks his wrist back, then raises an eyebrow at her.

"Really?" he asks, voice heavily skeptical. "We're in the middle of a snowy forest—you don't want me to take us back to the comfort of your house?"

She shifts in her snow boots. "I'll take it off when we get cold?"

His mouth does a thing, like he can't decide whether to scowl at her or to grin.

"We could walk?" Lyra says, at the wooded area around them, at the pristine and untouched snow. "To see if it comes loose at all."

"Is that how you're planning on taking down Terese?" he asks, examining his wrist, at the thing she cannot see. "Stop her from doing anything?"

"Seems like a good idea." Lyra shrugs, and the air is rather cool on her heated cheeks. "Better than letting her kill or anything."

He considers that for a moment, then reaches for her again, tugging on the edge of her snow jacket, pulling her in.

She lets him, and he wraps his arms around her, a better hug this time.

"See, I would've suggested tossing me out of the body, make me go take a different one," he says, and even though he's just in the one shirt and jeans his skin is warmer than hers. "That'd be a bit more tricky, but probably more useful."

"I like this body," she blurts out, then flushes deeper against his chest.

His laugh rumbles through his chest, and it's almost nice, before he pulls away, looking around the forest. "You want to walk? There's a trail about a hundred yards away."

It's a bit more difficult of a walk than she anticipated, with the knee-deep snow, but he just keeps on next to her, examining every bit of landscape like it might bite him.

Once they're on the trail, he breathes a sigh of relief, then eyes her. "This is more disorienting than I thought," he says, but the scowl doesn't seem real. Like there's actual glee, tugging behind his features.

"Describe it to me," she says, pulling him over to a cleared off bench, sitting and stretching her legs out.

"You didn't order me to follow directions this time," he says, and it's almost flirty. "It's like...having a thin scarf pulled over your eyes. You can still see through it, but everything's a little fuzzy. Like details are missing."

She studies him, but he's looking around, at the snow laden trees, at the thankfully blue sky above. The light illuminates his golden-brown curls, the slight scruff still on his cheeks.

"Do you still see all the gold?" she asks, looking at her still normal hand.

"Not as much," he says, then, almost compulsively, grabs her hand. "Even your hand feels different, less like a brand, more like..." His lips turn downward again, like he's trying to pick words to describe something and finding them wanting. "You're still warm, you're still vivid, but you're not...glowing."

"So I look like a person," she says, mostly joking, but he nods, eyes shrewd. "So doing this also took away how you see. Just leaving the human body?"

His eyebrows raise, and he looks around again, like the world is dawning anew for him.

"So the body might just be short-sighted," she says, trying and failing to stop from smiling in amusement. "That might be the blurry details."

He swipes his thumb against the palm of her hand, then, gentle, like he's telegraphing his motion, puts his other hand behind her head, tangling it in her hair. His lips part, like the world is something strange, something different.

"Even your hair feels different," he says, whispering like someone would overhear them, "is softer."

His eyes flicker down to her lips, and her heart gives a thump.

"You kissed me before," she says, half scared and half emboldened. "Do you want to see how that is now?"

He hesitates for a split second, then crushes his lips against hers.

Gone is the tentativeness, gone is the slow exploring of her, instead he presses kisses to her like a man dying, like she would be taken away from him at any time.

His lips are cold in the air, and he pulls her closer with the hand in her hair.

She rests her hand on his thigh, leaning up more into him, and he makes a startled sound in the back of his throat, breaking the kiss.

"This is massively different," he says, lips still so close to hers that they touch. "Like night and day." He smiles, like she's something worthy of discovering.

"See, that's actually interesting," she says back, and gets rewarded with another smile. "Just how differently you process the world." She sounds like Alette, all scholarly.

His eyes fall over her, like he's seeing her for the first time. "I think you're beautiful," he says, and he's almost tentative, "like this, even without all of everything else."

She kisses him again, and he reacts like he could stay there and kiss her all day and not think for a single moment of anything else. Like all that matters to him is where they touch, out here in the snow, and how he could continue enjoying those small delicacies.

It's intoxicating. Even without any demon powers or pleasures, her heart pounds and her blood thrills and her stomach tightens.

He pushes her hair back behind her ear, and, suddenly, shivers once.

"Wait, are you cold?" Lyra asks, pulling back herself. "Are you actually cold?"

He examines himself with detached wonder, at the goosebumps rising on his skin, before looking back to her.

"Scan me," he says eagerly. "What can you tell, what can you do?"

It's a bit strange to go from kissing someone to sensing them, but she shifts close to him, letting her eyes flutter shut.

Air draws in through his lungs, like it always does, and blood courses through his veins. He's warm, he always is, but something is subtly off, subtly different.

"Hey, man, put a jacket on," someone says, and Lyra's eyes pop open.

It's a pair of hikers, all kitted out in snow gear, trekking past with their ski poles and cleated boots, and they both wrinkle their nose at Lyra and Melekai, obviously judging.

Melekai twitches underneath her hand, a vicious motion, and she digs her fingers into his leg to stop him from jolting up and doing...something.

His eyes are wide, much wider than she's seen them, and they both watch as the hikers continue on, deeper into the snowy woods.

"They can—" Lyra starts, but—

"Untie the rope," Melekai interrupts, an undercurrent of panic in his voice, "Untie it!"

She grabs at his wrist, fumbling with the bracelets until her fingers graze the unseeable cord and she tugs it undone. He shakes his wrist, before gripping her arm back and—

They're in her house, the snow from her boots is still crusted along the soles of her feet, and he stands up straight, pulling himself to full height.

"Okay, so that was weird," Lyra says, heart pounding. "So that makes you just..."

"We shouldn't do that," he blurts out, swirling away from her and pacing the length of her small kitchen. "I don't...I don't...too much danger."

"I won't," she says, still a bit thrown. "Did it make you just...just the human body?"

"They could see me," he says, and she can tell that his heart is pounding, even with his demon powers returned.

His eyes reflect the light back at her.

"They could see me, and they could've attacked you and I wouldn't have been able to do a thing and—" he cuts off mid-sentence, pacing away.

Her cat looks up at him and mewls, but he doesn't bend to give it attention.

She can see his pulse jump, from all the way across the room.

"They didn't," she says, bending over to take off her boots, because she can't deal with a demon having a panic attack if she's tracking snow all over her house. "We're both safe."

He stares at her, frazzled, and his face twists. "Terese could've found us, could've hurt you."

And he's right, he fundamentally is, but that's not going to help this. "She could've found me at any time in my life, but we're safe, we're indoors, you're back." She hangs up her snow jacket, then shakes out her hair, her mind racing. "All your protections are still up, yes?" she says, guessing, because it feels right. Her house feels unchanged.

He nods, still pacing.

"Then we are very safe," she says, and her cat meows up at her this time, since Melekai hasn't given him any attention. "You've ensured that."

He doesn't stop pacing, eyes focused on the window outside.

So she lets herself breathe, lets herself think.

Jackson had panic attacks, in the first month after the accident, when she had to relearn to walk and he had to relearn how to sleep and how to deal with crutches, and she never quite figured out what to say to him. How to talk him down.

But Melekai's different.

So she grabs his hand, and he flinches, before gripping back, hard.

Without saying anything, she pulls him towards her bedroom, down the hall. He doesn't resist, still looking everywhere, for some sign of danger.

"Here," she says, flopping sideways onto the bed in a decidedly not-sexy way. "Sit with me."

For a second, she thinks he's going to protest, before he crawls next to her, curling his body around hers, like he can protect her even there.

His pulse flutters against her skin.

Her words fail her again, so she just rests her head against the bed, and lets him hold her.

If not for the panic, it would almost be nice. Some sort of advanced cuddles.

After a few minutes of not getting attention, the cat wanders in, jumping on the bed and curling up on an unoccupied pillow. His purrs fill the silence, and for a while it's all that she can hear. Just the purrs and Melekai's ragged breathing.

He unwinds, one muscle at a time, like it takes conscious effort.

"I didn't mean to leave you helpless," she says, after his breathing evens out. "I thought it would be good, for when dealing with Terese."

He exhales. "You're not wrong," he says, and she can hear the tension in his voice, "it might be a perfectly valid tactic."

She twists so she can see him, see his face. His freckles are stark, this close, and even though he's not smiling she can still see the faint hint of the dimple on his cheek.

"Still, this is me apologizing."

After a moment, he nods, then pulls her closer, tucking her head underneath his chin. "You did a clever thing, and it was excellent, until I realized it," he says, and with a breath she realizes that he's not angry at her, not at all, but at himself. "If there wasn't a threat, I would have you do it again and again, just for how different everything is, just to see people and interact with them, just to..." He presses a kiss to the top of her head again. "Never apologize for being clever."

She's not apologizing for that, she's apologizing for making him feel like shit, but that's splitting hairs, so she nods against him, and it ends up being mostly a nuzzle.

She can still feel his heart pound, and it doesn't stop until after she's drifted off.

HE'S GONE when she wakes.

23

———

Three days later, without a hint of Terese anywhere to be seen, and three days of putting in applications to local jobs in between check-ins with Melekai, Axel and Alette pull up in Axel's fancy Mustang right outside Lyra's home.

She waves through her kitchen window, at the grimy snow clinging to the tires, then looks down at herself.

She hadn't planned on leaving the house any more that day, after handing in applications to the diners in town and was therefore in her sweatpants and a ratty t-shirt.

LYRA (3:58 PM): I'll be out in a sec, gonna change.

And she dashes back into the bedroom to change, only to almost run into Melekai, standing stiff.

"Uh, hi," she says, then edges by him to get to her dresser, pulling out a pair of corduroys and a chunky sweater, "how long have you been here?"

He turns and looks at her, his eyes reflecting the light back at her, but his face doesn't move.

"Right," she says. "Alette and Axel are here, I think they want to do something,"

"Don't go to the headquarters today," he warns, and she stills. "I don't know why, but don't."

"Alright," she says, drawing the word out as she chucks off the ratty shirt and shrugs on the chunky sweater. "I'll let them know."

LYRA (4:02 PM): Where are we going?

ALETTE (4:02 PM): There's a research library south of Bellingham, can we show you?

Melekai's shoulders unwind with that. "I'll meet you there," he says, pulling himself to his full height and finally nodding at her, like he wasn't pretending to be a statue just moments ago. "I'm not in the mood for a car."

"That's fair," Lyra says, pulling on a pair of proper pants. "Uh, you okay?"

He blinks at her, like the last time they spoke for any length wasn't a panic attack for him. He tilts his head at her, as if reading through her intentions.

"You're unsure if I'm angry at you," he says, almost declaring it instead of asking. "I'm not."

"Oh, okay, good," Lyra says, grabbing a hairbrush from her bookcase and attempting to untangle her waves.

He hesitates, head tilting in the other direction this time. "Just ask," he says, voice a bit milder, "sometimes it's difficult to guess what you mean."

That, she can do. "Then where have you been the last few days?" It feels confrontational, it feels too much, but he said to ask...

"Trying to track down Terese's hiding places," he answers, immediately, and there's a sense of relief coming from him that's stronger than she anticipated. "She must have some, they must be protected, not even I can go for forever without rest, and she is much younger."

She ties her hair back the best she can, then grabs her snow jacket. "Safe for me to go outside?"

"Very," he says, smug, then disappears from in front of her.

"Alright," she breathes, then tromps to her front door, where the car idles.

Deftly avoiding her cat trying to escape, she meets them at the car, sliding into the back seat, next to Alette.

It takes Lyra a moment, before she realizes that Dr. Frisse is in the passenger's seat, leaving Alette and Lyra to the back.

It's almost unnatural to see her in a car.

"You guys need to text ahead," Lyra says, fitting herself into the warm quiet of the car, as it rumbles over the snowy potholes of her street, "that way I'm not in my pajamas or anything."

"Impulse," Axel says, breezy, and his too slick, too fashionable facade is back, and he probably doesn't know that she's seen underneath it. "We realized that your street was literally on the way."

"I didn't think," Alette says, but she hears the apology. "Have you ever seen a magical library? They're fantastic."

"Obviously not," Lyra says, and the idea that there's one so close to her, that there's been one this accessible for so long grates at her nerves. "I would have definitely tried to do some research there."

Just the idea of bringing Jackson there is delicious. He would lose his mind.

"It's hardly impressive," Dr. Frisse says, and Alette wilts, just a little, as Axel pulls onto the main highway. "Do you really live in that hovel?"

It's definitely not the worst place she's lived, so Lyra bristles.

"I inherited it," she says, instead of all the swear words she wants to say. "I'm not gonna turn down free rent."

"At least that's pragmatic," Dr. Frisse remarks, and even that sounds like an insult.

"Hey, it was your demon threat to end the world that blew up my work," Lyra replies, staring hard out the window.

In the reflection, she sees Alette wince.

"She would have come after you at some point," Dr. Frisse continues, as if that makes it better, "with how many people she's killed, she would have stumbled on you eventually."

"Thanks," Lyra says, sarcastic, "but I'm not gonna move when I'm broke and I have free rent."

Through her peripheral vision, she sees Dr. Frisse's head turn towards her, like she's actually contemplating Lyra's financial state. "Lyra," she starts, and Lyra's stomach drops at her tone, "what is your level of education?"

If they knew she was in foster care, they sure as hell know that she didn't graduate college.

"Well my brother's in law school," she says.

"Education doesn't transfer between siblings," Dr. Frisse responds.

"Only one of us could go, thought it'd better be the one of us that didn't miss school all the time," Lyra says, which isn't quite true, but truer than she usually wants to give people. "I have some community college."

Dr. Frisse turns and stares at Axel. "First necromancer you've ever found, and she didn't graduate."

The doctor is trying to make some point, Lyra knows, but she's not here for it.

"And yet, you have already raised two people, and seem to be growing in abilities each day," Dr. Frisse continues, and the flip is so sudden that it almost makes Lyra's head swim. "Imagine what you could have done if anyone ever sat you down and trained you properly."

Lyra shoots Alette a look, hoping for an ally, but Alette's only scowling out the window, rubbing her brace idly.

"Are you trying to insult me into signing up for magic classes?" Lyra asks, and Axel snorts, before covering it up with a cough, "'Cause I want to learn but this isn't cool."

Dr. Frisse falls silent, and in the rearview mirror Lyra can see her purse her lips. "It would be easier on all of us if you were fully trained," she starts, lofty, and it's the same lofty tone that she's heard Alette use, but all of the warmth and fun is gone from it. Like Alette's been trying to copy her, but has too much character to get it right, "and it would be easier to train you if you weren't out looking for employment."

She's not wrong, not exactly, but Lyra still doesn't like it.

"If we arrange for a stipend until this is all over, with the understanding that you could then go and learn from the College in Europe, would you accept it?" Dr. Frisse asks, and it takes Lyra a moment for her brain to catch up with the words. "I'm certain someone there would love to teach you, to study to see what you can do."

And Lyra's stomach drops.

Not because of Europe, because that sounds awesome, and she's never thought she could travel before. Not because of money, though that sounds like it would get a lot of strings tied up in it really quickly.

But because of the tone. The idea that she could be so bought so easily, and so whimsically, with no assurances that this wouldn't turn out so poorly for her.

But her mama always taught her to take free money.

"I'd want to see that in writing," Lyra says, mulish, "and my brother would look it over."

Alette gives her a glance, like she's unsure what is going on in her head, and Lyra really wishes that Melekai was here. He'd at least have some insight into whatever the heck she just halfway agreed to.

Or find the entire thing amusing.

"That's fair," Dr. Frisse says, smug, "It'd be better if you could dedicate yourself to helping with this threat."

As if she could say no to stopping the End of the World.

"So this library," she says, instead of anything else, as the sun sets outside the window as they turn off the freeway, onto an almost abandoned bumpy road, "what's so special that you wanted me to be there?"

Alette sits up straighter, thankfully, and she knows she could actually get a straight answer out of Alette instead of any half insults. "A collection of sealing glyphs," she says, as if she's equally as grateful for the conversation changing, "both new age and ancient, some from the time when necromancers were more plentiful."

"And these two always want to go to a library," Axel chimes in, "with any problem, it's always let's go to the library and see what they can suggest."

"There's seldom any new knowledge, it's all things people have found before," Dr. Frisse murmurs, as if it's an afterthought.

"This place is neat 'cause they have computer runes," Axel says, completely ignoring Dr. Frisse's interjection as he drives, deftly avoiding potholes and chunks of solidified snow, "actual runes made on computer boards so the electricity activates as it moves through the little parts, and—"

There's a thunk, before the tires hit an edge of a pothole and the back of the Mustang swerves, and Lyra's heart is immediately in her throat.

"What—" she blurts, before the back-window shatters and glass flies through the cabin, a musical crystalline noise, and her hair gets flung in front of her face.

And then the world slows down, and for a second, it's like she's floating, the car spinning underneath her, and her breath catches.

Somewhere, Alette screams.

Lyra exhales, and shards of glass twinkle in the air, as the car spins out on its back, the cab tilting up, like something fell on the back and rotated it on its back wheels.

Axel's yelling, Alette is gasping, and all Lyra can do is turn her head, turn towards the broken glass, and stare.

The front end of the car slams back down to the ground, tires squealing, and Axel's head slumps down over the steering wheel, and everything is so loud that Lyra can't hear a thing.

Someone's yelling, someone's screaming, and the glass still tinkles through the cabin, and all Lyra can do is look.

Like a goddamn supervillain, Terese stands behind them, illuminated by the setting sun off the snow and the shards of glass.

Lyra twists—it's good, she can twist, nothing is broken—and fumbles with her seatbelt, but her hands are slick.

There's blood on Axel's head, his eyes are closed, but he's not dead, not yet, there's no pull towards him. Alette's mouth is stretched open, and she's frantically trying to undo her seatbelt, like she's yelling, but Lyra can't make sense of anything.

Dr. Frisse opens her door, calmly, like this is no big deal, and steps out, facing Terese.

Terese's eyes reflect back at them, and she's untouched by whatever she just did, not even a fleck of grimy street snow on her leather jacket.

There's blood dripping down her hand, though, and it's a visceral human blood, vivid red mixed with black.

She bleeds.

Lyra scrabbles at the handle to the door, her fingers sliding around and unable to get traction, but it's bent weirdly, and Lyra can't get it open, so she throws her shoulder into it, before tumbling out onto the icy pavement, hitting it shoulder-first.

She rolls with it, then shakily slides to her feet.

Terese's eyes immediately cut to her, and she tilts her head.

It's such a familiar motion, one she's seen from Melekai hundreds of times, and her blood goes cold.

"I didn't think you'd—"

Her words cut off, as Dr. Frisse slashes something against the smoking bumper of the car and sparks slide off, ricocheting at Terese, forcing her back a step.

And Lyra's out here, standing on the icy road, her heart pounding.

There's nothing dead, nothing that she could sprint to, just some roadkill about a hundred yards away. Nothing she could pull from and tie Terese up with, nothing she could use...

She exhales. They're in a forest, there are plants everywhere, she could—

Terese raises a hand, and her chest moves with an intake of breath, her eyes narrowing, directly at Dr. Frisse.

And Lyra's the only other one out of the car.

And she's survived this before.

With less finesse than is probably necessary, Lyra stumbles into Dr. Frisse, knocking her back and down, so she skids away, right as Terese clenches her fist.

Immediately, Lyra's ears pop, the pavement below the two of them dents, then shatters, and everything stills.

Terese's eyes widen, as Dr. Frisse safely scrambles away, and it's just her and Lyra in her little death bubble.

Lyra's hair floats around her face, her chunky sweater fluttering against her skin, and some of the blood on her hand drips upwards instead of down. Chunks of grimy snow stir around their feet, like it can't decide which gravity to follow.

There's a dead bug, deep underground, some sort of worm, but Lyra doesn't know if she can grab it through the ice and the pavement and the frozen dirt.

Terese ducks her head, eyes reflecting, as if inviting Lyra closer, but she knows better than that. "You have to help me," she says, voice just as musical, just as pleading, "please, they're just making it worse."

Lyra doesn't know what to say, but keeping her talking is much better than having her start to kill people again, so Lyra just nods, letting her eyes scan around the bubble.

The last bubble was made from all sorts of rope and threads.

In the back of her awareness, she sees Dr. Frisse scramble to the car, and a small, disassociated part of her wonders if she'll just drive away.

"Tell me," Lyra starts, without knowing the end of the sentence, "what do you need?"

It's a trick she used to use on the belligerent drunks, on people too distressed and stoned that they lose all perspective on the world and can't figure out a way out of their problems until they end up at her store. Get them to talk, get them to have a single moment outside of themselves, until she can get away or get someone else to handle the problem.

She reaches a hand to the edge of the bubble—to where she thinks is the edge of the bubble—and lets her own breathing slow.

Terese's colorless eyes watch the motion, moving too fast, jerking around, like she can't fully commit her focus to one thing. "Everything hurts," she says, but her voice is back to cunning. "Everything hurts and they won't let me stop it."

It's nothing Terese hasn't said before, and that...bothers Lyra.

Pushes at a part of her like a hurt tooth, like something she can't help but worry at.

Lyra's legs don't hurt in the bubble. Her hand, whatever's wrong with it, whatever caused so much blood, doesn't hurt either.

Like Terese is trying to wrap herself in a blanket of no-pain and isn't quite succeeding.

Lyra's fingertips graze on a brief, immaterial texture in the bubble, so much finer than the other one. Like a gauze, something so deftly woven together.

Lyra's blood hangs in the air, caught on the invisible fabric, illuminating the texture.

Terese immediately tracks her hand, almost as if Lyra struck her.

"How would you?" Lyra asks, as if she could pull Terese's attention away, distract her with what must be incredibly obvious.

Behind her, a car door clatters open, but Lyra doesn't risk looking away.

Terese straightens, as if unsure what Lyra's doing, which is fair, she doesn't even know what she's doing, before she takes a deliberate step forward. Closer to Lyra. "There might be a way you could help," she says, and alarm bells go off even further in Lyra's mind. "Can you come with me to see?"

Lyra takes a breath to respond, her heart pounding, before—

A bang, so loud Lyra can swear she can see it, and blood blossoms on Terese's front, black and red intermixing.

She gasps, and for a brief, brief second her eyes are entirely human.

Lyra flinches back, grabbing a fistful of the threads of the death bubble, feeling the cords in her hand, coated with her own blood.

Behind them, leaning staggered on the car, is Alette, a small pistol incongruent in her hands.

Terese lashes out, and Lyra dashes in front of whatever strike is going towards Alette, and it hits her like a gust of wind, knocking her back.

But.

She remains alive.

Terese snarls at her, dripping blood from a gaping wound in her chest, and Lyra swipes her hand, full of the cords, until she can scrabble at Terese's arm.

The moment she does, a gold flash echoes around the abandoned stretch of road, and Terese grips back, digging in her fingernails, baring her teeth.

And three things become apparent.

One. There's a bullet punching through Terese's lung, and yet they still flex, black blood pooling around them, sticky and visceral and not at all what should be bleeding from that wound.

Two. Red blood, normal blood, pumps through her veins, despite her heart stuttering and the electricity in her brain firing off in wrong directions.

Three. She's in so. Much. Pain.

Another bright flash, and Lyra's legs almost buckle.

But.

What can be given, can be taken away.

"No," Lyra says, and, desperately, tries to imagine reaching into Terese and taking back the gold flash, pulling back what is hers.

After a moment, it's easy to see, the gold separates from the black and the red, but the longer she takes the more it absorbs into the black, into the lungs with the pooling blood.

And.

Terese's heart stops.

Her nails dig in deeper into Lyra's arm, as she stumbles, bracing against Lyra, her eyes wide and bloodshot.

Terese's brain fires off again, and again, but nothing reaches to the heart, and now Lyra can't let go.

She's never touched something—someone—at the moment of their death before.

But somehow, Terese grins at her, baring bloody teeth at her, as her heart doesn't pump and her brain tries desperately to restart it.

"That doesn't work," she hisses out, and, as she uselessly grips against Lyra's arm, her muscles spasming, she jerks herself upright.

As Lyra still holds on, the brain stops firing. The lungs stop flexing, and all the sparks in her spinal cord go silent.

The death punches through Lyra's defenses, taking her breath away. But still, they cling onto each other, and Terese's still blinking, still baring her teeth.

She shouldn't be talking, she shouldn't be standing, she shouldn't be fighting, but—

With a gasp, something more tortured than Lyra's ever heard, Terese's heart spasms. One beat, then another, then...

Terese coughs, and blood, black blood, splatters on Lyra's face, then grins. "Not today."

She's in so much pain.

She—the body, at least—just came back from the dead, without any other outside influence. Lyra didn't do that, Lyra didn't restart the heart, none of it.

She has a moment, a split second inside the death bubble, where she despairs. Where she doesn't know what she can do, if anything, against the power that just came back from the dead.

But somehow the cords from the bubble are still in her hand, and Lyra desperately tries to imagine them as a rope, winding around Terese's arm like a vine.

"You need to stop—" Lyra starts, before Terese shakes her off, batting her aside like one would a fly, sending Lyra careening to the ground and smashing into the broken pavement and ice shoulder-first.

Terese turns away, back towards Dr. Frisse leaning heavy against the car door, and Alette bracing herself against the trunk. There's blood on the side of her temple, coloring her glasses.

Lyra's head rings, but she kicks out her legs, her foot connecting with Terese's ankle, and Terese staggers, instead of whatever the hell she meant to do.

And with that little kick, she tries to pour whatever power she has, whatever little bit of energy, and—

With a bang so loud that Lyra sees double, something hits Terese, knocking her to the ground.

Melekai stands over her, looming, without even a glance to Lyra, as Terese scrambles to her feet.

Another narrowing of Terese's eyes, and another explosion and a dent in the pavement, and the bubble blasts out again, enveloping the two demons and Lyra on the pavement.

There are bugs caught in this one, somehow, their moments of death bright against Lyra's awareness.

She could use that.

Something inside of her hurts, in a sort of distant way, numbed by the presence of the demons and their power, but in a way that Lyra suspects is going to be very much not okay later on. She drags herself towards the bright little bits of death, something, anything, she can do to add to Melekai's power. Tip the scales of whatever battle is happening.

The two demons circle each other, with Terese still with a gaping bloody hole in her chest and Melekai standing tall, and Lyra tries to crawl away, get as far away as possible.

Her ears pop, and pebbles of pavement and ice fly around her head, spinning within the circle as...as something unseeable happens, as something hits Melekai and he doubles over, as something rakes across Terese and she staggers.

Melekai had said he wanted to avoid battle.

Lyra can't see whatever it is hitting them, can't see the points of impact, but for the pain on both of their faces and the reeling from the blows.

The very earth around her shakes, and she ducks to avoid a shard of ice, flying in towards the two of them, just to see it imbed in Melekai's back.

Black blood sprays from it, but he pays it no mind, hurling something at Terese hard enough to make her shriek, high-pitched and inhuman.

Something whirling through the air, and Melekai stumbles, head snapping back. If he was human, if the body was alive, it would've broken the neck, it would've severed the spinal cord, would've left the heart to wither almost immediately.

But he lashes back out, with a surge of power that almost feels like wind, knocking Terese over until she slides away on the broken pavement.

Her chest is heaving, heaving around the gunshot wound and the power against it, and she scrambles for purchase before she disappears in a snap.

Leaving sudden silence.

Lyra gasps for breath, as if the sudden lack of power steals away her ability to breathe, and Melekai is still, still standing, black blood oozing from his back.

Slowly, he turns towards her, and his eyes reflect back at her, and he wobbles.

Wobbles, then topples over, right there in the street.

24

For a split-second Lyra can't move.

She's paralyzed, laying on broken concrete and ice, staring at Melekai.

He's facing away from her, his golden-brown curls coming free from the bun and darkening with the grimy snow. Blood seeps from his back, black against his Henley shirt.

Then, from the car that's still steaming, someone moves, and Alette stumbles forward.

"Lyra," she rasps out, "Lyra is—"

Lyra pushes herself up, and the cut on her hand bleeds, but she's still inside the bubble and can't feel a thing, just the edges of her skin tugging against the gravel.

She stumbles upwards, and Melekai turns over, flopping onto his back, and the blood mixes with the snow and she doesn't know if demons can get infections or if that's just not how it works.

His eyes stare up at the setting sun, before locking onto her, wide.

At least he's blinking. If that's good. If that's a sign of demons being alive.

There's so much she doesn't know.

He struggles to sit up, to scramble away, and he throws a hand out, blocking her.

"No," he gasps out, and he pushes himself away, scooting on the broken concrete.

She freezes.

His eyes are wide, panicked. "No, Lyra, back away," he says, and his voice cracks in the middle of her name, and there's something...off.

Lyra swallows. There's still blood dripping down her hand, she can feel the liquid moving sluggishly over her fingertips but can't feel the pain.

She doesn't know if he's feeling any pain. He said they don't, not like humans, but.

But his eyes are stretched open wide, and his upper lip trembles.

She looks back at the car. Alette's helping Axel out, and his eyes are open, but there's blood on his temple. He leans against her, heavy, woozy, and Dr. Frisse guides him to sitting down on the ground.

Even from this far away, she knows. They'll live.

"Melekai," she starts, and takes a step forward, and he shakes his head at her motion, golden curls flying.

There's black blood welling up around the corners of his lips.

"What's wrong?" she says, and with every word she feels a bit more of herself, feels a bit steadier. Like the shock of the accident and the shock of whatever it is that Terese did is wearing off and wearing off quick.

She probably shouldn't feel this good. Not while she's actively bleeding.

He shakes his head again. "Back away," he says, and his voice breaks, "don't touch me."

She can feel Alette's eyes on them, but Alette's not going to step into the bubble, she's not stupid. Not after what happened last time.

Every part of him rubs on the edge of her awareness, like the fight took everything that there is about him and turned it on edge. Spun all of the familiar energy out, leaving him raw and empty.

"You're hurt?" she asks.

The dead bugs are bright against her senses, too.

And Melekai's looking up at her, like he's horrified, like he's scared.

"Mel, tell me what you need," Lyra says, pitching her voice down low, her heart starting to pound. "You've been stabbed, tell me."

His eyes race over her, like if he stops and stares at one thing for too long, he'll get stuck, and a trickle of blood trails down his chin. "Don't come closer."

She takes another step, instead, and his breathing hitches.

"Don't," he blurts, "if you touch me, I won't be able to stop."

And his eyes lock onto her, like he's begging her to understand, and in that moment, she does.

Whatever injury he has, where he can breathe this well and speak this well through a stab wound that should have punctured his lung and stopped him cold, it's still serious.

She exhales again, breathes out the feeling of wrongness, and inhales something resembling confidence. Not real confidence, goodness knows she'll never have that, but a sort of resolve that forms up in her bones, winding through her veins, dripping out with her blood on her hand.

She casts a glance to her hand. There's a gash in the palm, like she cut it on some flying glass.

Wouldn't be the first time that happened.

Taking a moment to steel herself, she gathers up the threads from the dead bugs until they blink away from her awareness, trails her hand along the bubble left behind until the cords coil up in her hands and mix with her blood, and steps forward again.

Melekai pales. "Lyra," he says, and it sounds like a prayer and a sob.

Without looking down at her hand, she twists the threads of the bugs with the cord from the bubble, until somehow, she can feel the end of the string.

He shakes his head, pushing himself away, but his arms give out, like he can't muster up the energy to move, and she can see his chest tremble.

She takes another step.

This close, everything feels discordant. Like she wasn't aware of how attuned she is to his being until the wrong note gets struck.

Her heart pounding, she crouches next to him, and he cringes away.

"I don't want you to die," he whispers, and there's blood sticking his shirt to him.

"Thanks," she says, then, as quick as she can, winds the cord around his arm.

There's a brief gold flash, where her fingers graze his skin, and a strangled noise breaks from his throat. Her hands almost go numb from the lack of sensation, fumbling with the edges of the cord, before yanking it close in a knot.

He winces away from her, and there's a gaping hole in his back, and she can almost see the edges of the wound pulling away.

"Melekai," she starts, and his attention snaps away, pleading, "this is an order. Take enough to save your life, but do not kill me."

His throat works, and he looks at her as if she's going to kill him, going to drive that wound deeper into his back.

And then she lays her hand on his cheek. Feels the stubble against his chin, the grime of the fight, the inherent wrongness of whatever the heck his energy is doing, there's a flash of gold, and—

She wakes in a strange bed.

She wakes alone in a strange bed, in a strange room that doesn't have her cat in it, that has none of the sounds she associates with home, and light worms its way underneath her eyelids.

She breathes out, listening, as if she could hear better if she keeps her eyes closed, but no familiar creaks or rustle of her windows meets her ears, and the bed is too hard, even for her.

Careful, still not opening her eyes, she stretches out her legs. No pain, and her legs meet the edge of the bed. A twin bed.

She's definitely not at home.

Taking a deep breath, she opens one eye, and finds herself in a softly lit, small room, laying on a cot.

It's not quite a hospital room, with none of the beeps or machinery, but it gives off the same vibes. A room of rest, of recovery.

She pushes herself up, and she's still not in any pain. There's a bandage on her hand, and it's meticulously cleaned.

The light comes from a series of written glyphs, glowing lightly against the wall. Without even touching them, without even getting closer, she can tell they're from Alette.

She's wearing a set of gray sweatpants that she definitely did not get herself into after the crash on the road with the ice.

The crash in the road.

She swings her feet over the side of the bed, standing with only minimal wobbling.

Melekai.

Melekai's out there, and she's in here, and how did she get here, and is Alette okay, is Axel, is Melekai still alright, and—

The doorknob grows warm against her hand, before twisting open easily, revealing one of the byzantine hallways of the headquarters, with its fancy carpet and expensive track lighting and magical moving glyphs.

She has no idea where in the building she may be.

"Hello?" she croaks out, and her throat is dry, parched. Like she hasn't had a drink in days, which doesn't bode well.

How long had she been out?

There's no answer, so she pads on bare feet over the carpet, down the hall, and the recycled air is soft against her skin.

Is Melekai still alive, did her gambit work, did they make it out?

Someone must have, if she's here and not laying out in the grimy snow.

She turns a corner, and nothing is familiar.

Her purse hadn't been in that room, there are no pockets in the sweatpants, but she stills, tries to listen.

When there's nothing, she lets her eyes flutter shut.

The colony of dead ants still grabs her attention, a few floors down, further away than they were in the grand hall. The dead mouse, skeletized by years of pain and the passage of time, is closer.

So she takes a deep breath, exhales, and turns around, using the map of the dead to guide her back towards the conference room, feeling around to the elevator, and punching down to where she hopes the room will be.

It's like only having a map based on smell, and it's disorienting at best.

The elevator whirrs, and that, at least, is a familiar sound. It's the same elevator she's taken quite a few times now, and the familiarity settles her hackles down.

The door beeps open, revealing the hallway to the grand mahogany gateway.

"Great," Lyra whispers to herself, and the words get stolen away from her the moment they leave her lips. Like Alette's sound-cancelling spell continues this far out.

With another steadying breath, she pushes the doors open.

Inside the cavernous space, treating it like it's just her office, Dr. Frisse sits in one of the plush conference chairs, papers spread haphazardly over the grand table.

She glances up at Lyra, standing barefoot in the doorway, and blinks, a single moment of a double take before the mask slides cleanly into place.

"Oh good, you're awake," she says, business-like and official. "You must be starving."

She is, but that's not the most pressing issue. "Where's Melekai?"

"I don't know," Dr. Frisse says. "You've been out for two days."

That explains the dry mouth and the headache.

"Is everyone okay?" Lyra asks, drawing deeper into the room. There's the collection of water bottles in the corner, as well as what looks like a pack of the energy bars Axel's always handing out, so she snags one of each on her way in.

Dr. Frisse looks up at her over her glasses, then folds them up and places them on the table in front of her, on top of the multitude of papers.

Lyra didn't even know she wore glasses.

"Axel will have a fetching new scar that I'm certain he'll magic away, and Alette is very terrified about what she saw in that battle, but she's fundamentally okay," Dr. Frisse says, like she's reciting a grocery list. "Axel spent the night in the hospital in Vancouver, and he'll have a headache for a while, but he will recover."

Lyra lets out a breath she didn't know she was holding, and all but collapses into one of the fancy chairs at the table. It's comfortable, at least.

"He's already futzing with his car, trying to figure out how to replace all of the magic that Terese so unceremoniously broke." Dr. Frisse drums her fingers against the paperwork, studying Lyra until she feels self-conscious downing the water. "Your demon disappeared."

"Physically disappeared or just you haven't seen any evidence of him?" Lyra asks through a mouthful of disgusting granola bar, though her heart pangs.

If he's gone, would she know? Would any of them know? Would there just be a gaping hole in her psyche and a horde of unfamiliar demons if she ever used her power again?

"Well I've seen no evidence, and Alette hasn't seen him actually," Dr. Frisse says. "I expected him to take you away, after what you did, but he left you."

That smarts.

She examines the water bottle, to avoid looking at the table or at Dr. Frisse.

"You had quite a concussion and your hand got some stitches, but other than that and whatever it is your demon did, you seemed to be fine," she continues, still as if she's reading off a list. "I was worried about the concussion, but you reacted quite well, so I didn't take you to the hospital."

"Thanks, that'd be too pricy," Lyra quips, and only gets a raised eyebrow in return.

"This is twice now," Dr. Frisse says, "that you've been the one to deal with Terese and come out alive."

"Yeah well, her death bubble doesn't hurt me," Lyra says, picking at the label of the water bottle. "I didn't want to have to raise someone in a street in the middle of nowhere, it was chilly."

She can feel Dr. Frisse's eyes on her.

"You saved our lives, almost certainly," she says. "I don't know what you did, I don't know what your demon did, but she hasn't resurfaced."

For a split second, Lyra hopes, before disregarding it. Her life could never be that easy.

"I think she teleported away under her own power," Lyra says, ripping another strip off the bottle, "and other than the gunshot, I didn't see other injuries...how did she come back to life?"

"Pardon?" Dr. Frisse asks, face so carefully bland.

"I felt her die? I was trying to tie her up and she grabbed me? I felt...I felt her die." She's rambling, part of her brain fuzzy after sleeping and the lack of food and caffeine, but she can't stop. "Her brain stopped, her heart stopped, all...all electricity between the two just stopped. Then started again."

The doctor watches her, so very careful, like she's waiting for Lyra to reveal a secret so grand.

"It wasn't what I do, that feels different, but it just went back and started up, I don't know how it happened," Lyra keeps going, and she wants to stop her words, but can't. "It's like she couldn't die."

"Interesting," Dr. Frisse says, then leans forward, almost clinically. "Do you want some coffee?"

TURNS out there's a fully functioning kitchen with not one, but three different coffee machines as well as a startlingly wide variety of teas, and Lyra's able to get some toast started and a cup of brutally hot coffee poured for herself as Dr. Frisse sticks what looks like a luxury meal to be reheated in the microwave.

"When you touched her, did you feel the demon, or just the

human?" Dr. Frisse asks, after Lyra's comfortably munching on some really great toast. "Or would they feel different to you?"

"I don't know," Lyra says, tucking her feet underneath her and marveling at the utter lack of pain in them.

Melekai must have taken a lot.

She scowls at her toast, for a split second.

"Let me rephrase, when you touch your demon, does he feel human?"

It's a much more revealing question than she would want to ever divulge over toast.

"He feels pretty normal to me," she says.

"That rope you created," Dr. Frisse says, and her voice is so casual that hairs rise on Lyra's arm, "what was it from?"

So she can see that.

"She did that death bubble thing, right?" Lyra starts, and Dr. Frisse nods. "She uh...caught some bugs in it."

Dr. Frisse tilts her head, like she's evaluating Lyra through a different set of eyes, and Lyra doesn't like it much.

"When things die, you can use them?" she says, clearly jumping to that conclusion. "That's how you blew up the plant, that's how you turned offensive with your power."

"Well, yeah," Lyra says.

She leans forward towards Lyra, and it's a cross between her worst school teacher and the lawyer who would occasionally work for the foster system. "Is there any downside to it?" When Lyra doesn't immediately answer, she extrapolates. "Are there any negative effects to you or to the dead when you use this power?"

Lyra stares down at her steaming coffee and realizes Dr. Frisse is definitely more like the lawyer than she would like, the urge to just...not answer her growing.

But this could be very applicable information.

"I can't bring the thing back, after that," she says, like it's a confession, "even if it's something I should be able to, it's gone forever."

"A sacrifice," Dr. Frisse says, then nods. "Something final like that, it must be daunting, especially for someone who could otherwise be in control of death."

Lyra doesn't like this faux counselor side of Dr. Frisse. "Anytime I had to practice on Melekai, a bug or something had to be dead near me."

"We can prepare for that," Dr. Frisse says, and it sends a chill down Lyra's back. "We just need something that can die whenever you're about to go into battle."

"Bugs, bugs are good," Lyra blurts out, before Frisse starts to sound even more like a serial killer.

"But the bigger the death, the more power it would have, right?" Dr. Frisse presses, and Lyra's skin crawls. "Terese is powerful, if we want to bring her down, there might need to be a bigger sacrifice."

Not for the first time, Lyra wishes Melekai had a phone, and— "Shit, my phone, my brother's going to be worried—"

"Alette already called him," Dr. Frisse interrupts. "He's going to be taking care of your cat. Said being at the house would give him an opportunity to study."

That's almost too neatly convenient, but Lyra nods her thanks.

"He definitely wants you to give him a call when you are awake, but we can arrange for Axel or Alette to drive you home," Dr. Frisse continues, and Lyra hears the giant 'but' at the end of that sentence, "though we do want to make sure you're well protected."

"Melekai put up wards," Lyra says, but the words feel dryer than the toast.

Would they survive even if he was gone? Would there be some existing protection to her?

What if, instead of dying, he just...leaves? Washes his hands of her, of her problems and the problems of the little trio of magicians, runs off to whatever other world he inhabits when he's not around her? Shows up once a year and then disappears?

It settles poorly in her stomach.

She takes another bite of toast, and, somehow, she's on the edge of tears. On the edge of crying, past the toast and the coffee and the exhaustion and the surreal lack of pain.

Crying is the last thing she wants to do under the watchful eye of Dr. Frisse.

"If those are gone, do you have any plans?" Dr. Frisse asks, voice still carefully bland. "A place you can go, protected in some way, if you're no longer under his spell?"

"I'll be okay," she says, though there's a lump in her throat. "I'm always okay, can I go home and check?"

If there are no wards, and Jackson's there alone, there's nothing stopping Terese from stopping by and ending him. Or hurting him, if she so chooses.

"Is that wise?"

And fuck if she knows.

25

Shortly after the driest of toast she's ever had, Dr. Frisse summons Alette from somewhere else inside the building, and she very gracefully drives Lyra back. A scrape adorns the side of her face, but otherwise she looks okay, if spooked.

Terese isn't outside of her house, but Alette still idles up slowly, like she's dreading it.

"Alette," Lyra starts, "how do you see your magic?"

They sit in her very reasonable car, staring at Lyra's little rundown mobile house, with its faded plastic siding and faux brick plaster.

"Differently, since you...you know," Alette says, like she's unwilling to discuss what Lyra does, "but generally it's more of an emotion than a vision thing."

That doesn't answer her question in any reasonable manner, but Lyra still nods, staring out at her house.

"Melekai did this thing, to show me how magic moves through the world, so I could uh"—Lyra waves her hand, going for trying to show the cords and rope and twine and probably looking like an idiot —"see what I was doing, and when he did, for a little bit of time, I could...I could see all the magic that had been done. The line of protection he made around my house. The...the edges of the death bubble. His actual face." She looks at Alette, and, thankfully, Alette's watching her, nodding thoughtfully. "I think that's what you see when you look at him?"

"Can you still do that?" Alette asks. "Can we test it?"

"Not right now it's...it's just temporary, and he has to be here," Lyra says, staring down at her hands. "But...what did you see during that fight?"

Alette swallows, then politely folds her hands in her lap, keeping them away from the steering wheel. "Terese is worse, with what I can now see," she starts, before tucking a strand of her thick black hair behind her ear. "It's so much clearer that she's stuck in something she does not want to be. But..." she trails off, pursing her lips, not out of distress but out of some frustration at not phrasing things correctly. "It was like they were warping the world around them, twisting space and matter to disrupt each other, I'll have to study it more." A hint of a smile. "In less awful circumstances."

"But everything doesn't look gold?" Lyra asks, watching her boring house and imagining how everything shined. "Also, I think I saw Axel's real face, did you know he changes it?"

"Oh yeah," Alette says, and it's almost flippant, "he figured out how to do it when we were fourteen and went crazy with it. I haven't seen what he actually looks like since then." She falls silent, then sighs, heavy. "I wish we could have shown you the library. I think you'd take to studying of all of this rather well, and I think you'd enjoy it."

"But not gold?" Lyra asks.

"Not gold, but I want to read recorded history of people in relationships with demons because I know those exist, despite the uh...dangers." Alette gives her a smile. "I'm glad you're okay."

It's heartfelt in a way that Lyra seldomly is with other people. "I'm glad you guys are, too."

Before any more exchanging of feelings can take place, she ducks out of the sensible sedan, so much less flashy than Axel's car, and climbs the steps to her house.

It's a bit awkward, manipulating her key with her hand so heavily bandaged, but she manages.

Only to open the door and find Jackson fast asleep in her green chair, a book comically open on his chest and her cat in his lap.

He looks decent, he looks healthy, if a few circles under his eyes, and it's roughly two in the afternoon so she tiptoes past him to her room to change out of the boring gray sweats.

By the time she's in her own comforting pajama pants, however, he's awake, reading the book, and he visibly startles when she exits her bedroom.

"Jeez," he says, after a split second, "how long—"

"Only a few minutes," Lyra says. Her cat raises his head to blink at her, then resumes his snoozing, the traitor. "Uh...thanks for—"

Her brother stands up, upending the cat who scatters away with a mew, and wraps his arms around her in a giant hug, stopping her words cold.

She stands there, awkward for a few seconds, before hugging him back, patting him on his shoulder.

"I'm okay," she says, after he just squeezes her tighter, like he doesn't believe her. "Seriously, I'm fine."

"Sit," he says, guiding her over and dumping her in the chair with all of the finesse a little brother would have, "sit and let me make food."

Jackson's a horrible cook, but she lets him putter around the tiny kitchen with her ancient two burner stove as he attempts macaroni and cheese, and her cat eventually joins her with a put-upon purr.

Jackson's silent, and he's frowning the entire time, and the books and papers spread all over her dining room table look to be boring, but she glances at them, out of a lack of anything else to do.

"So Melekai hurt you," he says, eventually, bringing over a bowl of gross orange macaroni and cheese to her. "He hurt you and then you were...unconscious for a few days."

"That's misleading," she says, and he stares at her fork pointedly until she starts to eat. "If they told you that, then they just wanted to get you angry."

He gives her a sidelong look, one that she saw many times while he was studying to get into law school and noticed something sketch about their background and growing up. "They said there was a battle and he was injured and knocked you out to heal himself," he says, which is a lot more precise, "and that you offered yourself to him for that."

He sits in the kitchen chair across from her, obviously strict, and she sees where this is going.

"First of all," she starts, then trails off, because where could she even start, "that still sounds bad, doesn't it."

"Yup," he says, popping the p sound. "Still sounds bad."

"Does it help if I say I put a magical leash on him and told him he couldn't kill me?" she asks, poking at the radioactive macaroni and cheese. After the toast and the energy bar and the coffee, she's not the hungriest, but...but Jackson's here and he was distressed enough to cook. "I'm not stupid."

"That's...good," he says, then leans towards her, and she feels like she's being lectured again. "Jesus, Lyra, don't do that? He's not worth it?"

"Does it make it better if I say he begged me not to?" she asks, and he rubs his nose, obviously frustrated. "Because he was more willing to die out there than hurt me?"

Jackson stares at her, and she takes another bite, as if that would avert the disapproval.

"Look, my life's gotten weird," she says. "I thought he'd die, he was bleeding, do you know how weird it is to see a demon bleed? I knew I could stop him from actually killing me, I knew he didn't want to kill me, I thought...I thought it'd be a good enough risk. To keep him alive."

"Let me be clear," Jackson starts, "I would much rather you let him die than put yourself at any risk."

"That's 'cause you're my brother," Lyra says, and he nods, as if that's obvious. "I haven't seen him since then, I just woke up a few hours ago, who knows where he is."

"Do you think I could punch him? Do you think that's a thing I could do to a demon?" Jackson asks, and she raises an eyebrow at him.

He's not just disappointed, he's not just scared.

He's furious.

Lyra sets her fork down, because this is new territory for them. They've always both had everything under control, you had to, with how they grew up. They were always too fragile, in too delicate of situations, to lose control for even a few moments.

Like she's been doing anything different.

"You might," she says, because she doesn't know the actual answer to that question, "but I don't know if it'd do anything."

"You're telling me that my big sister saved his life, and he left you there on the street?" he says, and his voice doesn't even waver. "I think he'll feel my punch."

She looks away, the attention all of a sudden overwhelming, and lets her attention fall around them, on the papers spread on her table, and lets him seethe.

And seethe he does, banging around her kitchen to get his own bowl of macaroni and cheese, until her cat jumps off her lap and skitters under her bed with a thump for all the noise.

"How are finals?" she asks, after he sits back down with one of her mixing bowls full of pasta. "That's what's coming up, right?"

He stares at her, flat, like he can tell she's deflecting.

"Anything I can help with?"

"Don't get dead, that'll help with my finals," he snips, and it's at least more like the little brother she knows. "I mean, I got to sit in an empty house for two full days and just focus on papers, that was good."

"Good," Lyra says.

"Good," he repeats back at her, still scowling at his bowl of macaroni. "Yeah. Good."

~

MELEKAI DOESN'T COME BACK that night, and her bed feels cold. Even though they've just spent one night actually in bed together, the lack of it that night is so much worse. Even with her brother asleep in her chair, she misses him.

JACKSON REFUSES to leave for that night but has to go back into town the next day for a class tutorial and scowls all the while.

"Call me," he says, after fussing over her bandage on her hand for a bit longer than strictly necessary. "I don't want to find out you're in trouble by these rich strangers, call me yourself."

"In my defense, I was unconscious," she says, but nods as he wraps her up in another uncharacteristic hug. "I'll call, I'll call if I can, you focus on passing your classes."

"It's going to be a bit harder if I'm worried that the next unknown number is a weirdo telling me my sister's hurt," he says, and makes her stay in place, walking to the bus stop by himself.

She watches him go through the window, before she twitches the curtains closed to the outdoor world.

SHE HEARS NOTHING OF MAGICIANS, nothing of magic, nothing of demons or possession, for three whole days.

26

O n the fourth day, she wakes up with a text message alert that someone deposited a rather large sum of money into her bank account and, of course, it got flagged as suspicious.

She peers at the number on her phone, at the suspicious amount of zeroes, before flopping back onto her pillow face-first.

LYRA (10:46 AM): Did Dr. Frisse give me money without talking about it first?

Her cat cuddles up against her chin, insistent, so she curls around him, snuggling him back, and lets the light of the weak sun reflecting off the snow play over her small room, instead of getting up and dealing with whatever the hell this is.

ALETTE (10:49 AM): She says not yet.

ALETTE (10:49 AM): But she has a document to send to you, when you are ready.

Lyra frowns at her phone, because that's not the easy answer, and she's certain she'll have to account for the money somehow.

You can't spend money that's not yours, someone'll always come looking and it's way worse to owe than to have.

LYRA (10:51 AM): How's Axel and the headache?

ALETTE (10:52 AM): He says it's manageable, and he regrets being unconscious so he couldn't blow stuff up. How is your hand?

Lyra glances at it, as if it would tell her under her bandage. It aches but she's still not quite in the place where she is feeling pain, so that tracks.

LYRA (10:53 AM): The stitches feel tight, but it's okay.

But now...now she has a problem to deal with, and the problem involves money, and she doesn't want to have to deal with that.

So she chucks on her favorite sweatshirt and fleece-lined leggings, and drags her aged laptop to her kitchen table where she can plug it in and take a look at her bank account.

A bank account was nothing her mother ever had, so she tries her hardest to keep on top of hers, but it's a lot easier to keep track of it when it's under five hundred dollars as opposed to...whatever the hell this amount is.

While her coffee is brewing, she boots the laptop up, before poking around on her bank account website.

It appears to be cash money left by a secure deposit drop with her information, including name and account number, in a city in Texas she's never been to. Non sequential bills, not all the same denomination, barely skating under the maximum deposit amount before someone brings in the feds.

It's far more than she's ever had in an account, even including the time they deposited the first check of Jackson's scholarship into her account so she could pay his first month rent for him.

And it's all in there. With her name and account info and everything. Even has the answers to her security questions written on the deposit form, which isn't anything she's ever told anyone, even Jackson.

She takes a deep breath, then another, as her coffee machine percolates and snow falls lightly on the steps outside.

She can't ask Jackson, his final is later that day and she's not going to sabotage that when he helped her so much earlier, but she sits back in the green velvet monstrosity and stares numbly at the computer screen.

In terms of rich people money, it's probably not a lot, but in terms of her, it's...literally life changing.

She could help Jackson with his books, she could pay to go see a doctor, she could actually maybe pay down some of that medical debt that still hounds her. She could take her time looking for a job, actually take time and figure out how to do something she'd want to do instead of just surviving.

She could figure out how to study with Alette, instead of having to sneak in sessions between looking for jobs and whatever retail work she can find.

The number still sits wrong.

It's too exact, with too real of information on her. A computer error wouldn't know her security questions, wouldn't have hand-written them on the deposit slip in the middle of the night.

Melekai might.

She mulls over that, stretching her legs and grabbing some coffee.

He might, it seems like something he'd do. Just go out and get something for her anonymously, leave it for her to find and deal with, if she ever looked. Like whatever house protections he might have, like how he apparently saved her life many times while leaving her unaware.

Like he heard the conversation about her needing a job and decided to take care of it. And now she owes a phone call to a branch in Texas so they can take proper notes about where the cash comes from.

"Any bugs you could catch?" She glances down at her cat, who's sleepily winding around her feet. "I need to talk to Melekai."

He meows quietly, but that doesn't help with anything, so she sighs.

Or he could come and visit.

Two days and several uncomfortable calls with the bank later, with nothing else to show for it, when she walks by her kitchen window, Terese is illuminated in the blowing snow.

Lyra stops, clutching her cup of coffee, and Terese watches her with her colorless eyes. Her leather jacket still bears the jagged edges of the gunshot, though her body underneath it appears whole.

Terese dips her head, some strange acknowledgement, before trying to take a step forward, but being rebuffed.

Well, at least her protections are still in place. At least, wherever Melekai went, however he's doing, his magic is still there.

The coffee cup hot in her hands, Lyra slowly, ever so slowly, reaches for her snow jacket, before cramming her hair under a beanie and shoving her feet into snow shoes.

Terese lifts her chin, at that.

Lyra's cat meows, loud, once at Lyra, but Lyra just grabs her gloves anyways.

"I'm not leaving, I'll just be on my porch," she says, like the cat could understand her, before she opens her door and steps onto the rickety wooden railing.

Her father had left a plastic chair out on the porch, next to an old ash tray, and while Lyra had thrown that away she kept the chair out of some sort of odd loyalty, even if she rarely sits in it. It's just under the awning enough that it doesn't have a pile of snow on it, though grime clings to it.

Terese doesn't stop watching her.

"What do you want?" Lyra asks, wrapping her snow jacket around herself like a blanket.

The awning does little to protect from the wind.

Terese's mouth opens, then closes, twice. Like she never thought Lyra would actually ask her, would actually try to talk.

Lyra lets her ponder, though her heart pounds.

Terese tries to take another step forward and gets jerked back from whatever barrier Melekai had put into place.

"You can't come in here," Lyra says, after swallowing down the fear at Terese's attempt. "But...why do you try?"

"Maybe he'll get sloppy," she says, and her eyes reflect back at Lyra, "maybe he won't be thinking so hard, and maybe he'll leave you unprotected. Maybe he'll die."

That's a bit comforting, as it's a little confirmation that Melekai's probably not already dead, that he survived the battle.

She pulls her jacket tighter, all of a sudden feeling a pang of missing him. A pang of fear, a pang of upset, that he hasn't come to see her.

And Terese has.

"Can I ask a few questions?" Lyra blurts out, and again, Terese blinks at her, like she caught her by surprise. "Why all the targeting? Why kill all the random magicians?"

"None of them could help me?" Terese finally says, and her voice is small. Like she's whispering, like she's scared.

"I don't think I could, either," Lyra says, and Terese immediately shakes her head, as if to contradict her, "not without dying."

"That's okay," Terese says lyrically, "everyone dies."

"Cool, so you're a psychopath," Lyra says, gathering her jacket up to stand up, and Terese puts her hand up, like she could stop her from leaving. Urgent.

"Why would you get in the car with that doctor?" Terese asks, and it's just enough of a unique question that Lyra sits back down, tries to listen. "I wasn't trying to find you then, just them."

It's almost an olive branch, as much as an olive branch as one could get with a homicidal maniac who tried to flip their car, who blew up the Buggees, and upended Lyra's life. Who killed a small village in Canada, which somehow didn't make the news.

"We were just going to a research library," Lyra says, hoping that doesn't give away anything that shouldn't be given freely. "They picked me up because I was interested."

Her brows furrow, and she shrugs in on herself, like she's cold from the blowing snow.

"They wouldn't need a research library," Terese says, confident, though Lyra doesn't know where that could even come from, "I'm certain everything they would need to know is somewhere in that dark-haired spell weaver's brain." Her eyes flash up to Lyra. "Did you know I killed her?"

"Yeah," Lyra responds, unsettled. "I brought her back."

Terese nods, like it's common knowledge. "I saw the flare, but I couldn't track it down."

It's something akin to talking to someone in code, and Lyra wishes she had brought out a notebook, though her fingers would probably freeze if she tried to grasp a pencil.

"She was trying to..." Terese gestures with her hand, as if grasping for words, hoping Lyra could substitute them, "separate me into two."

"Stop the possession?" Lyra asks, and gets a surprised light in Terese's eyes. "We know you're in an alive body. I felt it."

"She's not really alive, she's mostly dormant," Terese continues, which isn't any less creepy, "all she does is hurt and occasionally wants food."

"That's sad," Lyra says, and means it. "Can you let her go?"

Lyra doesn't know if that means killing her or just vacating the body, and she doesn't know how any of it would work.

Terese just tilts her head at her and doesn't respond.

"If she's just hurting you," Lyra tries again, and hopes she's not advocating for someone's death, "wouldn't that mean that leaving the body, going to a traditional body for a demon, a dead one, mean you wouldn't be in pain?"

The snow kicks up a bit, and Lyra can't read Terese's expression from so far away.

"That doctor told you nothing," Terese says, finally, and for the first time her voice isn't musical, but flat. "I can't."

"Why not?" Lyra asks, and her skin starts to crawl.

She should go inside, she should stop speaking with this person who tried to kill her twice now. She should definitely think for herself, instead of this awful gnawing sense of curiosity inside of her.

"The doctor bound me to the body, not me," Terese says, her face sharp, her voice plain. "Her and with the research of the dark-haired spell weaver and that invention from the pretty alchemist shoved me in this body and kept me here. They're why it's only pain."

Lyra resists the urge to recoil away, to wince at the sentence.

She can't trust anything Terese says is true, but...but it's very interesting.

Melekai would probably have a different word for it, and then she misses him anew.

"So how can she undo it?" Lyra asks, instead of any of the hundreds of things in her mind. "How can she—or I—undo it?"

Terese's shoulders suddenly relax and she gives her a glinting grin. "Let me kill you?"

"Uh, no?" Lyra says.

"It might stop everything," she continues, "I haven't had necromancer before this." She gestures, widely. At Lyra, at herself, at the world around her. "But it just might work."

For a split second, Lyra thinks it might be a joke. That this demon, this demon that's been twisted around and completely beyond any sort of logic or reason, might've joked.

"Anyway, can I ask you to leave us alone?" Lyra asks, almost joking herself. "None of us particularly want to die, myself included."

"No," Terese says, and her voice is back to having the musical lilt, like it's an affectation she puts on to convince people, to appear more like a normal human. "Though you should run."

"What?" Lyra asks, and they lock eyes, as Lyra's nose starts to go numb in the cold and Terese's face blurs slightly with the snow.

The top of her head, on top of the pale blond of her pixie cut, there's a pile of snow building up, clinging to the strands.

"If I don't get you, you should run," Terese repeats, "or that doctor will do to you and your demon exactly what she did to me."

Terese falls silent, at that, her face pale, like she didn't mean to reveal so much about herself. Like she didn't want to give the warning, like she didn't think it was fair.

Like she didn't get any warning.

"She offered money, first, to the human," Terese says, like the words are being pulled out of her, "rescued her from poverty, told her she would be safe from me, then tied me up and captured me with a rope around my wrist." She shivers, once, the only indication that the body feels cold. "We thought we were learning powers, not..."

"Were you a necromancer?" Lyra asks, quiet, unsure if her words will be heard over the wind and the pelt of the snow.

"I don't think the body was, she wasn't as bright as you," Terese says, just as quiet back. "I can't communicate with her, I can't tell, other than she just won't die. She's just there, on the edge of my awareness, screaming in pain and hurting me." Her face is pale, pale in the snow and the cold. "I want her to stop."

At that, Lyra sits, for about three seconds, then gathers up her jacket and steps inside.

Terese's eyes follow her, reflecting back in the same way that Melekai's always do, and even when Lyra closes her curtains, she can still feel her gaze.

She breezes past her cat, heads straight to where her phone lays, from where she texted Alette about money.

Then stills.

For all of Melekai's ability to read her mind, to see what she's seeing, there's no guarantee that Terese didn't do the same, from the time she destroyed the Buggees. It could all be a lie, all be a warped fiction told specifically to scare her. Seen or heard the conversation about money with the banks and used that. Could have seen the rope that Lyra tried to tie with magic and tried to manipulate that information to her own use.

Or.

Lyra takes a deep breath, then another, well aware that she's on her way to a truly irrational panic attack, but it doesn't help.

Alette wouldn't do something like that, not knowingly, and it's hard to imagine the same Axel who offered her a jacket would do something so harmful intentionally.

She has no such faith in Dr. Frisse.

Which really is the problem.

She yanks the pillow off the couch, and sits cross-legged on the floor, her hands shaking.

There are no dead bugs, nothing dead near her, but she squeezes her eyes shut, and tries to...feel. Sense.

Imagine, or whatever the fuck they keep on telling her.

Her cat is brilliant against her awareness, as he creeps close, then skitters back away under the bed with a thump. Whatever she's doing, it scares him, his heart fluttering and the muscle in the back leg tight.

He meows sadly and she can't hear him from the kitchen, but can feel the rumble in his vocal cords and the tremor in his whiskers.

Further out, Terese seems to glow, and the demon shifts the moment she feels her reach out, like her power burns. She moves her weight from foot to foot, deciding if it's a threat or not or if she'd even be able to fight back, from this far away. The nerves up her back ratchet in pain, blistering in their awareness.

With a twist of pain, she vanishes, leaving behind two footprints melted in the snow. Like it's not worth the fight.

Beyond her, the ground is cold, and all the animals are hidden away, and she strains, trying to sense any bugs or dead birds or —

"Stop," Melekai says, his deep voice rumbling behind her, and her eyes pop open, and she trembles.

She's still in her snow jacket and boots, and underneath it she's coated in a thin layer of sweat.

He's scowling, his mouth downturned and his eyes dark. He's still in the same body as before, though there's no black blood on the Henley and his hair is immaculately in place.

"What were you doing?" he demands, but he doesn't make a move to sit next to her, to join her on the floor.

"Terese was just here," she says, after a long moment. "We spoke."

His face twists suddenly, before he smooths it out, and he stalks over to the curtains and twitches them open.

Terese is gone, just like Lyra felt.

"And you felt the need to send up such a huge flare that everyone who might be looking for necromancers would see it?" he asks, before turning back to her, his brows furrowed. "Why?"

"She said Dr. Frisse did that to her," Lyra blurts out, and his hand jerks towards her, as if to comfort her, but he stops himself, "said that she took the human Terese and the demon and tied them together."

He's still, so still, he's not even blinking. Not even breathing, and she's still deep in her concentration so she feels it, feels the lack of motion.

So she looks at him, meets him right in the eye. He might be angry at her, for whatever risks, for doing something he forbade her to do, but she has to say it.

"I wanted to warn you."

27

H e doesn't move, until, abruptly, he does.

All at once, he exhales, then he grabs her by her arm, smoothly pulling her up to standing. A hand curls around the small of her back, and she gets a brief moment of peace, before...

Before they're no longer in her home.

Her feet hit stone floors and the sound echoes. It's warmer in this new place, but not by much, and the warmth feels empty, far away, instead of cozy.

Still, she strips off her snow jacket, looking around.

It's a grand room, with vaulted stone ceilings and dust motes high in the sun, and bookshelves crowd the edges, but still the room feels abandoned. Bereft.

But sun spills through stained glass windows, lending it the feel of a church or some holy land, and rugs cover half the stone floor. A giant fireplace burns, with a giant sheepskin rug in front of it. There's a modern leather couch, out of place with the rest of the environs, with a plastic side table and a stack of books next to it.

The sun's at a different angle than it was back at her house, closer to late afternoon than midday.

Melekai steps away from her, like he's worried she'll harm him, and she tries hard not to feel hurt by that.

"Where is this?" Lyra asks, drifting further into the room. Her voice echoes.

He doesn't answer immediately, instead methodically scanning the windows and entry points, as if checking to make sure they're still safe.

"Don't do any necromancy in here," he says. "I'd like this place to stay hidden."

She eyes him, but he's still checking all the windows and the eaves.

"Okay," she says, scuffing her snow boot along the stone floor. "Where are we?"

His eyes flicker to her, just briefly, before back to his task. "My home," he says, almost begrudgingly. "It's the safest place I could think of."

"Oh," she replies, then takes a harder look around.

It's barely lived in, besides the books and the fire and couch, no evidence of a place to sleep or eat, but of course he wouldn't need all of that. Instead it's just books, books upon books of knowledge.

She needs to figure out a way to get him a smartphone, if he's this voracious of a reader.

"Repeat to me," he starts, then frowns, like he's unsure of himself, and it's an awful look on him, "what exactly did she say?"

He holds out a hand to her, like he always does, but startles when she takes it. Like he had been so unaware of his actions that he acted by rote.

Still, he grasps her hand, glancing down at it as if it's fascinating.

Lyra tugs him over towards the giant leather couch to relieve the pressure of standing, and it's gloriously comfortable. He lets himself get pulled along, though his prickliness radiates out from his every movement.

She exhales, leaning back against the comfort of the couch, and it's like it was designed for her. Like it's custom made just for her issues, for her body.

"Thank you for keeping me safe," she starts, and it's horridly stilted, before pressing on. "I saw she couldn't get through your barriers, and I...I wanted answers."

He sits next to her, the couch sliding them together, but his face is still drawn. "She could've been doing that for show."

"Yeah, but..." Lyra trails off, unsure what to do with the frustration and the anger and everything inside of her, "you disappeared, Dr. Frisse doesn't answer anything straight."

He picks up her hand again, begins tracing it, and something like relief unfurls in Lyra's gut.

"I didn't disappear, I went somewhere to recover," he says, though his hand skips along hers, like a break in his thoughts. "She could've killed you."

"She almost killed you," Lyra throws out, and he breaks his gaze at her hand just long enough to give her a scowl. "And then I didn't hear anything from you for..."

"We don't need to talk about it," he interrupts, and it might be the most irresponsible thing she's ever heard from him, "we could pretend I didn't disappear, pretend that didn't happen, and work on keeping you safe and stopping her."

For a moment, she's tempted. She's honestly tempted, to ignore the last few days and the tension and the horrible pit in her stomach whenever she thinks of him, but...

"No," Lyra says, and his eyebrows flash up, "no, I don't want to get pulled around like that. Why didn't you at least stop by, at least let me know you were okay?"

He looks caught in the headlights, eyes wide. Like he didn't actually expect her to disagree with him, like he had actual hope that he could get away with saying something like that, that she would let it roll off her back just as easily.

Then again, he's probably not had much long-term experience dealing with people like her.

Lyra sighs, then scoots close to him on the couch, so their legs press against each other, and every motion causes another muscle to relax in his shoulders.

"I didn't...I didn't want to take more," he says, like he's fumbling over his words, "or if you would make me hurt you, or..." he trails off, looking away and wrinkling his nose in frustration. "I could have killed you."

The words, laid bare, hang in the room, heavier than any heat from the fire.

"Even with your tie and your command, one misstep and one weakness in a technique you've only done twice before, and you would have died. It was an incalculable bad idea, too much of a risk, and then I'd be without you."

He snaps his mouth shut at that, mulish, but still grips her hand, still presses against her on the couch.

Lyra exhales past that one, past that declaration, and presses her knee against him in a little motion, one that he nods at.

"You've lived for...god, I don't know," Lyra starts, in what she hopes is a soothing voice, but it still echoes in the large room, "you'd be fine, eventually."

He recoils, actually recoils, away from her, dropping her hand like it'd burn him.

"And if you died, and I was left there...there'd be nothing to stop Terese from just killing me instantly," Lyra continues, willing herself to stay in place and not wince away. Let him do that, let her show him that she's still there. "So if I didn't take that risk, I'd be dead soon anyways."

That's how she's justified it to herself in the last few days, at least. It definitely was not in her head when it happened.

He stills, and she just lets him sit in that. Lets him think.

It's a pretty statement, at least, for how slightly untrue it is. Or, rather, how incomplete.

"And I like you," Lyra forces herself to say, though it goes against everything in her body to say, "and I didn't want to think about you being dead, and I panicked."

His gaze on her is like a brand, but she doesn't let herself squirm away. If he could say uncomfortable things, then so could she.

Slow, as if telegraphing his movement, he curls his hand on the back of her neck, an old familiar motion.

"I would not be fine," he says, voice low, and her stomach turns over at his words, at their implication, and at his touch. "I would very much not be fine."

"So that's what these last few days have been?" Lyra asks. "The running away, was that you panicking about me dying?"

It's awkward, it's horrible, saying these things out loud and so plainly. All her life, there's been things that you just don't give words to, and all these awful feelings are definitely among them.

He looks just as spooked, but he nods.

"Okay," Lyra says, then exhales, shaking out her arms, startling out a grin from him. "So if you almost die and I do that again—"

"Don't do that again," he interrupts.

"—And you disappear for a few days, I know to expect it?"

He scowls at her, but his hand is still on the back of her neck, so it feels less severe, and it's strange, how she flipped from being afraid of him to needing him in her life so strongly.

"I guess," he says, like it's been pulled out of him. "I'll see about notifying you, so you're not just…"

"Worrying," she finishes for him.

And they sit like that, for a few seconds, with the only sound the pop and crackle of the giant fire.

"But you're better now?" Lyra asks, into the silence. "The wound was…"

"We heal different," he says, flippant. "The wound that made me bleed was not the critical strike."

"Creepy," Lyra replies, and he smiles at her, a small, almost understated smile, and her heart flops all over herself, before he leans into her, placing a kiss on her lips.

"I want you to never do that again," he whispers, lips still touching hers, "I want you to never be in danger again, danger from me or from anyone."

"No," she whispers back, then kisses him again, stronger this time, "I make no promises."

He makes a noise, prodding her closer to him, and she lets him, until he pulls her onto his lap, still kissing her.

It's not how she usually kisses people, if she could have a usual, but he tilts her head back, like she's more captivating than she could ever imagine. It's like kissing a dying man, like kissing someone so desperate that they may not even breathe, like being the only thing keeping him together.

She's never felt that important before.

She pulls at the hem of his shirt, pulling it over his head until he has to break the kiss to finish taking it off, and sits far enough back to inspect him.

There's a faint mark, almost the hint of a scar, where the ice hit him. Like it's the vague memory of a wound, instead of something so concrete. Like years upon years had actually passed, instead of just a week.

He scowls at her inspection, then pulls her close to press a line of kisses on her throat.

"You haven't tied me back," he says, tugging the neckline of her sweater down to best kiss on her collarbone, "do you need to?"

"I thought you said no necromancy," she breathes, trying not to squirm under his touch. "You won't hurt me."

He hesitates, his lips a ghost over her skin. "I won't hurt you," he repeats, like he's trying on her trust for size. "I won't hurt you."

Suddenly, a hand against the small of her back, before she can do anything, he has her in his arms and lowered down onto the rug, warm against her skin, and he kneels down over her, still wearing his jeans, his knee between her legs.

She wiggles out underneath him, then takes off her sweater first, and he bends and places a kiss in the middle of her stomach, his scruff scratching her just enough.

A heat grows in her, and she locks eyes with him, just as his hand goes to the fly of his jeans. The roaring fire lends a reddish tint to his skin, and the freckles dusted over his collarbone stand out.

"Do you want this?" he asks, and she knows he's not just asking about his cock.

It's about all of it. About all the messy emotions and the confusion and the frustration from the conversation, about his fear and his difficulty talking about it, about his fleeing and his utter inhumanity.

But in exchange, it's about all her skittishness, about all her pain, about how she still doesn't like to think about connecting with people. About how the idea of being with someone more than once still scares her, still pulls at her fear that she's going to have to leave, have to disappoint them, have to watch as they distance themselves and leave her behind.

"Yes," she says, as he undoes the front of his jeans, and the heat inside her grows even more. "Yes, I think I do."

She's not used to this, being desired like this, so obviously, but, if this is how it always is, she could get used to it.

She tugs him up to kiss him, open mouthed, her other hand going to his cock. It should be cold, with how cavernous the room is, but with the fire and the rug, it's almost exhausting in its heat.

"I want," she says, soft, so he has to lean in close, "I want you on your back, instead of me."

His eyebrows flash up, but he sheds his jeans.

Half waiting for him to stop her, she presses her hand hard against his lean chest, pushing him down in a long, smooth motion, until his back is against the rug instead of hers.

She sheds her own snow pants, so she's just there in her underwear in front of him, but he looks at her as if she's clothed in the finest of jewels, in the finest of silks.

She surges forward, kissing him, flicking his lips open with her tongue, and he groans against her, a hand tangling in her hair, holding him against her.

He's hard, that much is already apparent, but it's difficult to figure out how, even when it's not the first time they've been together, and a small part of her marvels at him, marvels at the weirdness that she's sleeping, she's fucking, with a dead body. A dead body that belonged to someone else, once.

"Stop thinking," he mumbles against her, tugging off her panties and tossing them aside in a more than practiced motion. "Stop thinking and just...be."

It's great advice for someone who hasn't had to worry their entire lives, but she leans against him, her knees on the sheepskin rug, and kisses him back.

He kisses her like he'd die without her, and with just a few motions, his cock presses against her, and she sighs, high and breathy, before leaning back on top of him.

The air crackles around them, with some strange electricity, some strange discharge of power between them, and without warning, she's consumed by it.

It's different from being drunk, at least on the surface, though her blood fizzes and her skin tightens, and all she can see is him, all she can feel is his hands on her hips, thrusting into her. His legs against hers, as she rides on top of him, his eyes on her breasts.

It's glorious, it's sublime, and she lets her eyes flutter shut until the emotion and the sensation carries her away, sparkling behind her eyelids until it's all she can see.

28

After, she's panting and there's a thin sheen of sweat on both of them—why he sweats she doesn't know—and she snuggles up against his chest on the sheepskin rug.

A hand rubs down her bare back, halfway between a caress and the touch of a feather.

He exhales, and he's staring up at the vaulted ceiling.

"This place is much more warm with you in it," he says, and it's dreamlike, his voice in the open space with the crackling fire. "I should have brought you here ages ago."

She presses her nose into the crook of his neck, against that one spot he has three freckles close together.

They're going to have to talk about all this, sometime, and she doesn't want to ignore it.

"Did you put money into my bank account?" Lyra asks, pushing herself up onto her elbows so she can see his face.

"No?" He wrinkles his nose at her, before his face smooths over into something thoughtful. "Is that something you'd want?"

"Well, Dr. Frisse offered money but then said this didn't come from her," Lyra says, and he props himself up at that. "You were the only other person who might have big sums that would give me any."

"And Terese said Frisse got the trust of the human by giving her money," he muses. "Too convenient."

"Everything is too convenient," she says, and he nods his agreement. "Everything is too convenient and too easy to suspect."

"This is why I say you're smart," he says, easily, "a more foolish magician would fall headfirst into that trap."

"You really think it's a trap?" Lyra asks, resisting the urge to tangle her hand in his golden-brown curls, splayed all over the sheepskin.

He stares up at his vaulted ceiling, at the stone pillars and the stained glass.

"If I wanted to take down a group of magicians, I would sow seeds of discord between them however I could," he says. "Especially if one was new and the rest were established." He tilts his head towards her, and the tops of his cheeks are still flushed. "Especially if it was a necromancer. I would want to get you alone, immediately, without any additional protection. Make you want to withdraw from your demon protection"—he gestures to himself—"and from other magicians."

Lyra pillows her head in her arms, content to stare at Melekai. He's open, when he's like this, mellowed out, the mischievous glint a little bit softer in his eyes.

He's handsome.

And she can't tell if it's the body, or just the knowledge of him inside of it.

"But," he continues, "I don't trust Frisse at all."

"Me neither," Lyra supplies, and gets a bare-toothed grin. "I can't tell if she's just snobby or like...actually malicious."

"I wouldn't put it past her to have pulled some less than ethical experiments," he says, and he inspects his hand, as if he expects it to change just from sitting there. "And if it was from any other source, I'd believe what Terese says. It fits neatly in what I think of her."

"Before I summoned you, she was casual about Alette dying," Lyra says, and Melekai snorts. "What, it's applicable."

"I'd be surprised if she's ever felt affection for anyone," he says, then trails off. "I doubt Alette is malicious at all, and I don't think Axel has the capacity."

Lyra nods, even though he's looking up in the room, and they have a moment of peace, a moment of quiet, just the two of them.

"How'd you find this place?" Lyra asks, rolling over and staring up at the ceiling with him.

It's almost church-like, at least her limited understanding of churches from the media. Like he took an old church, took out everything that made it holy, and stuffed it full of books instead.

She could deal with that.

"Eh, it's been abandoned for...centuries?" Melekai says. "I found it when they were bombing everywhere."

"Bombing...Melekai, are we in America?" Lyra asks, propping herself up.

He shrugs.

Of course he wouldn't be concerned about something like that.

"I don't like Terese knowing your bank account," he says, begrudging. "I haven't even put effort into knowing your bank account. That's human stuff."

She pokes him in the side, and he wrinkles his nose at her. "I'm human."

"Yes, and that's why you caught it," he says, poking her back in the side. "If you need money you can just tell me, and I'll make it appear."

"Actually appear or just..."

"I'll find a way to give you stacks of cash," he says, "I know it's possible, I've seen Wights do it all the time."

Lyra tries to imagine actually going into the bank with a stack of bills and fails.

Somewhere in her contemplation, he lets his head fall to the side to stare at her, and his hand drapes over her hip. It's a tender motion, and, somehow, it brings tears to Lyra's eyes.

"I missed you," she says baldly, and his eyes briefly panic. "No really, I missed you, when you were recovering."

"Terrifying," he drawls out, but she can hear the marvel behind his words. "What sort of necromancer actually misses a demon?"

She pokes him again, right in between the ribs, and he rolls over, draping his entire arm over her in a squashed embrace.

"Can you stay here for a few hours?" he asks, and it's much more vulnerable than she thought it would be. "I want...I want to make sure your house is safe. And your brother."

"Is it easier when I'm here?" Lyra asks, and he nods. "Or is it just that me being there is a distraction?"

He rolls his eyes, then sits up, reaching for his pants, before he disappears.

Leaving her alone in the grand cavernous hall.

She shivers, once, though she is plenty warm, before rolling up herself.

Without him, the entire place is quieter. Less severe.

Half tempted to remain naked until he comes back, she nonetheless pulls her clothes back on, making sure to pull on her socks to protect her feet from the stone floor.

This place is his, has been for...a while now, if his bombing comment was any indication, and this is an unprecedented chance to actually get a glimpse of what he would be like if she's not here.

So by god she's gonna browse.

The books by the couch are all in what appears to be French, if her understanding is correct about it, and the covers are an eclectic mix of pulpy science fiction and textbooks about some sort of biology.

Like he's trying to learn something.

She picks up the first pulpy book, entranced by its cover of an astronaut shooting a laser at a fleeing spaceship, with a planet blowing up in the background. It's so far beyond what she would think he'd like, but it's so well worn that he either bought it used or read it many, many times.

She needs to show him some TV. If he likes books like this, he's going to love her binge-watching shows from the mid-eighties, where the space is high and the hair is higher. Where everything glitters and everything is optimistic and shiny.

The first bookcase is covered in dust, and none of the books are in a language she's ever seen. Her fingers tingle when she touches their spine, like there's some magic in them, magic to make him be able to touch it easily, to remain here. To remain intact, when they're so obviously so old.

The next shelf is pristine textbooks, in every subject and every language. Lyra pulls an English one—*Modern History of the Americas* —and the palm of her hand tingles against it.

She cracks it open. Published in 1961. And yet it is as new and as unvarnished as if it's from this year.

She trails her hands along several more bookcases, coming across one of more science fiction pulp novels, one stuffed full of pink romance books, and another of stuffy looking literary fiction, then one full of compilation books of New Yorker magazines.

There are glimpses of strangeness, too. A bookmark of blond human hair, neatly braided, almost crumbling at her touch. A collection of miscellaneous human teeth, lining a shelf full of old mystery novels. A gold chain that sends a chill down her spine in a decidedly unfriendly way, coiled in a corner of the bookcase as if it was forgotten. A skull of a rabbit, staring at her and giving her the faintest wisps that she could bring it back, even though the rest of the body is missing. A dried plant arranged in haphazard bundles, one that she can't bring herself to touch out of the belief that it'd probably kill her.

In the back corner of one shelf, tucked between the wood and a book about geology, there's even a blurry polaroid of her, and by the bad dye job she would say it's from when she was about twenty-two, right after she dropped out of college. She's looking over her shoulder, like she's talking with someone, and fully unaware that she was photographed. There's a strange effect over the picture, like Melekai wasn't fully able to develop it correctly, but kept it anyway.

There's nothing written on the back, no commentary, just...just the one photograph in this entire place, and it's a blurry one of her from long ago.

She carefully tucks it back in its place.

Of course, he'd probably know she found it, based on whatever gold trace she seems to leave behind, but there's no reason to be disruptive.

There are a few dead birds hidden in the roof, she can tell without even trying, just the vague pull in her stomach, but she promised no necromancy, so she doesn't try to pinpoint where they'd be.

If Melekai thinks she's safe here, she's safe.

From where she dumped her snow jacket in the middle of the room, her phone beeps, so she pads on socked feet to go fish it out.

ALETTE (3:02 PM): Are you safe?

LYRA (3:05 PM): Yes? You?

There's no reply, which isn't comforting, so Lyra cradles the phone, bringing it back to the couch, where she flops onto with less finesse than she would have hoped.

She thumbs open her maps, and sure enough according to her GPS, they're somewhere in farmland France. Close enough to a population source that she'd still have signal, but obviously far enough from her system that she'd definitely have roaming charges.

Well, if whatever money she has is still hers when she gets back to the States, that might not be that big of an issue, and a part of her psyche shies away from thinking about it that way.

She pokes around on her phone, flipping between the social media she rarely uses and her library app, until there's a crackle in the air and without even raising her eyes to glance up, she can tell that Melekai's back.

"You touched my stuff," he grumps, but there's no spite in it, not really.

"We got to use this magic"—she waves at the room as a whole—"to get you a cell phone."

"Why would I ever want a cell phone?" he asks, flopping down next to her on the giant leather couch.

"Because then you would have all the world's books in a portable little square," she says, wiggling her phone at him, "and it's easier to dust."

"Every generation has their replacement for the physical book," he says, but nonetheless leans over her, draping his limbs over her. "It's exhausting to keep up when one moment you blink and there's a new technology that's irrelevant again that you just got used to." He tugs her over to him, until he can bury his face in her hair.

She snakes her arm around him, holding him just as tight. "How many things in this room could kill me?" she asks.

She feels him make a face against her neck. "I thought you'd be smart enough to not get dead."

"Yes, but I'm curious and there are weird things."

"Probably three, if you don't count the bookcases falling over," he says, shifting so they're practically laying down on the couch, then— "I like having you here."

She lets her eyes flutter shut at those words, lets herself feel the emotion behind them.

"I've...contracted with people," Melekai starts, slow, like he's unsure, "that if something happened to me, you won't be completely unprotected."

She lifts her head to glance up at him.

"It won't be perfect, and you might have to lay low for a little while, but you won't have to worry about...other demons."

There's something fragile, in his words, something so insecure, so she rests against him again, and he sighs against her hair.

"Is my house safe again?"

He nods against her, but makes no movement to bring her back, and honestly, she could lay like this for forever, just the two of them. A lull of peace, before everything could go wrong. A single crystalline moment, the sort of moment you remember forever.

29

He takes her back to her house a few hours later, and her cat twines around her legs, meowing loud enough to let Lyra know that he is rather displeased with her absence, until she swoops over and picks him up, cradling him like a very spoiled baby.

"You should name him," Melekai says, even though his eyes are focused on the window sills, as if double checking his work. "I like things to have names, then I don't get things mixed up in my own head, and I have known too many cats to just keep thinking of it as 'cat'."

"I'm not hearing any suggestions," Lyra says, as the cat purrs, then wiggles out from her arms so he can wind around her legs again instead. "Anything I think of just sounds silly or stereotypical, and I mean..." she trails off, after a particularly loud meow. "I mean he's been dead, I feel like his name should reflect that, but calling a cat something like Hades just seems mean."

"Hades works," Melekai says, and the cat immediately starts begging for love from him instead, "or you could just call him something normal."

"How would you know what a normal cat name is?" Lyra asks, this time actually hanging her snow jacket.

Outside, in the dark of the late evening, the snow's been blown off her yard and driveway, as if it's never been there, and there's a perfectly delineated berm at the end, where Terese stood.

It'll block some traffic, but when has she ever cared about that?

"Smudge?" Melekai starts. "Max? Charlie? Chatters? Momo? Peter? Leo? Jiji?"

She squints at him, then back at her driveway. Fresh snow has fallen on her yard, but it hasn't stuck yet, despite the few hours that have passed.

The cat just winds between the two of them, without a care in the world.

"I could do Max, that works," Lyra says, still squinting at her driveway. "What did you do?"

"Made it inhospitable for any demon that's not me," he answers.

Even her dead lawn is showing.

"It'll get covered eventually," he says, petting the cat like the sucker he is. "Max, will you respond to that?"

Of course, the cat meows at him.

"He'll respond to anything you say in that voice," Lyra comments, still raising an eyebrow at her yard. "The neighbors are gonna be super weirded out."

"One of your neighbors cooks meth and the other one is three steps away from a heart attack, they're not concerned with your yard," he says, and he has a point. "It's no danger to you, it's no danger to them, and if Terese comes back it's going to be so unpleasant she's going to go literally anywhere else." He scowls out at the yard, like it personally irritates him. "It's a bitch and a half to set up and I shouldn't have to, but I don't want her thinking she can just talk to you and say those things until she weasels her way inside."

"I wouldn't let her in," Lyra protests, but he just looks at her side-eyed.

"Little Lyra, you want to help everybody, and just because she's in pain doesn't mean she's not going to kill you," he says, and when she opens her mouth to protest, he holds his hand up. "You kept a cat that you brought back because you felt bad. You raised Alette when you barely knew her. You almost died to save my life even though it was incredibly risky. I know you."

She snaps her mouth shut.

"It's incredibly endearing, it's incredibly dangerous," he continues. "All the necromancers I've ever seen or known have been combat-oriented but you apologized when you left someone with bruising, you're that much of a healer."

"I like that," she blurts out, before she could stop herself, "healer." The moment she does, she definitely feels like she should be taking offense to it, but...but no. Healer. Sounds good.

Sounds a hell of a lot better than the creepiness of her powers. Sounds a hell of a lot better than blowing stuff up, than whatever the heck they want her to do to Terese.

He gives her an amused sort of smile, one that's almost embarrassing in how tender it is.

Her phone buzzes, and she has to dig it out of the pocket of her snow jacket.

ALETTE (7:22 PM): Still good?

"This is foreboding, right?" Lyra asks, turning to show the phone to Melekai.

"Yes," he says, without bothering to read what's on the screen.

LYRA (7:23 PM): Yes what is going on?

"You want to help them, even though Frisse lies to you and talks down to you," he points out, like that hasn't already occurred to her. "Your greatest flaw is your drive to help people."

"It's not a flaw," Lyra protests, but halfheartedly.

HE STICKS around the rest of the evening, but it's a companionable evening. A quiet time where it's just the two of them. She makes food for herself, and they don't hear from Alette for the rest of the day. He vanishes after a brief kiss, but it doesn't feel like the last time. Doesn't feel like he's abandoning her. Doesn't feel like she did something horridly wrong, like she stepped on his toes and insulted him.

Just feels...normal. Sustainable.

Like she could do this for the rest of her life.

A COMICALLY LARGE stack of money is left on her kitchen table the next morning, and a brief bubble of laughter hits her.

THE NEXT DAY, after hearing nothing and worrying for far too long, her phone finally buzzes and it's Alette.

"You better have a reason for all those texts yesterday," Lyra says, in lieu of a greeting.

"We thought you might've gotten kidnapped," Axel says, instead of Alette, and she really wants them to stop switching phones—it makes her entire stomach drop out. "We were just on a wild goose chase with Terese from here to literal Alaska and eight people died."

Lyra sits up straight, despite her legs cramping. "Anyone—"

"No one you know," she hears Alette say, in the background, like they're driving. "And Terese started burning the bodies so we can't bring them to you."

Again, Lyra wishes for a cell phone for Melekai, because she'd totally text him.

"But at least one grandmaster of spellweaving up in Hyder is dead, and all of his knowledge with him," Axel says, voice tinny through the phone, "and we thought Terese used someone with a massive amount of necromancy energy, so we thought you."

Lyra blinks out at her yard, now barely covered with the thinnest layer of crunchy snow, despite the dumping her neighbors received. "Isn't it like Christmas in three days?" she says. "Why wouldn't she, I dunno, wait until after Christmas?"

"It is?" She hears Alette wonder in the background. "Really?"

Lyra can't really respond to that, so she sits on the velvet green monstrosity, and the cat— Max?—jumps to join her. "Well I'm safe."

"Can we pick you up?" Axel asks, and she can hear the familiar crunch of gravel underneath the car wheels.

It's not the Mustang, that's for sure, and for a few seconds she contemplates what must've happened to the car.

"What for?" Lyra asks, warring between suspicion and the hope to see them alive and well.

"Well I want to make sure you're not just a copy of yourself that Terese has seeded—" Axel starts.

"Axel," Alette says in the background, chiding.

"And Dr. Frisse has ideas for a trap."

A trap.

"She can't really make copies, can she?" Lyra asks, heading towards her snow boots.

As if her longing summons him, Melekai appears next to her, and if her longing can do that, they're going to be having way more sex than before.

He raises an eyebrow down at her

"She doesn't need to come," Alette says. "She might still be resting."

"No, let me come," Lyra says, with a glance to Melekai.

He tilts his head at her, like he's evaluating, then gives her a sharp smile.

"What? Okay," Axel says, puzzle in his voice, and—

"I want to help, and I don't want to be in the dark about a trap," Lyra says.

"And we can determine if they're actually going to hurt us or not," Melekai says, softly, and Lyra doubts that the phone could pick him up. "Test how trustworthy they are."

She nods at him. "I wanna help with this trap," she says, locking eyes with Melekai, who just grins deeper, "and I don't want to be the bait this time."

≈

MELEKAI WATCHES THEM ROLL UP, then puts a hand on the small of Lyra's back. "I'll keep track of you, and intercept if you're in danger," he says, low. "I want them to think you might be helpless, to see if they say anything." He shifts as they get closer, so they can't see him, so they don't have a line of sight on him.

She tilts her head up to him, but he's just idly touching her, not doing anything serious. "I'll see what I can find out," she says, and he nods, absent-minded. "Ask some questions."

"Be your best self that pretends to not know anything," he says, and this time it's her turn to grin at him. "The doctor would buy it. Alette might not, but Frisse would, and Axel would find it funny."

Lyra nods at him, then steps outside.

Alette pulls up, driving her sensible sedan, and Axel looks like he's going to shake out of his skin as he tumbles out of the car, before he freezes the moment he steps on her lawn.

Alette follows suit, but instead of freezing just pokes at the ground. "What did he do?" she asks, still sitting in her car and nudging the snow with her needle case. "This is..."

"Terese was here again, Melekai got irritated," Lyra says. "I think he might've gone overboard."

Axel lifts one foot off the ground, as if testing if he'd stick. "Just when I think that I understand what demons do, he does something weird like this and I can't keep it straight," he says, then, ridiculously, waves at Max the cat in the window. "You look conscious."

"I could say the same to you," she says, and he shrugs, then points to his hairline, where not even a hint of the wound remains.

"Still hurts, but it's a lot better," he says. "Car's wrecked."

"I shudder to think what protections he'd put inside, if this is what he did to your lawn," Alette says, then gestures Lyra over.

"Frisse thinks that we can trap Terese, with enough warning and a sufficient enough lure," Alette says, succinct, as she drives out of her neighborhood, past the house with the rusted-out cars.

"I'm not gonna be bait," Lyra says again.

Alette and Axel lock eyes through the rearview mirror.

"I think Dr. Frisse is going to be," Alette says, though Lyra can tell she doesn't like it, with her hands gripping the steering wheel tight. "We know Terese wants revenge, we can use that, and have you be the surprise in the corner."

"Now, I wasn't conscious, but I thought that you did a great job with her last time," Axel says, flippant. "I could tell you staggered her, and that's not with much prep."

"Why," Lyra asks, sitting forward, intent, "does Terese want revenge?"

"We couldn't help her," Alette says. "My theory is she blames Dr. Frisse."

"My theory is she has a bunch of misplaced aggression and Dr. Frisse is difficult to kill," Axel says. "She's killed so many other magicians without any barriers and she's tried like five times with Dr. Frisse, it's got to gall her."

They pass the blasted-out husk of Buggees, and there's a construction van in front of it, with plywood piled up against one of the walls, and something like satisfaction thrills down Lyra's back. Even her job is healing.

"Still, revenge is a weird word," Lyra says, watching Buggees until it disappears out of view. "That sounds like just a regular grudge, not revenge."

Axel shrugs, but Alette glances at her, thoughtful, through the rearview mirror.

"It's the word she uses," Axel says, drumming his fingers against his leg, his perfect skin glinting in the light. "I never thought more."

"Me neither," Alette says, and she's definitely more skeptical, which is nice. "I wonder what Aunt Frisse would say to that."

"Probably something pithy," Axel says, then sits up straighter, like he's imitating her. "I can't imagine into the mind of this poor misguided demon creature, why should we waste our time on such theoreticals?"

Alette snorts, then covers it up with a cough. "She doesn't...like to extrapolate on stuff like that," she says, apologetically, like she needs to defend her to Lyra, "she's not the most forthcoming with details she thinks we don't need."

It does little to help Lyra's opinion of Dr. Frisse, but at least she doesn't think that Axel and Alette would actively know about something bad and participate in it, and that settles something inside of her.

"So we're going to the compound?" Lyra asks.

INDEED, it is the compound, and Lyra is almost getting to know her way around it now, with the dead mouse and the dead ants as a sort of bizarre compass that is solidly working for her.

Alette and Axel, of course, walk as if there's no doubt they know where they're going.

"Do you guys live here?" Lyra asks.

"Might as well," Axel says, turning around and walking backwards so he can converse with her, "my workshop's here and my stuff's too explosive to actually do outside some careful wards."

"I don't," Alette says, and she gets the feeling that this is a long-standing argument with them, "I live in a perfectly reasonable apartment in the next town,"

"Yeah, just like you drive a perfectly reasonable car," Axel says, then throws a wink at Lyra, "and end up commuting here every day and crashing on the couch on the third floor when you think nobody knows."

"It is a perfectly reasonable couch," Alette says, and Lyra can see the twinkle in her eye at the argument. "I doubt Dr. Frisse would keep it if it wasn't so reasonable."

"She just knows that if she offers you one of the apartments, you'll refuse," Axel says, then again turns to Lyra. "I'm sure you could take one, if you wanted."

"I have a house," Lyra says, instead of cussing him out at the idea of living somewhere so remote. "I inherited it and everything and my phone works there."

Without saying a word, Axel lays his hand out to Lyra.

"What?" she asks.

"Give it," he says, making grabby hands. "I'll make it work."

She raises an eyebrow at him.

"I won't do anything else, I promise," he says, and she pulls it out and places it in his palm. "I'm just gonna make it so the magic doesn't block out the signal, just like...this."

He taps the backside of her phone, and there's a disconcerting crunch, before it beeps, once, and he hands it back to her.

"Now it'll get signal everywhere," he gloats, and Alette rolls her eyes. "What, it will!"

Alette pushes open the grand mahogany doors to the conference room, and the table is pushed to the side, all chairs along the side, with a giant elaborate circle painted in gold paint on the carpet.

Lyra stops, every instinct in her body flaring up, like she's in immediate, obvious danger.

Off to the side, Dr. Frisse stands, and she's in rough jeans and a tank top, gold paint everywhere, like she painted it herself.

"Oh good, you ended up coming along," Dr. Frisse says, wiping her hands on her jeans, smearing more paint everywhere. "We need more prep time, but you might be able to help." She gestures towards the giant circle. "What do you think?"

Alette and Axel file in behind her, and Lyra follows them, edging around the room, as far away from the circle as she can get while being in the room.

"Feels dangerous," Lyra blurts out, which is probably not the best course of action.

Dr. Frisse waves her hand at that. "Not to you, just to demons," she says, "and your demon should be smart enough to avoid it."

"I'll tell him you said that," Lyra says, still staring at the lines in the carpet.

At the very least, it's going to be a bitch to get out, and the paint shimmers bright in the overhead lights.

"Looks magick-y," Lyra says, because it does. It looks like someone took a magic circle out of any movie or TV show and made a few tweaks but then painted it onto expensive corporate carpet.

"There's a reason why movies always look like this," Alette says, like she's trying to fill in Lyra, "there's some basis in truth to all fiction."

And Dr. Frisse just looks so pleased with herself, staring at the magic circle.

"I thought you said you'd send me a contract before sending me money," Lyra says, and both Alette and Axel blink up at her in confusion.

"I did say that," Dr. Frisse says, not pausing in her pleased look at the circle, "and I still have not sent any."

"Uh cool, 'cause then about thirty-grand showed up in my account that Melekai has nothing to do with," Lyra says, and that gets everyone's attention.

"Bank error," Dr. Frisse says, almost dismissive, "didn't come from us."

"That's one hell of a bank error in the favor of the poor person," Lyra says, edging around and sitting in one of the comfy chairs as far away as she can get.

"I would notice if that amount went missing overnight," Dr. Frisse says, with a shrug. "Maybe insurance over the work building."

Because Lyra's totally the person who'd have that insurance and not the owners of the store, and like any insurance would just deposit the money without trying to withhold it for forever.

"Well, Merry Christmas, I guess," Lyra says, sarcastic.

"Are you religious?" Dr. Frisse asks, and it might be the closest thing Lyra's gotten to curiosity from her. "I didn't get that impression at all."

Lyra just eyes her, not wanting to get into churches or anything like that.

"Hell of a way to ruin carpet," she says, instead of anything sarcastic.

"Oh, the paint won't stay here," Alette says, bending over and poking at one of the edges. Her wrist brace is slim, now, almost entirely just for some additional support by the look of it.

Like it's almost all healed.

"Once a circle is cast, so to say, we can transport it anywhere we would need it," Alette continues, then tosses her long braid behind her shoulder. "This room is just the easiest to map out large enough circles—you can use almost any space."

"This is why I'm not a spell weaver," Axel says, as an aside to Lyra. "Too much fussy components, too little fun."

"What does it do?" Lyra asks. "To demons, if it's so dangerous."

"It should significantly weaken her, if we did it correctly," Dr. Frisse says, "which I did. It'll keep her restrained within its lines, it won't decrease her offensive power—that has too much potential to backfire of course"—Lyra didn't know, but whatever—"but this would make them much easier to make mortal. Make her body permanent, and if you kill the body, it would kill her."

The sickening feeling of Terese's heart stopping, then restarting, drops into Lyra's mind.

"So it'd kill the human Terese, right?" Lyra asks, and Dr. Frisse blinks at her, like helping another human isn't high on the priority list. "You weren't planning on saving her, were you?"

"I don't think she can be saved," Alette says, soft. "We tried."

"But you could walk through it without any real issue," Dr. Frisse continues, as if a glaring humanitarian issue hadn't been just pointed out. "You could walk right up and stab her, pour unlimited power into her, with no bad side effect."

"And it won't go away until both of us lift it," Alette says, beaming at Dr. Frisse, like she's proud of herself for helping.

"Great," Lyra says, then rubs her arms as her skin crawls, "I'll keep that in mind."

"We'd absolutely plan to actually cast it in the open, where there's plenty of animal life for her to kill and you to use," Dr. Frisse says, which doesn't help Lyra's stomach. "We would never bring her here, where there's nothing dead or living."

"There are ants and there's a dead mouse," Lyra says, helpfully, and everyone gives her the 'creepy' look. "What, they're kinda hard to miss."

"I don't think I will ever get used to that," Dr. Frisse says, then, in Lyra's pocket, her phone rings.

A call, an actual call, from Jackson.

Everyone stares at her as she holds it in her hand. "Probably saw my phone in Europe the other day and wants to see why," Lyra says, ignoring their double take, holding it up, before answering. "Hey, what's up?"

"Hey," Jackson says, and the hair on the back of her neck raises at his tone, "are you okay?"

She looks around the room, but everyone's staring at her, which doesn't help the feeling of disquiet.

"Yes," Lyra says, cautious. "You good?"

Axel and Alette glance at each other, and she sees Alette mouth 'brother'.

"Yeah, yes, I'm okay," Jackson says, and his voice is cautious, cautious in a way she hasn't heard in many, many years, "I have a crick in my neck."

It's the old code between them, tied from when they were both starting to hit adolescence and had to keep secrets from their mother and, later, any foster parents, so Lyra stills.

It means, Jackson needs help. It means Jackson needs her help and didn't want to say why out loud. Didn't feel safe.

"Where are you?" she asks, already starting the mental calculation. She's about an hour north of her house, well into Canada, and if he's still in Seattle, it'll be at least three hours, more like four, unless she brings in Melekai—

"Oh, me and my friends are in Vancouver, we were catching drinks," he says, and that's significantly closer, "right outside of the city, at a cabin on the beach."

"Cabin on the beach," she repeats, trying to figure out if that's another bit of code. "I can come pick you up."

Axel raises his eyebrows at her, and even Dr. Frisse looks mildly concerned.

"It's not my normal friends, but she said she wanted to see you," he says, and his voice dips down into almost a whisper. "She's odd, she has short blond hair, and her eyes are just like Mel's but everyone else can see her—and I thought you'd want to meet her." His voice abruptly changes in the middle, tilting back up to cheerful and normal, and Lyra's stomach drops.

"I'll be there," she promises, and, just like that, he hangs up the phone.

JACKSON (7:45 PM): 4800 Sechelt Inlet Rd.

"Terese has him," Lyra says, staring hard at the address. "Terese has my little brother."

30

After just enough time for her to memorize the address, Lyra shoves the phone in her pocket, looking up at the room.

"I'm going to go get him," she says, fully intending to march down to the greenhouse and kill a few bugs to bring Melekai to her, then steal Alette's car if she doesn't offer a ride. "He was scared, he snuck the phone call to me, and was only able to tell me a little."

"How do you know?" Dr. Frisse asks, sharp. "How would he know?"

"Because he's been raised from the dead so he can see demons, and he told me that there was one there that everyone else can see with short blond hair and she's making him uneasy and said she wanted to talk to me, so yes, it's Terese, and I'm going." She pivots to Alette. "I'll take the car, I won't wreck it."

"No, we'll go with," Dr. Frisse says, still wearing a paint-covered smock and holding a paintbrush, but her eyes gleam with something resembling greed. "We can use it, we can surprise her, we can trap her there."

"I don't care, we're just going to get him," Lyra says, then, as fast as she can, lets her awareness drop, drop towards the dead mouse and the dead ants and pulls, and—

Melekai appears beside her, and she twists to see him. Alette gasps, a small sound, before quickly smothering it.

"Can you bring me to Jackson, can you focus on him?" she blurts out.

His eyes scan her face. "No," he says, but she can hear the seriousness in his voice. "What's wrong?"

"Terese has him," Alette says, as Lyra whirls towards the door, but Melekai catches her by the arm with a reassuring grip.

"And you have a demon trap here, all ready to go," Melekai says, turning his gaze to Dr. Frisse, and Lyra wants to tug out of his grip, pull her way free. Jackson needs her.

There's a pause, and Lyra realizes that Dr. Frisse doesn't have the earpiece that Axel made, no one else can hear him but her and Alette and everything's taking so long and—

"We were crafting it, it's mobile, we can bring it to her," Alette says, sharp, then nods at Lyra. "You know what they do?" At his nod, she lifts her chin. "Let's see how close we can get."

Alette turns towards the door, and Lyra pulls out and follows her, Melekai trailing behind her.

To fit them all in, Dr. Frisse gives the keys to Axel to a sleek black SUV that looks like something out of a goddamn spy movie.

Melekai snarls at it, his face pulling back, but he still squeezes in after Lyra, into the back seat, and Lyra's about to vibrate out of her skin. "He's still alive, I can tell you that," he says as Axel starts the car and they rumble out of the parking garage and out of the complex. "I would be able to tell that."

She sees Dr. Frisse fit the earpiece in her ear, before turning in her seat to look at Lyra.

"You need to come to an understanding that this may be a trap," Dr. Frisse starts, and Lyra can't help herself, can't play nice.

"No shit," she snaps, and Melekai grips her arm tight as Axel swings onto the freeway. "I know it's a fucking trap but it's my fucking little brother."

To her credit, Dr. Frisse doesn't flinch. "Yes, but this may not go as well as we all hope."

"I don't care," Lyra says.

Her eye contact is intense, way more than Lyra wants right now.

"If you have the chance to take her down, do it."

Lyra stares back, and Melekai's arm tightens around her.

"Why do you think I'd be the one who could?"

"You can survive her. If one of us falls, if someone out there dies, use us."

Axel sucks in a breath but doesn't say anything.

"I won't if it's my brother," Lyra replies, hotly, and Melekai squeezes her.

"Of course," she says, as if suppressing an eye roll. "But we know what our magic does to demons, we don't know about yours."

Her phone says it'll be less than thirty minutes until they get there, and she has never wished for a faster car.

It might be too late. It could be too late, if she's destroying bodies after she kills them.

She shuts her eyes, hard, against all the noise of the car against the road, of the three living and breathing bodies in the car all thrumming with energy, of Melekai besides her, bright and vivid against her awareness, of the cars that pass them and—

"Breathe," Melekai murmurs, into her ear, "we're on our way, breathe."

She forces herself to exhale, but it doesn't help.

"I'm more worried that she's imitating his voice," Alette says. "That he's fine, that we're rushing off for nothing."

"She would have to know the code," Lyra says, then shuts her eyes in frustration. "Look, we were on our own a lot, we had a code when we were in trouble and needed the other. I doubt she'd know that."

"That's more conclusive than I would think, but she's copied other private things," Axel says, in his distracted-because-he's-driving voice.

"She knew the name of my second-grade teacher, was able to find her and imitate her."

Melekai is a vibrating mass of energy next to her, almost over-whelming her, so she turns into him, pressing her face against his chest. He hesitates, for a brief moment, then wraps his arm around her, awkward with her seatbelt.

"I don't care," Lyra repeats.

"No one is saying we're not going," Alette says, and it's almost unbearably kind. "We're just trying to prepare you."

Melekai glowers at her, but Alette doesn't even waver under his glare, holding Lyra's gaze.

"I'll stop her," Lyra says, and her stomach feels sick, feels like she's going to puke. "If she doesn't have Jackson, then we'll stop her there."

There's silence in the car, and Axel just grips the wheel tighter.

The car winds its way up the beautiful coast, coated in a layer of fluffy snow that glitters in the light of the full moon. The street lamps get further and further away, as it turns from suburbia to vacation homes to cozy cabins worth more than any of the money Lyra's ever seen.

And her brother escaped there, three days before Christmas, to drink with his pals.

They had loose Christmas plans, they always do, where they get drunk on cheap red wine and attempt to bake a ham, but now that she's learned about this trip it's like she never even knew her little brother. Like each winding road in this interminable long drive just emphasizes how much she doesn't know him anymore.

Still.

The cabins up here are all deep-set, away from the road, almost entirely obscured by trees. Just leading to deep driveways and far away lights in the windows.

Christmas lights twinkle along the street, however, a cheery mockery of her worry.

They turn a corner, and Melekai sucks in a breath.

Lyra cranes her neck out the window but can't see anything.

"Wait," he mutters, then grips her arm tight.

The vision of gold blooms, bright against the night sky, and she inhales.

There's a pillar of the red-black power and a bubble of worn golden threads, near the road in the expansive yard of one of the deep-set houses. There's shattered Christmas lights sparking on the ground, an evergreen tree reduced to splinters, and—

And Terese, standing in the middle of it, one hand on the back of Jackson's neck, nails gripping tight into his skin.

Lyra's seen that exact motion enough to know what Terese is at least trying to do. Or trying to appear to be doing.

The car's not even stopped when Lyra's kicking open the door.

She's not wearing gloves, and her own skin glows gold in the moonlight. Melekai's right behind her and he radiates power, like the very wind flows through him, like he could grasp the air and thrust it back at Terese like a knife.

Jackson's eyes are wide, and he's mouthing something at her, and she knows it's probably a warning, probably something about how she shouldn't have come, some sort of machismo bullshit about self-sacrifice, but he's not even wearing a snow jacket, and the hem of his jeans are soaking in the melted ice, and he's barefoot.

He's barefoot.

She must've pulled him out of the party, from whatever is going on in the cabin behind them, and he didn't even have time to put on shoes.

Lyra's rage solidifies into something cold. Something hardened, something vicious.

Terese's eyes light up when she sees her, though the shadow self beneath her skin is still frozen in pain.

But.

But her eyes trail back, trail up to the car, to the sleek SUV. To Axel and Alette, climbing out slower. Where Alette's unravelling a golden thread, looping it among her fingers. Where Axel's gripping something in his hands, something electronic.

To where Dr. Frisse climbs out, the picture of smooth control, despite her paint-stained smock. Her hand is in her bag.

Terese exhales through her teeth, a hissing noise, and her nails leave red marks on Jackson's neck, stinging half circles that Lyra can feel all the way away.

Jackson's feet are frozen, long past the point of pain, and panic coats the inside of his veins, pounding his heart and hurting his head.

She's hurting him.

Lyra can't even think, she can't even feel, but there are dead ants in the base of a tree, and she yanks them to her in one smooth motion. Instantly, there's a ball of cord, a ball of power, in her hand, and it's bright in the dark night.

Terese gasps, delighted, and merely shoves away Jackson, who stumbles towards Lyra.

She catches him, off balance with her much larger brother, and Melekai uses that moment in Terese's distraction to hurl the wind at her, to flood her with power.

Jackson's a mess of sensation, his head pounding, his heart jack-hammering away, and Lyra shoves her shoulder underneath his arm, propping him up, one hand still full of the energy from the bugs. She can't drop him, she can't let him go, but—

Terese strikes at Melekai, an awful rush of vicious red-black power, and Melekai staggers.

Jackson pushes off of her, staggering to get his feet underneath him. "Go!" he says, and he's barely audible over the roaring in Lyra's ears, in the panic.

So Lyra uses the mass of power in her hand, and, trying desperately to imagine it as a knife, as something that can stab, lobs it at Terese.

It strikes Terese in her hand, and Terese shrieks, her melodic voice piercing into the heavens. Blood, black blood and red, sprays out from her wrist.

Lyra can see bone.

A part of her mind still tracks Jackson, who scatters away from them, deeper into the yard, still barefoot, still hurting.

But the other part reaches out, further, trying to find the dead.

Trying to find any bright bit she can use, anywhere she can draw power.

Alette starts casting something, and Lyra's never seen her power through Melekai's eyes before.

Glittering gold threads gather around her hand, some sort of kinetic fire, and in one controlled motion she thrusts it at the ground.

It spirals towards Terese like a lightning strike, the very earth moves, as if Alette has the power to shake the ground, to move mountains and tectonic plates.

At the same time, Axel runs away from the car, drawing the attention and lobbing something over his shoulder. It explodes, a vivid bright sun of sparks, and Terese covers her eyes, off-kilter.

Lyra doesn't know what it was, but she knows it wasn't originally a grenade.

Without a word, as if they've practiced, Alette's golden lightning spirals up the ground and into Terese's feet, and Axel slams his hand on the ground and the dirt beneath Terese transforms, morphs into something else, then solidifies around her feet, like asphalt.

A quick and easy trap.

Dr. Frisse thrusts her hand into her bag and then casts it out, and the same golden paint that was on the floor of the grand conference room is now on the forested floor, with the snow and the pine cones and the sparking Christmas lights.

With Terese and Melekai within its sphere.

They both freeze, and Lyra's heart jumps.

Immediately, like it was never there, her ability to see the magic around them stops, leaving the world darker.

Melekai's eyes snap up to her, a warning. A vow. Something.

He straightens, pacing as far away within the circle as he can from Terese, circling back towards Lyra. Every line of his body is tense, like a predator stalking his prey, like a beast protecting his wounded mate.

There's a moment of silence, as everyone takes collective breaths. As Terese struggles, her feet encased in concrete, her eyes wild. She's in pain, it's obvious with her clutching at her wrist and with every gasping breath.

Even Jackson, hanging back, watches.

(And Lyra really wishes he'd go back inside, go put on socks and shoes, resume the party with his friends and forget they were at all out there. Leave her to whatever this is, whatever is going on, and be a safe and healthy law student.)

Axel strides towards the circle, and in his hands are two batteries, just the run-of-the-mill batteries they sold at Buggees.

Terese strikes out at him, a jagged snap of energy that she hears rather than sees, and he deflects it, sparking it off one of the batteries.

The battery smokes, and he drops it, shaking his hand out, then he slams the other battery into the ground, right next to the circle.

Lightning, actual sparking electricity and not magic, spikes up through the air, dropping and striking Terese, and this close, Lyra can feel all of it. Every spark of pain, every spasm and burn and crater, until Terese shakes herself, gathering electricity into the palm of her hand.

Terese twists, as much as she can, and sends a snap of that same electricity towards Melekai, who jerks away, and the power crashes into the trees above Lyra's head.

She ducks away. There's nothing dead, there's nothing she can pull off of, there's nothing she can do.

She's useless.

"See, Terese," Dr. Frisse says, and Terese flinches at her voice, at the suddenness of words in such a wordless situation, "there's nothing you can do right now, you're trapped."

Terese sends an arc of something, only visible by the air it moves and the branches it flutters, towards Dr. Frisse, who neatly sidesteps.

"Don't waste your power," Dr. Frisse chides, and there, in her paint-stained smock and jeans hastily shoved into snow boots, she looks powerful. "We can give you a choice."

Terese stills, though her eyes jump from Lyra to Dr. Frisse to Melekai, like she's trying to tell who the bigger threat is.

Alette draws next to Axel, and both their faces are pale. Like they can't believe what's happening.

"Let us try to help you again?" Alette says in the silence that is their section of the woods. "Let us—"

Terese directs a shattering blast of power to her feet, the asphalt around them fragmenting around her, and she charges for the edge of the circle, directly at Alette.

And gets stopped short, like a leash has been jerked on a chain.

"Please," Terese says, and it's the same beg she made to Lyra, all those weeks ago, back at the gas station store. "Please, you have to stop her—"

Melekai, his back to Lyra, clasps his hands behind his back. It's almost an innocent motion, almost idle.

Then he crooks his finger to Lyra, invisible to Terese.

Dr. Frisse said nothing bad would happen to her.

Lyra approaches the circle, with its glowing light, and reaches across the barrier, laying a hand on Melekai's arm. Lets a trace of herself go into him, just a trace, and it gleams faint in the twinkling of the Christmas lights.

He straightens, like he's squaring his shoulders.

Again, she can see the magic, see the trace of golden threads left behind by what Terese sent to Dr. Frisse.

Terese's breath hitches. "Please."

Alette's lips part, and Lyra realizes it's working, that Alette is buying it.

Terese sees it at the same time.

Terese waves her hand, and this time Lyra can see it happen. Sees the point of energy hit, then detonate, and the shining ball of golden thread appear.

Sees the power reflected, for a split second, in Alette's glasses and Axel's eyes.

Dr. Frisse sees it, too.

With a jerk, Dr. Frisse throws herself sideways, knocking Alette back, and Axel away, and—

Melekai charges, slamming down a smash of power into Terese, who jerks. Magic, bright, arcs into the trees around them, pine needles shattering everywhere.

The bubble, full of the gut punch of energy, hits Dr. Frisse in the chest, and she drops. Just drops, like a puppet that the strings have been cut off from, like a toy that's tossed aside without much use.

It strafes Axel's side, and he reels away, and, immediately, the double vision from him disappears. Gone is the polished smooth face and perfectly angled chin, and any sense that he has magic, like it's been winked out of existence.

He stumbles to the ground, gasping, and Alette drags him up, drags him away from the circle, though her eyes are wide at her aunt.

Terese whirls on Melekai, and there's so much magic in the air Lyra can barely see, but—

But there's a bright, shining death, right there, overwhelming in its intensity. It fills her nose, fills her mind, like there's nothing else in the world that could matter, could exist.

Back behind them, Jackson cries out, in shock more than anything else.

Because he's actually never seen someone die before.

Terese sees Lyra, sparks off more power, and Lyra ducks, the power ruffling her hair. Snow, shaken off from the tree, dumps on her, a shock of frozen water spraying over her.

Melekai snarls, and a spray of blood appears across Terese's face, bright red blood. She retaliates, and Melekai's arm snaps in the middle, the bone broken, and he cries out.

She needs to move fast.

Lyra dashes across the circle, and the magic doesn't do anything to her, doesn't even move her hair, until she's next to Dr. Frisse.

Her skin is already pallid, already gray, like death and the first few steps towards rigor mortis happened immediately, and Lyra falls to her knees next to her.

She could bring her back, she could bring her back and revive her and the death would go away, would stop clouding her senses, stop echoing around her, but -

From the other side of the circle, she sees Jackson move, and at the same time, so does Terese.

Wildly, Terese rakes something out at her brother, at her harmless little brother, who can't see any of the magic or any of what's actually going on, and—

Melekai jerks himself, right into the spasm of the energy.

Blocking it. Blocking it from ever getting to Jackson.

He flinches, his full body convulsing and bright red blood spraying, and his eyes have a split second to meet Lyra's, before he crumples to the ground.

And all awareness of his being, all awareness of him, blinks out of Lyra's gaze.

"No," Lyra whispers, and Terese spins to her, her mouth wide in something between a grimace and a smile and raises her hand.

So Lyra pulls the death from Dr. Frisse, pulls whatever death she can towards her, and lashes out, grabbing Terese by her arm.

Terese recoils and there's a flash of gold, Lyra's legs going weak, but—

"No," Lyra whispers again, and, using the death that's so close to her senses, wraps it around Terese, like a snake winding around, like she could unhinge her jaws and swallow her whole—

Terese jerks away, jerks back, but—

"No," Lyra repeats, and she can't look towards the ground, she can't do anything but pour the power, pour what used to be Dr. Frisse, pour everything she can, into that grip.

Terese flinches back, her eyes wide, colorless, until they reflect gold, and—

Like something ripping in two, Lyra can feel the demon coming loose, fraying apart at the seams, ripping the threads and apart.

Like the demon had been entwined, like a strip of yarn, and Lyra can ply the two pieces apart, fray them down, pick them until they're separate.

And, with her blood fizzing and rage in her heart, she does.

Terese's nails dig into her arms, and she yanks, like she's trying to use Lyra's power, pull herself back together, but blood vessels fracture apart and the two halves that made up the demon rip asunder.

Lyra just holds on. Lets herself sink into it, until she can feel the energy running through Terese's very being. Until she can see every little place that Terese had her fangs in the human and rips them up.

Terese, Terese the body in front of her, staggers, colorless eyes wide, gasping, and her nails draw blood on Lyra's arm. Digs into her skin, as the demon struggles against Lyra, struggles against all the energy of Dr. Frisse's death, struggles against the rage and despair in Lyra, until—

Until like a candle snuffed in the wind, the demon is gone.

For a split-second Lyra reaches out, reaches for wherever the demon might've fled to, but there's nothing, there's no one there, but—

The body in front of her stumbles, nails releasing, and, with a gasp, sags to the ground.

Just a human. Just a normal human, with a beating heart and blood leaking from many wounds and a pulse going too fast, gasping and coughing on the ground.

Terese—is it still Terese?—raises her hands to her mouth and comes away with blood, before she shrieks. Shrieks at the top of her lungs, then takes a big gaping breath and topples over.

Her brain is still moving, the blood leaking isn't going to kill her, so Lyra steps away.

Somehow, somewhere deep inside, she knows there are no more demons anywhere close. The gold circle around them flickers out, like it could tell, too.

There's silence, blessed silence, where the only thing in her mind is the willful lack of noise, where the wind and the rustle of the evergreen needles don't reach her ears, where she can just exist and nothing can touch her, nothing can burst her bubble, nothing can extend a hand and disrupt her, and—

Her eyes stray to the side.

He's still laying there, crumpled on his back, twisted away from her, so all she can see is the faintest hint of his profile and the mess of golden-brown curls and that the body is empty. Empty, like a vessel before Melekai poured himself into it.

Like she's been wrapped in fuzz, like everything around her is static and she's the only one who can move, Lyra steps over to him. To the dead body, if it even is Melekai. If it could be considered Melekai.

If he could actually be gone.

Her footsteps falter, like her brain didn't give the proper signal and misfired, and half of her gives a silent wail and the other half just recedes. Just pulls back from the idea, like if she doesn't address it, it didn't happen.

Outside, away from her, people are scrambling. Axel has crawled away, but his appearance is still rough, still imperfect, and he's staring at his hands, like he's desperately trying to do something and finding them lacking. Alette is clutching her aunt to her chest, as if the gray skin and lack of heartbeat could be brought back by something so little as hugging. There are tears, actual tears, with mascara running down her cheeks.

Jackson—

In two large steps, Jackson reaches her, wrapping her in a big hug, and she sags against her little brother, until they're both sitting on the icy ground. He didn't go back and get his shoes, his skin is actively cold, but he hugs her, and Lyra lets herself shake apart.

31

"Lyra," someone starts, and she flinches.

She's in the cold, the ground is cold, and Melekai's dead body is still next to her, and it's like she's been stabbed all over again.

"Does she need medical help?" Another voice—Axel, she thinks —asks.

"I called an ambulance," her brother says, and it's his in-control-lawyer voice, the one he only breaks out when he absolutely needs to. "At the very least, whoever that woman is needs the hospital." His voice is firm, like he knows what to do in such a strange situation. Like he knows how to talk to the police like this, how to explain away what happened.

Lyra lets her eyes open, and Axel's crouched near them, near Melekai's dead body, and even though Axel's face looks entirely different, she knows it's him.

Something's missing from him, she can tell.

"Lyra, are you okay?" It's Alette, and she's next to Terese, or the body that was Terese, taking her pulse, even though Lyra could tell her that her heart is fine, that she's just unconscious.

The only body against her awareness is the one that used to

house Melekai. Even Dr. Frisse's corpse is cold, completely bare of anything she could use.

"I..." Lyra starts, and she again lets herself look down at Melekai.

His body isn't even cold.

There's still some black blood dripping from the wound on his cheek, but sluggish, and the blood underneath it is back to red. Like now that Melekai's no longer in it, the blood goes back to its normal color.

Her brother hugs her tight, and he's sitting on the ground with her, like him hugging her could protect her from whatever turmoil is going on inside. Like he could shield her from her looking over at Melekai.

Axel shifts, and his hands are shaking, but his face is serious. "Is that him?" he asks, grave.

"Jesus, Lyra, is that who you saw when you looked at Mel?" Jackson blurts out, and Lyra nods. "Oh Jesus."

Alette makes a sound in her throat, then drops the body part that was Terese's arm, and walks over until she can sit next to them, leaning against Lyra.

"Can you bring my Aunt back?" she asks, small, like a child. "Did you use her death like she talked about?"

There are faint tremors going up her arms, and Lyra can tell she's injured, somehow, but not seriously. Like a sprain, catching on her still healing wrist.

"I can't bring her back," Lyra says, and Alette gives a little nod, like she understands, before her face twists once more.

"Where is he?" Axel asks, and his voice is somehow tilting up, like he's the one panicking right now. "If this is the body, where is he?"

Alette locks eyes with Lyra, and she knows. She must've seen, must've been able to tell, and Lyra shudders.

She's the one wearing the snow jacket, her brother isn't even wearing shoes, but once Lyra shivers she can't seem to stop.

Axel looks between them and touches a rock in a motion she's seen him do dozens of times, he's going to magic it into something, but nothing happens. Almost an automatic motion.

He withdraws his hand with a wince and a sideways glance to Alette. Something happened to him, something big, in the wake of Terese the demon's blast, but Lyra can't parse it out. Not like this, not with Melekai right there and dead.

Dead.

She gasps, like the thought is just occurring to her, like it's not what her brain has been screaming at her from far away, and unbidden, tears come choking out of her throat.

"Oh, hey, shhh," Jackson says, and he rubs her back, just like they used to do when they were children and got sick. "Shhh, I got you."

It's not enough, it's so far from enough, and Lyra flails out, her heart wrenching, until she can grab Melekai's hand.

And she immediately knows three things.

One. The body died from a lack of air, some subtle poisoning in its lungs, and there's a variety of small injuries, though there's a bone snapped neatly above the elbow, cleaner than any break Lyra's ever encountered before.

Two. There's no trace of any demon in him. None of the special taste of power that she got to know so obviously well.

Three. She could bring the body back.

She stares down at the body. At the freckles on his cheekbones, at the smooth line of his eyebrows, at the bracelets around his wrist, and a sob chokes its way out again.

From across the clearing, the woman turns over. Shifts in her sleep, and Alette and Axel both flinch. Alette grasps at her needle case, and Axel looks like he's about to scramble back, to figure out something, anything.

"The demon's gone," Lyra says, muted, at them, then, at their blank looks, points over at what used to be Terese. "That's just...that's just the human body."

"She's alive?" Axel asks, despite the fact that he just saw her move. "How—"

"I don't know," Lyra says, still holding onto Melekai's hand. The body's hand.

It would be so easy, to just reach inside, start the lungs again. To heal the bit of decay in the brain, because it was dead for at least two hours before Melekai found it.

To hear that same voice, with someone else behind it. To see those eyes blink up at her, even without the mischievousness that is Melekai.

Lyra can't decide if it's selfishness or not.

Jackson shifts, and he's still barefoot. "We should move inside," he says, which is entirely logical and entirely out of the realm of possibility for Lyra to comprehend. "We should move that lady inside, so she can be warm, and wait for the paramedics."

Alette pushes herself up to standing, though she wobbles, and she takes a deep breath, then another, as if trying to fit herself into her own shape. As if trying to push aside all of her emotions and grief and terror, to fit herself into the person who calmly takes control, who knows what to do, but it fits poorly. "We have the badges in the car," she says, voice trembling. "That will stop a lot of the police questioning."

"That's not legal," Jackson says, but it lacks heat, because how else will they explain this?

"We also have blankets and food, Axel," Alette redirects to her friend, who's staring at her with a lost expression. "Axel, come help me, let's get something to stabilize uh...not-Terese, and get Jackson more warm clothing."

Axel pushes himself up, and he's slower than he used to be. Like all the pep has gone out of his body.

And Lyra's still holding Melekai's hand.

She's certain it's a bad idea. That bringing back this body, this body she doesn't know and is otherwise unrelated to, would be a bad idea. To try to explain to a total stranger how he appeared in the woods, three days from Christmas, when he had last been alive sometime in October.

And if Melekai's dead, if he's truly dead, then there'd be nobody to protect her if she uses her necromancy, so this one act, stretching this one muscle she's barely learned how to flex, might rain down death and destruction on her.

The moment Axel and Alette walk away, Jackson rubs Lyra's back, like this is all an upset stomach that could be cured with soothing touches and some ginger ale.

"I'm so sorry, Lyra," he whispers, and it's just the two of them, in the cold, with the sparking Christmas lights and the stars overhead. "I'm so sorry. She made me call you, but she wanted you alone, I'm so sorry."

"You used the code, I was going to come," Lyra says, her mouth automatic.

Melekai had died to save her little brother.

She doesn't even know if the body would have memories of that.

In the multitude of small injuries is that shoulder tightness that she had felt all that time ago. It'd be easy to heal, if she did that before restarting the heart.

Fuck this.

Lyra exhales, as controlled as she can, and squeezes his hand in hers.

First, the break, as easy as socketing two Legos into place. It'd heal more just fine after that.

Second, the shoulder. It's as easy as finding the mass of muscle knots, of smoothing it over, so the shoulder blade rests properly in its place.

Third, his heart.

She hesitates, a brief second, before finding that spark of electricity and pushing it into place.

The heart flexes, firing off at random, before it settles on a beat. The lungs follow suit, and the blood reaches the brain, filtering out the decay like it was never there.

Jackson flinches, full body, as the body that was Melekai gasps, then coughs, before breathing normally.

There's still no demon energy, still nothing that would suggest that it is him, but the body curls in on itself, like he's sleeping normally, and it's exactly how Melekai slept next to her.

Tears crop into Lyra's eyes, as red and blue lights start to flash in

32

I t's a long few hours, of sitting in hospital waiting rooms, of watching as the unconscious body gets MRIs, gets CAT scans, gets blood test after blood test, before Lyra can sit in peace in a tiny little hospital room with the ceiling the color of cream and dots along the tiles.

Alette sticks with not-Terese, who hasn't regained consciousness, and Axel floats between the two rooms, still looking strange. Jackson stays with Lyra, getting her food and shoving bad coffee into her hand, until even exhaustion preys on him and he leaves to go lay down in the car.

They have the body hooked up to an IV, and some meter beeps softly around them, and Lyra just sits. Her back aches—these are no chairs for someone with nerve issues, but she can't leave.

It's been hours.

Somewhere, deep in the hospital, someone dies. It punches at Lyra, and she breathes through her nose.

She can't go save them. Even if she knew where they were, she'd be too vulnerable, too open for attack.

But that is the peril of hospitals, there's always death around them.

So she breathes through that death, and the next, a few floors away, and just...sits.

SOMEWHERE CLOSE TO THREE AM, the beeping in front of her speeds up, and she lifts her head.

Melekai—or the body, she has no idea of his name—is blinking up at the ceiling.

Lyra's breath catches in her throat, a single painful little hope.

But he turns his head at her, blinking at her, and it's just the golden-brown eyes. Nothing reflects at her.

He stares, a little bit numb looking, and there's fog in his brain and pain in his arm, so completely obvious. Even with her healing the broken bone, the muscles around it still scream in pain.

"Hi," Lyra says, and despite the many cups of hospital coffee her voice still rasps.

"Hi?" he says, then makes a face like he tasted something bad, and it's such a familiar face that Lyra almost starts crying anew. "What"— he lifts his arm, the one that's attached to the IV, and stares. "What the fuck?"

Lyra exhales, then extends her legs, because of course they're hurting. "You're probably confused—"

"Of course I'm confused," he blurts out. "Lyra, what's going on?"

Lyra's heart jumps, and in front of her, he tries to flick off the IV, and nothing happens.

"Lyra, this fucking hurts, what the hell is going on and"—he stops, actually stops, like his brain catches up with what he's saying, and he gives her a dumbfounded look.

She can't help but just stare back.

"What do you remember?" she asks, finally, small, though hope burrows inside of her, burrows deep. If it's him, if it's not just the body being aware enough to know her name, if it's—

"Where's Terese?" he asks, and there's that familiar panic behind him. "Where's Terese and why can't I do anything? What happened to my arm, why is everything blurry, and—"

Lyra bursts into tears, and, despite knowing that that's a really piss poor idea, flings herself onto him for a hug.

He freezes, then shifts so he can cling tight to her. "Lyra, what happened?"

"You were dead, she killed you, I brought back the body and I didn't know if it'd be you or—"

He grabs tighter, pulling her tighter, like he can't bring himself to be away.

"I can't do anything?" he says, and his voice is puzzled. "I'm just...it's like that time in the woods." He touches her hair, soft, like he's checking. "Lyra, is Terese—"

"She's gone," Lyra says, pulling back just enough to see his face, and he's furrowing a brow at her. "The demon is, the human part is alive I think, but in a coma, Dr. Frisse died, Jackson's safe, something weird happened to Axel, and you were dead."

He gives her a long look, then, sudden, grins, bright and strong and a little bit wicked. "You brought me back as a human," he declares, like he's trying it on for size, and he touches her hand like he's feeling her for the first time. "You. You brought me back, beyond all logic, and you're still here."

"Of course," Lyra says, and her voice cracks, but he's smiling so she's smiling.

He settles back against the pillow, then gives it a startled look, then rubs at the area around the IV. "And now I'm in a hospital? And now I have a body?" he marvels, then looks back at her. "And everyone's safe."

"Yeah," Lyra's heart is beating so fast, so fast she can hardly believe it. "And you're you."

He reaches back to her again, and marvels at her hand. "You did it."

THE END

EPILOGUE

Sometime, between when Lyra nods off in her chair and when the morning staff wakes them both up, Terese disappears.

Not like a demon, not quite, but she wakes from the coma, crawls to the window, and leaves.

Her hospital bed was on the 4th floor. No outside security camera catches her climbing down the wall, and no footprints are found.

IT TAKES three weeks until the pain, the real pain, the sort that leaves Lyra laying on the bed whenever she can, the sort that makes her call out sick from work, the sort that finds her staring at the ceiling and hoping that she could fall back asleep, hits again.

Melekai's long out of the hospital by then, and he curls his body around Lyra as she lays there, on the bed that is too big for the tiny room in the mobile home.

"I wish I could help," he says, after they lay in silence for a long time, and his voice catches in the back of his throat a little more. She can feel the ache in his arm, around the still healing blood vessels around the break, but he keeps the arm around her tight, despite the discomfort. His hair gets tangled on her quilt, now that he can interact with it, and she swears she could feel the drag of his curls against the fabric.

She turns her face to him, and he takes the opportunity to squish her in tighter.

She's worked through this pain before, she's dealt with it, she's survived with it, but it seems to be hitting Melekai just as hard.

And she can't just lay here, not that day, but she savors the contact anyways.

Because while it might not take away the pain, might not magic her into a relaxed comfort, it's solid. He's there, and getting him to budge when she might possibly need him, is not something he's about to do.

She flutters her eyes open, and he's watching her with all the same intensity as before.

"I'll be okay," she says, even though her legs ache and her back feels like it's about to spasm, "this happens."

He scowls at her, such a familiar motion, so she pokes him in the side, and he squirms away.

It was probably the fourth day of him being home from the hospital that Lyra discovered the body is actually ticklish, and she uses that whenever she can. There's a whole slew of new things for him to deal with in the body, but that's by far the most amusing to Lyra.

"Besides," Lyra says, sitting up despite the discomfort, "there's that Wight thing."

She swings her legs over the bed, and immediately, his hand is at the small of her back, stabilizing.

It's almost nice to be babied a little. To not have to be the sole person taking care of herself.

He grabs his glasses off the side of the bed - because the body needed them, badly - before stretching, long and luxurious. "Fuck them, I want to stay in bed," he says, but still climbs out, shrugging a hoodie over his shirt.

It's strange, still, to see him in different clothing.

She gives herself that moment, still sitting on her bed, to finger comb through her hair and stuff it back in a messy bun, as he putters around the small room. Everything's still so new to him, still so amazing, that despite the pain in her legs, she still smiles.

"What?" he says, after a moment, crossing the room to her, leaning over her.

"Nothing," she says, but tugs on the wrist of his hoodie all the same, "I'm glad you're here."

His face creases, briefly, and he smoothes down a flyaway hair for her, a small, tender motion.

"I would move the world for you again, if I could," he murmurs, "I would change everything, I would make it so you would never have to feel pain again."

"I know," Lyra says, and his face twists again, before he leans his forehead against hers, "I don't need you to."

"I know, but," he settles his hand behind her neck, like it's a bad habit he can't quite break, "I just want to, and I can't, but -"

There's a small tug, similar to how it feels to be close to Alette doing magic, and his lips part.

It's not a relief from pain, not like he used to, but there's a warmth, spreading down her neck.

It's not total, it's not even close to solving her problems or making her all better, but...

But it's something.

"Did I -" Melekai starts, and at the same time she says -

"Was that -?" she cuts herself off, and his lips split into a grin.

He tries again, pressing his palm against her skin, and there's a faint whisper of it again. Brief, disappointment flickers over his face.

She leans up, pressing a kiss to his lips. "Whatever it is, we can learn," she whispers, hooking her hands into his belt loops.

He nods, then pulls her close once more, in a proper embrace. "We can learn."

.   .   .

The End

Continue on the adventures in "The Girl Who Has Already Died"

SNEAK PEEK FOR THE GIRL WHO HAS ALREADY DIED

The moment Alette's car leaves the bubble of Aunt Frisse's failing protections, twin shadow shapes blur along the edges of her vision, keeping pace with her perfectly sensible sedan, even as she guns the engine faster than she usually goes.

She knows by now that if she looks straight at them, they look akin to giant dogs, like the hellhounds of old, cloaked with shadow and soot and grinning at her with giant teeth like they could bite her in half.

But instead, they just run along her car like it's a game of cat and mouse.

Her heart sticks in her throat, though, and she keeps her eyes on the road.

They first appeared in the month after Alette was raised from the dead.

At first, she ignored them, blaming their appearance on long nights and stress with Terese destroying parts of the magical web around them. She had always had an overactive imagination, or that's what her aunt always said, and maybe some trauma of actually dying spurned her brain into imagining monsters from the deep.

But then they continued appearing. Every time she glanced out a window of a car, they were there, running along. Sitting patiently at stoplights with tails wagging and fangs grinning, only to start running the moment she started moving again.

Axel never saw them. Or, rather, he never commented that he saw them, and she knows if he saw them he would never shut up about them, so she assumed.

Shortly after they started appearing, then...other people started appearing.

Melekai the demon had called them Wights, and none of her research gave her any sort of answer to what they were.

She pulls past the gates of the compound, and the Wight with curly black hair is standing, casually leaning against the aged chain-link fence, and the two shadow dogs circle around him, before continuing to follow Alette's car.

His brilliant blue eyes track her motion as she drives away, and she knows he can run to keep up with the car just as easily as the shadow runners, but he stays in place, not even visible in her rearview mirror.

She still doesn't know that particular Wight's name. He's by far the one who appears the most to her.

But giving him a name would give too much legitimacy to all her confusion about all this.

She never asked to be able to see them, though according to Melekai they were always there. Just existing next to her world, interacting with it, but never in a way she could tell.

One of the shadow runners veers close to her car, and it's only years of driving safely that makes it so she doesn't swerve, but her hands tighten against her steering wheel.

Melekai and Lyra had said that the Wights wouldn't hurt her. Melekai had even worked out a deal with them to protect Lyra, in case something happened to him, and that's about as close to trust as she could fathom from the demon, but something about them itches under her skin. Like she shouldn't trust him, that she should be warning everyone to run as far away as possible, except no one else can see the threat and no one else would pay attention to her rantings.

There've been a few times Alette's wondered if she's crazy, but this takes the cake.

He's under the first stoplight her sedan idles up to, pale in the glow of the heavy January fog, but he doesn't say anything, and she doesn't roll down her window to let him. He just watches her, eyes solemn.

When she could first see them, he wouldn't stop chatting at her. Sometimes in French, sometimes in English, but always chatting. Chatting through her car window, muffled gleefully by the glass and metal, but still talking.

Goosebumps rise up her arms.

There's no one else around, not that she can see through the mist, so she coasts her car to an abandoned gas station parking lot, the pavement cracked and pebbled beneath her car's wheels.

This far north, the sun won't rise for a few hours, and everyone else is asleep. The gas station parking lot is empty, like no one knows it exists.

That's silly, of course, and Alette knows it, but sometimes, when faced with someplace new, her mind seizes on the idea of everyone who's moved through there, everyone who has or has not passed in an area, and how it leaves a place different.

Like how she can tell if Axel's been into the compound's shared kitchen or not. Or how she could tell when Lyra stopped by, even if she had been deep in research the entire time and missed her. Or, before, when her aunt left her food and her favorite coffee and she didn't notice.

It had, like all of this, started when she was raised from the dead, and now she knows this little forgotten corner hasn't seen any other humans in too long.

Alette exhales, her car idling in the parking lot, only illuminated from a nearby streetlight.

Before she loses any will to try this, she shuts off her sensible sedan and delicately opens the door.

The mist swirls around her coat, and she swears she can feel the very magic of the gritty parking lot swirling through the spells she wove into it with her golden needle.

The two shadow dogs find her first, and they circle her in the trot of pleased animals who caught their prey, but they don't get close to her.

Still, she rests her hand against the secret pocket she sewed into her jacket, where her needle case is neatly tucked inside.

One of the dogs shies away at that, but the other stays in her orbit, never venturing a step nearer.

She doesn't see him walking, but between one blink and the next, the Wight appears, and the mist doesn't swirl around him—it envelops him. Welcomes him, like it knew he would be there, and it knew it could accept him.

He regards her, for a second, as if she truly caught him off guard by stopping the car. His hand rests on the scared shadow dog's head, and it relaxes, sitting down, its edges becoming clearer.

Once it's not in motion, it looks something akin to a cattle dog, a heeler, instead of a nebulous mass of shadow and movement.

The Wight's not speaking, he's not saying anything, so Alette steels herself.

"Why are you here?" she asks, and it's so late at night it's into the early morning.

The dog still circling edges closer, but she doesn't let herself look at it.

The Wight's gaze sharpens, and for a second she steels herself for some sort of attack. Some sort of something thrown at her, in case he is just as magical as Melekai was.

"Things are broken," he says, and his voice is raspier than the last time he chatted at her, the Quebecois accent deeper, "can't you tell?"

READ MORE in "THE GIRL WHO HAS ALREADY DIED"

ALSO BY ALESSA WINTERS

The Magic of the Living and the Dead

The Girl Who Brings The Dead

The Girl Who Has Already Died

The Girl Who Cannot Die

The Girl Who Inherits the Dead

The Ghosts of Riverside County

1. A Ghost of Her Own

2. A Ghost to Haunt Her

3. A Ghost to Free Her

4. A Ghost All Alone

Summer Merman Series

The Man of the Lake: A Merman Romance

The Man of the Isle: An Alaskan Merman Romance

The Paranormal Organization Series

Marked By The Demigod

The Succubi's Choice

Katya and the Young God

Follow her on twitter at @writerLyn

Want a Free book? Sign up for her Newsletter here and receive a previously
unreleased Novel!